THE
GENTLE RIVER

: : :

GORDON WILLIAMS

The Gentle River

Published 2024 by Gordon Williams
Copyright © Gordon Williams 2024
All rights reserved

Print ISBN 978-1-8383039-6-9
eBook ISBN 978-1-8383039-7-6

: : :

Set in 9pt Source Serif Pro
Titles set in Cinzel

CONTENTS

PART ONE

PART TWO

PART THREE

CHARACTERS

PIETRO FILIPPO ROSSETTI (1755–1828). Phillip Rossetti's father
ANNA ELENA ROSSETTI (1760–1828). Phillip Rossetti's mother
CAPTAIN PHILLIP ROSSETTI (1788–1841)
JANET ROSSETTI, née WATKINS (1807–1827). Phillip's first wife
CATHERINE ROSSETTI, née PRICE (1802–1863). Phillip's second wife
PHILLIPA ROSSETTI (1838–1913). Phillip and Catherine's daughter
RICHARD SPARKS (1831–1860). Phillipa's husband
GEORGINA ROSSETTI (1860–1934). Phillipa and Richard's daughter

JOHN PARRISH (1788–1858). Phillip Rossetti's Company Manager
RHIANNON PRICE, (1812–1897). Catherine Rossetti's cousin
BÉATRICE FLEURY (1794–1878). Lived in Antibes, France

PETER MATTHEW BENNETT (born 1914). Alice Rossetti's grandfather
CAPTAIN PETER BENNETT (1884–1942). Peter's father
CLARA BENNETT (1914–1988). Peter Matthew Bennett's wife
JULIA MASON (born 1921). Clara's sister, living in Fréjus, France

ALICE ROSSETTI GREERSON (born 1972)
JON GREERSON (born 1972). Alice's husband
ELENA LINDBERG (born 1949). Alice's mother
DAVID LINDBERG (born 1944). Alice's father

OLIVIER CANAC (born 1970). Living in Fréjus, France

TOM FISHER (born 1952)
CONNIE FISHER (born 1952). Tom's wife
RACHEL FISHER (born 1975). Tom and Connie's daughter

The story is set in 1996 / 97

PART ONE

So, if I dream I have you, I have you...

John Donne

ALICE'S WORLD

On a Sunday morning in late October 1996, Alice Rossetti Greerson, twenty-four years old and unhappy, muses on her life. She looks around her, at the leftovers of a happier time and feels, rather than thinks, *it wasn't supposed to be like this*. The room is heavy, with dark oak panelling to the walls and ceiling softened and brightened here and there with objects that were once new and refreshing, but nowadays are merely a part of the room – a tapestry made by Alice a long decade ago at school, a painting of a prince on a white horse, also from school; Jon's poster of his hero Eric Clapton, and a few thin colourful rugs laid on the bare boards that creak. All these things, and the rest, are now commonplace, and disregarded as she gathers her thoughts as best she can. Jon, her husband, sits in the next room beyond the wide open door, at a small table under the window, reading.

She looks through her own window at the distant fields across the river, and around their bedroom, at the dusty shadows on the floor from the window, and at the centrepiece – the bed, used these days for its fundamental purpose, to sleep in.

Jon closes his book and gets up. He walks past her, to the door that leads to the stairs down to the ground floor. "I'm off to see Peter," he says. "I'll be back for lunch." Then, as he opens the door and looks back, "Can't you do something Alice, *please?*"

But she watches him go, and Alice – called pretty by most – tries to think but she is, at the moment, pretty vacant.

To set the scene: for those unaware of it, the Wye Valley – the setting for much of this story – is a long and tiresomely lovely ribbon of land and water, the last twenty miles or so running down to the Severn at Chepstow between wide meadows and high wooded hills. The Wye itself from Monmouth southwards is quiet and heavy, well-behaved beyond the rare flood when she

1

serenely carries washed-out trees and other plunder and piles it all against bridges or delivers it into the muddy estuary far below, but mostly she is tame, and set in her ways. Below Redbrook, England ends at this river, and Wales begins. And deep in that same valley, Alice, an heiress, the owner-in-waiting of the old inn halfway along the Chepstow to Monmouth road, waits for something to happen. *The Wondrous Gift* – a hotel these days – is in Wales by the skin of its teeth, and sits under the forest that clings to the steep banks high along this side of the river border, across from the English village of Brockweir. Alice lives and works here, and her husband Jon comes and goes. In uplifting surroundings and under an exquisitely-framed heaven, she reflects on how they share the same resignation, of how they manage to step around each other – in the spatial sense as well as the intimate – while living together and sleeping in the same bed. It's not indifference for her, not yet, not after two weeks, but a still-fresh betrayal and in their wretchedness they miss each other, the way they used to be. When Jon's not in work – most evenings and weekends – he doesn't seek her out. She works downstairs while he spends his time upstairs, and they meet in the private kitchen for their evening meal in miserable wariness as the hotel works around them.

This happens within and without The Wondrous Gift, the Georgian-Victorian house turned inn turned hotel, which in its infancy appealed to the changing tastes of the time – two storeys, a low pitched roof and a wide frontage of stone and glass in almost equal measure, a symmetry which also pleased its architect and owner, Alice's ancestor Captain Phillip Rossetti. He cleared the old cottage that was there, then cut into the high bank behind and built his house with stone pulled and stored for a forgotten purpose from the local quarries in the early days of mad King George, when the ordinary people were united in exasperation at the unending wars with France, long before Phillip came here. In the peacetime of the 1820s the old stone was bought, cleaned and dressed, and the new house rose from the cleared ground alongside the coach road next to the river. Now, the hotel is settled in that old grey stone and slate, sitting in the perpetual dampness under the hill – the trees and rhododendrons, the deep greens of winter and summer pinks in profusion behind and to the sides giving shelter to all but the front, where the car park exposes it all, the white-lined tarmac wide open to the road.

Alice and Jon's rooms are in a row across the front, on the first floor. They have no need of a kitchen, but a tiny room tucked in next to their bathroom has a worktop, a sink, a kettle and a few cups and plates, and a fridge. The main rooms have wide windows looking out over the car park to the river and to England beyond – and they are largely original, the same oak frames, small-paned draughty iron casements and handmade glass put in by Phillip Rossetti's builders. Original, apart from the many repairs and patches, and a dozen pieces of bland easily-noticed modern glass. Inside, all the walls and all the ceilings are panelled in sombre dark oak, but the windows do their best and give a reasonable half-light on bright days, and Alice has put colour wherever she can. The bathroom and tiny kitchen are denied even this half-light, always needing lights to show off their white and blue tiles in the closed-in windowless rooms, begging the question of how they would have been lit in the old days. Suffocating candles, no doubt.

She will one day own it all, all eight bedrooms, dining room, conference room, kitchens, polished floors, all those oak-panelled walls and ceilings, staircases, attics and fancy chimneys – everything will be hers. But for now she is the Manager, managing her future pot of gold for her parents while her mother Elena manages above her. David, her father, is not a working part of the hotel; he'd come with his parents from Sweden – an immigrant baby – and grown up at Cleddon, deep in the forest a few miles above Brockweir. He teaches at Monmouth School for

Boys, dispensing wit and knowledge to an assortment of youths, most of whom are thankfully happy to share his love of English Literature. He therefore keeps school hours, apart from the evenings he's required to stay behind as caretaker to the boys still busy with whatever, after lessons are over.

Alice overlooks the cooks (two), waitresses (three), cleaners (two, in busy times three) and strives for the satisfaction of people working well together, which she manages to achieve, in good times. All these people are there, plus a parrot – of which more later – who also adorns the roadside sign, being the embodiment of the name *The Wondrous Gift* and sitting there, resplendent in grey and red, overseeing the passing traffic.

Alice and Jon – these two unfortunates – have known each other for three years, yet they share their rooms and their mealtimes but not much else. In the beginning her mother had fallen for Jon almost as quickly as Alice had – almost, because no one falls quite like Alice – but mothers also look for the extras their moonstruck daughters can't see, and she'd found them in this quiet boy who was pleasantly bereft of brashness, and even unsure of how to impress his girl. Out of his depth in so many ways, but open: a boy with promise, she'd thought. Alice had tried to describe him to her in the few days before he first came to the hotel – in the time when she didn't know him beyond saying hello – and *handsome* was too vague. Rugged, or sensitive? Well, a sensitive face. She tried to think of a lookalike, and because she liked the look of Jon Bon Jovi she thought he was a bit like him but with less hair, but the picture she found for her was unconvincing. She had unconsciously grasped at his name, and he didn't look much like her Jon after all, apart from his blue eyes... yes, their eyes were the same. And the eyebrows. So she had to settle for a nice face, those blue eyes, and a little taller than she was. Her mother would have to wait though and make up her own mind about him, so she waited, and when the meeting came and he was revealed to her, as mentioned, she was pleased. Nine out ten to start with. But was he really suitable? *An engineer? For Alice?* She could not explain her misgivings. Engineers can be soft, surely. They can dream. What exactly would she like for her anyway? Had she imagined an artist? A banker? He worked for Rolls-Royce, at Bristol, making mysterious things for aeroplanes – different, quite unexpected, but a promising future. Even so, getting a ten would take time.

His childhood was uneventful, as most childhoods are, beyond the small traumas that have to be got through. Nothing memorable. Happy, with safe parents, he said, without explaining what that meant, but he'd grown up without any obvious baggage. And it was clear he was ready to tackle the newness that was Alice Greerson.

Alice, meanwhile, had grown up some twenty miles from him in her own world, with her own safe parents. She had been called beautiful for all of her life but beauty, being subjective, is different for everyone. Most would agree Alice was special, like a film star – and weren't the best ones always blonde? Marilyn Monroe was, but falsely... the Swedish genes from her father had made Alice a natural blonde, so one better, the real deal – and that, along with her pale green eyes and delicate, almost elvish good looks, had made most who looked at her admit: *she's beautiful.* But the problem was that she came to deny the word when applied to herself, because one momentous day in her ninth year she discovered someone she thought truly worthy of the word. The name of this someone was Rhiannon – not the familiar Rhiannon of her father's Fleetwood Mac collection, but the original, the mythical ancient queen who may even have ridden alongside the river under the wooded hill on her white horse, many centuries before Brockweir's time.

On an afternoon of wind and rain at her grandfather Peter's house he'd said to her *come and see*, and she went to him, where he sat in front of a child's school book - fifty or so pages of rough paper filled with careful, childish drawings, and many fanciful illustrations cut and pasted. The book lay open.

"What do you think of this?"

It was a flawless lady in flowing white and gold on a magnificent white horse, her proportions not-quite-right, but the contrast of dark overhanging trees gave the picture an impact that startled the girl. She stared, lost for words. Her grandfather looked sideways at her as she gazed with big eyes, and he saw something memorable – a stirring of senses, a delight, a finding of treasure.

"Well?" he said.

"Who is it?"

"This is Rhiannon, a queen from long ago. Have you heard of her?"

"Dad's got a record about her."

"I know, She's probably the same one."

A thinking pause. "Where is she now?"

"Oh, she lived many years ago, hundreds of years ago, so she's not around any more. But she was once a great queen, not too far from here." A myth, but a child needs to be aroused, and he was not the one to bring her back to earth, not yet. They went through the book together after lingering over the heading on the first page, written with a child's wayward precision, in red ink:

RHIANNON.
However slowly she rides, other horses cannot catch her.

Towards the end, a few gilded princes appeared alongside the horses and the splendid, mysterious lady. And so many questions.

"Why can't other horses catch her?"

"Well, she was a queen and a goddess, and you could only catch her if you called to her. And only then if she thought you were special. She was magical, I think."

Another reflective pause. "Is this your book?"

"It belongs to us all really. It was made by a young girl – same age as you – almost two hundred years ago. And guess what her name was?"

Big eyes, again. "Alice?"

He smiled, and disappointed her. "No, it was Rhiannon. She had the same name as the lady in this book."

"Can I look at it myself?"

Her doting grandfather, expecting such a request, put her in charge of it. "But remember, it's very precious." So Alice held it close and took it home to her room in the hotel, where she sat at her window gazing at it, entranced. What soon followed was her overwhelming by the lady's beauty, and her own beauty was reduced to ordinariness in her eyes.

Later that day she said to her parents, having no doubts at all, "I'm not beautiful. *She* is beautiful," and her surprised father replied, "Yes, but you are also beautiful, Alice." But she turned and went up to her room, and the book.

This was ten days before her ninth birthday, and from then on she would grow up with a sense of not being perfect in looks, and with a balanced, healthy regard for not being quite so special. Beauty was being put in its place so later, before she was a teenager, Alice knew where happiness would be and that beauty and admiration were no guarantee of it.

She learned from her grandfather about the Rhiannon who had made the book, a cousin of the wife of their ancestor Captain Phillip Rossetti, who came to live at the Inn to help with his one-year-old daughter after his death and stayed for the rest of her life.

"She stayed," he said, "When she didn't have to. She was a helper to whoever needed one."

So this Rhiannon became one of Alice's heroes from the past, and would surely have been the soulmate *par excellence*. Apparently the child would introduce herself to strangers as 'Rhiannon, from the Red Book', meaning the *Llyfr Coch Hergest*, the Red Book of Hergest – Rhiannon, from the Otherworld, the old Welsh equal to Epona, the Celtic horse-goddess. Magical, powerful, dream-inducing stuff which steered Alice towards the magical, the easily-entered world of unreality and enchantment, the world of princes and princesses, of guaranteed happy endings. And as she grew into adolescence she took her baggage with her, because that's what it was – a many-layered eiderdown covering her life, a profusion of settled thoughts and expectations. She knew well enough her princes were not real – but how she wished they were, and at fourteen she was the dreaming girl facing the truths of school and the trials of finding a soulmate there, someone to share her layered lives and just accept her other-worldliness. She found one, a sallow, quiet girl who became a friend but only half a confidante, and faded from her after failing to *die* while being shown the book. Alice treasured it, and read elsewhere about the medieval Rhiannon, becoming firmly entrenched in the old Welsh tales of the original *Mabinogion* and preferring them to anything else she was expected to read, and so 'Have you done your homework, Alice?' became a regular and necessary question. There was no shifting her from her reveries, and her beliefs were absolute. Her own life, she knew, would work out in the end – but meanwhile the transitions into the realities of life were always hard, especially into her teenage years when the daydreaming began to include real people. She'd not yet loved and lost as cousin Rhiannon apparently had in her youth, so wondered as she grew about the reality of love, about how it would come to her and when. But her times were full of trickery and illusion; there were boyfriends – false, wrongly-motivated – and in her seventeenth year after indifferent sex with one of them she'd locked herself away from them all, in anticipation of real love.

There would soon be a lost boy in France, and four years after him was Jon, the one she chose as her husband and the one who would disillusion her and now, after that inexplicable event, the hotel shelters them both with their two-week-old sorrows – Jon frets and waits for the return of his lost love while the beauty that is Alice, on her thorn-ringed bed, forlornly awaits her prince's kiss.

The window of the bedroom Alice shares in separation with her husband overlooks the road and the river. The double bed takes most of the space in the small room – a double bed, but for appearances only. The one bed has become two: a double bed of the no-touching-please variety, with a cultivated strip of no-man's-land (meaning also no-woman's-land) which provides the un-happy luxury for these disturbed people, of not being disturbed. Sometimes, on evenings he feels are free, Jon lies on this bed, dreaming perhaps, desiring certainly – remembering the excite-ment, the smoothness of her, and wishing he could hold her again with impunity. Later, as winter set in he was to ask her, while knowing the answer, "Why can't we be close any more?" But she'd answered quickly, "We are close Jon, every night," and his irritation had flared silently inside him as he'd turned away from her, not finding the will to say *you know what I mean.*

So that's how it is with them, and it had started in a relaxed and hopeful moment when Jon had spoken his mind and in so doing made his first ever violation of her principles – he'd said, on a seductively pleasant evening in mid-October, "Let's wait a while, shall we?"

Those six words brought an unwelcome new world into being – a bewildering place of separation, of silence after all the warm, easy nights spent together, the low talking in the darkness, the agreement of two years of their life together before a child is started.

"Will you be happy, Jon?"

Jon had said yes, and never wavered – and so it was set for them: the special day of anniversary and conception was ringed in fluorescent rainbow colours on the calendar of Alice's mind,

9

ticked off month by month, day by day, while Jon's black and white calendar ticked off the same days with rising anxiety and when his plea for more time came, just before those two years were up, it destroyed her trust in him. From long before their marriage Alice had had her own ideas of what happiness meant: fall in love, marry for love, have children, stay in love forever – but this perfection made her open to the slightest uncertainty over Jon's responses, the smallest atom of doubt she may have had about his sincerity. If it were there she would find it. Yet her radar had failed and she hadn't seen it coming, and that's what hurt so much... he'd covered it so well, it made her wonder what else she was missing. She felt stupid, taken advantage of. Friendliness now would be an attempt to placate her – and above all, *I love you,* if she should ever hear it again from him, would not be believed. Alice was distraught, and Jon was bewildered.

'Saturday, a fine day, temperate, & the Westerlies hurry us home. Seven o'clock in the evening. Dearest Janet, I wonder shall You ever read these words I write while thinking of You, in this lonely room? You are so much in my thoughts, too much I think for the good of my Profession and therefore I have today resolved a torment that has troubled me for too long. I have become tired, impatient & sad of the sea, & out of love with it. My thoughts are more with You, & my 30 years of visiting the world are enough; having gained some Fortune, & having won Your Heart (so I earnestly hope) I have therefore devised a method to ensure Our Happiness & Prosperity, if You should be willing.

'I have a plan to sell this solitary Vessel (but to retain her Sisters, for Our continued benefit) & stay with You when next I am home, which will be & must be in the coming weeks when my work is done at Bristol. Janet, We shall make an Inn of Our house! Brockweir has many I know, but all too empty of decency so We shall be their rival & offer much more than they lack. Also, the new bridge will bring much trade from the North & We shall have it before Brockweir. These plans You know nothing of, but I come with all possible speed. My Love, my Janet, I miss You more than anything else I am parted from, & despair in waiting to come to You again & to give You the Gift I am keeping safe in my cabin. This Gift is for the most part a wondrous & tolerant creature & watches me as curiously as I watch Him. The Ship is making good head-way & We shall pass the Islands of the Azores to our Starboard, in the morning. I am coming home.'

So, a brief step away from the two fallen lovers. The above narrative was written in 1827 by Alice's ancestor Captain Phillip Rossetti, and is at present unknown to her. It will be found in time. It will transform her from gloom to elation, from isolation to belonging, and return her to her husband – all this, in time. But first a skim of history, and for that we need Peter Matthew Bennett, Alice's grandfather:

'Yesterday I went with my granddaughter Alice to Sea Mills, downstream from Bristol, and we stood together on the bank of the Avon. The river stretched both ways from us, filled with mist above the muddy low-tide, grey, desolate, and silent. The ships came through here on their way to the City harbour and out again to the world, but now it's back as it was, before eight hundred and more years of commerce and the Romans long before that, before Bristol began. John Cabot sailed past here to the new founde land five hundred years ago, and my father's ships a hundred times to and from a much wider world. Our ancestor Phillip Rossetti's affinities with the ways of this river, and the expertise of so many others – his knowledge, and theirs, is lost now and it's all but empty, the big ships gone for ever, the industriousness over with.

'Alice and I were quite alone on the muddy grass of the bank, and I stared upstream and down, filled again with the emptiness – the lack of everything that used to be. Yet I was also content with its return to its ancient self, and the beautiful calm greyness of the day comforted any regrets I had over the past. Alice was quiet, maybe surprised into silence by the emptiness, and after a while we turned back to the car and left for home.'

That is the opening of Peter's story, his family history from its start in Genoa in the north of Italy in the 1750s, up to now, to

Alice, his granddaughter and final character. He is eighty-two years old, and for more than fifty years, since the death of his father, he's been longing to tell that story, and especially to exorcise the doings of that father from his life. So he's writing it all down, with some pleasure, some revelation, some anger, and calling it his *History*, to fight it out with his father's own version, *The True Account of Our Family*. He wants to be fair, and fairness is easily found if looked for: from journals, letters, diaries, and the spoken memories passed down, but all adding up to an often different story than his father's biased tale.

Peter also lives on the Welsh side of the river, four miles above The Wondrous Gift and below the straggling village of Whitebrook – an improbable stone's throw from the forests and fields of England across the river meadows. He is alone but for the remembrance of his wife and the inflexible ghost of his father and he is an artist, a painter of portraits, still working in the studio he shared with that wife for so many years: Clara is gone, but still he senses her there beside him as he works, sees her touch everywhere.

Even before they came here, Peter had one hero from history: his great-great-grandfather Captain Phillip Rossetti, whose Private Journal will rescue Alice and delight Peter. He will not let him go. But he must not forget his own father, the other Peter Bennett, the heavy-handed *Captain* Peter Bennett, whose sins are there for all to see. His son has carried them around for most of his life – deeply-set, unshakeable burdens. Thus Peter's History begins in great detail with two thousand determined words to tell of a pivotal ten minutes, a short trip as a child in a rowing boat across Bristol's harbour – the Floating Harbour, the tideless expanse that Peter grew up overlooking from the hill above. Terrified of water, and having accidentally met with it twice before, he was no sailor. His Captain father was however intent on making him into one, and all the boy had to do on that day was to stand up in the little wobbly boat without holding on, and therefore without fear. A small thing, to please his father. He was ten years old. He failed. His dread of the water won the day, and his disgusted father marched him back up the hill to home in disgrace.

"You have a useless son!" he'd bellowed to his wife, and Peter remembers how she had come and taken his hand, his sad, reflective mother – and led him away from the man who cared little for either of them. Night after night he would fall asleep wrapped in his small bed and dream of the father he had and the one he wished for, nightmares of abuse, and dreams of proudly saying *this is my father*, and he never knew what the night would bring. Often he wondered what it would be like to be without him for ever... lost at sea maybe, a collision in sea-mist, a going-down-with-the-ship, a newspaper report, perhaps a hero's death – how sad would that be? Or how perfect? The ten-year-old would wait many years for an answer and now, as an old man, he knows that writing about it will not soften the memories he has, such is the permanence of things we learn as children. It will be a catharsis of sorts, but he will still go to his end with, as he writes, 'the unwanted ghost of my father above me'.

JON, AND BABIES

To return to the estranged lovers. Of all the things Jon Greerson had in front of him during his first two years with Alice, the question of children was the one he fretted over. The thoughts he'd long had about a precious son or daughter, of teaching and showing, of being appreciated and loved by a new human being – all that slipped, in favour of worrying thoughts of fatherhood.

His ideas of children, of babies, had once been positive. They came in the only way they could for him, from detached observation – he loved them from a distance, and in his teens always included them in thoughts of his future. There was no experience of growing up with them, no contact beyond being shown an assortment of babies over the years, but always he would stand back and be amazed.

There was his cousin Elizabeth – Lizzie, married at eighteen early one summer and giving birth at Christmas to a boy child, a tiny baby he found startlingly wonderful. Jon cared little about the unlikely seven-month pregnancy: here was a perfect, new child, delivered at the right time, not the wrong time. And Alice had been with him when he'd met Lizzie's new son, in the winter before their own marriage, and been delighted with Jon's response. What she didn't appreciate was that to him all babies were beautiful, but he only saw them at their best and least bothersome, and that, to Jon Greerson, was babies.

Talking with Alice later, his memories still intact, she was still delighted with him; in fact, his internal enthusiasm had lasted from the beginning, from their own summer of love, past Lizzie's child and into the following spring, when marriage was looming. Then he found, to his disquiet, that his thoughts were becoming closer to the reality of children, to all the logistical stuff that surrounds them, the *caring* for those beautiful helpless babies. He was aware that his feelings were changing. Could they really be a bother, a nuisance? A sense of foreboding came into him as he realised he hadn't thought it through, not much beyond the happy perfection of the new baby – wrapped, clean, warm, and silently sleeping in his arms.

His lot would not be like the rich with their nannies. He would be involved – *no nannies, says Alice*. He found himself going over and over the imagined scenario of pregnancy, of clinic visits, of changes to Alice, and childbirth and sleepless nights and noise and mess and being tied down, the disruption to his life – to their life together. The reality had become heavier than the rosy dream. He wanted to say: *I don't really want children. No, move that 'really'. I really don't want children.* Then he would waver: *Not yet, anyway.* And then he'd remind himself he'd always wanted them, and he should think only of the joy and not the hassle he'd dwelt too much on. He'd moved to the opposite pole, away from the contented, placid child to the demanding, bawling baby – missing everything in between – and it bewildered him, distressed him.

He kept his secret and struggled for a solution but the only one, apart from being stoic, would have been to not have married her, but that was unthinkable. He'd wanted to marry her. For all his intelligence, his cleverness, he could not work this one out – it was too abstract, with too many unknowns, and he loved her while carrying around the unfathomable problem in his head, dithering, wanting then not wanting.

His solution, if it can be called that, was to do what he thought was the best thing: face the inevitable, but ask her to put it off for a while, when he would surely feel differently. But would she simply say, 'Okay, no problem... let's think again in a few years?' He knew what he wanted, and it wasn't what Alice wanted, but a few years would make all the difference for him. *I'm only twenty-four, and surely a few years won't matter? But I need to ask her soon. Ask soon or go along with it.* And in the end it was a measure of his not knowing her that he was able to put the question so easily.

No harm in asking.

So on the evening of that fateful sixteenth of October, one week before the two years were up, he asked his question in the calmness of their bedroom. He'd come home shortly after six as usual, and they'd hugged and kissed, also as usual. It was a free evening for Alice, her mother doing the managing and giving her time with Jon, a gift that began with their marriage two years ago. It was rare for Alice to be called upon on in the evening, but it happened now and then. But not tonight. At that point Jon was two hours away from losing her, but his mind was set: *no harm in asking*. After supper, they were together in their bedroom. The lights were on, the curtains closed against the falling night, and Jon, seduced by the warmth and familiarity of the room and of his wife, judged the time to be right.

He turned to her and casually said, "Alice... let's wait a while, shall we?"

"Wait a while? For what?"

He'd thought she would understand instantly, not question him. Moments passed, as they looked at each other and both of their questions grew in importance.

"For what, Jon?"

In that moment he could have read her and maybe escaped from the question, but he was poor at such things and his hesitancy didn't help; anyway, she was light-years ahead of him. He did his best to remain casual.

"Shall we wait, for the baby? Another year? You know, some more time together, before..." And that's when the harm in asking was shown to him. He was stunned by how upset she was. She stepped back from him, wide-eyed as the tears came and she made sense of what he'd said. She stared at him in shocked silence. Her voice was deceptively soft.

"You said we could start now – two years Jon. You promised. Do you remember?" And in some alarm he said, "Of course I do."

"So be honest with me, please."

He quickly put his arms around her, but she didn't respond. He said quietly, "I *am* being honest, Alice. I just thought we could wait a bit, that's all."

Her voice was still soft. "But you promised me this year Jon, now, soon. We talked about it *yesterday*." She pulled back from him. "All this time you said you were happy about it. You promised me Jon." The disappointment in her voice was tragic, as she looked at him tearfully, in disbelief.

"It was just a question Alice – I'm still agreeing with you."

"But you're not, not any more. Why did you lie to me? Why lead me on all this time?"

"I didn't lie Alice, it was a question. Give me a chance." He felt desperate now. "Look, let's have the baby. It'll be fine, I know it will." And now his choice of words. *The baby*. Like *let's get the car fixed*. It's OUR baby.

Everything had changed, inexplicably. She stared at her new husband, now different from the one she had two minutes ago. Where was Jon, the man who agreed with all she wanted?

He could only look at her, so she turned and walked away from him and he said, "Oh Alice... we can't fall out over this." And as she left the room she said, without looking back at him, and in the quiet, accepting voice he was hearing for the first time, "No, we won't fall out. It doesn't have to be now."

She went downstairs in such mental agitation that she was unable to think straight and walked out unseen, in a daze, into the car park in the semi-darkness then around the hotel, climbing the steep path to the old wooden bench high up under the trees. She could see across the river from there, over the roof and chimneys of her home.

She tried to think calmly, but in the silence her trust in him punished her. She'd been totally convinced, so sure he'd wanted exactly what she'd wanted, for all the time they'd been together.

Another year was not an option.

So how did this happen? How could he do this? She thought

everything was fine when everything looked fine, but it was an illusion. Love was an illusion. But was it? *He'll agree to a child now, just to please me. Whatever. Better to be slapped with the truth, than kissed with a lie.*

Then she thought back to his cousin Lizzie's baby, and how happy and excited he'd been; but there was more to that meeting, a throwaway comment from Jon to Lizzie – banter, that's all, a funny thing to say. Lizzie, seeing how happy he was with her son in his arms, had said, "I suppose you want to take him home with you now," and he'd replied as he handed the boy back to her, "No thanks – that's got to be hard work!" It was a jokey reply, and Alice had laughed with the others and thought it harmless, but she'd stored it away nonetheless – *Yes please!* would have been better. Now, suddenly, that reply meant something different to her. Now, they were his true feelings. He wasn't joking.

And there were other memories, of times when his enthusiasm had waned a little, when he became tired and she'd thought that's all it was – he's tired, as any man would be with all this baby-talk. But at the time she'd never doubted him.

Her suspicions pushed her from upset and alarm to despair. Nothing was safe now, and she picked over their months and years together, recollecting trivial comments and rebuilding her husband into a different man – not the one she'd thought she had. She sat there, and the tears that began earlier with Jon still came, but softly, in her acceptance of things as they now were.

She wasn't noticed sitting on the bank, and as it became properly dark she went back inside and upstairs, to the bedroom where Jon was sitting at the table in the window, looking out. He turned as she came in and said, "Hello." She said nothing as she passed him by, with his hopeful smile, and went through the study to the bathroom where she ran a bath. She'd walked past him without acknowledging him, for the first time ever, the first time in her life she'd ignored him.

So they went their separate ways to bed, she not seeming to see him at all, and he afraid to confront her. He was about to say goodnight to her before the light went out, but she beat him to it – a feeble goodnight, but he grasped it and answered as he always had, not changing his voice, looking for normality but not daring to lean over and kiss her. *Let her get over it* was his first response. *I know what I've done.* It would be a new day tomorrow, and they would talk it through. He turned away from her as the hotel slept below them.

The next morning when the alarm woke him she was gone, silently from their bed, and when he went down for breakfast she stayed away, so he ate alone with her parents. Her mother observed, asked him where Alice was, and had the short downbeat reply, "She's around somewhere."

"What's happened? She's always here."

"She wants to be on her own, I think."

After a quick glance at his wife David said, "That's okay Jon. We all need time on our own."

Elena moved closer, but Jon looked down, sipping his tea. There was a crash from the next room, a metallic clatter as something was dropped, but no one looked towards it. She leaned on the table, across from him.

"Jon love, what's the matter?"

"We'll be okay, Elena. A misunderstanding."

And she didn't feel she could ask any deeper. She left him, and was in and out as he shared small talk with David and finished his breakfast, and as he left he said to them both, with another of his smiles, "We'll be okay."

He looked for his wife, and found her in the office behind the reception desk, standing at a filing cabinet with her back to him. She was facing the window and the early sun streamed through the glass, edging her hair with silver. His beautiful wife. He stopped in the doorway.

"Alice... can we talk?"

She'd sensed him behind her, and without turning round said, "No, not now. I'm sorry."

"Can I apologise?"

There was the merest turn towards him, then she said, softly, "I feel I'm slipping away."

"Away?"

"From everything."

"Alice..."

In this beginning crisis he wanted to hold her, to spin her around and pull her to him. He crossed the small room as she faced the window, put his hands on her shoulders and moved close to her but she would not be spun around.

"Not now Jon, please. Not now."

Astonished at the difference in her he stood, his head inclined, the side of his face in her hair.

He spoke very softly. "Can we talk about this?"

"Not now. Go to work, please."

Ten minutes later Elena had watched as he'd walked to his car and driven away without Alice being there to kiss him. When he'd gone she'd found her daughter, raised her eyebrows, and Alice said, without stopping what she was doing, "It's okay, don't worry."

"What's happened?"

But she wouldn't talk with her and after a very final, "Please Mum, leave it for now," she was left to her work.

Their shared mid-morning coffee was missed, as it sometimes was, and they went through their work guardedly, together and apart until lunchtime, when as always they sat in the kitchen at the big pine table with the sandwiches made for them that morning by the cook – their casual indulgence, the bonus of not having to prepare food for themselves.

There was low-volume music in the room – a hangover from the days when Elena would spend more time there than she does now – and Puccini was in the background as *One Fine Day* drifted from the old tape player by the window. Alice looked glumly down at the table, at the sandwich on her plate, the regular lunchtime coffee – all subservient to the questions she knew would come. Her mother poured her own coffee. They started to eat, then Elena said, "Have you seen that couple in room seven?"

"Oh," said Alice, pulled away from her thoughts, "...the tattoos?"

"Yes, extraordinary. I suppose it's all right, but I do wonder why they do it."

She could think of nothing to say.

Elena put her cup down. "Talk to me, darling."

Above all, Alice feared admitting she couldn't cope, feared her mother would maybe side with Jon. After a moment she said, "I don't think Jon loves me anymore," then looked to her mother for support, but all she said was, *"What?"*

"I don't feel it, and if I don't feel it, then it's not there. You understand that, don't you?"

"Yes, I do understand, but what's changed?"

"I don't know. Just something different now. I know he doesn't love me."

"And how do you know that?"

She hesitated, then lied. "Because he doesn't tell me."

"And that means he doesn't love you?"

"Well yes, it does."

Petulance, and a revelation that didn't fit anything that was familiar to Elena - yesterday these two were in love, and looking forward to so much, to their first child.

"There must be something else Alice - is there?" There obviously was, but then she went on, "Well, anyway, you know it's a man thing. Lots of men can't say I love you – they think it's soppy. You have to look beyond that. And don't forget, lots that do say it don't mean it." A mistake, and the look from Alice was enough. Elena quickly reached across for her hand. "No, sorry, that's too harsh. But probably most men find it difficult. And it's only words, after all. Give him a chance, Alice."

She said nothing.

"So... what brought this on this morning?"

Alice looked down at the table, and simply closed her eyes when her mother eventually said, "Darling... is this about the baby?"

Far away, Renata Scotto finished her song, and *One Fine Day* was over.

When Jon came home that evening he had a different Alice, a quiet, suspicious Alice, who kept a subtle distance from him and only spoke when spoken to. The difference was immense. Later he faced her as she came onto the landing outside their bedroom.

"Alice, can we talk?"

She was diminished, a somehow lesser Alice. Again, her softest voice. "Yes, we can talk."

They went in and sat down, he on the bed and she at her dressing table, a profound separation.

He said, "Alice, I'm so sorry. Can we have that conversation again?" She just looked at him. "Alice, please. I want to put it right."

"You can't put it right Jon."

"Why not?"

"You can't undo what you said."

"But I can tell you why I said it."

A shake of the head as her voice came back to life. "You told the truth, you really did. You should have told the truth sooner. There's no rewind button, you can't have another go at it."

"Well can I explain, please?"

"There's nothing to explain. I don't believe you want this child. That's it."

He said, "Well you're wrong Alice," but that was the moment he finally knew the gravity of what he'd done. She got up and crossed

23

to the door as he said, irritably, "Please, let me explain!" but she looked squarely at him and said, "Can you see how I can't trust you now? Do you understand that? Your mouth said what your heart felt, Jon."

He thought, *This is not right,* then about how to answer, but in those moments with his new-found guilt nothing came to him.

She went out and closed the door quietly behind her, then opened it again, stood there and said quickly, "Mum wants me to tell you that she knows."

"What? You told her? Don't you think it was private?"

"But she guessed."

"How could she guess that?"

"I don't know Jon. She's my mother."

His voice rose a few decibels.

"So what do I do now?"

He covered his face with his hands briefly then stood up, crossed the room and pushed past her, saying loudly to her face as he went by, "WHY did you do that!"

He went quickly down the stairs as she stood at the door in shock, his words ringing in the room.

Their evening meal passed with no mention of the problem that surrounded them. Being new, no one wanted to jump into it. In their dismay they would let things settle.

"Alice... room eight – have you sorted it darling?"

She looked blankly at her mother and saw her perplexed look. Her work would get done, but the shock of Jon's response the night before had been grave, because he'd never shouted at her before, not even raised his voice. She couldn't get it out of her head and later, when her mother said, "Alice, let's have a break," she felt less like coffee and more like running away, but as they sat in the oasis of the kitchen she admitted: "He says let's have the child, but it's just not right any more." And Elena was sure there was more to it, otherwise why wouldn't she just accept what he says? Why couldn't she forgive him? What is the matter with this girl? In the end all Elena could do was to urge her to find some compassion for him. They drank their coffee without words, to the background of whatever music was playing that morning.

It was the evening of that day and just before their supper, but tonight the togetherness was so in doubt that Elena went out to Jon in the car park, where he busied himself cleaning his headlights with an already dirty rag of the grime thrown up by the rain of the past days.

"Jon, love, have you got a minute?"

Yes, he would have lots of minutes for Elena. He faced her with the stoicism he was both blessed and cursed with, crossing his legs and arms and leaning back against his car, a picture of relaxed anxiety safely in touch with what was one of his few possessions. He felt wretched.

She said straight away, "I know what's happened," and he said, "Yes, I know."

Alice's mood was perhaps explained. He would not have liked that.

"Well, can anything be done, to put it right?"

"We could have a baby," he said. "She knows how I feel." His words were frosty, almost irritable, and he'd looked down as he'd said them.

"Jon, we all need to get on together. I'll let her have a break if she wants to. In time maybe she'll come round."

She moved towards him and he stood away from the car, grateful for the hug she gave, and while in her arms he softened and said, "I'm sorry Elena, really I am. I caused it all... I just wanted a bit more time."

"Actually, it was a crisis waiting to happen, my love. She needs to keep her feet on the ground. Let's move on if we can."

Her husband watched through a window and thought he would give some support, but as he went out they were hugging, so he turned smartly and went back in.

Their evening meal around the old pine table was a strained affair, kept alive by comments from Elena and David that would be acceptable any other time, but tonight were banal, and forced. When it was over, Alice had gone straight upstairs, without comment or apology. Things did not look good. Jon lingered, unsure of whether or not to follow her, and Elena said to him as he dithered, "Jon, we all know what's happened. Don't despair."

He looked at David, who simply smiled back at him and said, "No need to be embarrassed Jon. We're adults, we can talk about this."

"So what should I do?"

Elena said, "Remember your anniversary. Take her out."

"She won't go with me."

David was upbeat. "It's been one day, Jon. Give her time."

But now Jon's thoughts were with Alice, anxious over what she might think of him talking to her parents without her.

David cleared the table, and Elena said, "You must find more little ways of showing love – I think that would convince her in the end. I think it's what she needs now." But *in the end* could be a long way off, and those mysterious little ways may be the hardest work Jon had ever done, even if he could fathom what they were. Elena, being fond of him, hoped he would be strong enough, and willing enough.

"Yes," he said, "thank you."

Upstairs alone, whichever way Alice's thoughts ran, she could not get over her disappointment. She revisited their courtship, recalling the times he'd told her he loved her, and wondering whether he'd meant it. She thought of the months before they married, and the two years since. There were many times he'd said it, from the golden summertime when they'd first made love to just a matter of days ago, most of them too commonplace to recall precisely. But had he meant any of them? Were they all meaningless? Irrational thoughts filled her head. Even the baby was taking second place to her need for him to be sorry and to tell her he loved her – and she wondered if saying it once, sincerely, could be an instant cure for everything... but then, how would she know if it were sincere?

ONE MORE YEAR, JON

Three days after that fateful evening Jon had asked her, "What do you think about us going out on the twenty-second?" He'd found the courage to confront her. They were in bed, the light was off, and he said it quietly into the darkness.

After a long time she said, "How can we do that?"

"We book a table, and go."

How simple. "I don't think we can, sorry."

"But we can, Alice. What we can't do is carry on like this for the rest of our lives. Let's go, let's try."

She was trapped. He wanted to make things better but surely didn't understand how they'd gone wrong. He turned to face her, invisible in the dark. He tried not to sound upbeat.

"Shall we Alice? It can't make things worse."

Eventually she said, "I don't know that it would help."

"Well I think it would. We can't go on like this."

And she knew he was right – they couldn't go on like this. He'd noticed the softer 'I don't know that it would help'.

"Please think about it Alice," he said, then, when she gave no reply, bid her goodnight as she turned onto her side, away from him.

Alice was alone, and misunderstood, yet over the next day she thought about their anniversary, about whether there could be some salvation there. She'd had four long days of grief and separation from everything and everyone, but finally went ahead and booked a table for two without knowing what she expected from it, or what that salvation might be. She told him that evening. He was surprised and delighted, but she was cool and turned away after she'd spoken to him. Alice would be very wary of him, her estranged husband.

Elsewhere in the hotel, the parrot (here he is) suffers with Alice. He listens to her quiet ramblings and replies, in his silent parrot way, *I'm sorry you're upset... tell me about it.*

In his substantial cage at the bottom of the stairs he sees everything, misses none of the comings and goings around him, and is much visited during the long days on his perch... Alice is his favourite though, and she's the only one he calls by name. Her grandfather gets *Hello Grandad*, but everyone else, including her parents, must make do with a cheery *Hello*, usually followed by the vaguely offensive (but always forgiven), *What do you want?*

He's an African Grey, and his name is Aku – which means, boringly, *parrot* to the Hausa people of Nigeria, where his ancestors (not him, because he was English by birth) screeched through the treetops in freedom. He was the second Aku to live at the hotel, the first being the dearly loved companion of Captain Phillip Rossetti (and later, Rhiannon) during the mid-eighteenhundreds, the one that inspired the name The Wondrous Gift – because that's what he was intended to be, had fate not stepped in to spoil the surprise. The surprise was lost, but Aku lived on to a great age in the company of Phillip and the people who followed him, along with another parrot called Henry, brought in by Phillip to share the wonderment of visitors to the Inn, long ago now.

Alice adores them all, loving the memory of the first Aku and loving the second in the busyness of the hotel, where in better times she would wink as she passed him and he would follow her with a beady-black eye, and say, with perfect inflection, "Alice?" to which she would reply, "Aku?" But those were better times, and these days she cannot manage levity. She would use him even more now as a confidant, as Phillip had done with his own Aku a hundred-and-fifty years before, in the same cage in the same place – and he would listen, a perfection of stillness, of concentration, of taking on board.

: : :

On the second anniversary of her wedding day Alice sat with her husband in a corner of the *Misbah* Indian Restaurant, at the top of Monmouth – dressed up for the first time in many weeks, and stunning. She had made a huge effort without wanting to, not knowing where it would lead but she had done it anyway – for him, and because it was expected.

For Jon, tonight was hard and he was anything but relaxed. They'd driven up almost in silence, and walked from the car the same way, but now, as they waited for their food, he was determined to break through to her.

The first words must be banal, he thought, not heavy. *Don't say she looks gorgeous. Just don't. But start her talking. And don't sound desperate to engage her. She's not stupid. And she doesn't hang on my words, not any more. She wants to hear me say… well, what does she want me to say? To say sorry? I can't start with that.*

While he sat there thinking, Alice suddenly said, "One more year, Jon?" Shocked again by her. So matter-of-fact. "One more year, then we start our child? That's next October."

She looked intently at him, and at that moment their food arrived, so what she'd said was left in the air as the table was rearranged between them.

When the waiter left, Jon said simply, "Ok."

Alice looked down and began to serve herself as he watched her and wondered if this was it, and things will be fine now. She still looked down, and said, "But you must be straight with me. Otherwise I can't cope, I really can't."

He reached for her hand and held it, even though there was a spoon in it, and it was awkward. That would have made them laugh a little while ago, but now it was just awkward.

She looked up at him and said, "You can explain now, if you like."

So he told her how he felt and she listened, her antenna tuned precisely on his words. Always too sensitive, always too trusting, but that was Alice – but now also suspicious: *Tell me what I want to hear... please. Don't make me doubt you for ever.*

He spoke quietly, deliberately.

"You'll doubt me, but I do want children. I'm happy with them around... but I just wanted us to have more time together before everything changes. You know everything will change... and I'm so sorry I misled you."

And as he was talking he felt he began to tell the truth. The unhappy feelings he'd lived with and struggled over for so long were dissipating under the pressure of his situation, and babies – children – were beginning to seem not so bad.

She listened, and they ate their meal in the warmth, in the soft pinks and reds, to the distant sound of a sitar as the waiters quietly busied themselves across the room. She said nothing, sometimes looking at her food and sometimes at his face, trying to read him.

He said, "A year will make a big difference."

He told his story and for her, wanting to believe him, it was a reasonable start, a possible if thin foundation for rebuilding. At the end – as if she had not been listening – she asked him again the reason why, if he liked children so much, did he want to put off having them, and he found the patience to say, "As I said Alice, to give us more time together, just you and me."

She could doubt or accept, and the one was as easy as the other was hard. But as a reconciliation, the mood was hopeful. She would give him seven out of ten, perhaps. For two hours they talked and listened, and at the end there was some warmth between them again. As they left, an uncertain little voice from somewhere suggested she make the best of it: *perhaps he's telling the truth.*

They walked through the night to the car, and she took his hand in hers after he'd almost given up hoping she would – he'd dangled his arm close to her as he always did, when she'd always taken it. It was a little thing they did. They got in late, went straight upstairs, and in a short space of time they made love, and went to sleep.

So they made love on the very night she'd waited for, but the purpose had changed. To her they'd had sex because he'd wanted it, not to start their child, and that made all the difference; their child was a long way away, and it was in the sorrow of that fact that she'd taken her pill again that night.

In the short space of one day, the night of reconciliation, for Alice, had become unconvincing. She'd thought it might end as it did, but afterwards as she lay in his arms in the darkness she was disappointed that it had. *We had sex, so I hope he's happy.* And making love was the wrong term for it – it began wrongly, with lust. It offended her, but he also felt it, along with relief, and it made him too careful in the wrong way. He misunderstood her. All she wanted was to be made love to, but in his uneasiness he hadn't even told her he loved her. So the evening had not worked, and their lives slid quickly back to where they were before their anniversary; Jon's world was again both empty of his wife and full of her as she all the time rejected him, and the reason was simple: she had not really believed, nor forgiven. Her disappointment in him was too big to be overcome by a friendly meal and some hurried sex.

Jon would spend many of his evenings in their sitting room but Alice, whenever she had any spare time in the evenings, had retreated to Phillip Rossetti's old study in the next room. Separated thus by the thickness of a door, their evenings passed in a strange limbo of detachment, both secretly wishing for much the same thing yet both powerless to provide it.

THE HISTORY DEPARTMENT

Peter Bennett drove the few miles down from Whitebrook and found his granddaughter sitting on the bench high up on the bank above the back of the hotel, wrapped up against the damp chill and staring across to the fields over the river. It was late morning and she should have been busy inside but in the few days following Black Wednesday, as her mother was now privately calling it, she had gone from useful to hopeless and she'd been told to take a break, please, and try to get over it. So yesterday she'd walked for miles along the river and missed her lunch, and today she was sitting alone on the bench, ready to miss it again.

The trees above were dripping onto her but she seemed not to notice, or to care. Her grandfather had to sit on the wet seat next to her. He took her hand and said straight away, "Alice, my love, I have to say – I'm concerned because Mum says you seem to have fallen out with Jon."

There was a long pause then she looked back across the river and said, "Oh, does she?" *So much for privacy.* "What did she tell you?"

"She told me what happened. And I'm sorry."

"So does everyone know now?"

"Of course not. But she had to tell me. Don't be annoyed with her."

She looked back at him. "Well, we'll sort it out."

He went on, "So Jon is having second thoughts. Is he dead against it?"

With slight irritation she took a deep breath and said, "He says in a year will be fine, but I can't believe him any more. He's lied to me for three years." She looked down to the ground, at the wet autumn leaves and long grass on the bank below, and he thought she was about to cry. He put his arm around her shoulders.

"Alice, two things. Number one – men are different creatures, I'm sure you know. Number two – if you think he doesn't want children, you're almost certainly wrong. What would you say to that?"

"I agree with number one."

"But not number two?"

"Why would he want to wait for a whole year? Why would he be any different then?"

"Well, you're right. Why would he be." She felt a twinge of victory. But then he said, "You need to talk to him." He spelled it out for her. "I think he's putting it off because he has no experience of children, or babies, and he's afraid."

She looked back to him. "Afraid? Afraid of what?"

"Afraid of things changing. Afraid of losing his freedom. Afraid of losing you, Alice."

"But he wouldn't lose me... why would he lose me? That doesn't make sense."

"Not to you maybe. But he doesn't know he won't lose you, he doesn't know anything at all about how things will be. It's all new to him. And threatening."

There was a long pause. She still looked at his face.

"You mean lose me to the baby... I'd push him out?"

"Yes, just that."

She thought about it, then dismissed it. "That wouldn't happen."

"Well, it almost happened to me."

Still with his arm around her, he told her how he'd felt before her Uncle Patrick had been born, how he feared that Clara would be so besotted with the child that he'd be sidelined. It was a real fear. It didn't happen, he said, because they talked about it. But it hadn't occurred to Clara, and it hadn't occurred to Alice.

He said, "Maybe he hasn't lied to you. Maybe when the time came he began to worry about it. Lots of maybes. And you fear he doesn't want a child, Alice. You really don't know for sure. Talk to him."

"But what if he's lying about next year?"

"Let's assume he isn't, shall we? As long as you're reacting to him instead of trying to understand him, things won't get better."

"I understand he doesn't want a child."

"You *fear* he doesn't want a child. Talk to him. I know he loves you."

Her thoughts ran their course, in a rush: *I could say no, he doesn't love me. But then he'll ask me how do I know, and I'll have to say I don't know, I just feel it. And then I'll get all the man-thing stuff again.* She sat beside him, downcast and troubled. Nothing else was said about it as they huddled together under the trees.

Eventually he said, "Well, listen – something different. I've been thinking... you know I've been saying for years that I'd like to write a family history – well I'm going to make a start." She'd gone back to staring across the river. "I've got heaps of stuff from Bristol, going way back. What with my father's account as well, I think I've got enough to make a real start." She sensed what was coming.

"Would you like to help me with it?"

Her heart sank. Why do people do this? She knew why, but wished they didn't. All she wanted was for someone to rescue her by leaving her alone, by magic, by flipping some switch to take her back to the happiness of summer and make things better again.

He said, "Just for a few hours now and then. What do you think?"

She looked away again, and said flatly, "And does Mum agree with this?"

"She doesn't know yet."

A pause. "But I have to help her."

"Not all the time. She won't mind letting you go for a while."

Then Jon came back to her, and all the bad feelings came with him. Was this her life now? Having to be helped through it, having to be distracted?

He said, "You remember years ago, when you were, what...

seventeen? Before your trip to France? When we read up about Phillip Rossetti – how we both thought what a good man he must have been?" She closed her eyes. She remembered. "Well I've found his father's journal – fascinating stuff - and Phillip's own diary from when he built this place, when he first came over from Bristol. And John Parrish? His manager? Just about all the letters he sent to his mother when he was with Phillip – I've got them. It's really opened it up for me." She stayed as she was, expressionless, looking ahead.

"Thank you, Grandad," she said at last, then turned to him and said, in a fragile, faraway voice, "but I don't know... how, or what, any more. I'm sorry, I don't know." And Peter wanted to throw both his arms around her, to pull her closer to him, but the risk of tipping her over, of making her cry, stopped him.

He said, quietly, "Think about it Alice, please. A bit of distraction, something different, away from here... I think you may like that." There was no response. "And another thing – I'm popping over to Bristol on Friday for a drive around. Will you come? We could have lunch somewhere, take our time."

It was too much for her, his concern and his plans. And what about her work? She said nothing.

After a moment he said, "Well, will it annoy you if I ask you again some time?"

She simply shook her head and said softly, "No."

"The offers are there for you, Alice. Just call, any time."

He got up, gently squeezed her shoulder, and left her sitting on the bank. Hugging her in his head and in his heart he went home to Whitebrook, without going into the hotel.

She went back to her work soon after he'd had gone. In spite of her melancholy, a spark from somewhere turned her thoughts to Phillip Rossetti, his diary, and letters. Direct connections to the man. She was Alice *Rossetti* Greerson because of him, and like her grandfather had a great affinity with this sailor who had built the Bristol business. Within the hour she decided she would go and help him. The work would take her away from her situation with Jon, away to the affections of someone else, and she wasn't bothered by thoughts of adultery or disloyalty. This well-imagined man was long dead and no threat, but the spark drove her and she wished he were not dead: *where are the Phillip Rossettis these days?*

She mentioned the offer, almost in passing, and her mother said immediately, "That's good. You know I can easily find some-one to help."

It was half-expected. Her mother had plans to cover her if need be, and Alice felt the shame of not being herself, of being of limited use to the hotel. She was being excused, let off, and she could not lift her spirits beyond an exhausted feeling of relief.

"Go and see him, darling. Think of other things for a while." And her mother dared to wonder how long that *while* may be.

At four-thirty, in the lull before her work geared up for the eve-ning, Alice took her car up the valley to Whitebrook and *Celyn*, her grandfather's house on the rising ground away from the river.

She arrived unannounced, and found him raking leaves from his lawn in the semi-darkness. He stopped straight away and went over to her, and hugged her – it felt safe now, and she allowed it. No tears.

He said, "I'm so glad you've come."

"Grandad… I've thought about what you said."

He gave her a very intent look. "And?"

"And I'd like to help, if I can."

She spoke so softly, like a wounded person, almost without breath. Another hug, then he took her through the house to his studio. Surrounded by the stacked paintings of his shared life, the oasis of space in the middle of the room that usually contained his working easel was now filled by a big table. The easel, never standing empty in Alice's memory, was gone, folded away for the time being, to clear his mind of art and to free it up to harsher, necessary things; on that table, waiting for her, was the jumble of history that held the life of Captain Phillip Rossetti, as much as was known of him. She looked at the piles of paper. Next to them the flawed *True Account*, with its important, tooled leather covers and lying on top of that, a small notebook, a well-worn dark blue leather diary. Phillip Rossetti was waiting for her. Peter waved his arms expansively and said, "Welcome to the history department."

Two hours later, as she drove back to the hotel, Alice thought of those long-ago talks with her grandfather, when they went over the Bristol memories, when they discussed Phillip Rossetti and his philosophy: try to be fair, be honest, be generous, give love whenever you can. She was struck by the simplicity of this, even though as a philosophy it was hardly original. Talking with her grandfather had brought it properly home to her; she was seventeen then, full of hope for the future, open and impressionable – Phillip imprinted himself onto her, in spite of the scant knowledge of him. She knew of his loves and his tragedies, and she loved him because of them all. Then there was a French boy she'd met – Olivier, an almost-lover from about the same time, the two weeks of meeting and losing him, and the impression he left her with. Those two – one dead, one alive somewhere – formed her lasting notions of love while now, in the space of a week, Jon had become an estranged husband, a failed stand-in for the sincere love she craved.

Bristol. We could have lunch somewhere, take our time.

It sounded good, to take their time. So Friday was spent in the city he'd grown up in, going around the places he knew intimately – the docks, now used by sightseers and leisure boats, the only remains from his day being a crane or two on the quay where his father's ships had sat for days, while everything from sugar to tobacco to timber were taken off. All gone, even the old offices at Mardyke, gone and replaced with modernity. It was a different world, the only part much the same being his parents' old house in Charlotte Street, and Brandon Hill beyond. They walked across the Hill along with the ghost of Phillip Rossetti, over the wide view of the harbour once crowded with ships and masts, now clear and still. The water Peter had been forced to cross in a little boat with his father was far below and tranquil, glittering in the weak November sun.

They had their lunch somewhere, taking their time, then went home by way of Sea Mills with its silent memories of so many ships, with its lost Roman harbour, its abandoned mud.

"What a strange place," was all Alice had said, taken in by the bleakness of the river.

"I used to come here as a boy," Peter said, "ten or twelve, I suppose. I'd walk all the way, just to sit here and watch the ships. I knew the tides, when they came and went, and I knew the ships – the ones that belonged here anyway. Such memories."

He'd turned and smiled at his granddaughter, but she was staring away from him, along the river. He let her be. As they drove home she'd asked him about his life there and he'd told her so much, some of which she knew but most she did not; he filled in many gaps in his life, from his first remembered days to his arrival at Whitebrook, almost as a prelude to her involvement with his story.

∴

The greater part of Peter Bennett's artistic life was spent in cluttered, sunlit studios, first in Bristol and then at *Celyn*, where Alice now helps him. He is suited to the house. The first time he'd seen it he'd been alone with Clara, and he'd known their lives would be lived out here, everything being right except for the name – it was *Lower Barn*, a sprawling bungalow not ten years old, and built on the site of an ancient farm levelled for development in the thirties but left to nature until 1951, when the house was built.

From old maps, he'd discovered the name of the disappeared farm – Celyn, which is the Welsh word for holly, and they wondered how it should be pronounced: Kelline, perhaps, or Selline? But no, it was *Kellin*.

"There used to be a big patch of holly here," said their new-found neighbour, waving grandly towards the end of the house where the studio now was, "but all you've got now is a few trees in the hedges." He was a dour no-nonsense type, friendly enough but very to-the-point, a middle-aged failed farmer turned photographer who'd lived on the hill above since leaving the army in 1946. It would take them a year to get used to his bluntness, to realise he was simply speaking his mind instead of beating about the bush – he meant no harm, and anyway they found him to be pleasantly truthful. He showed them pictures he'd taken of the waste land before the new house was built, and agreed with them about the name. It would have to be Celyn.

Clara, Peter's lamented wife, was also an artist – a landscape artist, to contrast with his portraits, and they spent their adult lives in those studios, indulging themselves as only wealthy people can, in complete freedom. They were lucky with Peter's accident of birth, and also happy. It was largely his own money that provided: the huge inrush of riches he'd had from his father's Bristol business, *The Bennett Line,* sold after his mother's death in 1955, when what was left of the revered Phillip Rossetti's company disappeared after almost two hundred years.

They spent their days in the studio at ease and in harmony with the clutter and each other, turning out one a week or one a year for galleries in Bristol – it didn't matter much, and if nothing sold, too bad. The need to sell was always less than the desire to sell, and the safety net of wealth would turn them both into carefree amateurs by the time their children became teenagers.

Clara's parents moved in the arty and secular circles of London, and during their time together studying fine art at The Slade she and Peter had come to an understanding over his lingering doubts with religion, and her lack of them – they would simply strive to be happy and see what the future brought. He had struggled to free himself from the when-it-suited-him piety of his atheist Captain father and the protestant devoutness of his mother – and he would later write, 'I well remember the pull from my mother and the opposite pull from my father, leaving me on the middle ground where I've settled, unconvinced of either direction, and quite content, so far.' As it happened, the future did nothing to settle him, but with the thoughtfulness of Clara he drifted along, only occasionally troubled with his uncertainties.

They had moved to the Wye Valley, to that friendly house tied to the past by its rediscovered name, in the summer of 1960; their daughter Elena was eleven, three years younger than her brother Patrick – the son who became an accountant, of all things (with a father and mother both immersed in the fluidity of shape and colour, he chose the rigidity of numbers. A few sensible, stray genes from his grandfather Captain Bennett, perhaps).

Elena, who would be Alice's mother, was more in her artistic parent's mould; she would write poetry and dream of princes, as her daughter one day would, and end up running The Wondrous Gift. Her accountant brother would be Alice's Uncle Patrick, stay single, live far away and see them all every year at Christmas.

LOOKING BACK: FRÉJUS, AUGUST 1989

Seven years ago, when Alice was seventeen and a couple of months after those first talks with her grandfather, she'd spent two summer weeks in the South of France, and fallen in love. Phillip Rossetti was in her mind, put there during those evenings together poring over the slight details they had of his life, from letters, scribbled memories, and suppositions. This was long before knowing his diary, but still she took what she knew of him with her, and built him up into something rare: a perfectly formed example of her perfect man, and a presence that all others would be measured against. In France she thought she'd found him in reality, but all she'd got was a classic unrequited love and she came home without any bond except to the unshakeable notion of how love should and could be, and an also unshakeable resolve to reach this perfection when her own love came along.

From then on she set her whole life on a quest for that flawless love. To Alice, the road was flat, smooth and clear. It would lead her, via Olivier Canac of Aix-en-Provence, to Jonathan Greerson, closer to home, after a gap of four years – with every step on that long road guided by the spirit of Captain Phillip Rossetti.

On August 12th 1989, Alice left Bristol Airport for Nice, on the Côte d'Azur. She was met there by her great-aunt Julia, the sister of her grandfather's wife Clara, and they drove the seventy kilometres down the coast towards Saint-Tropez to Julia's home in Fréjus. She lived alone, the eldest survivor of her and Clara's family, left by her husband twenty years before and their only son the year after. She'd moved to France two years ago, and lived alone in what her brother-in-law Peter called her Mediterranean Paradise, in a small single-storey house on the Boulevard de la Mer, surrounded by oleander and bougainvillea, plane trees and stone pines, all in a perfect climate. It was a busy, touristy street in the summer, but a paradise for him, a different sort of beauty intimately tied to the warmth, the colours and the heavy scents, and a world away from his home and his life in the Wye Valley.

Clara had died in the summer, the year before, and he'd gone to stay with Julia soon after the funeral, feeling bereft of so many things, and they'd mourned together in the little house until he was fit to return. Three weeks of melancholy in Fréjus, helped by the vivid colours and the muted tones around him, the always-blue sky, and the vast welcoming Mediterranean, when he felt like wandering down to the sea. Sometimes they'd driven out and walked in the heat on the dry burnt-over terrain above Saint-Raphaël, catching glimpses through the stunted trees of the sprawl of houses and the glittering sea beyond, and gradually between them they began to ease their grief. Peter came home to the Wye valley, to his empty house, and tried to put out of mind what his Clara would have made of the bare bright landscapes and views he'd left behind.

He spent more time at Brockweir, with Elena and David, and Alice. And in the spring of the following year, after their Phillip Rossetti meetings, he suggested to Alice that she take the same journey south and stay with Julia for a while. An open invitation was there – regardless of the troubles that an appealing seven-teen-year-old may cause – and the summer break from school was coming. She would need to be prepared to be chaperoned by her great-aunt, but not, hopefully, to quite the Victorian extent the word suggested. Alice could have taken a friend but decided to go alone, looking forward to the sun and the sea and the lovely differences of France rather than a sweet romance, which two girls may have encouraged; certainly her best friend at the time was not to be trusted to stick to tourism. Alice needed time and space to dream. So she went, full of her grandfather's imagery of the place, and was driven south from Nice along the Corniche d'Or, the winding coast road to Saint-Raphaël, and Fréjus.

As she got out of the car, Alice felt the same blast of heat she'd felt getting off the plane at Nice, a different heat from the summer valley she'd left seven hundred miles behind her. The house was welcoming. Compact and square, with a shaded terrace at one end and a surrounding garden full of blazing colours and heady fragrances. She was exhilarated by the differences everywhere: the peach tones of the walls, palest green window frames and shutters – each with a small cut-out of a tulip's head in its centre – the orange of the roof tiles, the soft crunch of hot pebbles underfoot. There was warmth everywhere, in the walls, in the colours, in the night air, even in the sea, and in the comings and goings of the people on the street. She would enjoy this.

The boy she fell in love with was two years older than her, and she loved him at first sight. First sight for her, on the Monday after she arrived, was a slim figure crouching next to a rose close to her bedroom window, and she'd moved closer to the window then stepped back, watching him. He was looking intently at the rose, a special *floribunda* Julia had brought with her from England that she'd encouraged in the sometimes searing heat of her garden. He was touching the stems and the leaves, and she saw his mouth moving; she realised a moment later he was talking to the plant as he touched it, and she instinctively knew he was giving encouragement to this thing of beauty which was so important to Julia. She loved him, even then, moments after first seeing him, but if she were asked why or how, she'd have no answer. He fitted the requirements without her meeting him, or hearing his voice, or even seeing him standing up... somehow, mysteriously, she knew. The boy in the vivid orange baggy t-shirt (with *Fréjus, Coeur d'Azur* in blue across the front), with the black hair and olive skin, with the eyes she couldn't quite see the colour of – *he was the one.*

She stood motionless, loving him as he loved the rose, and

when he suddenly looked up as if he'd felt she was there and saw her through the glass, she stepped back, a half-step away from his gaze. His eyes met hers, and an instant later he smiled broadly at her. She smiled back and the moment was gone. He looked back to the rose. She couldn't bear to let him go, so went as far into the room as she could while still seeing him, and sat on a chair, hoping that if he looked again he wouldn't see her. But he didn't look for her again. She pretended to read a book just in case and watched him move around the garden, a tall slim boy without clumsiness, touching here and there, tidying around the plants, watering the shaded borders. When he went around the corner from her she dropped the fraudulent book into her lap, beginning to feel separate from her body, aware only of being taken over by something beyond her. Even her thoughts were stilled. When she could think again, it was only to connect with what had happened, the fleeting presence of her love, her unknown but certain love.

He came three times a week, apparently.

That evening Julia answered her nonchalant questioning about him, sensing more than Alice would have liked, and gave her a picture of the boy she'd fallen in love with: Olivier Canac, nineteen years old, a native of Aix-en-Provence to the west but living in Fréjus with his cousin, and a rare speaker of Occitan – the old language of Provence – as well as the regular French that Julia was almost fluent in, and Alice rather less so.

Anything else?

Alice tried her best to sound casual, as if the question didn't really matter: "So which other days does he come on?"

Wednesdays, and Fridays... an hour each day, just for the essentials.

"He's a lovely boy," said her great-aunt, "very knowing, about plants. I think he's saved my roses." But that great-aunt had no idea whether or not he had a girlfriend, and she thought surely she wouldn't be asked. She wasn't. Still, she would have to watch this, not wanting to be guilty of encouraging a love affair so far from home...

On Wednesday Olivier returned, late in the morning.

The day before they'd driven in the heat down to Saint-Tropez, and spent several hours there. Alice had had exotic notions of the place, but was a little disappointed with the fabled seafront and didn't find the glamour and exhilaration she'd expected – apart from the garish yachts on the quay and out in the bay it was just another lovely south-of-France town. They walked the back streets. She didn't feel like going to the sea, putting on her bikini, lying on the sand and being watched over by Julia; but she was also aware of her colour, her paleness jarring with all the tanned bodies on the beach. Not yet the colour of the south, she would maybe try a few days in the garden at Fréjus – on the days when Olivier was away; there would be time for the beach and the sea later. They came back sooner than they'd planned and walked in the cooler air on the hills above Saint-Raphaël, as Julia and Peter had done the year before. Wednesday saw a leisurely breakfast in the dry heat of the terrace, and Alice was asked about the unplanned day ahead – where to go, what to do – but Julia knew that young Alice would be happy just sitting there and looking at the garden. Or the gardener.

"I'm happy to chill a bit," said Alice, but she was the opposite of chilled when an hour later Olivier came through the gate from the road, nodded slightly to them, smiled and said, *"Bonjour"* – they both answered, and Julia called him over and did her duty with the introductions. He shook hands with Alice (Julia had warned her that kissing cheeks would not be right with strangers, regardless of what she'd heard), and said, "Hello, Alice," in the gentlest way, and she said, surprised, "Hello Olivier."

It turned out he could speak English better than Alice could speak French, and Julia hadn't known. He always spoke French to her and because she was able to respond he never mentioned it. So Bonjour became Good morning from then on, to them both.

But that Hello was all he would say to Alice that day; he smiled his goodbye and left with Julia to look at the garden. She sat back down, her heart running faster than normal (she thought – *so this is a real fluttering heart, this is what it feels like*). Her feelings for him were confirmed, with his touch, and his manner – and those eyes were brown, and soft, as she'd known they would be. So was this love? Yes, so far, it was. One-way love, anyway, but what had he thought of her? A blonde seventeen-year-old – beautiful, yes? – mixed English and Swedish blood, an heiress with great possibilities, into books and films and poetry and music, art and gardens – all of those things; but he didn't know any of that. Surely he found her attractive? – he'd only met her with his eyes, with two words and a brief touching of hands.

What should she do now? She sat and watched the two of them as they moved purposefully around the garden in the shimmering heat, talking quietly together, and when they disappeared around the house she got up and went inside. She went from room to room, heart racing, peeping at him through those tulip cut-outs in the closed shutters, at different windows as he went around the outside of the house with Julia, and when he was left alone she sat in her bedroom as she had the first time, and watched him through her window, bright and unhindered by closed shutters. So she adored him from afar, while he was there in front of her, and when he moved on she suffered the loss of him but stayed there, unwilling to expose her fervour to her great-aunt. After an impatient few minutes Alice returned to her chair on the terrace, and again pretended to read her book, waiting for Olivier to reappear, but when almost an hour later he did, it was only to pass across the pebbles in front of her on his way to the gate.

He raised his hand, smiled at her and was gone, into the busy street. *Gone. Why didn't he say goodbye?* And then, immediately, *why must I wait so long?* She could not see him again until Monday, as most of Friday would be spent with Julia's friends in Saint-Raphaël. On that day, at that time, Alice's *Olivier hour* would be empty of him, and she would sit overlooking the distant sea, in the dappled shade of a plane tree and smiling at strangers, longing to be back in Julia's garden.

Missing him had become unbearable. Her pain was constant, and her thoughts for the rest of that Wednesday took her far away from Fréjus, from the South of France – far away to the Wye Valley, as she saw him with her wherever she went – then brought her back just as quickly. Where she was didn't seem to matter, but she always reconnected with Fréjus as the place where he was.

He was gone now, somewhere out there, out of her sight until Monday, until four full days had passed as well as the rest of today, and she feared she might not make it, simply not survive the long hours. For the first time in her life, she felt the almost unbearable ache of a love she couldn't have.

After lunch she went inside and lay on her bed, exhausted by this new craving. She was asked again if she fancied going somewhere, but she said she would rather stay home. Julia had watched the watcher carefully, observed her sudden infatuation, her excitement and disappointment; she left the girl to her thoughts and went to her own bedroom, to her siesta. Alice stared into space, into the corners of her little room, and at the window now curtained against the heat of the day, at the glaring strip of sunlight where the curtains didn't quite meet. *A different world, this. Not at all how I thought it would be. All the looking-forward to sun and sand, the plans, the possibilities. The differences. But I've fallen in love. And what do I do now? What happens now that I can't think straight, want nothing except him, and he's four days – almost five days, more than a hundred hours, countless minutes – away from me?*

Thursday. A trip into the wilds of Provence, ending up in the foothills of Mont Sainte-Victoire, the mountain of Paul Cézanne, the mountain Olivier could see from his childhood home in Aix-en-Provence. Another hot day, and they sat for an hour in the shady cool of a roadside restaurant in Puyloubier, below the grey flanks of the mountain, before heading south for home through the stark shrubland to catch the main road, La Provençale, into Fréjus. For most of the day Alice had been quiet. Her head was full and they drove in silence, while in her mind she went through all the things she longed to know. *Where does he live now – where precisely? What does he like – what doesn't he like?* And the most terrible question: *Does he have a girlfriend?* Julia didn't mind her detachment, as it was friendly and didn't amount to sullenness... but she no longer doubted whether this girl was in love.

For Alice, it was a wonder, how it had happened. *But What if he's married? He must be kind, he just must be.* Thoughts came and went at speed. There was simply too much to know, and too little to base it on. The list of needs in her head was impossibly long by the time they walked from the car, through the gate into the garden.

The nights were hot, and that evening she stood at her window, as she had the evening before, looking out at the roses and oleander as the light faded, remembering him there. He was diffused throughout the garden; everywhere she looked, he'd been – every flower, he'd touched.

The dulling ache of love stayed with her, though she knew nothing about him. Yet she imagined him being alone, as she was. She imagined – beyond hope – that all she wished for would be hers, that things would fall into place and he would be her first earthly love. She was certain all would be well, and yet, way back in her mind, the slight doubt sat, ignored now, biding its time – pushed there in the hours since he'd gone, and almost forgotten behind all the weight of expectation. She didn't feel the need to cross her fingers.

Friday, and the weekend, had been slow, and she'd not slept well in the unfamiliar heat of the nights. And her plans of getting a passable tan had slipped. She'd lain in the garden in the afternoons but too much in the shade, and the need for that special attractiveness went out of her. She did not want the transition of pink, or red, so she lay away from the sun and settled for the palest tan – still an improvement, she thought. On the Saturday they both went in the sea some distance up the coast, below the high railway viaduct at Anthéor, and went back there on Sunday. Easy, casual days amongst the red rocks, warm sand and hot *Mistral*, but Alice's mind was always with Monday, and eleven o'clock, when Olivier would come again.

Monday arrived, the first day of her last week, and the sky was still an unbroken blue. Alice was awake early, the warmth of the day had already settled in, and she had a sense of being at the very beginning of something unknown and exciting, laid out in front of her, waiting. In good spirits, but careful not to overdo it for Julia, she carried their breakfast tray out to the little table on the terrace and they sat there in the shade, agreeing on their liking of small French towns, backstreets, crowded markets, leafy squares, the warm pink and peach of the buildings, and small cafés where they could sit outside and watch the world go by. Today they would walk around Fréjus, the old town, the narrow streets up to the amphitheatre, and spend the afternoon in each other's company. They were good companions, sitting in the morning sun.

"That's why he left me, you know," she'd said to Alice, "I wasn't serious enough for him." Her husband had simply walked out one spring morning twenty years before, and not returned.

"He was fifty-eight, and fancied a new life. Quite a shock, that was. All those years I thought we were okay. Never even came back for his best clothes. He had his new life, all worked out."

Alice knew none of this. "Did you ever see him again?"

"Six months later he knocked on the door and apologised for not taking his stuff with him, meaning his eighty-seven cassettes of medieval music. He was lucky I hadn't given them to charity. Didn't even come in, just took the box and went again. I tried with him, I really did, but no small talk even, nothing. Haven't heard from him since."

"Does Michael know where he is?" Their son Michael had left home the year after.

"He must do, but he's under orders, I think, to keep it a secret. I don't know why. He's alive, that's all I know. It's strange, how some people can't be open about things. But I hope he's happy... that's all you can do, isn't it?"

Alice thought deeply about such things, how two people choose to live together then go different ways because of something that's built up over the years, some difference that was small and tolerated – even celebrated – at the start but insurmountable at the end. *I will not let that happen to me.*

Julia's divorce had left her their London house, which she sold after fifteen years and moved to Fréjus, to her own new life. She was sixty-six when she moved, and never regretted it.

"If you ever look for a husband Alice, choose well," she'd said, "the first one should be the last."

Around ten Alice went back into the house, leaving her great-aunt at the little table in the shade. Julia thought about Olivier, about the obvious attraction – from one side, at least – and how to handle it, because she felt it needed handling. Keep them apart, bring them together, or leave them alone to work it out? *If I try to keep them apart, I'll probably push them together. If I push them together, who knows? I have no idea how Olivier feels... but she's a lovely-looking girl, and holiday romances are so tempting, and easy. At least while they're happening. But Alice leaves for home on Saturday, and she'll go with either a joyful heart or a broken one – I'm sure it will be one or the other, nothing neutral. So I leave them alone? Yes, I think so. From where she is now, Alice must find her own way out, and she will be wiser because of it.*

With that sorted out, Julia stayed at the table with her book. Alice sat in her room, unsuccessfully reading, until she heard Olivier's voice ten minutes before he was due. She put down the book and went through to the outside door, where she glimpsed him as he disappeared around the house in his baggy t-shirt, this time the colour of the sky. Julia was still at the table, reading. *So he knows what to do today.*

She ducked back in without being seen, and again crept through the rooms from window to shuttered window until she found him. She stood and squinted through one of the cut-outs, feeling silly, like a child trying to be invisible. He was tidying the border at the back of the house. After a few minutes she left him, went out with her book and sat opposite Julia, and waited for him to come to her, as he surely would.

"Olivier's here," Julia said, knowing it was no surprise. "I'll ask him if he'll have his coffee with us. He usually drinks it on the hoof, but I'll ask him." The concept of elevenses had come over with her, and Olivier embraced it – even in the heat he would accept *un café noir* from this quirky English lady, to indulge her.

They both read in silence, but Alice could not have said what she was reading, and Olivier did not appear. Soon Julia went inside and came back with the coffee then went off to ask him, and Alice was awaiting her fate as moments later they came around the corner together.

He smiled when he saw her, and sat between them.

Soon Alice said, "You live in Fréjus, Olivier?" *The sound of his name...*

"Yes. Up in the old town, with my cousin."

"What does he do?"

"She. My cousin is a...," he looked at Julia, *"fleuriste?"*

"Florist," said Julia. He nodded. "A florist."

They drank their coffee. Small talk about Wales, and England, about working in the heat, about what happens in Fréjus, and about gardens. Alice was interested, but knew hardly anything about gardens; nevertheless she could only agree with his enthusiasm over Julia's roses.

"They are lovely," she said. "Julia says you've saved them."

"No, I help them to survive, that's all. They need a little help, so far from home." He looked at Alice as he said that, and she picked up on 'so far from home'... *I am also far from home. Did he mean to include me in that?* She took it that he had – she looked for tiny details from him, anything at all to suggest he cared for her. She tried to avoid staring at him but found it difficult, to the private amusement of Julia, who was enjoying the scene.

After a few minutes Olivier made a move to get up, and excused himself. "I'm sorry, I have to carry on. The gardens of Fréjus cannot wait, and I have promises to keep. Excuse me."

So off he went with his unfinished coffee, after a deeper glance at Alice, and now he knew how she felt – something in those green eyes, something inviting in the look she gave him. The look was not lost on Julia and as he went the thought came, with a little conflicted sadness now, that maybe the *fleuriste* was more than a cousin to him.

They finished their coffee, and Julia read her book. Alice got up and wandered across the garden, then around the corner of the house, and Julia suddenly felt unhappy. *This will not work. She will force herself on him. She wants to seize the day, because there aren't many days left.*

But as Alice found him, he was walking towards her, on his way out. She stopped dead, and as he went past her she said, "Goodbye Olivier," and he replied, with a smile and a slight bow, and turning a full circle as he said it, "Goodbye, *Mademoiselle*." She was again hit by him – a rushing, electric, frisson. She stood and watched him go away from her, around the corner. As she heard the gate close she went back and sat with Julia, who carried on reading, offering nothing. After a few minutes, Alice could keep it no longer.

"What do you think of him?" she asked.

Julia looked up from her book, and smiled.

"*So*. He's a nice boy... and a good gardener. But you need to be careful Alice."

"Why careful?"

"Well, if I were you I would be more cautious, probably. You're going home on Saturday, remember, and it's safe to say he won't be going with you."

Her bluntness was a shock, as if she hadn't thought of that, because only now mattered. Saturday spoiled things. Of course she'd thought of it (she still dreamt, bizarrely, that he *would* go with her), but there was no explanation that would fit, no caution to be observed, only the fact that she loved him, and the certainty she had that he was falling in love with her – nothing harsh or spoiling beyond that.

"Just be careful, Alice." And then, more seriously, "You know in France it's not so unusual to marry your own cousin. Just a thought. I don't want you being hurt."

She looked hard at her great-aunt. *His cousin? The florist?*

Her slight doubt shifted in its slumber, but still she said, "Oh, I don't think so."

And after a moment Julia smiled and said, "No. I hope not."

"You don't know anything?"

"No. And I can't ask him directly – it will sound like I'm setting you up for him, which he wouldn't like."

"Of course not."

They talked in the heat of the garden, both more relaxed now the anxiety had passed, but the talk hardly touched on Olivier. Privately, Alice didn't think she needed to be careful, but she saw that a sixty-eight-year-old would think differently. Julia would have been seventeen in 1938, when Alice imagined moral behaviour to have been rather more genteel and cautious than it is now. And she was her acting guardian, so that brought with it the need to guard. So yes, she understood why she was asked to be careful.

But for the rest of that day, and the whole of the next, she exhausted herself with the intensity of her feelings. She thought about 'being careful'. Did it mean don't get too close, and therefore, don't hope for too much? She wasn't even sure that she wanted to be careful with Olivier. She would say and do what was needed, he would know that she loved him, and if he loved his florist she would cope honourably. She would wrap him up in her love, whatever.

Julia felt the need to speak with Olivier, to somehow sound him out or warn him, but she wasn't sure which. Or at least to find out if he and his cousian were a couple. She tried twice to ring him from the house on the Tuesday morning, when she could see Alice safe in the garden, but there was no reply. Then they'd walked down to the seafront at the end of their road, and sat beneath the palms on the hot sand for much of the morning, then taken a taxi around the marina to the Boulevard d'Alger and sat outside a restaurant looking out across the road and the sea.

La Sirène was chosen by Alice, from a row of open-fronted restaurants along the beachside road. There were young people there. Less well-to-do, less formal, and more lightness and authenticity than she judged would be in the others. Julia was amused by her silent decision-making but always content to share a space with the young, and they spent a relaxed hour people-watching in the warm seaside breeze.

She'd noticed the looks Alice was getting from the boys and men whenever they went anywhere, and as they sat outside the restaurant looking through the tourists and the cars to the sparkling blue of the sea she wondered how heavy she should be with her 'be careful', with her so-far unspoken thoughts about men, and boys, and their errant ways – *but she's seventeen, not such a child. I was so aware at seventeen...*

She tried again in the evening to call Olivier, and again without success; she would have to leave Alice to her fate, good or bad. She would have liked to know about the boy and his cousin, or anyone else, and to save the situation would have asked him straight out if she could. Infatuation easily overcomes warnings, but if necessary Julia would have given her more than a warning.

She could even have stopped him coming for the rest of the week, but it was too late now: *tears tonight, or tears tomorrow*. She was uneasy.

In Fréjus the early morning light was pure, and washed with pale blue and fading pink as the sun climbed in the sky. When Alice woke it was already warm, and the traffic in the street across the garden from her window was increasing, with sudden rushes of noise ending the almost-quiet of the night. She'd woken early, around six, from a dream which had ended with her lying on her back on a beach, staring up to the scorching sun as it burned her pale skin. She'd wanted to move but couldn't, unable to stop the burning as billowing un-Mediterranean waves crashed in her ears. She would have liked to resolve the ending though, to have seen where it led, and fretted over the loss of the dream – unfinished business, and never satisfactory.

She got up at seven after hearing Julia moving around the kitchen, and got herself ready for the day. And for Olivier. He would come at eleven, and she would be ready for him; she was not a child, and she believed she would win, whatever happened. It all sounded good to her and she was positive as she went along to the kitchen. Julia was putting down the phone as she heard Alice coming – in the skimpiest of shorts that had raised Julia's eyebrows too slightly to be noticed.

She'd been speaking to Delphine, Olivier's cousin, and been incapable of asking her what she'd wanted to know; he'd gone already, and asking her of all people if he had a lover would be dreadful. She hoped Delphine would never know about Alice. They got breakfast ready between them, and took it out to the garden.

There was small talk about the day ahead, but they were both keyed up, with different apprehensions, as they waited for the morning to pass. When Olivier inevitably became the subject, Julia probed as best she could about Alice's plans, feeling desperate for a happy outcome, but Alice gave nothing away. She wanted to see him again, that's all – and yes, she thought perhaps he has a girlfriend. But her words did not match her thoughts.

Julia said, "These holiday romances don't usually turn out well, Alice. You can't take him home with you, you know. I hope you're prepared for disappointment, darling... are you?"

She lied. "Of course I am." She forgave Julia her unease. She didn't want to dwell on going home without him – she could take him home in her heart, if she couldn't take the boy himself, and they would breathe in different worlds, waiting for each other. Her perfect love was coming, and perfect loves do not disappoint. Had Julia known these thoughts, she would have been more fearful than uneasy.

Eleven o'clock came, and with it came Olivier. He was wearing the same orange t-shirt he'd worn the first time she saw him – and Alice's heart leapt again at the sight of him, an uncontrollable leap of joy. He was tall and lean, with no fullness, no awkwardness in him – tall, dark and handsome? Yes, all three. And the olive skin, that had refused to become darker in the sun – could she ever be that same colour? He crossed the open space towards them, carrying a tattered canvas bag that rattled with a few gardening tools.

"Good morning, ladies," he said, with another of his slight bows, and Alice stood up without meaning to. Her beloved had come to her at last, and he had little inkling of it. She held out her hand to him, and he took it – *should I kiss him this time?* But they shook hands like English friends, not embracing like French lovers.

"How are you Olivier?" asked Alice. Julia sat there, in some sad wonder at her eagerness.

He said, "Fine, thank you. And you... are you well?"

"Yes, I am. It's hot again today."

He smiled. "It is Fréjus." He let her hand go, and turned to his employer. "Anything special for me today, Julia?"

"No Olivier, just the usual."

"Then I will make a start." He smiled at Alice, excused himself and went off around the house. She sat down again. It was over. Julia looked at Alice, who was intent on pouring more coffee for herself and making a fair attempt at being unbothered, taking her cup and relaxing back into her chair as she looked across to the gate. The same thought suddenly came to them both – *Well, what next?*

Some time later Julia made more coffee, and poured a mug for Olivier, who was still at the back of the house. She said she'd take his coffee to him but Alice said, "I'll go with it," and she had to let her go.

He was amongst the roses again, outside her room, and he thanked her. She tried to think of the words she'd planned to say, the beautiful phrases that would endear her to him, but they'd gone. Suddenly her mind was empty. Then silence for a few seconds, a lifetime, until Olivier looked down to the roses and said, "They really are beautiful."

"Yes... they are."

"They are not very common here, so they are a treat for me. And they are in their second bloom now, of course."

Of course. She wished she knew more about roses.

More moments of silence, then she said, "You're from Aix-en-Provence – Paul Cézanne's town." She knew something of art, and that Julia's sister Clara had been a lover of Cézanne's work.

"Yes, his house is not far from my father's house. You can see his mountain from there."

She told him of their trip to his mountain, and they talked for a little while as he worked. Olivier was aware of many things in Julia's garden, but today it was full of something else – an overwhelming sense of adoration coming at him that was impossible to miss. He'd never felt anything like it before. It was both pleasurable

– to have this girl paying him such attention – but also vaguely troubling. And she had nothing in her head except that same overwhelming love for him.

They were less than a metre apart, and she could barely resist the urge to reach for him, to pull him to her, to run her fingers through his hair, to kiss him. After little more than a minute of this turmoil, and after a few more disjointed comments and a few more silences, she felt she should leave him to get on with his work.

She came back to the table, sat down, calmed a little and pretended all was well. She agreed with herself that he was right for her. Everything was good and she'd felt no irritation or dislike, only the silences – but he needed to get on with his work, after all. *So is this it? Do we part company today, like this?*

Time passed, and soon he would be finished, and go. Julia was in and out of the house, thinking about lunch, and Alice could not leave things as they were. She got up and took the coffee pot into the kitchen and refilled it.

Julia's heart sank. "He won't want it."

But Alice took it to him, and her timing was bad. He was gathering his tools and about to leave, but accepted a small amount of coffee from her and they stood together in the shade. Julia watched them. It was her turn to spy from the house, and she silently urged them to resolve things amicably, without tears or hurt. They were talking and seemed easy with each other. Then it was time for him to go, so they walked together around the corner towards the front and in some hopeful desperation Alice said to him, "What's *La Sirène* like?"

After too long a pause he said, without enthusiasm, "It is a nice place." Then he took the coffee pot from her and put it down on the pebbles, along with his mug, reached out, took both her hands in his, and said quietly, "Alice... I am very happy that you like me, but I don't think my girlfriend will be happy if I go out with you. I'm sorry."

She was startled, and couldn't quite grasp that he'd said the thing she'd feared most. A double blow, because he'd guessed what she'd wanted, and rejected her, all in one; she was in shock, but smiling, not quite believing what he'd said.

He added, "But we can be friends?"

She sounded surprised. "Yes... of course."

Julia was inside the door, straining to hear what sounded like the disappointment she'd felt would come, and if she'd seen him holding Alice's hands like that it would have confirmed her fears. Alice's shock was profound, and she felt herself slipping quickly away from what had happened. Shattered dreams, an instantly broken heart and an empty future.

But Olivier was also shocked, by the intensity of her reaction; looking intently at her, and still holding her hands, he said, "Shall we finish our coffee?" and Alice was caught between doing that and bursting into tears.

"Come on, Julia won't mind," he said. He picked up his mug, gave her the pot and led her to the table where he sat her down, like an uncomprehending child, opposite him.

"Alice, I'm sorry. I don't know how to make this right for you. I don't think I can." She sat across from him, struck dumb. Out of kindness he reached over and poured more coffee for her. She lifted the cup to her lips as a robot would, without awareness, and sipped from it while looking down at the table, towards him. It had been two minutes of the greatest disappointment she'd ever felt.

He was fading from her, even as he said, "Alice. Come on."

He reached for her hand and held it, and as she looked at their hands together, as the seconds passed, she gradually came back to him. She felt the hurt, the offence, slipping away, replaced almost by relief; he was there, he was touching her. It was inevitable from here on, and she couldn't bear to lose him entirely, so – *it is how it should be. Of course – I accept that you love someone else.* In the end it was a short step from disappointment to acceptance, to coping with the alternative ending she'd been warned about. *I love him, so I can do this.* And he'd been silent, allowing her to have her own thoughts, and later this would reinforce her love for him. He was not impatient with her. She was looking at his face now, stepping over the chasm, finding words for him.

"Olivier. Thank you. You're very kind."

"But you are upset. What can I do?"

She finally said, without smiling, "You can pardon me. And we can drink our coffee."

He smiled at her, and they drank their coffee, in silence.

After a short while she looked in his eyes, and found the strength to smile and say, "I know you have to go now. Don't be late." *Don't hug me, please... don't kiss me.*

He got up, saw her eyes shining with tears and after a moment he walked away, found his bag, crossed to the gate and went through. She'd turned it around in her head, around to acceptance, but it didn't last. Julia left her there in her distress for a few painful minutes until she thought Alice could cope, then she went to her, leaned over and hugged her. And that made her cry, at last.

In her bedroom, Alice went over it all, again and again. Even after Julia's warning, she really hadn't given much thought to the possibility of him having someone already... *how stupid was that?* Blind optimism, crazy. She should have listened to that little doubt. She'd lost him yet she'd never had him, not for one moment, and she felt foolish, like a silly girl. She was in tears that evening, angry with herself for ignoring what should have been obvious – the fifty percent chance that he had someone already. She'd been so certain. *But I love him. What else could I have done? Asked him? Yes, asked him.* And Julia hadn't known. Olivier had phoned her early in the evening to ask how Alice was, and to apologise for what had happened. French manners, and genuine concern. Later Julia told her she really hadn't known and that she wished she'd asked him outright before any of this happened.

Alice went, after a barely-touched supper, back to the gloom of her bedroom. There could easily have been a discussion on the perils of falling in love on your own, but that should have happened before she'd even met him. *Anyway, this girl has drunk an awful lot of coffee, and gained only heartache.* Julia commiserated as best she could, and left her alone.

The next morning Alice again woke early, and went out into the waking street and down to the sea. She hadn't slept well. The beach was already warm, and empty apart from an old woman with a bedraggled dog on a lead, walking across in front of her at the water's edge, skirt flapping around her thin, over-tanned and shrivelled legs. Alice sat on the sand for half an hour, going over and over the events of yesterday, and was getting somewhere with coming to terms with it when a rabble of young teenagers spilled onto the beach and pulled her away from her deliberations. *What worries do you have?* she thought, as they did stupid things with each other, childish things; they were only a few years younger than her, but a world away from where she was, with her deathless concerns. *I have a secret love. You know nothing, you children. Be careful who you give your love to, because, you see, it needs to be accepted.*

A loud, stern-looking man suddenly appeared, broke into her reverie, and rounded the youngsters up. He took them off towards the marina, and she was alone again. Soon it would be seven o'clock, and Julia would be getting up. She went back to the house, slowly, going over what had happened with Olivier, and driven by her broken heart to find some solution, some way forward from here.

They had a whole day away from Fréjus. It had been loosely arranged as a shopping trip before Alice left for home, and it was to Cannes, the home of the wealthy, half an hour up the coast towards Nice. They went early, found a shady spot for the car and walked through the town. Julia's task for the day was to keep Alice occupied, distract her by taking her around the expensive shops and boutiques. By lunchtime it clearly wasn't working well. They ate in *Le Fouquet's,* this time Julia's choice, surrounded by the wealthy, the chic, the tanned posers, and the wannabes that Julia enjoyed pointing out to Alice – it was a game she always played, never really sure or bothered if she was right or wrong. Alice was hard work for her, not being slightly impressed by the thought of film stars or the other luminaries who'd been there, and lunch passed mostly in silence.

While the world turned around her, Alice's thoughts, when left to themselves, were with Olivier and her new life without him. There was a long day-and-a-half before going home, and it was too long – she wanted to go home now, but would sound like a hopeless child if she said so. She would be strong, then next moment slip almost into despair again, but always now she longed to be home in the safety of The Wondrous Gift, telling her sorrows to Aku, who would understand.

After lunch they returned to the round of air-conditioned shops and the oppressive heat of the streets, until Julia felt something else was needed. Alice was far away, and not interested in shopping. Rather than drag her any further, she asked her, out of the blue, if she knew about Alberto Giacometti. Alice knew the name from somewhere.

"He did the *walking man* sculptures... do you know what I mean?" She didn't. "He was a favourite of your grandmother Clara's. You'd know his stuff if you saw it, I think. She came here with your grandfather long before I ever did. There's a museum, a gallery actually... would you fancy going? It's not far."

Fully aware of how hard Julia was trying, she said, "Yes, I'd like that."

So they found the car and drove north, above Nice, to Saint-Paul-de-Vence and the *Fondation Maeght,* a collection of modern art, a place of refreshing beauty that Julia hoped would stir the girl a little from her closed-in reverie. And for the first time that day, Alice felt her spirits lift and her thoughts move away from her troubles as they walked in the fresher air through the trees, and in the courtyard of the museum she saw those walking men for the first time; it was as if she knew them from the past, yet knew she'd never seen them before. She couldn't remember ever seeing a picture of them, but thought she must have, somewhere, sometime in her life. From Clara probably, or her grandfather Peter – for years, as a child, the piles of art books in their studio had absorbed her, sitting in a corner going through the some-times strange and sometimes wonderful images from different times, and different worlds, while they worked away in front of her. Peter had said, 'Art should take you out of yourself', and the walking men did it for her; she was mesmerised as she ap-proached them – their spindly bodies, the fixed movement in them as they strode soundlessly across the courtyard, sculptures rooted to the ground yet full of some life, some determination, wanting to get away, to move on. She stood in front of the first one, and her obsession with Olivier stepped back.

They spent two hours there, amongst Miró, Matisse, Chagall and all the others, and again with Giacometti as they left for home. She would never forget how art had indeed taken her out of herself that day, and how simply by looking at it she'd got herself under control, and moved Olivier from the front of her mind. He was still with her, still the biggest thing, but her eyes had opened again to colours and shapes and allowed them to temper her single-minded focus on him. She'd moved back into the light.

In the car she felt better, delivered from her dark corner and resolved to make the best of this calamity that had overtaken her. They talked easily together for the first time in days, Alice feeling slightly ridiculous for taking things so badly. So Julia had a different, reconnected great-niece to travel back with, and they again took the Corniche d'Or rather than the motorway, to be dazzled once more by the wide and glittering sea.

The evening was almost as enjoyable for Julia as the first few evenings had been. They sat together on the terrace, sharing a supper that they'd had once before but which to Alice tasted now of everything around her, all the tastes and colours of Fréjus, of the Mediterranean. She was blessed, returned to life, and though she didn't talk about Olivier he was never far from her thoughts. Julia thought about calling him, to stop him coming tomorrow, while alone in her room Alice argued with herself over whether she should see him again, or not; the truth was, she wanted to keep him as he was – perfect, even in his love for another. She would remember him and take him home with her like that, but tomorrow, the last opportunity to see him, she would spend away from the garden and from him. It was for the best. She was more at peace now than for the past week, and to risk that peace for a fleeting look or some difficult conversation was a risk too far. She would be sensible and not face him tomorrow. She told Julia, who was grateful not to have to make that phone call.

Her last day, and she wanted it to go quickly. She planned to leave the house well before Olivier arrived, but it didn't work out like that – Alice was in her room when he arrived, shortly after ten, much earlier than his normal time, and tapped on the kitchen door. She heard Julia talking with him, then the voices faded as they walked into the garden. She sat on her bed, suddenly, and very surely, in disarray again.

"I want to see her," he said to Julia, "is she still here?"

"Yes, she is. How did you know she was going out?"

"Because it is what I would do."

"Olivier, I don't think she'll want to see you."

He stood with Julia, not knowing what to do. "Shall I bring flowers for her? Tell me what is best."

"If you do she'll cry. No flowers. Better if you just go, I think."

He couldn't just go. He left her and walked around the house to Alice's window, hoping for some sign that she had forgiven him, a brief goodbye, if she were there. He looked into her room, and saw her sitting on her bed, staring out at the garden. She saw him. He went over, stood among the roses and motioned her to the window.

She opened it and he said, "I'm sorry." She simply looked at him, with a faint smile. "Alice, I'm sorry this happened."

She shook her head. "Please don't be sorry. All my fault."

There was a moment of silence, then he said, upbeat and in the Occitan language of his childhood, *"Que pouguèsse ana'mé tu!"*

He said, "It is a blessing. It means... have a happy life."

She said nothing. They looked in each other's eyes for a long moment, then he turned and walked away. And now, after all her coming-to-terms, she was again full of all that had happened. There was too much to overcome. He'd filled her life with desire, with longing for a future together, with a thousand little hopes she'd foolishly allowed to take root. Alice stood at the open window and she didn't cry. She left the house soon after, and spent the rest of the day alone, sitting by the sea.

She went home the next day.

: : :

Alice took home with her the strongest reinforcement of the values she'd had before she went to Fréjus, painful as they now were – his refusal to stray from his chosen love, to be virtuous, even in that famous French atmosphere of heat and sex and *laissez-faire*. He could have deceived his lover, and taken Alice. They would have dodged Julia, found time and space to make love and be joyous for the few days she had left. But he chose not to; it was him, not her, who made the decision, and that's why she loved him, and admired him. It was how she imagined Phillip Rossetti to have been, and now it had been shown to her. This was love – promises are to be kept, not turned off and on.

At Brockweir, she settled back to school and friends and hotel, and over the months the aching loss of Olivier eased; she loved him from afar, making him into an object of desire much greater than he really had been, but what she couldn't know was that this infatuation would turn into an obsession – his rejection of her would see to that. She couldn't have him, so he would become, like Phillip Rossetti, a symbol of ideal love, a template for any future relationship, an almost impossible-to-reach standard. So she made him perfect, as perfect as Phillip already was in her mind, and she imagined his life with his lover without needing to wish him happiness.

But she hadn't known him at all, and she also had no idea that the words he'd said to her at the window did not translate as he'd said, and that all he could bear saying to her was *have a happy life*. If flowers would have made her cry, the true meaning of his words would have done far more – he'd said, unhappily safe in that old language, *I wish I could go with you*.

HANDSOME IS AS HANDSOME DOES

Peter Bennett's History begins with cruelty, and the tale of his forced trip in the little boat. "I fear you'll be shocked by this," he'd said to Alice when he showed her the first few pages, and she duly was. "But leave it as it is," she'd said.

The setting was the Floating Harbour in Bristol – *The Float*, made non-tidal for convenience in the early 1800s, the centre of Peter's world as he grew up and the source of the wealth that his mother would one day leave to him. His memories of his father were still vivid, fifty-four years after his death, a blend of the wished-for father and the real one – tall and powerful, both magnificent and terrible in the heavy blue and gold of his uniform. Unbearded, and handsome to many who knew him, and with the blue eyes that had surely diverted his wife in their early days together. But to the child he was a giant, a baffling, loud, harsh, unforgiving giant of a father.

Peter was not the son he'd wanted, and the fact that he never followed his father in looks or ambition made things worse as he grew; he had the lightness and sensitivity of his mother, and his father never got over it. And Peter describes him as he remembers him, with nothing invented: handsome is as handsome does. Alice understands this perfectly, and tries to imagine how it was for him, her lovely, soft grandfather.

He'll come to nothing, this mockery of a son, this weakling, this milksop! The hateful words of his father, in no particular order; small wonder he longed, with his mother, for the day the man would set sail again, off across the world, out of reach and far away. In the time Peter could not remember, in his babyhood, those farewells were already secretly joyous occasions, and the child would be held as light as a feather in his mother's arms, watching with big eyes as the huge black ship crept out from the harbour and into the river that led to the faraway sea. A month and more of peace was ahead of them. Later, as Peter grew up, the secret joy remained as his father became his dream-father, very different in his absence.

He remembers falling in love for the first time, with his father's ship, with everything about her – her size, the wonder of how she went around the world and found her way back to Bristol, and above all her name – *North Star.* Alice shares this love through his enthusiasm, from photographs and description, and from the romance of the name – the one fixed star in the heavens above them looking down on the restless oceans below.

He found much beauty in his surroundings in Bristol, and balanced it with the un-beautiful reality of his father for another eight years until he left for London, where he met Clara, and his new life began.

The he recalls his father's death, far away from Bristol and the people who, regardless of his failings, would weep for him – for the man he could have been, and he finishes with him for the time being:

'He died somewhere in the darkness of the Atlantic Ocean – went down with the ship (my beloved North Star) in the wartime spring of 1942, caught with a hold full of corned beef while racing for the Western Approaches and the hungry bellies of England. I was twenty-eight years old, and tearful for that proud wasted ship. I wept for her who once filled my baby eyes, for the loss of my dream-father, the blameless crew, and the corned beef. Now we can move on.'

Sitting across the big table from her grandfather, Alice weeps inside for him, for his fragile attempts at humour and his en-during pain at losing both father and beloved ship at the same time. Yet Alice wishes she could have known that father, the raging Captain of *The Bennett Line*, and told him what she thought of him. Two nights ago she'd dreamed of a strange ship in the harbour (not Bristol, not quite) then found herself on deck with a man she knew, but who had a captain's beard, which was inaccurate. She could say nothing as he went past her, calling gruffly for his son Peter, and was powerless, struck dumb, anchored to that insubstantial deck. A disappointing dream, hardly a nightmare, and the closest she could ever get to telling him anything.

So working together in the dusty studio, still cluttered with Peter's and Clara's paintings, they go through the untidy pile of papers and letters, sliding them across to each other and back as one seeks to delve deeper into his life and the other to escape from hers - because she is changed from the girl he knew, and shares nothing of herself. He longs for her return to the simpler times of sunshine and weddings and love, but all that seems out of reach now. He glances across to her when she isn't looking, and she reminds him of his lost wife Clara: a different, but profound, beauty; a clever and restless imagination with a guileless character, too easily hurt, and for that reason precious, even more precious in her distress. But Peter was also being opportunist, using Alice as a receiver of his lifelong sorrows over his father, something he could never do in depth with Clara in all the time they were together, for simply fearing to burden her.

And it worked, while they were together. But apart, things were different. Alice's distraction was only part-time. The other half of those days, away from his studio – the evenings, the nights, the mornings – were spent in wretchedness like the weeks before, since the middle of October, had been spent. She moved around the hotel, trying to work with her replacement – Jenny Jones, a patient, steady woman she knew from school, who needed that patience to work around Alice, who mostly got in the way on those days.

'Jenny, I'm sorry,' she'd said, 'tell me to clear off if you like.' But in the end she cleared off herself, and left her to it because as

November progressed the darkening days mirrored her frame of mind and her work at the hotel was slowly abandoned, along with the studio, in favour of Phillip's old study – her place of safety.

On mornings when she couldn't rouse herself time passed slowly and without meaning or memory, the link with her grandfather broken until the hours or days later when she would find the enthusiasm to visit him again. Often, during her barely-motivated wanderings around the hotel she would stand in front of Aku's cage, sliding her fingernails across the bars as he sat on his perch, his black eyes on her, first one then the other, his head the only movement – *You're a deep one, Aku. Will you stay with me?*

: : :

November. A darkening month in the Valley. Leafless trees, damp mornings, sharp mornings, and Alice went up to Celyn less and less. That November would forever hold her lost days, and later in her life she would remember little of their substance, her memory mired in confusion, in pleas of *let us help you* while drifting stubbornly alongside Jon with her certainty of *look what you've done to me.* But as for making him pay – no, she never thought she was doing that. And passivity was no longer easy for Jon. Most evenings after supper, when Alice had gone upstairs, he talked with Elena and David, sharing the feelings he could not share with his wife.

"Can't we get her to a doctor? Or does she need a *psychiatrist*?"

But the word alone was too shocking, as if the end were nigh, the end of everything Jon had. His marriage, his work, his life, all would change... all was changing. His wife has a mental problem – depression was a mental problem, but what should they do?

"Her grandfather is good for her," said Elena. "It's what she needs. Distraction. I don't want her moping upstairs all day.

I can't bear that."

Her intolerance of Alice's behaviour was surfacing, after many days of leaving her alone. And they all agreed they should not let her do what she wants, while having little idea of how to make that work – surely their family doctor should be consulted, but there was reluctance all round. Too soon, perhaps. As for a remedy, her father stated the obvious – that only one thing would bring her back to them: the recovery of what she once had, the impossible turning back of the clock. *Piece of cake.* And all this as Jon soldiered on, knowing he'd caused it all.

Aku was of little help. If he could rationalise and as a result talk some sense, he would have encouraged his devotee, his Alice, to continue her efforts with her grandfather. There was a change of routine, a lack of toings and froings when they would share a little banter; all she did now was to sometimes stand in front of him, tinkle the bars of his cage and look dolefully at him. He was not a happy parrot.

HISTORY AS REMEDY

Peter sat across from Alice as she pored over the thin journal lying open in front of her, trying to find English words amongst the Italian. She'd returned to the studio after losing another day to her despondency, and her grandfather had tried her with the precious scribblings of Phillip Rossetti's father after she'd said she knew some Italian. Her Italian would not be of much help.

This journal was written in 1788, the year the Rossettis left Genoa for good. Having lost two children they wanted better for the third, and later that year Phillip was born on board their ship *Florence* as she waited for the tide into Bristol. Many months before, they'd met an English captain who'd urged them to leave the travails of Italy to the simmering French or whoever and come to England, and they called him their *Ammiraglio*, their Admiral. No gold braid or cocked hat about him, but he was very persuasive. Phillip's parents crossed their fingers and took his advice.

"You know," Peter said, "they even changed the ship's name to *Florence*, for the English. It used to be *Firenze*, a pretty name."

Alice agreed. She found the whole thing agreeable, the telling of what they took with them, and their hopes and dreams as they left the Mediterranean behind, flying the flag of the Genoese Republic, identical to the Cross of St George – surely a good omen; and Phillip's mother had dressed in her finest, looking back to Italy as it was lost in the haze. But the writing was difficult, an almost unreadable flowery scrawl of old Italian and broken English, and Alice was feeling inadequate. She apologised. Peter's dreadful father had taken it to Brindisi – the other end of the country from Genoa – in 1936, and had most of it translated but he'd been short of time, and now they think they must be content with close-enough translations that make reasonable sense.

"It only covers one year, after all," said Peter.

"Just as well," said Alice.

So it went back and forth a few times as he wrote it all down.

The evening after reading about him and in the isolation of her room, Alice sat on her bed and thought about their Admiral. If it hadn't been for him they likely would not have come to England and she would never have appeared at all, or if she had, could now be living in the north of Italy, in the sunshine, amongst the wooded hills and vineyards, the slow-growing olive groves, speaking Italian and flaunting a hotter spirit quite different from the one she had from her more recent blending with the coolness of northern Europe. And that made her think back to Fréjus, and warmth, and French olive trees, and olive-skinned Olivier – *Where is he now, at this moment? Who is he with?* The heavy scent of oleander came to her from those two weeks of knowing him, so long ago. And the heat, the crunch of his sandals on the hot pebbles, their brief touching of hands. *But enough of that. All that is gone.*

Next day she went back to the other treasure: Phillip's diary, a pocket-book, a meagre record of his travels from Bristol to Brockweir, before he'd met Janet and up to the end of the year of their marriage. And again Alice is diverted to somewhere more comfortable by having in her hands something he'd held and carried about with him for years; the scuffed corners, the old pages – the delicate, living handwriting, the outpouring of his thoughts as they came to him all those years ago, took her entirely away from her troubles for as long as she was holding it. But above all she wanted to find a letter, something written in love by him for his wife Janet, and she wanted to hold it in her fingers and imagine it folded, unfolded, read so many times by candle or daylight, a precious irreplaceable thing. And through it all she found herself slipping from the real to the unreal, in her awakening world of Phillip Rossetti.

The Rossettis flourished. After their arrival on that October morning, with their half-day-old son, they settled into the modest house found for them by their *Ammiraglio*, and vowed to make good. The sounds and smells of the still-tidal harbour were not too different from the ones they'd left in Genoa, but the huge tides of a Bristol ruled much by the moon were very unlike the slight tides of the sun-ruled Mediterranean. New ways had to be learned, rules of tides, of river navigation, and of falling in with Bristol ways in a city that never slept.

Phillip would grow up around the harbour – part of the tidal river then – and learn to be safe in hostile and uncaring sur-roundings, being ignored by most and casually abused by some. The personal struggles for survival meant there was little soft-ness, and a clear lack of compassion. It was the downfall of the weak, and he would have been tough, even as a child. As the century turned, he was at sea most of the time aboard *Florence*, having first gone at ten years old, safe, according to his father, but lost to his frightened mother – there were even more dangers now for her beautiful boy, her *bel ragazzo*: the off-and-on wars with the French, the terrible anger of heavy seas, the accidents, the tropical diseases waiting for him – and she lived through the long weeks and months of simply not knowing.

It was in Jamaica, when he was fifteen, that he was first traumatised by the sight of slavery. His father had deplored the slave-carrying that had built much of Bristol, but not enough to prevent him profiting from sugar, cotton, and all the other fruits of the Trade, but after that time in Jamaica Phillip denounced that brutal trade to all around him even while working with his unheeding and determined father.

At nineteen he became captain of their second ship *Pensive*, which had replaced *Maddalena*, the schooner that came with them from Genoa, but still he bided his time, obediently bringing the tainted sugar and cotton. The scraps of information from Pietro's journal give a broad picture of what must have been a very divisive situation – a capable son, rebelling against a father unwilling to risk change. Were there arguments? How did Phillip cope with the hatred of what he was doing, needing his father to die before he could change? Alice tries to put herself in his place, to imagine having a father she loved, but whom she thought was behaving badly while he believed he was doing the best for his family. She is impressed with the depth of Phillip's feelings, with his patience, with that biding of his time.

Phillip was twenty-seven, when on an October day in 1815 – one of the days leading up to Waterloo – his father crossed the Floating Harbour in his small boat as a hundred times before, and unaccountably fell into the open sewer that the harbour was, dragging himself back out to die miserably from dysentery four days later. And this after he'd always told his intrepid son: *If you fall in, keep your mouth shut.* Then that son, after his father's death, took *Florence* out to Portsmouth and then to Morlaix, in Brittany, to buy two ships, one from each side, left over from the wars recently ended – a couple of solid, roomy transports, built to last forever, but in truth, some forty years. (And as he was there, in France, while being wary of any lingering local hostility, he found the opposite – something new and quite unhostile... but he was to tell no one. In Morlaix he found a ship, that was all).

After inheriting the company, Phillip vowed never to profit from slavery – beyond utilising the impossible-to-ignore city around him, with many of its buildings built from its proceeds – and it appears to Alice and her grandfather that he kept his vow. And the apparent truth of that is one of the reasons he's loved and admired by them, this maverick with even his mother's black hair, a long step away from the red Rossetti hair of his father and grandfather.

So in that sad October in 1815 Phillip took over as Master of *Florence*, purchased those two ships then moved his entire business into the shipping of timber which he brought from Canada and Newfoundland, from Sweden, from Finland and Riga and Talinn, and from Archangel, on the White Sea in Northern Russia – even venturing to the Far East. He took on an associate, John Parrish, an act which would save his livelihood and probably also his life in later years; he went on, with John's help, to make a huge success of his business.

The letters John Parrish sent to his mother are all there, researched and traced by Peter to John's great-grandson in Gloucester... and they are by far the best source, the most honest account of his employer from 1815 to the end of Phillip's life. But we are most concerned with what Alice thinks of all this: well, she is seventeen again, falling for Phillip Rossetti again, and her thoughts leave no doubt: *I am in love with this man, and I ignore the absurdity of it. Can I not love someone long dead, love the life they had and the way they lived it? Can I not feel love for him as well as distress? I can, and I do.*

And she loved him for many reasons, but especially because he longed for a family. His little diary began, on the fifteenth of September 1819 – and in the middle of his most successful years at Bristol – with the disquieting words, 'I am tired with this life,' but in the space of the first page that weariness turned into hope, the words lifting him away from his loneliness and towards the possibility of leaving the sea for the promise of a wife and children.

He was thirty-one, and felt it was time to realise his apparently unrelenting dream of a peaceful new home away from the port, a warm house for a family, in a new place of calmness. This would have been a mighty secret, needing changes not yet imagined... a new master for *Florence*, more help for John Parrish, and running his business from wherever home would be. It was an outlandish plan which he kept to himself until the following summer, when his friend John gave him exactly what he wanted – the chance to go from Bristol and find his dream, without guilt, and without worry. He went north, crossed the treacherous

Severn at Aust, set out along the road that followed the river into the Wye Valley, and found Brockweir.

And now Alice sits with his diary on a November day in 1996, and reads from the twelfth of June 1820, after he'd found and bought *Lower Carreg,* the tumbledown cottage that would grow upwards and sideways and one day become Alice's home:

> 'I have done this thing, but only from my Heart, which is now shared between Bristol & Brockweir. I am not able to hold it up as a good Investment of my Money, but I cannot help but take notice of the Happiness it provides Me.'

She races on, impatient for his time with Janet, and finds the beginnings of it in one of John Parrish's letters from 1825, after Phillip Rossetti had met Janet Watkins (beautiful, of course, by all accounts) at his new house in Brockweir – a house, not yet an inn:

> 'My Employer is beside Himself with the unmistakable Joy of one who is In Love. It cannot be otherwise. I have seen Him but once before like this, but I consider this to be different for Him. He is not Himself, and any Business is not safe in His hands, so I gladly carry the burden for Us both. He will recover, and return to Us presently.'

Phillip had fallen in love with Janet after meeting her just once, as she worked in his new house – a kitchen maid, a skivvy, soon to be lifted from there to the unimaginable heights of being her master's beloved. And Alice is once again impressed. A wealthy sea captain, a successful merchant from the metropolis of Bristol, a landowner, shipowner, gentleman... for such a man to fall for a barely-educated girl of little means – and for her status to mean nothing to him – was a wonderful thing to Alice, and surely unheard of at the time. Love crosses all boundaries, overcomes, and casts another solid reason for her to love him.

The story continues, and the True Account gives details that add to the very sparse details from the little diary: they were married in the early spring of 1826 in Phillip's cabin on board *Florence* in the Floating Harbour, and the story introduces the necklace, above all the symbol for Alice of his love for his new wife: a silver chain, and a delicate silver pendant pierced with the form of a medieval ship, – a best-guess at John Cabot's *Matthew* – a fragile and exquisite token of love. According to the True Account Phillip had had it specially made, and placed it around Janet's neck on that wedding day in his cabin, and the accepted story is that she wore it every day after.

The custom became, years after Janet, that each Rossetti bride would be given it at her wedding by her new husband straight after the service, and after that first day it would be kept safely for the next bride... which is what Alice is doing, in the autumn of 1996, while dreaming of her own daughter. She keeps it in its box in her dressing table, as another of those things Phillip had touched, along with the very fabric of the rooms she shares with Jon – the desk, the door handles, the window catches, the old elm floorboards he walked on, the ordinary things all used and touched by him during his life there.

But the tragedy of Phillip's life was that he lost Janet, a year after their marriage and before she could give him a child, and it happened while he was returning from sea, four days out from Bristol.

The sadness of this is apparent to all, but for Alice its significance is huge – the love of his life, taken from him as he was planning to leave the sea and settle down with her in Brockweir. She feels the distress of desperately wanting to give comfort but being unable to... so love and tragedy were there for her, two apt ingredients for an enduring obsession. All she can do is grieve with him so many years after his death, and it's this pain that has been with her since a child, since first being able to understand the story.

He came home to find Janet had drowned while crossing the Wye, going home to Lower Carreg. The ferryman and his boy were also lost after their boat capsized in the flooding river, and some days later when Phillip came to Brockweir he was given her necklace by the vicar at the little Tintern church where she'd been buried. It was taken from her body when Phillip knew it should have stayed with her, as her wedding ring had – but instead he took it home to his study at Lower Carreg. So Janet's silver necklace lay in Phillip's desk drawer, a long rest during which Peter and Alice both imagine its keeper lifting it and holding it close – but maybe they imagine too much of him.

It was years later that Phillip decided to give the necklace to all the future Rossetti brides, to let it go at last to begin its journey. And now it waits close to Alice for its uncertain future, but also keeps its secret – kept apart from the known details that she and Peter are aware of. The truth is it's older than they think, but a little time will pass before one of them knows the whole story.

So in that sad September of 1827 Captain Phillip Rossetti had been returning from the West Indies, from Kingston in Jamaica, with a cargo of Newfoundland softwood, having touched the old slaving port briefly. He brought nothing from Kingston except a parrot, the first Aku, as a gift for Janet – a *wondrous* gift.

He'd found him for sale on the waterfront, a splendid bird, a fine grey and red *Psittacus Erithacus*, in the prime of his life and apparently an excellent mimic. He was sitting in a wicker cage with one leg attached to the bars by a leather strap, as if the cage alone were not enough for such a wily creature. He shuffled along his perch, head cocked to one side, fixed a beady eye on Phillip and muttered *Buenos Dias* in a scratchy conspiratorial tone. After politely replying the Captain took charge of him for two gold crowns – a small amount (of course) for such a creature – after being assured it was caught locally and that it would soon begin to speak perfectly in the language of its owner. He would take it home for Janet, and hoped he could teach it to say her name before reaching her.

So Aku, who was actually born somewhere in the uncivilised forests of West Africa, was thus kept in his civilised wicker cage and taken on board *Florence* to travel again across half the world, condemned by his beauty and cleverness to a life of captive scrutiny. He travelled in the Captain's cabin, his cage moved around by Phillip or his First Mate to catch the sun through the small-paned windows, and covered at night (as recommended by the vendor) to keep him quiet. A bond of sorts was quickly made – his crew unkindly thought that their Captain had lost part of his mind, as during the months of that return voyage he had been heard talking to the bird, and not in what we would now call parrot fashion. He conversed with Aku. He told him the events of the day, where they were, how many miles they'd covered, what the weather was like, and so on. The bird fixed an eye on this chatty confidant, trying to make parrot-sense and picking on the odd word to stow away. *Janet* was no problem. Nor was *Hello George* (the Mate) and any number of seafaring terms, along with various ingrained Spanish obscenities which Phillip vainly hoped he would forget.

But as they docked in Bristol this splendid bird was forgotten in the tragedy of the moment, then remembered in the days after, being the receiver of much sadness from his master. He was left on board when Phillip went to the grave at Tintern and on to Brockweir, and on Phillip's return made the upsetting, innocent slip of saying *Hello Janet* to him.

From 1827, when he lost Janet, Phillip closed in on himself; he became withdrawn, left the running of his business largely to his manager John Parrish, and stayed for long periods at Brockweir where a decision was made that would lead directly to Alice's life – he went ahead with plans he'd made before Janet's death, to make their house into an inn: The Wondrous Gift was born, reflecting the undelivered gift that was Aku, and carrying out his promise to her for their future together; he would continue as if she were there and involved in the planning, the designing, the decorating and furnishing.

The strong, unshakeable Captain had broken down in his sorrow, but strove to keep his wife alive by making the new inn the way he imagined she would have liked it to be. He covered up the plain walls and ceilings with heavy oak panelling, which he knew she admired... the new, light oak which would darken and set with age, and the colours, the furniture, all the things they'd talked of, and that she was fond of. So he got through those years, and gradually came back to his Bristol life, his business, and John Parrish. The Inn was left in the charge of a landlord and his wife, and Phillip went back and forth.

'He made a fool of his Pain,' John had written to his mother a few months after Janet's death, 'and became an Example to all, of Grief overcome, and of sadness lived with, alongside Duty. He would not be cast down'.

Alice and Peter know little of these details, but they feel their hero's pain as he works through the years, and they know from John's letters how he feels about a family. His diary, begun in 1819, ended in December 1826, in the winter of the year of his marriage to Janet, with the determined words, 'I am leaving the Sea,' and all they have from then on, apart from John's letters, are time-worn memories, and a single letter of Phillip's written in 1837 to Catherine, his second wife-to-be.

Each time Alice looked from her bedroom window across the river to England, she saw an unchanged scene, apart from the few new houses on the other side. The river was still as Phillip would have seen it, and a little downstream was the site of the old ferry crossing where Janet was lost to the water that dark day, and close to where Phillip met his next love nine years later – but Catherine Price was not another Janet. She was older, more settled in her ways, and would learn before long that her husband had not given up his first wife when he married the second. But a family, a child, were still what he wanted.

Phillip had almost given up the sea before that time, sold his beloved *Florence*, spending most of his days at the Inn and visiting his Bristol business only once a month, where John Parrish was in charge of the office at the side of the Floating Harbour, set in his own ways as the ships came and went. Everything at Brockweir was precious to Phillip, especially Aku. Catherine would do her best to become friends with him (Phillip was grateful for her lack of Spanish, as Aku never forgot those early obscenities). She was interested in this man-bird relationship, and marvelled at their unembarrassed affinity – she would watch as they were together, observing their intimacy... a cocking of Aku's head, a shuffling along his perch to be closer to his friend, and the ritual of the broom: Aku had been given his freedom, first by accident, then by design, and his return always involved a favourite broom, a well-worn perch to which he would fly – but only if it were held out by his friend Phillip Rossetti, and only if it were his voice calling him.

Aku became a celebrity, with newspaper accounts of *The Wonderful Bird of Brockweir* – due to his daily outings ending with the broom routine and his sometimes racy talk – and before long the clamour to see him outweighed any advantage for Phillip. So in came *Henry*, another African Grey, brought across the Atlantic by and named after Henry Parry, one of Phillip's captains. He was given a crash course in English and in time took the spotlight off Aku, who retired to his master's bedroom, spending his remaining half-century in the space that Alice now shares with Jon.

The last writing they have from Phillip is the letter he sent to 'My Beloved Catherine' at her home in Hereford, a month before their wedding in August 1837, asking her to wear the necklace that Janet had worn. Understandably, Catherine did not look favourably upon it. To wear something intended for his first wife, and taken from that *dead* first wife, was beyond her. He put it away in the hope that a future bride would wear it, and he would be spared the disappointment of his own daughter also refusing – it was his undreamt-of granddaughter Georgina, fifty-four years after his death, who would wear it at her wedding and properly begin the custom.

Phillip and Catherine were married in the autumn of 1837, and the following year a daughter came, giving him his longed-for family. Phillip was elated. At the age of fifty he'd arrived at the place he'd waited for, for so many years. The sun shone at last through the valley and life was different, with new ways of getting through the days – the days that now included a new person, Phillipa Anna Elena Rossetti, the child with his own and his mother's names, his real and wonderful daughter. They would have each other for a few days more than a year.

That year later, as Phillipa passed her first birthday, the June was very dry, the gardens and fields calling for rain – and when it came Phillip was far along the riverbank. This sailor, long used to reading the weather, had ignored the signs and allowed himself to be caught, and soaked to the skin. So a summer storm gave him pneumonia, and in a few days took him away, leaving a distraught Catherine as owner of everything – Inn, business, and all. John Parrish came from Bristol too late to talk to his employer and friend, and he prepared, in astonishment, to carry on the business for a new employer – a female employer (rare, and untrusted in those days), an unbusinesslike thirty-five-year old showing no tendencies as yet for ambition, nor any as a competent mother to one-year-old Phillipa.

: : :

It was a hundred and seventy years later, as she reached the point of Phillip's death, that Alice's enthusiasm left her and on a very grey afternoon, with snow threatened, she left for home knowing that coming back tomorrow would be difficult. She simply wanted to lie down for ever, close her eyes and drift away to somewhere safe with her thoughts ~ and with her new knowledge of the untainted man who had possessed her. From now on, there would be very few days she would share with her grandfather.

Later, as she sat at Phillip's desk in his old study shortly before Jon would come home, she stared through the window at the darkness and the flurries of snow gusting without sound against the glass. Yet she thought of Jon, not Phillip. The snow had reminded her of the year before, before any of this had happened. She thought of a day like this one, but later, in December, when in the morning after a light fall of snow she'd traced a heart in the thin layer on Jon's windscreen – he was going into Monmouth, she couldn't remember why – and she'd drawn the heart complete with an arrow and the letters A and J, for him to see as he got in. But it went wrong – he was delayed, and when he finally went the snow had thawed and slid down the glass into an untidy ruffle at the bottom, and his indifferent wipers swept away the remains of it. She was disappointed, but it wasn't a big deal – things like that happened now and then, when her confidence in him was solid. There would be other things she could do for him.

So it was Jon on her mind in the quiet of the study after all, and she stayed there as she heard him climbing the stairs and opening the bedroom door. He came through to get to the bathroom, knowing she would be at the desk.

"Hello Alice," he said as he crossed the room behind her, "It's trying to snow."

She turned to look at him, gave him a feeble smile and said, "Oh," but he was gone, and that was it. That was their life – not empty, but sprinkled with weak, unengaged efforts. She got up then and went alone, down to the kitchen for tea, like most other days.

LITTLE PHILLIPA ROSSETTI

Phillip was dead, yet the day after that snowy evening Alice rallied herself and went back to the studio, some hours after what began in the late morning as detached thoughts slowly brought themselves together, surprising her – memories and sounds of heat and sun, of blue skies and glittering snow or glittering water. She felt safe and set aside from harm. Her holidays and good times gathered inside her head, an almost spiritual thing, filling her completely. It lasted until lunchtime, an hour or so that came unannounced, and lifted her mood. So in that filled state she went down to the kitchen, detached in her private euphoria from any reality beyond the automatic need for food, and afterwards went back to Celyn – still wishing so much for something and somewhere different – and back to the project as the euphoric vision finally left her. It lasted just long enough to tip her the right way and she was to have more of those episodes, and became grateful and miserable for them at the same time – grateful for their diversion but miserable for their brevity. And it was during those brief times that she found a little warmth for Jon: uncertain feelings of hope and recovery, but just feelings – she enjoyed the euphoria, and indulged herself, surrounded by that false hope.

One character leaves, another enters: the physical presence of Phillip left the story and his year-old daughter Phillipa took his place, a child that would become impossible, in every way. There was a fundamental lack of guidance from her mother and probably also her father, the sainted Phillip, who in any case would likely have found it unnecessary in a child barely able to walk, blinded as he no doubt was by the child's very existence. Alice thought it fair to put the blame onto Catherine, who had many more years than Phillip to get it right, and failed – the girl was to go her own callous way with everything.

John Parrish, Phillip's now-beleaguered manager, looked on with alarm as the child grew. Phillipa all but ruled her mother, and before she was a teenager she had firm ideas about the family business – it would be more profitable to return to Phillip's father's business plan, to again bring sugar, and more importantly by then, cocoa and tobacco, into Bristol. This was directly against the agreement John had made with Phillip in 1815 and he was resolute in standing up to Phillipa as she became older and more persistent. John Parrish's mother warned him:

'You must be strong, & You must think of giving up that Profession. Save Your money & be frugal with life, for I think She will let You go when Her Mother passes. Heed me, & see what a dissolute She is becoming. She will have no fairness, no pity. She will dominate You or destroy You, & both are to be avoided.'

Her son, at sixty, feared for his livelihood under the darkening cloud that was Phillipa – a precocious and demanding presence. At ten years old, very aware of the other merchants at Bristol, and madly envious of what she saw as richer pickings from the West Indies and North America, she was spoiled enough to want more and strong enough to override her poor mother, who could only watch helplessly as her lost child set out her demands to John:

'The Child, after hearing the month's returns, questions the wisdom of trading in Timber. Her manner was loud and noxious as ever. She (at ten years) wishes Us to trade in Sugar and Tobacco, for the Profit of the Business. She demands to know why this is not done. Understand me. She demands to know.'

And Alice finds another hero, in John Parrish. A steadfast man, with a wife and two daughters, and all four afraid for their future.

During the days of discovering him through his letters, and his mother's letters, and feeling the anxiety in their words on the paper, she was briefly lifted out of herself and dropped into the very different world of 1848, a world of revolutions, of industry and hardships, a world largely devoid of social care. She allowed her thoughts to drift away from her problems in the lovely valley, to John's day-to-day existence in the noise and grime of his bleak situation at the Floating Harbour in Bristol.

The True Account was bereft of these letters, Captain Bennett having been unaware of them. What he saw was what his grand-mother Phillipa saw - a man stubbornly refusing to change his ways for the better, and refusing to be dictated to by Captain Bennett's heroine, as a teenager. But John was refusing her because of her father, and the promise he'd made with him. The spoils of slavery were everywhere in Bristol – even Phillip's house in Charlotte Street on the hill above the harbour was built with the indirect proceeds of the Trade – but they refused to add to them. Phillipa did not understand such things.

John would write many times to his mother over his concern for Catherine, whose power within the Company was minimal, but John's words – had he known of them – would have meant nothing to Captain Bennett, who put his real feelings into his truly-less-than-True Account; Peter and Alice are unforgiving of one particular paragraph, even though in harsh business terms it made sense:

> 'It became time for John Parrish to move aside, & to allow a Younger mind to apply itself to our Business. My Grandmother Phillipa (at Eighteen years old!) was to set a more Profitable course, previously denied Her by this wasteful, blinkered man.'

So in 1856, when the blinkered man was sixty-eight and his

nemesis eighteen, he was indeed cast out. He had held on to his and Phillip's resolution for eight difficult years, and Catherine had found the strength somewhere to refuse to replace him, but at eighteen Phillipa took on a manager without her mother's knowledge – to take John's place and do her bidding until she reached twenty-one, and could take over the Business herself; she took on Richard Sparks, a well-off twenty-five-year-old who had come to Bristol looking to get into the shipping trade. It was done. Catherine gave in and withdrew to Brockweir, to live her remaining seven years in the company of her cousin Rhiannon and the two parrots.

Two years after leaving, John Parrish was dead. One of his daughters had married and moved away, but his wife and their remaining daughter lived on in the house given to him by a grateful Phillip – his parents' old house, in Queens Parade, on the bank behind the quay. They lived on John's income – more a contractual allowance from Phillip before pensions were commonplace, and in the event much reduced by legal trickery from the revengeful and vindictive controller of Rossetti Shipping & Trading, Miss Phillipa Rossetti.

: : :

As bad as her treatment of John Parrish had been, there was another matter which threw all else into the shade, because hanging over Phillipa's story was a dark, scandalous rumour of her being involved in the death of her husband, Richard Sparks – the manager she had brought in to replace John, and then married. It was a story Peter would love to prove, and he gives a whole chapter to his musings on whether or not she brought about her husband's death. Peter's father would have none of it, and the rumour was only ever passed down by word of mouth. After researching the Bristol records he found what he considered to be many pointers to her guilt, inadequately (he thought) looked into at the time, and anyway it added up for him: she inexplicably married a wealthy young man, which in those days gave all her assets to him; he gave her an heiress, their daughter Georgina; he then died mysteriously, returning her assets and giving her all of his, and her business prospered.

For someone like Phillipa to give everything away on her marriage was absurd, and accidental pregnancy by her manager was not the reason for their marriage. Two plus two equals five, perhaps, but Alice is intrigued, even in her distraction, and wishes her grandfather could be right... it would round off Phillipa's despicable life for him, and justify all his thoughts of her. But there was no way it could be proven without reopening a cold case from long ago – which even now could have repercussions for his family – so he finishes with Phillipa Rossetti and her iniquities; but how close was he to the truth? He would perhaps never know. But apart from all that, for Peter this was still the woman who made his father into the man he was. She could not be innocent of *that*.

: : :

So Alice's return to her grandfather's project had been brief. Phillipa, Richard Sparks, their daughter Georgina, John the beleaguered manager and Catherine, the ineffectual mother; the whole sad tale had held her too loosely and on a wintry day of lingering frost Alice could see and feel little beyond her closed-in self, and wanted to leave. She managed an hour from that point then told her concerned grandfather she wouldn't be going back, not for a while, and without giving a reason. She drove home in a more-than-usual numbing haze of *I don't care any more,* knowing it was over.

Elena greeted her as she went in, a greeting tempered by her daughter's appearance, her obvious discomfort.

"Darling… are you all right?"

"Yes, I'm fine."

Then the shortest of looks and the faintest smile as she went through to the staircase, leaving her mother to stand and watch as she went, unable to cope with such a meeting. As Alice moved along the dim corridor she had a glimpse of herself in a mirror, an astonished moment of seeing herself as she really was, hunched and drab in her heavy coat. She hurried away from her life and her mother (and bewildered Aku, ignored for once) to the safety of upstairs.

Any attractiveness had gone, and the shock stayed with her while she sat on the bed, still in her coat, and in some moments of clarity wondered how she had come to this. But there was no answer beyond feeling wretched. It was well beyond the middle of November, and the winter days stretched ahead.

LOOKING BACK: ALICE AND JON

In 1993, the year he met Alice, Jonathan Derek Greerson worked every weekday and every Saturday morning on the northern fringes of Bristol, at Filton, in his job at Rolls-Royce. He lived in Ross-on-Wye, and every weekend would pass through Monmouth on his way north from his lodgings in Bristol, or back south on the Sunday afternoon, sometimes taking the Wye Valley road, sometimes at the last moment going via the eastern edge of Newport and the tedious M4 that connected with the Severn Bridge. The decision was related to his senses and the seasons. Spring, summer and autumn routes were decided as he approached Monmouth or Chepstow – an open blue sky sending him along the winding road through the Valley, for the sublime views on clear or misty afternoons of the river as he crossed it or followed alongside, and for the canvas of changing colour – the bluebells, the wild garlic, the autumn reds and golds that were the backdrop for his journeys. Winter often kept him on safer roads. His weekdays were spent in lodgings a mile from the factory, in a cramped bedsit where he was allowed posters on the wall and music, within reason. His live-in landlady insisted on making him breakfast – though he never paid for it – on the grounds that it was a sin to go to work hungry, and being a young man he surely could never be trusted to eat properly. In the evenings he fed himself, warming up food on the grubby little hob then sitting at his table, hearing faintly through the walls Jo Stafford singing *Haunted Heart* or *I'll Be Seeing You* – songs his landlady had lived with and couldn't bear to be parted from. *Real music,* she called it. He would sit and listen to the pure and far-off voice, imagining her sitting alone and going back over her life in the forties and fifties, the different world of his own parents that would soon become the rock'n'roll era, when everything changed. He'd missed all of that, arriving in 1972 and driven home from the hospital with his twin sister Diane to the sound of his father's Eric Clapton tapes, and it was Eric for ever for him after that. His father would never admit to giving him his middle name after Clapton's alter ego in *Derek and the Dominos,* but Jon always believed he had, and when he was young wished his sister had been *Layla*. Diane, however, was happy to be Diane.

The aviation bug had caught his father, and Jon and his sister had been taken down to Filton with him in 1979 to see the first flight of the last Concorde, an extraordinary experience for seven-year-olds, and the impetus for Jon's future choice of work. He'd clung to the chain-link fence next to Diane, and they had both stared and trembled at the thunderous sound, uncomprehending of such a thing.

"Did you feel it in your stomach?" asked their father, and yes, they did. In their stomachs, and their heads... but only reaching Jon's heart, not his sister's. From then on it had to be aeroplanes for him – and it had to be Rolls-Royce – so Filton was the place, but even when he'd got the job of his dreams he would never lose his regret at not having been there during the Concorde years. His expertise developed into Systems Instrumentation, part of the intricate task that was aero-engine manufacture, and a logical course for an aviation geek with a fondness for complexity. He was content.

Alice had fallen for him heavily after meeting him at a party in Monmouth – a summer reunion of sorts, and Jon was there with his sister, who'd been at school with Alice. She was in finance, and Alice pretended to be impressed. She was impressed with her brother, though. Their home at Ross-on-Wye was ten miles up the A40, and when they parted that evening – after sharing no more than a dozen words and a simple handshake – Alice thought he was gone for ever, those ten miles becoming ten million in her mind. She drove down the valley to Brockweir in a state of miserable panic at having found and lost someone the same evening.

She hadn't known how shy she could be, how tongue-tied... *how stupid to keep quiet! Why didn't I ask to see him again?* She would think of nothing else for two days – the same aching misery she'd had waiting for Olivier four years ago – until a joyous phone call: after Jon had noticed Alice, his sister had noticed *him*, and she phoned the hotel, thinking it would be a good idea for them to meet again sometime – a bit of matchmaking that would decide their future.

"He'll go right past you," she'd said, "unless you invite him in..."

So three days after that, Jon called at the hotel on his way south to Filton on a dreamy Sunday afternoon they would never forget, and had tea. They were both twenty-one years old. Two years ago Jon had started at Filton as a mere Technical Apprentice – with the intention then of being head of his department – and he impressed her with his ambition. She'd been lost with his work-talk and smiled patiently when he raved over some engine or other, or some impenetrable detail which in his uncertainty with her he hoped would be of interest, or would at least impress her; she was impressed enough to take to him, for his mystery and his affection: she wondered, *Jon, will you stay with me?* Yes, she felt he loved her, but it's best to believe that Jon's affections were split, his heart shared. Aviation was his life before Alice, but when she appeared he helplessly let her into his tight little world, and had to allow this astonishing creature some space. She attracted him, fascinated him, threw him off course: he was in love, surely, or something very like it – and would have seen his mind taken over more than he would have liked perhaps, had he pondered it too deeply. He was analytical, essential for his work but a hindrance to a love affair yet he applied his mind nonetheless, and decided he could manage both.

: : :

Her first shyness with him on that evening in Monmouth had surprised her. She'd had boyfriends and not been shy with them, been able to talk, to ask questions, even when those boyfriends were new. (And her virginity departed years ago in an unmemorable affair at a friend's party, the only time in her life she'd drunk too much. She was sixteen then, and after that experience, and even after her time with Olivier, she went out with other boys but never let them get that far). She had become careful, saving herself for the one she would instantly recognise, the one who would give her love and respect rather than wandering hands, and that one was to be Jon – quiet, handsome in an unthreatening way, and the required small amount taller than she was. The handshake they'd shared was enough to light them both up, then almost close them down to each other in shyness.

So what they had taken away with them that evening were glances, the most basic knowledge of each other's lives, the single, soft touch of their hands, and a very new feeling of lightness and excitement. For Jon, that touch of hands had been extraordinary, a light baby-soft touch that thrilled him; it was the first time he'd touched a girl and felt something coming back at him (in his school years his own shyness had stopped any real involvement with girls, and in his confusion and pain he'd given out the false message of *leave me alone*. So he was indeed left alone, and waited for that handshake).

After she was introduced to him as Alice *Lindberg*, he'd put her name to her looks and thought she was surely Scandinavian – and as thoughts of Nordic blondes had always instantly connected with sex in Jon's mind, he vaguely wondered how long she'd lived here, and how much several possible English generations could have changed her... his sister filled in the gaps for him later: *only fifty-percent Swedish*. The much-diluted Italian blood in her veins was not worth mentioning, not even thought about – but it made no difference to him anyway, because he was smitten. She could have been any percentage of anything from anywhere.

: : :

Alice had been an almost-drop-out from Monmouth School for Girls, the rambling spread of buildings up on the Hereford Road at the posh end of town – she was bright, but had other ambitions than commerce or academia: she would join her parents at The Wondrous Gift. She would work hard, learn the business of hotel-keeping, and one day inherit it all. She was lucky to have parents who loved her, and who were willing to pay her to learn the skills they themselves would one day be happy to let go; also lucky that they would willingly forego her school achievements, which promised quite a different future. She defied the contemporary idea of the dumb blonde, the empty beauty. The prizes and awards she'd picked up during those six years were, to some eyes, wasted: *a degree is surely the way to go... then step back if you must – do something below yourself like running a hotel, if you really must.* So the early nineties were no different to other years regarding career advice from friends, but she'd ignored it all and had tea with Jon and her parents that afternoon safe in her choice of profession, and safe in her choice of man: she'd fallen again, fallen into love before she really knew him, a repeat of her enslavement to Olivier. In the space of an hour she'd known, and so had her mother: the slim quiet boy was evidently the one for her.

They got on together. On that first day Alice showed him around, and they walked along the river for a while, talking, sounding each other out. It helped that she was awed with his choice of job, which cheered him.

"It's beautiful here," he'd said, unsure with her as they walked, and she'd said, "What do you like, Jon? In general I mean, what makes you happy?" Then she smiled. "Apart from engines."

"Oh, all sorts." But he was never sure of what to say with new people, and Alice was still new, and female, and a little scary. He said, without much thought, "Books, films, music. And this place." She would, in time, need more detail – which books, which films, which music, and why? – but at that point all she needed to know for sure were his responses, before going forward. But what they really had in common was their unexplored attraction to each other, hers largely cerebral and dreamy, his a mixture of the same and wanting to undress her. They decided together to make this a regular thing, that he would go home on Saturday afternoons to Ross as usual, and call in every Sunday on his way back to Filton, to have lunch and spend the afternoon there, with Alice. So he dreamed of her. She was breathtaking, in every way - so novel, so new, and he was aware of being pulled away from his work. Alice had taken him over. But he was slow to realise that he'd also taken *her* over – he didn't know she'd waited, kept herself for him through years of hopefulness, of smiling through life while watching the radar. And when this day was over she would be convinced he had fallen for her personality, her likes and dislikes, for the way she was and not just her incidental beauty. But they had not even kissed. They had returned to the hotel, still with their arms around each other, and her mother observed – different, closer, holding each other. *They didn't leave like that. Fingers crossed, for all sorts of reasons.* But time had been short, and after a slight ill-at-ease kiss in front of her parents he'd left for Bristol.

Alice had planned that first day of courtship as a guarded, modest process, almost worthy of a Jane Austen affair with beating hearts and vested interests, but they both wanted more and she knew the next time would have to be different, so she planned accordingly. Her file on Jon was filling up. She would have a week to dwell on him, a long six days of preparation and difficult-to-end evening phone calls – mobile phones were a new thing, and within a month they would both have one, but meanwhile he monopolised the phone box down the road from his lodgings, not daring to talk to her from anywhere else where he may be overheard. And she realised this shy boy was only shy about certain things.

The following Sunday Jon drove into the car park full of wanting to see Alice again, and as he pulled up she perfectly acted out what her mother had told her as a child – walk, don't run. A big hug, and a very light kiss. He had no idea that things had moved on with her. She'd worked it all out, before she'd slept and while she'd worked, while wondering if it was a mistake to plan for two while knowing the real wishes of only one... Jon was quiet, but not a dark horse – but could he be? Could he be hiding his true feelings? She thought not. On that second Sunday they left straight after lunch, crossed the road, and gripping each other's hands scrambled down the bank to the path where the old railway track had been. They went further, to the edge of the river, and stood there looking across the soundless water, the chirping of grasshoppers mixing in the heat with the buzzing of tiny unseen wings, a profound and sensual moment. They stood a little apart, still holding hands, and she moved closer to him, took her hand back and put her arm around his waist. He did the same to her, and they waited there, looking ahead across the river from the rough grassy bank. They stepped back onto the path, walking slowly upriver, away from the boundaries of The Wondrous Gift. As they walked she leaned towards him and rested her head on his shoulder, a surprise that struck him harder than any declaration of love could have done... it suggested so much: it was love, and trust, and he'd never felt closer to her. It filled him completely. He pulled her tighter to himself and they walked on, like lovers after the event, after the lovemaking when heads are full of each other. The heat was oppressive, and he looked at her, and longed for her.

The afternoon was quiet, with only the occasional sound of a car on the road above them as they walked. After a while the path closed in and they moved away from the river, and in a small gap in their conversation he turned and put his hands each side of her face and kissed her, taking her by surprise but she didn't pull away. After a moment she put her arms around him and his hand found her breast, which she hadn't expected, and a very short time after that they made love in the long grass that bordered the path. Shy Jon had taken the lead, and surprised her after all. He'd fumbled with buttons and was mildly shocked by her lack of underwear: she'd looked intently at his face as he'd undressed her, simply wanting no holdups on the way, no inelegance, no hindrance beyond those few buttons. The deeply serious realisation of all her wishes had arrived. And no, he wasn't shocked much by her directness, but slightly amused - it was different, unexpected, the sweetest shock. So he fumbled again, with his trousers (*his* inelegance didn't matter) then the touching, the overwhelming of the senses, the brief, urgent act. For him it was the exquisiteness he hadn't seen or felt before and it went beyond the rest of her, beyond all the things he already knew, and he was helpless, like a child without thoughts. Alice had quite simply arrived at her heaven: it was done at last, this long-awaited thing of hers, and it was successful beyond words.

Afterwards, as they lay under the cloudless sky in their pro-tecting circle of grass, he looked at her and touched her and she woke as if from a deep sleep, but all she saw was him, and all she wanted was him. She was entirely unembarrassed, and watched him as he caressed her, also marvelling at this new lover, at his nakedness... but his shape was vague, even in the sunshine. He was next to her, talking quietly, caressing her, loving her while she felt away from the world, seeing and hearing him from a distance. She was full, with no room for anything else.

But soon their wider surroundings mattered again, and when they had slowly got themselves dressed and were lying together in the sun, reality had returned too soon for them both. Jon pondered that she appeared not to have been a virgin, but he was no expert. It just appeared that way to him, and he knew it didn't really matter. Jealousy and possessiveness were strangers to him, so it wouldn't make any difference if she'd had someone else – he was just certain now that he was in love with her. And days later Alice would think back to what had happened, but she would only remember certain moments with clarity, everything else blending into a sensuous dream, and as the days passed she became possessed by the fierce love she now felt for him.

That afternoon would be the first of many that summer, though never as carelessly, and never again without the spoiling condom Jon had brought and she'd refused that first special time – "I want you, not that," she'd said. The big risk had become small for her; even before she'd known him a couple of days she'd thought through the scenario of pregnancy and an earlier marriage. She was so sure of him, even then. So any outcome was good with her, because they would be happy together – a child of an extra-ordinary event, or the same event without a child. Come what may, at that time it was the lovemaking that mattered. Parents could be won over, brought round, and Jon could have the child he'd already said he'd like to have someday, a little sooner. In her seriousness, Alice was taking control of events, and of people she believed she knew. So her dreams were turning out nicely; she'd put him on like a new dress, a perfectly-fitting dress without imperfections or flaws – it was as simple as that – and there wasn't much to get used to. He was right for her, so all was well: they were in love, the sharing of their bodies the final proof, and as they'd walked back that sultry August afternoon into their new world they'd held each other closely, she wanting him for ever, as his mind touched lightly on the possible outcome of what had happened. From then on she made her private plans while he tagged along and wondered, in the midst of his love for her, what was coming next.

: : :

August, unusually hot and humid in the valley air; the hotel tucked under the bank sweltered at midday and waited to lose the sun as the afternoon progressed. The shade brought relief to some and regret to others. Sun-lovers were unhappy, workers generally the opposite. Alice and her mother were used to the sun moving around away from them, and were still able to look across the river to England in the sunshine, to lift them and remind them of the brightness they'd lost. They were busy every day, the rooms booked and the dining room mostly full, the waitresses coping with breakfast, lunch, tea and evening meal as the cooks sweated in the kitchens. The same every day, one after another, a solid routine lightened by the quirks and pleasantries, the occasional awkwardness of customers, the always-surprising differences between people. And Jon worked the summer far away from it all, at Filton. The ladder to his ambitions was in place and he was on it, surely taking him from his green overalls to the white coat he coveted in those early days, and he worked in a warm haze where everything suddenly looked better - and where the complexities of his work could be coped with alongside Alice, who now took up a lot of space in his mind. He'd always thought that love and sex should go together, but until recently he'd experienced neither, and this conflicted with his workmates who'd all (apparently) experienced sex yet never spoke of love – that would be soft-headed, and not something to be discussed for fear of losing face, so he'd kept quiet. And now, when he looked ahead ten years (he would be thirty-one, still young), his life could be good, and settled, with children and a loving wife. Yes, love was necessary, and he felt the comfort of the idealist when thinking about it as these thoughts flowed around and through him during their first weeks together.

Alice had not become pregnant after that first intoxicating episode on the river bank, but still he'd wondered at how she could have been so casual about the risk. But he didn't wonder about his own carelessness. Lust had taken care of it, and his remembrances of that afternoon would always begin with their first real intimacy, with the extraordinary softness of her breast beneath his open hand. So he loved her, and all the physical revelations that came with her, his first girl; she was new, strange, and so very *female* in shape, this truly natural blonde (later, "Are you sure about that?" would be the tiresome question at work). And she was clever in different ways to his own cleverness, which he found interesting, and acceptable: *We'll get on, the two of us.*

Three weekends later, Alice asked, "How do you feel about Jon staying Saturday night, Mum?" The question was a formality.

A small shock. "Oh... I suppose so. Yes."

Would it matter if they shared a bed now and then? These were liberal times and if Elena and David had concerns for their fair daughter, they didn't show them (but still they fretted: not so fair now? As if it had been any different with them, in 1971), but if pregnancy could be avoided then all should be well - and anyway she knew if they didn't do it here, they'd do it somewhere else. Jon, meanwhile, was out of it as Alice pushed ahead with their life together, without a thought that he may not be ready for that particular step – she was certain, always certain of her man. In spite of any misgivings Elena had said yes, and David, almost laid-back, had said yes. Jon, after the deal was done, had said, "Are you sure?"

So they started living together from Saturday afternoons to Sunday afternoons, with the delight of Alice's bed in between – except for the one weekend a month when he went home to Ross on Wye – and poor Jon, while loving the nights, struggled with this openness on the Saturday evenings spent around her parents in the bustle of the hotel. He couldn't avoid the embarrassment of being with their daughter in her bed ("Goodnight, sleep well...") and to him Sunday mornings felt like the old morning-after-the-wedding-night, with imagined knowing glances and the unspoken *everything all right then?* He would get over this, his imaginings replaced after a few weeks by self-confidence and acceptance of his new life, his new parents-to-be, and his still-dazzling lover. So this new beauty, at first a serious rival to his love at Filton, became a separate and important part of his life, and after two months he was relaxed and off-guard enough to agree to their engagement: "Let's get married," she'd said straight out of the blue one beautiful autumn day, and he'd looked into her eyes, hesitated for a second, and said yes. But it was a very big yes, and a few hours later, while driving south to his work, he tried to make sense of what it meant and why it had been so easy to say that *yes*. And shouldn't it have been him, proposing to her? It didn't matter. It was a result of the Love he'd been aware of for years that after all its familiarity had taken him by surprise. The next day, though, was one of quiet panic and his unease lasted into the evening until he had to face the fact that he would be a married man – a husband – probably within a year; seeing no other course than the one he'd agreed to he managed at last to put it out of his mind, and, without dwelling on her beforehand, went to bed and dreamed of Alice.

Christmas came and went, and plans had been made. It was to be Saturday, October the twenty-second, hopefully (surely) a brilliant late-autumn day, ten months away, and counting. The date was auspicious, and almost perfect for Alice... just one October day away from her parents' marriage, twenty-three years before: if they could be as happy as they were, all would be well, and choosing the same day – almost – was the best start. Jon's parents had come and gone over Christmas, after being impressed with the treasures possibly in store for their only son. Diane, the twin, had the credit for the situation, her matchmaking no secret by now, and Jon, the other twin, had the prize – and the prize was Alice Rossetti Lindberg, soon to be Greerson, soon to be a married woman, a wife. And an heiress. A beautiful soft blonde clever agreeable willing heiress... what could possibly go wrong? Jon had little idea of what could go wrong, and Alice wasn't looking for problems. The future was rosy.

: : :

When Alice appeared, she was Jon's secret. At work, whenever girlfriends were mentioned – which was often – he excluded himself, avoiding questions while fretting over whether to tell his workmates or not. They were content with him being wedded to his work, a sexless guy with no time for girls. So his reserve kept the secret until his engagement, when – knowing it couldn't last – he lost his nerve and settled for writing his wedding day into the office diary, which turned out worse for him when it was discovered: there was a rush, an unbelieving rush of crude comments as they sought him out, and Jon the Dark Horse suffered for his privacy. He was obliged to show them photographs of her, and he would never forget first his embarrassment, then his edgy pride as they stared wide-eyed at Alice, with one offensive loud-mouthed comment instantly shouted down. They would have let him know very quickly had she appeared tarty, or cheap. She was more than acceptable – she was almost *exotic* – and through the banter he felt the satisfaction of envy coming at him. He'd been top of his class for some time, and now she'd put him unreachably beyond them all.

But as the weeks and months passed, Jon sensed a change. He struggled with his ambition. *What do I want? I want to work with machines and fine tools, that's what. I don't want to be led away. I don't want to be turned by money or a push from anywhere or anyone. Sure, I can oversee people, but don't take me away from the shop floor... Alice works in a hotel, after all she did at school, after all the promise, so I can do the same and stay in the job I love, surely. So that becomes my ambition.* Ambition, he discovered, was not always the same as following one's dream; it could be imposed, and driven by pressures from others, expectations, the need for more money (no longer a necessity for him, with Alice and the hotel), and he felt it happening: "You could be head of your department," his instructor had told him, "you could easily get there." But as time went on that carrot tempted him less. He wanted above all to keep in touch with what made him happy, and not end up in a suit and an office somewhere; his instructor's job was as far as his ambition stretched, and even that would keep him at a desk for longer than he'd like. Those were his feelings now, but the route he'd chosen would not give him many shots to call, and if at the end of his training he felt uncomfortably pushed towards higher things he would jump ship; he was thinking beyond Filton, beyond Rolls-Royce, to a place as yet unknown where he could use his skills without feeling a need to move upwards and *better* himself. Yet all this was a struggle, to realise he was like this, and he tried not to worry what others would think of him. He'd said nothing to Alice, but with her he felt more hopeful for his future. "I want you to be happy," she'd said, many times, and sure enough that made him happy.

They were married at last on an unseasonably warm Saturday in October – a real Indian Summer – under the wished-for blue sky; the morning went by, ordered and cheerful, as Alice Rossetti Lindberg married Jonathan Derek Greerson, and they were properly joined together by law, as midday passed. Their union was sealed with Phillip Rossetti's necklace. She'd dreamt of it the night before – glittering in some unknown hand, and spoken to it in the strange way of dreams: *After one hundred and sixty-nine years you come to me, and I shall give you to the daughter I shall have, in time.* She knew what she wanted, and convinced herself that she would have it all. Her dreams would come true. She'd had the morning sunshine and the empty blue sky she'd wanted, and the full church she knew she'd have. The little church at Tintern Parva, at the bend in the river, was truly full; close and far-flung family, vaguely familiar relatives... and too many friends to get inside for the service and crowding around the building and across the grass of the graveyard, threading between the hallowed ancestors of the new bride as they went. A few distant and unfamiliar cousins came over from Sweden, to view their own – albeit fifty-percent diluted – distant cousin, and Julia was there from Fréjus, seeing a different girl from the one who'd left her in such disarray five years before.

Jon went easily through that first crowded day – even with his nervousness at being one of the leading players; he was caught up, and fell easier than he thought he would into the *newly-married man with loving wife* slot. His Best Man had been as nervous as he was, walking around the busy churchyard deep in thought with the words of his speech going round and round in his head, silently mouthing the words, oblivious to all and without realising that when the time came he would read it all anyway. Jon's own so-dreaded speech turned out better than he'd expected; his shyness converted all those good people into a friendly inanimate mass and he looked at no one in particular – or at least *saw* no one in particular, only a roomful of blurred and unthreatening faces. As for Alice, she was in the grip of euphoria, her head full of the day with no space for anything else, and they had all spilled out onto the grass after the service and in the midst of this rapture – in front of everybody there – she had grabbed and kissed her new husband passionately, and they had almost fallen over as he'd coped with this unforeseen embarrassment while trying not to step on her dress (*the dress: ethereal, flowing, delicate, sensual...* all the words that mattered to her, and the low neckline to show off the necklace he'd given her in the church. And white, of course, pure white. Those words meant little to Jon, simply adding up to *beautiful,* but there was certainly enough on the floor to be careful of).

They had come out from the church, and they were *married,* but the sky, as if jealous of their happiness, had turned while they were inside from clear and blue to covered and grey. Within five minutes of them coming out it had rained on them all (which was a good omen to Alice's English mother, but a bad one to anyone Welsh, and they were in Wales. Misgivings scratched lightly at her but she ignored them. Promises of bad luck were not welcome on such a day, and anyway they were only just in Wales... only half the river's width into Wales).

Please let us be happy! It was impossible to imagine Jon wanting anything else. Their wedding day, from sunshine into rain on that crowded riverbank, was a huge success and there could be no spoiling of it later. Guaranteed happy endings, that's what she wanted – the destiny of princes and princesses; she had that, and free admission into the never-ending pleasure of an excellent marriage. Or so it seemed to her as they all drove alongside the river to The Wondrous Gift – kept free for the weekend and transformed with flowers and lights and glitter in the best show since Elena and David's wedding in 1971.

It was also the night that British Summertime ended.

"An extra hour in bed tonight," said the Best Man, "so that's why it had to be today..."

It had to be today, but the extra hour was an unthought of bonus and they shared their familiar bed, leaving the next morning in the remnants of a slight frost for Bristol Airport and two weeks in Spain, to the exhilaration of Seville, a place strange and new to them both; Jon's new wife was a traveller with experience, flying every year to somewhere hot or cold with her parents or friends, but for Jon it was a first – first flight, first trip abroad, and he would remember for the rest of his life his very first step onto foreign ground at the foot of the steps down from the plane: *a warm breeze, in October!* Everything new, bright and strange. And more than a thousand miles from home.

It was to be a time they would always look back on as one of the best of their life together, two weeks of no timetables, no pressures, and long lazy days in the agreeable October sun. They both thought that if only they could keep what they had in those two weeks – and feel as happy as that for the rest of their life together – then all would be perfect. But it was a honeymoon, a holiday, and they returned happy with each other to Phillip Rossetti's old rooms at the front of the hotel, now very much their own; from now on Jon would commute each day to Filton, and Alice would await his return each day; and that's how 1994 ended for them, with new lives and a two-month marriage that looked like it would last.

ALICE NEEDS TO KNOW THAT SHE IS LOVED

The last day of November 1996, two years on from their marriage, and Alice's slide continued. There were few consolations, and as the month ended and December began she was upstairs most of the day, leaving the downstairs work to her mother and Jenny, her now settled-in replacement. Lonely, empty days, extraordinary for their difference and Alice, once so in charge of her life and her work, was now spending her time in a cloud of anxious reminiscences, coming down only for meals, begrudgingly facing her family, forcing a smile or the odd word while they wondered what to do with her.

Alice, once so in charge of things...

She lived in the past on those days, revisiting happiness and certainty. She recalled her school prizegiving, remembering the smooth, plummy voice of a well-fed and unappealing school governor – *"The Bullinger Prize, Alice Rossetti Lindberg."* The whole name. She'd asked for it. Not Greerson yet. The confident walk to the stage, the shaking of an over-fleshed hand, the "Well done Alice" breathed too closely at her to overcome the applause. But now she's dead, it's all past, and gone; the optimism, especially, is gone. A shame, she now thought, not to take advantage of one's talents. But also a shame to have made the wrong choice, years later, with Jon.

: : :

Jon would try Elena's little ways of showing love to her, but it seemed to him those ways were not much different to how he'd always been with her. He made a special effort to smile at her, while fearing it would make him appear shallow and make things worse. It was all too complicated, too confusing, and when he tried with her and she made no response he despaired of ever getting it right. *Little ways.* Like always saying hello, always being gentle, always trying to understand how she felt. Of tidying their rooms, or cleaning her car without being asked. Of always saying goodnight while lying next to her, while longing to hold her again in his arms. And of course, *I love you* – the words that now had an even greater significance, and must be said, regardless of how they were received. But saying those words to an unresponsive, out-of-it Alice was difficult, and it seemed to him that it would be easier to say them to someone in a coma in the hope that in some tiny way they get through. Yet he said them, judging the moments as best he could and telling himself not to be discouraged. He even brought flowers one evening, but was almost too fearful to give them to her, feeling foolish and weak while taking them upstairs; she'd given him a faint smile and an even fainter thank you, and he'd had to search downstairs for a vase after she'd left them lying on her dressing table and gone into the study next door. It was going to take a while.

On one of those evenings he was sitting in their bedroom when Alice came up from some aimless wandering after supper. He got up quickly as she opened the door, and said, "Alice, please – talk to me." She stopped in her tracks, and he faced her in the middle of the room. Her beauty had gone to some blank, lost expression; her eyes were heavy, not fully open, and reluctant to meet his.

"Alice... look at me." He put his hands on her shoulders and looked hard at her. She lifted her head.

He said, "Tell me how I can put this right. Help me, please."

She scarcely shook her head.

"Come on," he said, "this is no good. Talk to me."

And from somewhere far away she said, quietly, "I'll talk to you."

He spoke gently to her, told her he'd never lied when he'd said he loved her.

"You lied about the baby."

110

"I've agreed to next October, or whenever... even now, Alice, even now."

"But you lied to me for three years."

"I misled you. I'm sorry."

"If that's what you want to call it."

It was crazy, this grudge, to be still solid in her after so long. He said calmly, "Look, It's been over a month now. We really can't go on like this. Why won't you believe me when I say I love you? What's this problem you've got?"

He instantly regretted using the word. And there was no way she could explain this *problem* to him. Seven years and more, from her adolescence, from princes, from Rhiannon, from Phillip, from Olivier, from the perfection she'd dreamt of, which he'd provided and then betrayed. It was too much, but no one would understand or agree with her. Everyone would urge her to make peace with him, forgive him, be flexible... and there was the rub: she could not be flexible, no matter how much she suspected it would help. She was a fundamentalist, and not for turning.

He spoke softly as she stood before him, this different person, his lovely wife with untidy hair who needed to bring herself back to life.

"I know what I've done, Alice, I really do." Then he sighed. "I lied to you... I didn't tell you how I really felt, but I can't just keep saying sorry, can I?"

It was impossible; he'd even lied about lying. Misleading, or lying – what's the difference? Why did he even have to think about it? So it became harder for her: forgiveness, then that leap of faith – two huge obstacles to overcome. She said nothing.

"I could tell you I love you twenty times a day and you still wouldn't believe me. How can I get over that?"

And she simply replied, "I don't know." She moved away from him. "I'm sorry, I just don't know."

She went past him and into the study, closed the door between them, lay down on the couch and slipped back into the fog she'd slightly moved out of while speaking with him, as everything he'd said went from her mind and the devil in the shadows took her back – yet she'd reached a truth before that dark moment, that she was being unreasonable to her husband and that she could do nothing about it. By now she knew that anything good coming her way would not last, even a perfect reconciliation would inevitably fail, the best outcome would be damned by fate.

For Jon it was extraordinary to be annoyed then immediately full of love for her. He should have simply been firm, perhaps, and as he sat back down he went over a very brief scenario in his mind:

Me: I want us to have a baby now. (Bold. So far, so good.)

She: But do you love me? (Oh...)

That scenario ended abruptly, right there. It could have continued like this:

Him: Yes, I do love you.

Her: I don't believe you.

Him: But I do! I do love you! You can have your child... our child! Open your eyes – see what I do for you, what I try to do for you!

Her: Sorry, I don't see too well any more. Do you love me?

So befuddled Jon sat there, ruled by his uncertainties, while Alice lay in the next room and, unfortunately, allowed herself almost none.

That night she stopped taking her pill. The last time they'd had sex was the night of their anniversary, more than a month ago. Why was she still taking it? Why bother with something so unneeded? Something so against her wishes anyway, a thing to stop what she desired. After the talk with Jon, her future was even bleaker to her, and she could not forgive him nor believe him so there her fixation rested, quite intact. And she wasn't even mad at him, but sorry for it, for the hopelessness of it all... *this is how it is now.*

Jon saw the foil pack in the bathroom cupboard. He'd been in the private habit of checking it every day – he would probably explain this particular meddling with her privacy as part of the attention to detail he lived with at work, rather than the lack of trust it really was – and he was dismayed over the following days to see that she'd stopped. He suddenly thought how vulnerable she would be now. It was absurd, but it worried him. He felt afraid for her, as if she needed to be more careful from now on, but without knowing why. Had she given up on life? Or was she wishing to become pregnant? So did she have someone else, a lover? It was ridiculous, but for him she had taken a huge step away from the woman she was.

For Alice, each day was the same as the last. She slept late into the mornings then stayed in her room, only coming out reluctantly to eat in the kitchen. Her mother insisted on that. She failed to be sociable, even with her good-natured and ever-unmarried Uncle Patrick who, after being told of her predicament, had driven many miles in bad weather to be met by his unhappy niece, almost unrecognisable in her melancholy. It was an early visit, to see her, as if she wouldn't last until Christmas – and he left again the next day in sombre mood, after much discussion with his sister Elena, and David. Nothing had been resolved, but he would visit again on Christmas Day as usual, when things would hopefully be different. So as November turned to December, and more than two years on from their marriage, the Greersons were on parallel tracks, each incapable of making a first move closer, and their bemused bed kept its twelve-inch gap.

Alice had slipped – first, a few hours here and there spent away in her mind, then the odd day when she couldn't rouse herself in the morning and in little more than a week she'd gone from being involved to almost complete detachment, to the dismay of her parents. She'd stopped visiting her grandfather. She was gone from them all, into her own world. She wandered the streets in her daydreams, met people with different minds who would sweep her up, for better for worse, regardless. She would slip into those dreams, then slip out of them even further away, ending up in a soft thoughtless world where nothing mattered, a deep numbing snowdrift of non-feelings... *I don't know what's happening. I don't care any more.* Her parents observed the changes. They saw Jon distressed by his wife's detachment. They saw her slipping away, from her husband, from the hotel, from life, and she would not talk about it with anyone. People were consulted, discussions had, but she flatly refused to be involved with anything, especially counselling; she told her mother there was nothing to talk about, and it seemed that kindly faces or helpful thoughts were not going to put anything right.

Her grandfather's lifeline had failed – he'd been quietly upset to see her go after such a promising start, so upset that he stopped writing, left his History alone and went back to the solace of his painting. In a matter of weeks everything stopped for him, through sadness for Alice rather than anything else. He didn't tell her. It could rest for a while until he, and maybe she, were ready again.

She barely spoke with her parents, and then with a detachment that scared them. Things came and went without her. As her moods changed, her mind was either empty or restless, either crushed and quiet or craving something unreachable – and she wasn't sure what, in spite of the events that had got her there.

Jon carried on with his life through those winter days. His job took him every day to Bristol, and he would leave early, going with the flow across the sleepy Severn, away from her, his thoughts already with his work, and set for the day. When he came home she was always up in the study, sitting by the window or lying on the couch, and he always said, "Hello, Alice." There was usually no reply, and that was it, until he could build himself up to say *I love you* to her again... the hardest thing for him these days, and never sounding genuine.

As winter set in with its frosts and bitter winds, their lives followed the season and became colder. On most of those mornings Alice stayed in bed, with no reasons in her head to get up; she would lie in their room in the pale light, curtains closed, without knowing or caring what the day was like outside, and only shifting when she had to. *Tomorrow*, she'd say to herself, *I'll make a start tomorrow...* Her days were empty of anything important, and went by unremembered. Unremembered, that is, until the day of her Great Discovery.

On that extraordinary morning she lay in bed alone, gazing blankly at the covered window to the outside world, the muted rectangle of light, the only focus in the unlit room. The strange cravings for something – *anything* – made her move. She got up, crossed to the window and threw the curtains wide. Over the river the fields were clothed in frost, the few trees still and dead with cold. Nothing moved over there, beyond the invisibly moving water. Her mind was light and restless. Unable to face the drawn-out day, she felt a slow craving: something now, please, to fill her mind, to start the wheels turning... and the need led to a new thought: *Happy Lives – that'll do. Other people have Happy Lives.*

Calmly, she followed her need. She pulled on her dressing gown, found the step-ladder and clattered it across the landing. In the rough spidery loft above was a wooden box, pushed back under the rafters. The box was not the discovery. She knew it was there, and what was in it – invoices, bills of lading, relics and remnants of the old family business, boring yellowing lists and things of little interest to hotel owners, despite their history. She knew because she'd rummaged through that box at the start of her time with her grandfather at Celyn, when she'd thought it not worth bringing down. But now, there were human connections there.

So in her barrenness she climbed into the loft with a torch. The hotel busied itself far below as she crouched in the darkness under the roof, pulling out invoices, receipts, notes and scraps and wondering at those lives long over with, and the people that had made them... *and who were you, that wrote so perfectly? What was your name? And how did you feel, to be writing so perfectly – were you happy? Were you married? How did you die?*

For the first time, she dug to the very bottom, and found the book. Out of sight, buried, waiting – an inch-thick, with heavy covers bound in black leather. Taking it from the box, she felt its weight, turning it in her hands in the awkward torchlight. She sat down on the boards. Holding the torch, she turned to the first page. There, in thin elaborate script, she saw:

The Private Journal of Phillip Rossetti
Owner & Master of the Barque FLORENCE
of Bristol, England.
Begun this 12th of September, 1825
Omnia vincit Amor; et nos cedamus Amori.

Oh.

A rush of coldness.

She stared at the words, a frozen soul in the darkness above the pool of light, as seconds passed; afraid now to turn the page – afraid of disappointment, of her eyes taunting her with lies, of being cast off within reach of some deliverance. Hardly breathing, she turned that first page, revealing the treasure –

'This Journal begins with such Happiness as I have never felt before. I have found my Beloved, my Darling, my Angel, my Janet. I am certain We shall be Wed, as all is so Well between Us...'

It was real. She jumped a quarter-inch of this man's life, and found herself by chance four years later at the side of a river on a summer's afternoon: '...this disloyal River, which stays with me & must now sustain me with its Beauty alone.'

The book was almost full, the last three pages empty, the last words: '...this Book is filled, & finished. My Beloved & Wonderful Daughter is born into the world 3 days past & We are a Family. Omnia vincit Amor.' The last date, 30th June 1838. Another lump of pages, filled with close writing, then another – she went backwards and forwards, breathlessly jumping the years and reading odd lines, as something momentous came to her. She realised what she'd found: here, six generations back, was Phillip – her Rossetti namesake, the person she would choose above anyone else from the rabble of history. She occupied his very space above the page, touched lightly the ink of his thoughts just as they were put down, untainted and genuine, and fell properly and helplessly in love with Captain Phillip Rossetti; at eight twenty-four on that dead morning in December, Alice Rossetti – *forget the Greerson* – leapt to salvation from her desultory life.

Down in her bedroom, she consumed the book from end to end – all day lost to the world and long into the night – and found the Latin of the first page (she knew it would be perfect) – *Love conquers all; we too give in to Love...* and Alice gave in to love.

The love she already had for Phillip intensified in that time to fill her completely, and she gave herself to that long-dead lovestruck captain who had walked and slept a century and a half before in the room where she walks and sleeps. Transformed thereby she found new purpose, moving from death to life, overtaken by a great and pure love that filled all the gaps – *You'll never let me down, Phillip. We are the same.* She was, indeed, transformed.

WHAT'S HAPPENED TO YOU?

The hours after finding Phillip's Journal were a time of secret euphoria in which Alice read and re-read page after page, but dipping in here and there, into a vast store of treasure and it would be early evening when she'd properly begin from the first page. As breakfast time had passed she'd stayed in her room and had to be reminded to eat, and when her mother came and tapped on her door she scrambled to find a place for the book, unwilling to show excitement, of being too easily cured of her malaise. The book was already beyond precious, a Holy Grail unable to be shared, her glittering lifeline. She went down to the kitchen, and sat with her mother in a pool of distracted silence as things went on around her.

"You should eat, darling."

So she ate, slowly, while her mind was upstairs with Captain Phillip Rossetti. She would read for the rest of today and through the night and into tomorrow, every word, from beginning to end, and she couldn't wait, could hardly eat for thinking of him. She was awakened, and sharply aware that she was properly in love again, while her mother and husband knew nothing of it. This was real and constant, not flesh and blood; it would not let her down.

: : :

'Monday the 12th of September, 1825

This Journal begins with such Happiness as I have never felt before. I have found my Beloved, my Darling, my Angel, my Janet. I am certain We shall be Wed, as all is so Well between Us. My life is already Changed by Her, which was my Hope & Expectation & We look forward in the way only Lovers can Understand, with such Elation, to the Joy We shall have when We are Together again. Our Love, made in Heaven, will Surely Endure & be a Pillar to hold Us up.'

She read his words, page after page of lavish adoration for his bride-to-be, a rambling, over-romantic outpouring of feelings and wishes, and it was true that if it had been written by anyone else she would have closed the book, squeamish with the horror of someone else's sentimentality. It was the kind of writing she disliked. Give her Daphne du Maurier, or Rosamond Lehmann, or any of the stuff from history she'd grown up with, the authors who could truly write about love without the slushy idealism. In spite of her own idealism she felt she was deeper than that, but this was Phillip, and what she already knew of him before today would allow her to forgive him his exuberance for Janet – his beloved, after all.

Jon's own mystery deepened. He was aware on that first night of her reading by torchlight, something she never did. She was confident of not being bothered by him, as he lay awake wondering at her, listening for the turning of her pages, and falling asleep soon after the old clock downstairs chimed midnight; Alice heard it chime two o'clock, then three, then gave in to the night as the torch batteries faded, pushing the book as far under the bed as she could reach.

In the morning Jon's alarm woke her as it always did, but this time she did not try to go back. She pretended – as usual – to be sleeping, and as he left the room for his breakfast she reached for the book again, ready to push it under her covers if he came back in. Later, as she heard his car drive off she got up and dressed; her four hours of sleep were enough, and she read for the rest of the day, wide awake, around the distractions of breakfast and lunch downstairs. By the end of that day her transformation was complete, her recovery from depression quite miraculous: she was over it, saved. Her old life of the past month was finished with.

But still at the edge of it was Jon, and her parents, all the people she'd lost, and she didn't know what to do about them. Yet at brief times on that swirling first day she actually wondered about starting again with life and using her elation, her new strength, to overcome the problems – but she was spoiled by Phillip and could see no one else for more than a few seconds. These were the moments when her troubles with Jon could have been removed but she let them pass. Later on, when it was too difficult to change, she would think hard about that day and wonder if she should have been open about the journal, forgiving Jon, restarting work and life in a saving atmosphere of wonder at Phillip's life instead of the unreal and unhealthy secrecy she chose. The jewels of so many possibilities were before her, and she would choose unwisely from them.

After supper on the second evening, her reading of the journal complete, she went up to the study again before Jon came up, and sat on the couch in her new state of alertness. At supper she'd appeared the same as ever – quiet, withdrawn, separate from them all while in her mind she felt very different, and she'd had to put on an act for them to show the same Alice rather than the reborn Alice who could suddenly manage her life again. She was afraid of being thought shallow – too easily mended – and she kept her secret.

So she chose unwisely, and after some thought came back to the same point with Jon, to the impasse of not believing or trusting him. In her euphoria she compared him with the new Phillip she'd discovered, and easily found her husband lacking; she made her choice and left him as he was.

: : :

Two days after finding the journal, with Jon already gone, Alice went downstairs to her breakfast, and stayed. She sat with her mother, and with the hotel in the hands of her schoolfriend Jenny – by now quite settled – she talked, and opened up about her transformation, without giving the cause. She was relaxed, and so much closer to her old self that Elena was almost in denial, fearing a relapse at any moment. But there was no relapse; Alice gave in and for most of that day she moved around the hotel again, and spoke to people who'd had nothing from her for weeks. She was a new person, in many ways. She wanted to work, to get back into things while being under Phillip's wing, to live for him, and the madness of it all never bothered her... she would take back most of the realities she'd moved away from, but Jon, especially, would be left more bewildered than ever. It was the undeclared *coup de grace* for him. He saw her change. With her love – her reason for living by now – safely tucked-up in her bottom drawer, the world threw open its arms, the hotel ran sweeter than ever and all around her were amazed, but he despaired, because the changes were for everyone except him.

He'd come in from work on that second day, and there she was, smartly dressed, going through the check-in book in reception. It was a shock. He'd faced her and said, keeping his voice low, "Alice, what's happened to you?"

She was cool. "What do you mean?"

"What do you think I mean! What's happened?"

She'd looked away and said, after a pause, "I feel better."

He was cheered. "That's great, Alice!" Then, his deepest wish: "Do you feel better about me?"

He'd moved around her, to see her face, but she couldn't answer him. She looked away again, then walked away, leaving him standing there in his winter coat, clutching his briefcase.

None of it made sense now, as it had before today, when at least there had been a reason for Alice's depression. Elena had asked her what had brought her back again, and Alice had said, "A different outlook. I need to get on with life," and she'd replied,

"So what about Jon – is he a part of this now?"

"If he wants to be, yes."

"Why would he not want to be?"

"He needs to change. I've told you before."

"And you can't forgive him?"

"Not if he doesn't love me."

Elena looked at her daughter, exasperated. She said, "Do you have any idea how strange this looks, Alice? You were depressed for a month and now suddenly you're not – why can't you try harder with him now? Where is all this leading? To divorce? Is that want you want?"

Alice's eyes widened. *"Divorce?* I'd never want a divorce! Why do you say that?"

"Because, darling, if you can't forgive him, the road you're on ends there, or somewhere just as bad, that's why."

But Alice closed down to her then, as Elena almost regretted what she'd said. It occurred to her that this very sudden improvement could be fragile.

: : :

Alice kept the Journal in the bottom drawer of her bedside cabinet, underneath (amongst other things) two new bras in their wrappings. Safe enough, Alice had thought, unless Jon was inclined to take those bras out for some reason, to feel them in his hands, maybe... *why did she think of that?* – and find what was beneath. She felt safe with her Captain's hiding place, trusting that little space between the two men; and anyway, if Jon – or her mother, perhaps – were to find the book it would not be the end of anything. Alice would simply admit to finding it, but at a much earlier time than she did, to steer away from making any connection with her almost-miraculous recovery. The only problem may be with her grandfather, if he were told, who would wonder why she hadn't shared it with him. *Best if it's not found.* But she was surprised and a little ashamed to realise, in those early days, that there was pleasure in the slight risk, the small thrill at getting away with this – her new love so close to her old love, each unaware of the other... she was unbothered by the deception and that was a measure of her separation, mind and body, from Jon. She was often on the edge of not caring what he thought or felt, and only held back from going right over by occasional disconcerting bouts of guilt, short-lived. Any compassion for him was uselessly kept for the nights, when she would lie in the stillness of their bed and wonder at how it had all happened, before shying away from the answers and giving in again to the easy and welcoming fantasy of Phillip Rossetti. They were the early days of her new love, and as with Olivier – and after him with Jon himself – she found herself in the consuming realm of obsession, with little emotion to spare for outsiders. And Jon had become an outsider.

She talked with her grandfather and was surprised to hear he hadn't progressed with his History after she'd left him. Neither had raised the subject since then. In her new self-assurance she tried to think of a reason why he'd stopped. *I couldn't do it without you* was likely, but when he admitted he'd stopped when she had, on that same afternoon of snow flurries, she almost melted with the realisation that he'd stopped for her, given up when she had. This was special, this was solidarity – to support her by waiting for her... that's how she saw it, not that he couldn't do it alone. He never told her how upset he'd been.

So now Peter returned to his tyrannical father, and Alice returned to him most days in the quiet time after lunch. She could come and go because her friend Jenny Jones still worked at the hotel – Elena was thinking ahead, playing safe. Alice drove up to Celyn and worked with her grandfather for two hours on his beloved project. But she was still not properly connected, still not the old Alice he remembered; her depression had gone, but in its wake came something different – a happier, capable Alice, but still sometimes distracted, hooked on something unknown to him – and it wasn't Jon.

∴

'There was a Voyage to Port Royal, the old Capital of the Isle of Jamaica when at the behest of my Father I left Our Ship & wandered the town, as it was considered a safe place & empty of pirates long before that time. This would not be done at Kingston, where greed & violence held its place in that town owing to the great many slaves, & hardened men intent on their own profit. My age of 13 years He considered sufficient for a safe journey of 1 hour & with the condition that I keep close to the Harbour & keep company with none but the Carpenter Henry Dawes who would accompany me. Henry Dawes would have no harm done to me & was a good man who remained faithful to my Father until too old for His trade, & gave up the sea at near the time of my Father's death, when I would rise to Master of the Florence. The horrors I witnessed with Mr Dawes on that day but a short distance from the Harbour would give me great concern & also my Father, as He had deemed the town safe for me. The sore state of humanity there & the ill treating of so many poor wretches was hard for me to look upon & my Father was concerned thereafter to keep me on board until Our Ship sailed. This was Port Royal & the life there I was told was easy compared with Kingston.'

It was 1801, Phillip was thirteen years old, and if it hadn't occurred to him before, then that day at Port Royal changed him for ever. That was when his compassion overcame any thoughts of profit from those abused people, and the shock of that day never left him. He would tolerate his father's business, with its dependency on sugar, until 1815 as the wars with France finally ended; his father died, and everything changed after that.

She went over that paragraph, in the certainty that it was the crucial event that shaped Phillip's character, but before this, she'd read Captain Bennett's version in the *True Account,* where he has Phillip wandering abroad in Kingston, not Port Royal. And where he also blames Phillip's youth for his reaction and says, '...his Character was forming & He would harden as the years went by.'

He no doubt did harden over the years, especially in his resolve to not support slavery, and Alice felt this was the boy becoming a man. Out of the whole Journal, the Port Royal paragraph was the one that convinced her of Phillip's goodness, an important reason for her and her grandfather's admiration, and she was sorry she could not show it to him... she was sorry about the whole matter of her secret Journal, sorry but resolute; she could not share it – share *him*, with anyone.

While he had Janet, Captain Phillip Rossetti was a very happy man. He first saw her in his kitchen at Brockweir, on one of his visits from Bristol in the late summer of 1825. She and another girl had been hired for him by her father George Watkins – also Phillip's caretaker; he found her scrubbing the table in the white-washed room (something she would never do again) and he fell for her without caution. It was mutual, and for her it went beyond the romantic falling for the handsome Master cliché. She loved him, simple as that. So without fuss he took her away from her previous life that same afternoon, and with her apprehensive father's permission and quite against the etiquette of the day walked alone with her along the river, trying to remove her shyness and awe of him, taking her hand in his and convincing her that his intentions were honourable. When they returned, her anxious father was asked to find another girl to replace her, *because this one is not working here any more.* He was also asked again, but this time for permission to court his daughter. His wife had left him some years before, so poor George struggled alone with the need to please his master and protect his daughter, just eighteen years old.

It was all a bit sudden. Phillip had fallen for her in a moment: the lightning bolt to head and heart, the instant knowing – and Alice, the spellbound reader, knows it, because she's been there. And it was the same for Janet, though she was as shocked as her father by Phillip's haste. She went quickly from table-scrubbing kitchen girl to favoured young lady, walking alone with her wealthy employer, and in a state of perplexity and disbelief.

Despite the love she felt for him her thoughts were uneasy as they began their walk: *This cannot be true. He will harm me, use me then cast me off. This is how it happens. Sweet words, but this will be a different dream. It is sad, but he will cast me off.*

Yet as she shyly answered his questions, not daring to talk freely, she sensed he was genuinely interested in her. He was more grown up, more considerate than the raucous boys who'd pushed themselves at her, teasing and taking liberties. She didn't know then, but Phillip saw only that she was right for him, the country girl in the dowdy work clothes repaired at the elbows, the pretty bonnet she'd insisted on wearing, her diffidence, so refreshing after the superior wealth-obsessed women he saw around him in Bristol. He was twice her age, but it didn't matter; he'd waited such a long time – so many years of dreaming of someone like her, and as they talked his foremost thought was to keep her.

It was late summer and the riverbank was overgrown, the path almost lost in the ferns, and she knew as they followed the quiet river that she loved him, only that. On that perfect afternoon she wished for him to be safe, to love her, and to tell her so; but words of love? So soon, two hours after meeting him? So many wishes cluttered her head, so many hopes. But against his need, he did not tell her he loved her. It would be a step too far, he thought. *This must be slow. I want her to believe me.*

The unexpected journey had led not to disappointment and despair for her, but to barely-contained excitement as they returned to the house. The Captain appeared to be honourable. He hadn't talked flatteringly then thrown her to the ground beneath him, hadn't *used* her (a word so full of threat) but returned her safely to her father.

A week after their first meeting, Phillip took his new love to Bristol. They left in his carriage in the early morning, Janet still not recovered from the swiftness of events. They arrived some time in the afternoon and drove straight to the harbour through the clamour of Bristol, through the noise and the hurry, past buildings bigger than any she'd seen, past people more numerous than she'd ever imagined. The quiet country girl was amazed at everything, and the love story continued.

Alice had sat in the study upstairs with the Journal, watchful of Jon coming through, ready to cover the pages with a magazine if he did. He left her alone. In the quiet she sat at the window overlooking the car park, the occasional rush of cars on the road beyond going unnoticed, the faint sounds from the busyness of the rooms below not bothering her. She read of how Phillip courted Janet, how in the September and October he'd taken her in his carriage along the old coach roads, up over Whitebrook and down the Lydart to Monmouth, then down the other side of the Wye towards Chepstow. This was a few years before the new bridge at Bigsweir was built, the bridge Alice herself had crossed a thousand times. The account was a more detailed version of the one she'd discovered with her grandfather in Phillip's thin diary.

His description of The Kymin Hill above Monmouth was exactly as she imagined it had been before the houses and cars, the hedges and gardens. Phillip had taken Janet there in that year of 1825, on a late September afternoon of watery sun, and sat with her at the end of the ridge at a place Alice knew well. The trees, the stones and the solitude. It would have been the same, she thought, when those two were there; *but then again, maybe not.* He wrote:

'The horses were much exhausted by the climb & were grateful for the provision of water at the top. We left them & walked forward along the hill, passing the Temple & the Banqueting House & entering the Grotto, now much neglected & forlorn. The whole aspect I knew from reading Mr Heath's Descriptive Account some years before, was changed as the place had been taken over previously by men cutting wood for charcoal, their work now being done in the woods further down the Hill. The Vistas along the Top were grown over & spoiled & the seats no longer in use, with many removed. I was sad for my Love, as I was not able to show Her the delights I had described to Her. However the part furthest from the summit was agreeable & unspoilt & We passed an hour in solitude there with the high trees around us, the noise of the men far away. It was a time of Joy for Us both, my Love being the Sum of all I could Wish for in a Woman but the hour was short, before We were advised by the diminishing light to descend the hill & return to Brockweir.'

She thought of them on that hill, in the place where she'd often sat and thought about life. She wondered if they had made love there in the quiet of that hour. She actually asked herself, did people do that in those days? But she thought of them together and hoped they had, then decided they had; reading between those few written lines, her need for perfection in their love convinced her.

They were married on the fifth of April 1826, in the morning, in the room where Phillip was born thirty-eight years before – the Captain's cabin on board *Florence*, as she lay at her berth in the Floating Harbour.

When Alice had visited Bristol with her grandfather Peter in October – one hundred and seventy years after that happy day – she'd stood with him on the quayside at Mardyke, at the very spot (they reasoned) that *Florence* would have been tied up on that spring day long ago. She'd imagined them walking arm in arm off the ship, then riding away '...in a Fine Coach, horses all Plumed & Belled,' according to John Parrish's account. Phillip's Journal would soon give her the detail she craved:

'Our journey was necessarily long to avoid the dangers of crossing the Severn to Chepstow & We were taken through Gloucester & continued on Our way alone in my Carriage from Beachley, arriving at my House in darkness that evening. It was later than I had hoped as Our journey was

unhurried for the greater part. The whole House was
alight with lamps & many Decorations to welcome Us, a
Wonderful display not expected but arranged by Janet's
former colleague Annie & some friends, all of whom were
present as We arrived. There were Celebrations the
following day & We were joined by my Mother & Janet's
Father, all in a mood of joyfulness. Our Happiness from
those days went forward with Us for the 2 weeks We spent
there together, before I was required to spend time at
Bristol again.'

Her first reading of those lines, sitting at the window in Phillip's
study, had brought her back to the necklace, the central symbol of
love for her. There was no mention of it, and yet according to
Captain Bennett's *True Account* it was given to Janet on their
wedding day, and her grandfather Peter had duly put that into his
History. She was puzzled by the omission. As she read of their
early days together, through the weeks and months of 1826 and
into 1827, her disappointment at not finding it grew; but
something else was growing – Phillip's unhappiness at leaving
Janet at Brockweir. He had not married her to desert her for long
periods, even though that was inevitably what would happen. Alice
knew this was how he felt because she'd read his thin diary, and his
determined 'I am leaving the Sea' written a few days before
Christmas 1826 when he was indeed at sea, and desperately
missing her. The tone of his Journal was changing, from the joy of
their marriage to unhappiness at not being with her.

She had read on into the night, expectant and hoping for
some explanation of the necklace, but found none until the time
Phillip set out on his last voyage before losing Janet, on the
seventeenth of May 1827:

'Tomorrow I must leave my Beloved Janet & will not
return for many months, but it is with a gladdened &

settled Heart that I have decided to give Her the Pendant
& Chain as a binding together of our affections, after
much searching of my deepest feelings over its past.'

Its past? Another puzzle, another flare of curiosity, but it was not
mentioned again during the account of his voyage. It sat there in
the back of her mind until she could stay awake no longer; the
necklace, and Phillip's return to Bristol, would wait for tomorrow,
but what she'd read brought back in a blaze what she'd already
known in her heart, but had lost because of Jon. *No regrets now. I
was always right, it is possible to find a perfect love. It is possible.* It
was the feeling that had made her feel alive all those years ago,
when it gave her a childish sexless longing for happiness, for
sweet endings, for boys she knew but reimagined to suit her
needs, even then. So what did she think would happen now? She
was halfway through the journal with no idea of what was coming
next, but already she knew Phillip and Janet would sustain her
like Rhiannon and her stories had. They were a part of her now,
and they would never leave her. The necklace would be explained. There was time now for everything.

   She had lain in the dark, hungry for a sunrise so brilliant, so
full of promise, and as three o'clock sounded in that first night
she'd given in to sleep, at ease and unreachably alone in her
shared bed.

The next morning Alice picked up the journal and read of
Phillip's return. In 1827, on the fifteenth of September he was
close to the Azores, fast approaching England, and impatient -

   '...to come to You again & to give You the Gift I am keeping
   safe in my cabin for You. This Gift is for the most part a
   wondrous & tolerant creature & watches me as curiously
   as I watch Him. The Ship is making good headway again &
   We shall pass the Islands of the Azores to Our Starboard,

in the morning. I am coming Home.'

He was coming home to Janet, bringing Aku, the wondrous creature that was to be her wondrous gift. His anticipation in seeing her again ends with the joyful words of a single paragraph written as Phillip came into Bristol before meeting John Parrish, the bearer of such impossible news.

'We are in the Avon & will reach the approaches of the City Harbour within the hour. The Severn holds no terrors for me now & I shall take the shortest road to Brockweir.'

This was followed by another single paragraph, the last he would write for almost six months, where everything has turned around:

'There is nobody here. I sit in my room, above an empty & cold house, without cheer or any sign of hope. This long awaited Autumn has become a dead weight upon me & I have no expectation beyond sleep this night. She is gone from me.'

Two disparate paragraphs on the same page, separated by an inch of space and ten hours of time, the difference between barely-contained joy and utter despair. Phillip's writing had stopped. His grief had shut him down, and after those very few words on the horror that waited for him he would leave his Journal until the following spring, and then begin on a different story than Janet's, as if to clear his mind of something heavy.

Alice knew where the best parts of the Journal were, the writing that moved and excited her, and she'd begun to mark the pages with what would become a small forest of colour-coded paper strips: blue for Janet, red for thoughts of love. Very special pages had yellow, and there were many with both red and yellow. But she would find, weeks later, that she had used so many that the book was a mess, and she would spend several hours thinning them out, making herself sad in the process but ending up with only the best pages marked. She sometimes marvelled at her own behaviour, the time she spent with the book, but got over it by telling herself it was all she had. In truth it was a very big part of what she had.

: : :

In the spring of 1828 Phillip had picked up his journal again and written of the time he had crossed the Channel to Morlaix, in Brittany, to buy a ship from the French Navy at the end of the wars. There was to be another colour: *green would be for Béatrice.*

Béatrice Fleury was twenty-two when she met Captain Phillip Rossetti in the market place at Morlaix one afternoon in the spring of 1816, and he began writing of her on the third of April 1828, on a fresh page after the sadness of Janet and his six-month abandonment of his Journal. Twelve years after meeting Béatrice, he wrote:

'Now I must begin with another time, when I crossed to France with the intention of purchasing a Ship from their Navy. Which Ship it would be, I had no idea before landing there. It was at Morlaix, a Port with a river entrance like

Bristol but on a rugged & dangerous coast. The Wars had ended & peace had returned but it was with certain trepidation that I journeyed there, knowing of the anger of Sailors & especially the fury of those Frenchmen who had lost the Battles with England & now were obliged to sell their Ships. However the strength of the French Ships was well known & I was keen to choose for myself a solid & dependable Vessel that would be of help to me.

'The vessel I found was named Montclair, which to me was a pleasant name & improved the Purchase. She needed 12 men to work Her & She in time proved to be well suited to the trade. Of the Frenchmen I cannot complain & having an understanding of their grievances & a small part of their Language, I was indebted to them for their honourable manner in regard to the task before them, viz. the selling of their Ships, in many cases to their former enemies. On completion of the Sale & while my new Ship was readied for the voyage Home, I wandered the Town & with some relief found it to be friendly. It was largely built of stone, as in Bristol, but of a grey colour & with numerous wooden houses small & large, the entirety being most pleasing to me.

'There was a Market there every day & on my second day as I waited for the Ship I found myself with time to spend as I pleased. It was in the morning shortly after one of the great Churches had struck for eleven o'clock. The day was warm for April. As I passed among the vendors I saw a Lady dressed in Green Velvet flowing almost to the floor, as pretty a Lady as I had ever seen, without coat or Pelisse & more Beautiful in style & form than any Lady I had encountered anywhere. In my clear memory Her hair was covered by a simple bonnet also of Green Velvet without feather or trimmings & around Her shoulders was a shawl of a deeper green. Dark brown ringlets were each side of Her Face & gave Her an aspect of great Beauty. Her features I observed from a short distance away & Her face is so defined in my memory even after the 12 years of not seeing her, a most Beautiful Face, balanced & delicate & without severity or blemish.

'She was looking at silks & ribbons & holding them up against the sky as if to see through them, which I found fascinating, reasoning that the colour would not be seen well in that situation. In some boldness I approached Her & asked Her how She could see the colour but my French was wanting. She smiled at me. She said that She thought my English would be better than the French I struggled with & She said it in good English. She said the holding up is done to ensure that the weave is constant as the light will be troubled to come through in places if it is not, & that the colour was approved of before She did that. I thanked Her without knowing why, & not being certain of how to proceed moved a little away from her whereupon She asked me if I had come to the Port to see the Ships. Fearing Her response I nonetheless said the truth to Her, that I was an English Captain & I had purchased a Vessel the day before. She asked me which Vessel I had purchased & when I told Her it was Montclair She smiled again but with a greater radiance than before. Then to my utmost surprise She told me that Montclair was Her Father's Ship & was taken by the Navy & She was now sold because He had no interest in taking Her back.

'We could converse without great difficulty. Her eyes I remember were brown & I found it difficult to look away from Her. Her name was Béatrice Fleury & her Father was a Merchant visiting that town & having Business in some other towns in France. Even at that time, in those first minutes, I was in Love with Her.

'We talked a good while together, & wandered the

Market and harbourside. I found her to be a Wonderful person, a Young Lady of Wit & Intelligence. As evening approached & it was necessary for me to sail that day, I asked Her to meet me 8 days hence when it would be possible for me to return. She was willing, & I think eager, for this. We parted an hour later & in a state of Affection for each other, though for myself I had no doubts of my Genuine Love for Her. As I left the Port I resolved to return with a gift for Her, & imagined a Pendant of Silver on a Silver Chain which I intended to have made in Bristol.

'My time was short. The voyage was 2 days & I would see Her again in 8 days so what was left was 4 days for the making of the Pendant, which I considered an utmost necessity to have. After impressing upon the Silversmith Thomas Farr the urgency of my request, I was pleased to hear Him say that He would make it in 2 days, especially with my offer of an Excellent rate for His work. The Pendant when I first saw it, was sublime in its detail & finish. Mr Farr had faithfully formed my request into an object that I was unable to fault & it was with great Happiness that I carried it on board Florence in good time for the return voyage. We berthed at Morlaix in the morning of the day We had arranged & in the early afternoon I went to the Market & found my Beloved Béatrice waiting there. We walked beyond the Harbour & climbed the hill above the town, at the place where the whole Harbour could be looked down upon through the trees around us. In that place we felt safe & as We were alone I was bold & easy enough to Kiss Her, & in this state of Love we spent some hours together. The Pendant was given to Her & Her joy in accepting it & wearing it was Wonderful to see. Her Beauty was matched by the Beauty of that Pendant, & She wore it for the rest of Our time together. The radiance of Her Character & the things She told me about Her Life were a Wonder to me. After some time We came down the hill and walked along the quay, She being not willing to walk through the town & preferring the Harbour. Though the light would linger for many more hours, She saw fit to leave for home & for Us to meet again the next day, to which I readily agreed. The night was spent on board Florence & it was with great anticipation that I awaited the coming day. I believed She loved me, as I Loved Her. But the day that followed was a disappointment of such magnitude I can barely tell of it, even now.

'It was Her Mother that came instead of Béatrice. She met me at the Market & after enquiring of my name gave me the pretty box with the Pendant & Chain. She said Her Daughter had gone away & I must give up all hope of finding Her. The shock of this meeting was very great to me & though I pressed Her for the reason for this She would not answer but to say that I must forget Her Daughter & go home without seeing Her. Her manner was firm in the way She told me these things & she left me then, alone in the Market crowd. I knew not what to do. Through the afternoon I walked everywhere We had previously walked, in the vain hope of finding Her there. In spite of what Her Mother had said I was certain that She was still there, somewhere in that town. As I went from place to place, asking strangers about Her, I imagined that many looked upon me as an enemy though the War was ended, & no Person in that town could offer Help to me. Her name was unknown to everyone I asked & as the day passed I was drawn to accept my distressing Fate.

'Time was short & the evening tide would not wait. The hopes I woke with that morning were dashed but I resolved to return & follow this Lady who had taken my Heart from me in such a way that I could not ever forget Her, but it was a full month & more before I could again undertake a voyage to find Her. In my dreams Béatrice was my Lover.'

Phillip went back to Morlaix determined to find his love. What he found, after sheer persistence and after again scouring the town and asking whoever he met, was the information that Béatrice had left with her parents for the South and was in the area of Antibes, on the Mediterranean, where her merchant father owned property. He left Morlaix, once again in low spirits but once again determined to find her. He would go to Antibes as soon as he could.

: : :

So Alice had found Béatrice, and the shock at discovering her disturbed the comfortable position she was in with Janet – it connected with something she'd read in her grandfather's history though: John Parrish knew of his Morlaix visits, and must have suspected an earlier romance as he'd written to his mother after Phillip had found Janet, saying, 'I have seen Him but once before like this'. Nonetheless it was a complete surprise to find this rival for Phillip's affections, and to see the depth of love he felt for her. As she started reading of her she was briefly thrown off course, but she told herself, *don't be jealous.* As she read she had to agree that he loved Béatrice but she was gone from him, lost somewhere in the vastness of France, and Janet was here and he found her, married her and loved her. Béatrice does not threaten Janet. They were not rivals. *Embrace Phillip's other love, the one he never really knew, as you embrace Janet. This adds to his worth, not takes from it.* So in the end, her delight was doubled: the story of Janet is joined by the story of Béatrice, and after reading about her she went to the drawer and took out the necklace. It was different now. The pendant and chain in her hand had travelled with Phillip to France, been worn by that same green-velveted

Béatrice then given back to him. It had travelled the seas, witnessed life in England and France, and this some ten years before Janet had known of it. And after all that, more than a century-and-a-half later, Alice herself had worn it, and now holds it in her hand. So for her the story is improved, and her head is full of high regard and wonder for Phillip Rossetti as she finishes reading of Béatrice:

'I sailed to the Mediterranean Sea & docked at Antibes, but the 2 days I spent there were not fruitful & I returned Home without any hope of ever finding Her again. The memory of Her is fixed in me & I wish that my Imagination, which flies everywhere in Her Name even now, would fold its wings & rest. After 12 years of not seeing Her, the unknown has become my enemy. She is somewhere in this World but were it possible to find Her I am almost resolved against doing so, in fear of disappointment in seeing Her life as it is. So I continue my own life without Janet or Béatrice, but often I wish that those Ladies were able to give me peace.'

INFATUATION

Alice's falling for Phillip was quick and helpless, but she had nonetheless fallen properly, not like some lovestruck teenager at a dance. It was infatuation, though she would never call it such, and each time she thought of him she had a craving for more that was impossible to disregard. A raging sleepless secret in her head, giving her no rest, allowing her no doubts and because Phillip was dead there was nothing to spoil him – no new behaviour to cast doubts for her; he was set in stone, unchangeable, and she gave him no peace as she stalked him through the pages of his journal. She read his words every day, a few minutes here and there, choosing from the colour-marked pages, boosting herself like some desperate addict and she would go back down the stairs to her work feeling lifted, revitalised, ready for more hours away from him while carrying his thoughts everywhere with her. And often, knowing full well her position but being in no state to challenge it, she thought, *please, let me not be mad.*

One of the first things she read, on that first day in December, had been *Omnia Vincit Amor; et nos cedamus Amori*, and she passed it by, knowing the first part but not the second. When she found it in one of her father's books later that day, its specialness was confirmed: *Love conquers all; we too give in to love.* She followed it up and read it in context, marvelling again at such writing that came from so far back, two thousand years and more, the older narratives that fascinated and held her. From the classical ages of Greece and Rome, to her early obsessions with the *Mabinogion* and Rhiannon, through the dark ages and stopping at around 1700 – those were her times; through medieval English, Celtic magic and the exhilaration of Shakespeare's capricious kings, queens, fools, lovers and villains

140

to the other great Elizabethan poets. Her father tried to show her a bigger world, to interest her in more modern writers, to no real avail. Forget the Victorians, *please*, and apart from a few writers from fifty or sixty years ago she found it all dull, and despite her father's pleas and her teachers' efforts through her school years she stayed rooted in the past – a slower and deeper world, she thought, with more time to observe and reflect. She was comfortably stuck there, seeing most contemporary writing as being without permanence, and lacking the seriousness of history.

It was that ancient Roman virtue of *gravitas* she needed – the sincerity, the depth, the honesty, and all of those were there with Phillip. During his empty years, between losing his first wife and finding his second, he wrote in solitude of his life and his loves, human and otherwise. After telling of Béatrice, there was a gap of many months and then, on the first anniversary of Janet's death, came a page bare except for a date, and lines which Alice already knew well:

September 14th, 1828
Since she must go, and I must mourn, come Night,
Environ me with darkness, whilst I write:
Shadow that hell unto me, which alone
I am to suffer when my Love is gone.

John Donne. Phillip had taken his words, and put them onto his own life. Alice was overwhelmed and lifted away from life and reality, and from all her doubts about love; elated, she rushed through the pages hungry for more quotes from Donne, more four hundred-year-old delights. He was the greatest of her heroes of literature and had caught her years ago, after her father introduced him – for which she would be forever grateful, and he forever regretful at having given her yet another long-dead writer to enthuse over. She would find many more disconnected fragments in the Journal, after an explanation from Phillip, dated September 20th, 1828:

> 'I am past the Anniversary of losing my Love & I am better
> disposed now to write of brighter things. I am at my
> window & it is pleasant to see the sun through the branches
> of the trees, playing upon the margins of this book &
> making dancing shadows there. My other books are beside
> me as I write, and give me great support at these times. I
> have a Collection of Poems & other writings by men I
> admire, all by the kindness of my Friend Joseph Cottle, the
> Publisher in Bristol who has given much thought to my
> likes & advised several Collections of writings & poetry that
> He considered suitable for me. I have five books in all, the
> best among them being a Collection of John Donne which
> fits very well my demeanour at this present time, even
> though He often confounds me with His doubts & disdain
> for Women. John Donne will excuse me for choosing from
> His writing only the words that please me, for I find my
> own feelings put better there than I ever could tell of them
> myself. It is the occasional lines that I Love, & their fitness
> for my Life.'

Alice thought there was not much happiness in that life, and
she was happy for him to take his words from their context,
simply for their fitness, while fearing her father would not be impressed by such wantonness. Her father, however, was not
involved.

The sad anniversary and Phillip's time of 'brighter things' passed,
and before long he would fall again into the abyss of grief which
would plague him for nine years, until he met and married
Catherine. He took lines and verses from that one book without
mentioning the others, and dropped them into his journal
narrative as and when it pleased him, and on the verge of meeting

her he wrote a single line that summed up the sorrow and dejection of his life at that point; aware of his mortality, he finished with John Donne's deep reflections – at least in his journal – with the line:

'I here bequeath ... to women, or the sea, my tears.'

In his wretchedness and private self-pity he'd taken the words and addressed them to his women and to the sea, the two most important elements of his life, and mourned the loss of them all while Alice, who shares the words, mourns the tragic compulsion that had made him put them there.

: : :

On that same December morning, after Jon had left for work, the whole day was hers. She sat in their bedroom, only leaving it for the food she didn't want, and late in the afternoon went out and walked along the river in the half-light as the day began to close around her. She walked the path she'd followed many times as a child, and then with Jon, the path usually infused with memories of love, of hot afternoons, of unfamiliarity and getting to know each other – but now the path was empty, of people and of memories; it was familiar only by its geography, its twists and turns as it went close to the river's edge then veered away again. She walked now with Phillip Rossetti, her mind crammed with his words and all other space filled with love for him. She was reprogrammed, lost from the world. Then after ten minutes her father's childhood warning came to her – *remember, it will take you just as long to walk back*, and she turned for home in the failing light.

Soon it would be fully dark, the closing-down of the winter's day even before evening had come. As she walked towards the lights of the hotel – the only lights this side of the river, losing then finding them again through the leafless trees between her and the

143

road – her focus was complete, yet an abrupt thought came and possessed her. It was the lights ahead, and the sudden realisation that this was the home she loved, where her parents lived, and her husband – all of them loving her but she was apart from them all, living separately while amongst them. How strange – how stupid, almost, and she was suddenly sorry that the other loves in her life were kept apart, unused, unappreciated.

They were twenty seconds of forced reflection, a slap from somewhere telling her to wake up, to see what she already had before this nonsense began. She stopped on the path, waiting for some unsought revelation perhaps, and stood there until the interruption faded. It was a brief distraction though, and before reaching the bank up to the road any misgivings had gone and she crossed to the hotel, welcoming and brightly lit for the evening, knowing that Phillip would be there.

Back home, her joy at returning to him tempered by the overall sadness of his mood, she turned to the page she'd left an hour before, the page she could already recall half of from memory, the page given over to John Donne. It was part of a Meditation from the *Devotions* that finished with what she'd always thought of as a poem, something separate, and it was a revelation to find it wasn't, it was just the well-known part of something bigger, and the paragraph Phillip had copied gave her a different perspective. She was thrilled to know he'd thought the same as she had – that the poem he'd also memorised had apparently been so special to him long before he'd been given those collected works in Bristol, and she read again his careful handwriting, the long passage, and the ending: *'...any mans death diminishes me, because I am involved in Mankinde; And therefore never send to know for whom the bell tolls; it tolls for thee.'*

She ran her fingers over the soft, pale paper. The black ink looked new, the words fresh from the push and scratch of his pen but which had lain in the darkness of the attic for a hundred and fifty years, and she had grown up in the rooms below, unaware; words put down in pain or happiness – and she could never know which, never be sure if a rare cheerful phrase was truly written in happiness or in some desperate attempt to be so, and as her fingers lay on the page she longed for the impossible – to be able to comfort him.

: : :

Christmas Day came with stillness in the valley, crisp, snowless, and a clear blue sky. The cosy Conference Room was decked out for Christmas, for lunch, and tea. Both families would be there, and as in previous years an effort had been made to make an impact on the Greersons but not to overwhelm them; the decorations were therefore toned down but were still enough to make an impression, the dark oak walls garlanded in green and red, the tree heavy with tinsel and glass and real candles in holders, and a log fire burning in the centre of the back wall.

As well as Alice's grandfather Peter and her Uncle Patrick, Jon's parents and sister were there. They had been told of the problem in October, soon after the event, and it explained their son's mood during his few phone calls up to then; he'd been evasive, so his mother had talked with Elena. Meetings had been secretly arranged then postponed in fear of Alice's response, and in an atmosphere of rising anxiety they at last decided to wait until Christmas Day when they would all be together at Brockweir, and maybe the problem would resolve itself by then. There was no plan B.

After lunch they all left the hotel while the big mahogany table was magically cleared, to wander along the riverbank for an hour. However, the day brought a problem for Jon: in front of his parents and sister he had to do his own bit of acting, to show how things were not quite as bad as they feared. But they knew well enough how things were, and when they saw him with Alice, he didn't fool them for long. She played along with small talk but fondness was missing, and indifference from her and awkwardness from him were in its place. Later, in front of the bright fire, presents were exchanged. All eyes, and all thoughts, were on the gifts that Alice and Jon had for each other but there was a surprise – two surprises, because it appeared they had both taken trouble over them, rather than cheapen the occasion with token gifts.

Alice had given Jon a fountain pen, a stylish *Caran d'Ache* she'd found for him in the spring, before events had made her forget. It was perfect, and quite unexpected; he smiled at her and thanked her, thinking how strange this all was. He watched her open his present – a silver pendant on a chain, an almost-copy of Phillip Rossetti's necklace, as near a copy as he could find, and a note with it said: *Because you can't wear the real one.* It was different enough not to be mistaken for the real one, but still beautiful, and as she saw it her heart missed a beat. It was with great effort that she held on to herself, keeping the little note private, and in her hand. It rattled her, and made her think outside the world she'd put herself into. Jon was sitting there, the same Jon she had lost, and she briefly looked him in the eyes and said an almost-shy *thank you.* Her mother held back from suggesting she put the necklace on, for fear of spoiling the moment, so after being shown around it stayed in its box on Alice's lap.

Before they left for home that evening, Jon's parents were put properly in the picture over their son's marriage. It was more puzzling than shocking, and his mother especially wanted to dive in and talk to them together. There were no secrets now, so why doesn't Alice climb down? What possible reason could there be for this?

Meanwhile in several minds was the awful fear that Alice had taken a lover, a well-concealed lover, but Elena knew her daughter and had watched for signs and seen nothing, and no one wanted to confront her with it. And no one at all had doubts about Jon – it was impossible to imagine him having someone else.

Their gifts showed that whatever this wall was between them, it was less than solid, so *wait and see* became the policy as they said their goodbyes that evening, with the New Year before them.

: : :

"Thank you for my pen," Jon said that Christmas night as they lay in bed. Alice was facing away from him, and said quietly, "You're welcome." And then, after a few moments, "Thank you for my necklace." Jon smiled into the darkness. Times were desperate, but he smiled. He would leave it like that for today, and not risk spoiling it. Eventually Alice fell asleep, some time later than Jon.

: : :

The Journal consumed her. Thirty-four thousand words, and before the end of the year she'd read them all several times. But there was something else on her mind. Since Christmas Day she'd been troubled by a feeling she couldn't help... a feeling of compassion mixed with guilt, for Jon. The present he gave her – a necklace of all things – pierced the shell she'd made around herself, and brought him back into her thoughts.

Since the moment she opened the box, she felt herself sliding in a direction she'd thought was closed... a necklace, like Phillip's, and beautiful. She'd given him a pen she'd bought almost a year ago, an easy present she'd forgotten she had. There was no comparison. It almost made her cry that night, cry with confusion, lying next to her husband in the dark. And the days that followed were different. Although she did not allow herself to climb down from anywhere and still treated Jon with indifference, there was a germ of something inside that sat there and niggled her. Such a beautiful necklace, looked for, chosen carefully, then given. And the note proved its thoughtfulness. But over it all the blanket of disappointment remained, and still she felt she was not prepared to trust him. So she gave nothing away, and she would continue into January with those new feelings. Jon felt nothing new.

THE SONG IS ENDED

A door opened along the landing outside Alice's room, and it was easy to tell which one. All the doors in the hotel had their own sounds, their slight differences, and she knew this one was to her parent's room. The muffled voice of her grandfather mixed briefly with her mother's, and the door closed again. It was reassuring – she felt safe, people were kind to her, and even the familiarity of the doors added to her belonging there.

Alice was at her dressing table, and open in front of her was Phillip Rossetti's journal, when someone tapped on her door. She closed the book, put it on the floor and pushed it under the dressing table with her foot.

She turned and said, "Come in."

It was her grandfather. They hugged, and he asked how his favourite granddaughter was.

"Your *only* granddaughter is well, thank you."

Familiar banter, but she was nervous, without knowing why; they met in his studio on a few days each week, and also downstairs at odd times, but this was the first time he'd come to her room. They sat down, he on the bed across from her, and they talked for a while about this and that, the weather, the state of the hotel and the world, about progress with his *History*, and she waited. Then in the middle of it he paused and suddenly became serious.

"Your mother's still concerned about you Alice. We all are, in fact. Is everything really all right? She thinks you're... well, you know what she's worried about. You need to talk to her."

Sent by her mother. She suddenly felt sad and irritated that he'd been asked to do this.

"I'm okay – really."

"It's about you and Jon." Her smile had gone. He said, "I should say it's not my place to ask these things, but we love you Alice.

We want you to be happy – both of you."

"I am happy, and you know I talk to Mum. We talk all the time." There was a significant pause. He waited, watching her, until she said, "Jon doesn't change – we're all right really. She shouldn't worry. Nobody should."

"But you two don't talk any more. You're better in yourself, we can all see that, but what's happening with Jon?"

"We're *okay* Grandad." She'd closed her eyes briefly as she'd said it. Peter looked at his granddaughter, struck yet again by her, and he thought how sad it would be for she and Jon to be really out of love with each other, while knowing they must be. How could an outsider ever make that right?

He said, "Just try to share your problems with her, if you can."

There was the barest hint of frost in her voice. "Yes, but I don't really have problems. But thanks."

"Don't be cross with her."

"I'm not cross. Just nothing to worry about."

He persisted. "Well, you surely can't be happy with things as they are?" He waited. "Are you?"

After a pause she said, softer, "No. I'm sorry."

"Don't be sorry, Alice. Let's all care for each other, shall we? Can't you two work it out? Can't you forgive him?" She was looking down at the floor. Then he said, "Okay, it's private, of course it is."

She stayed as she was, so it was time to go. He got up, went towards her and they stood together, and he hugged her, then looked into her eyes and said, "Look after yourself, Alice." She barely nodded her head. Then she smiled. "Don't worry about me Grandad. Tell Mum I'll talk with her about it again."

"You should say that to her yourself, Alice. She's afraid to ask you any more, and I'm a poor go-between."

She said again, "Sorry," and looked helplessly at the old man, all at once afraid of everything, at the cost of everything.

He said, "Just talk with her now and again – or with me, if you like. What's private is private... but we're all concerned." Then as he turned to leave he brightened. "Will you be able to give me another day or two?"

She pulled herself back. "I hope so."

"Good. We should finish it this week, you know... unless we've missed anything up there." He pointed to the ceiling. "Should we have another look?"

He was well past his attic-crawling days though and would have to leave that to Alice, but she said truthfully, "Only invoices up there, that's all – I've been very thorough." *(But I'm sorry. I found the biggest prize of all).*

"Well, we've got enough invoices, I think," said Peter, unaware of that prize lying in the shadows across the room from him. She said she'd see him tomorrow, hopefully. They embraced again and he left, and through the door and from far away she heard *Bye bye Grandad,* and her grandfather reply, *Bye bye Aku.*

She loves them all very much, but she doesn't need this. *They don't know, so they don't understand, and I can't possibly explain. These people all love me, yet I'm unloved.* She was aware of how bizarre it would sound to anyone else, this secret of hers. A mental problem, no doubt. Maybe so, but it harmed no one, she thought, while leaving Jon out of those thoughts – he really was out of her loop now. And she was pulling her weight in the hotel. So j*ust let me get on with my life.*

But soon after her grandfather had gone she thought again of Jon. There was no life with him. He was an acquaintance, a familiar face with a backstory that still had a warm place in some recess of her mind. She pondered her two lives, the hard reality and the beautiful distraction... *can't you forgive him?* Her grandfather's words had stayed with her. There was a song he sometimes played while working in his studio – Nat King Cole, *The Song is Ended.* She remembered the times as a child when she'd sat and watched them both as they worked, with some heavy book on her lap, usually with music as a background. Did he think of Clara now, while he worked? – of course, why not? If the song had been good, and it had ended, then why not... but it had been hard to bear that her own song with Jon had ended so soon. There was no music she would like to play now, no melody lingering on to remind her of her own earthly love. Nothing came to her. He was still a part of her life, but he'd been replaced; the greater part of her was sure it was his own fault, and now in spite of her years of certainty she doubted that such an earthly love could ever last. It would always fail, sooner or later. *But Phillip, you will never let me down.*

In that mood she went back to her youth – when she was able to make the world she wanted, in thoughts and words, at any time – to a story she'd written in the intimacy of her room when she was sixteen, a tale she'd called *The Man Who Stayed For Ever:*

'She took him home with her, the man who'd grown up in the city, dressed him in blues and greens, washed-out reds and yellows, and showed him the land. They lived together, she teaching and he learning, and after a while he thought he would stay with her, because all she ever asked of him was that he love her.'

: : :

Early that evening a door opened somewhere on the landing, then closed again, but Jon might not have been sure which one. Unlike Alice, he felt he didn't belong, not really. He lived there, but his heart was sometimes elsewhere, and he didn't know where that would be – apart from his job at Filton, but that was his other heart, the one safely wedded to his work. Perhaps he should stick with that one. He knew that what he'd said so long ago had made her fall out of love with him, and then perhaps he with her, but how would that feel, being out of love with someone – does it feel like this? He feared his real heart, his human heart, was emptying of love for her and becoming vacant – or was he just fed up and wishing for his old Alice to return. So in its despair, his suffering heart waved at any passing female, and there weren't many of those. He worked with men, but the evenings and weekends sometimes put him among girls, or women, who moved around the hotel or were staying there; none waved back beyond a glance – or a smile, sometimes. He wasn't looking for anything beyond some playful female banter instead of the endlessly boring male stuff he endured at work. He wanted them to like him, and perhaps it would have been nice to have the opportunity to turn them down if they ever did go too far with him. He suspected, in his wretchedness, that that would feel good. So a female smile would occasionally stir him, and he would save it.

With the best ones, he'd had good times in his mind, enjoying easy relationships with a crowd of eager smiling females... they were real to him, and took him away from the austerity of his marriage. Poor Jon – or not so poor, perhaps. He easily made up conversations, situations, feelings – all he lacked was touch, and he could even imagine that. In his sadness he'd perfected his imagination, and everything was there for him, now that Alice wasn't.

His evenings were busy, one way or another, and tonight he was in their bedroom at the little table under the window with an open folder and papers laid across the surface in front of him, a lamp giving a pool of brightness and blinding him to the darkness outside. He'd left the curtains open, not wanting to close the room completely, feeling the need to connect with the comings and goings of the car park and the comfort of passing cars, their lights striping across the ceiling as they went by unseen. He was distracted. *Aspects of Digital Signal Processing for Flight Control and Evaluation* had failed to hold him as it normally did. He was thinking of Alice, then of his work that day, of his work tomorrow, of some song or other, of some girl he'd noticed, then

153

of Alice again. It was difficult to get her out of his mind, to think around her. He was in another extended interlude – he'd had many – of wanting her back in spite of everything, without apologies, without conditions – an intense week-long period so far of trying to understand their situation, but failing. Her smile was very bright amongst the others in his head, but it was different with her: real, and hopeless. This relationship really was impossible to analyse, and if it couldn't be analysed, how could it be put right?

In the middle of this particular evening's quiet turmoil, he heard her voice from outside. He quickly turned off the lamp and stood up, moving to the side of the uncurtained window, and there she was, in the brightly-lit car park below, talking and laughing with someone. He stood back and watched her. She was leaning against a car with her hands on the roof above the open window, talking, and he caught the odd word; he didn't know the car. She must know this person, he thought, otherwise why be so friendly? Why lean on the car like that? It was a short scene, and soon she stood away and with a little wave of her hand the car drove off. He didn't see who was driving. As she walked back she glanced up at the window – a quick glance, like a guilty hope-he-didn't-see-that glance, and was gone. She was his wife, his Alice, and it was wrong... but no – why is it wrong? Why can't she talk with other people? But she looked happy doing it, and that's what hurt. It wasn't wrong, but saddening. He really wasn't a jealous man.

He then thought maybe that glance meant *what are you thinking about up there?* Or that she'd seen him at the window, and her glance was something of an apology. All these doubts summed up his life now – removed, not properly connected, and especially not to his wife; and yet he loved her at that moment, standing alone in the darkened room. The memory came to him of how he would lie alongside her, or with her in his arms, matching his breathing with hers, – to be entirely with her – falling into sleep together; but those were old times and he didn't think he knew her any more, and often wondered if he really ever had, or would ever again.

: : :

Sometimes in bed I touch her, you know, across the zone; I really can't help it, we move about. That's the best for me now, but the worst of all. I touch her gently, I feel her skin for a moment, soft and smooth and warm, like a baby. Sometimes I can keep my hand against her if she doesn't stir. And sometimes I just want to grab her and pull her towards me. Longing becomes lust and I can't think of anything else – she's naked beside me but I'm too afraid... the risk of being turned away from, of having no response except coldness, of her pulling away from me. Where is she? What's she thinking about? It's not helping me, sleeping next to her... but maybe it's best like this, because I can't bear to think of her not being there.

It was a gap in her work, ten minutes or so to grab a coffee or sit somewhere quiet – usually with her mother, but today she was alone. A Friday morning – the first of the new year – with the weekend ahead of her, and Alice had spent those ten minutes in their bedroom reading Phillip's reminiscences of Bristol in 1836, when he'd met Isambard Kingdom Brunel as work properly began on the Clifton Suspension Bridge. He'd walked boldly up to the man in the workings on the clifftop above the sheer gorge, and shaken his hand in simple admiration. *That's real history.*

She closed the book, left it on the bed and sat at her dressing table, enjoying the morning and watching the clock. Ten minutes were all she ever allowed herself. The Journal lay where she'd left it, the sunlight sweeping a broad band across the bed and the book. She glanced at it, suddenly thought she saw something, and looked harder. The back of the book was not flat. It was minutely raised in the middle, the merest plateau revealed by the sunlight; she would never have seen it but for the coming together of those particular circumstances – the bright light, the angle of the book on the bed, and her precise viewpoint across the room. *There was something there.*

She picked up the book and ran her fingers over the back, but felt nothing. Only by holding it at the flattest angle to her eyes, and into the sun, could she see it – a vague rectangle, some three inches by four perhaps, quite flat under the leather. She sat down again at her dressing table with it in her hands, but now it had gone, the back perfectly flat, the *something* invisible. She squinted into the sun again, and it reappeared, and now she thought her fingertips could feel the edges of it, the tiniest, most subtle gradation. Her imagination took over. *It was a page, a letter, something secret and hidden, and Phillip had put it there to be never found.* She looked inside the back cover, at the heavy paper neatly fixed to the board, trimmed around the three sides leaving a margin of leather an eighth of an inch wide. There was no unevenness – it was perfectly flat, neat and untouched. She compared it with the inside of the front cover, and it was the same. Untouched. *But someone has disturbed this. Phillip has opened the back cover.*

Again she held it against the sun, ran her finger very lightly over the surface, and again felt the slightest edge. A single leaf, a delicately thin piece of paper, surely. She didn't know what to do. She wanted to open it now, peel back the leather and find what was there, but after a few minutes of pondering realised that she would probably destroy the cover and whatever was under it in the process. Everything was glued together, she knew that. She would have to take her precious book to a specialist, decide to leave it with someone – and risk them reading the whole journal, as they no doubt would. Her ten minutes had become fifteen.

Later that day she found a bookbinder in Cheltenham, far enough away she thought, and called him. Yes, he would take a look at it, but could not guarantee the safe removal of a thin sheet of paper glued to the leather and the board, as it must be. She would take the risk; she liked his voice and his manner and took the book the next day to the other side of Cheltenham, to a small Dickensian workshop smelling of animal glue and leather, and dim, with pools of light over benches and daylight struggling through small dusty panes.

She left it with a middle-aged man who'd been so far from the image she'd conjured from his voice she'd doubted she was in the right place. Why had she thought he was tall? Can you get that from a voice? She met a small man, then waited for the man she'd spoken to.

"It's just me, I'm afraid," he said, seeing her waiting, maybe sensing her surprise that such a slight figure could manage something like this on his own. Then she knew the voice was right and she felt stupid, and apologised for her assumption.

As she stood with him she still had concerns over sharing

Phillip Rossetti's private thoughts with someone else. It felt wrong, as if she were betraying his trust in her, his chosen confidante. *Don't mind this, Phillip.* The man took the book and examined it through a loupe under the glare of a lamp, gave a little huff and said he'd do his best.

"Trouble is, my best may not be good enough," he said, but with a smile that reassured her. She was sorry she'd doubted him. She gave her mobile number, not wanting any calls to the hotel, then left for home, and waited.

On the Monday morning he called her.

"It's not too clear, but I can read it."

"Please tell me what it says."

"Well, it says, 'Mon Cher Phillip, I pray that this note will reach you safely. I am sad to not be writing a letter of love to you, with all the joy that comes with it. It is certain that I am unable to see you again, Phillip. My father and mother are so strongly set against us being together, and a life I could have with you would be full of worry and pain for us both. They will be sure to spoil any happiness we could have. I ask you to forgive them, as I will, and become reconciled to their way of thinking, which is to care for me, as perverse as that appears to be. I am well looked after, and want for nothing except that which the Lord sees fit for me not to have. Therefore I ask you to let me go, and I will let you go. Béatrice.'"

She excused herself from her work, got into her car and left for Cheltenham.

An hour later she stood next to her man. She looked down at the Journal on his bench, the leather peeled back and the note still attached to the board. It was too risky to detach the note, he said, but he would try if she wanted. It was an unexpectedly-white rectangle of paper, and he'd done well to make it readable. The words were there, magically, before her. She leaned over it, read it, touched it, and fell into a dream of seeing the young woman in green at the market in Morlaix, feeling her grief as she wrote it, and her absent beloved's grief at reading it.

Finally she looked at the man standing silently beside her, and thanked him, wondering what he was making of it all. She had taken her camera and took a few pictures, as closely as she could, then touched the paper a last time before asking him to put it all back as it was, a decision she knew was right. *Goodbye, Béatrice.*

The note, she knew, would affect her very much. Behind her small talk with the bookbinder was a great wave of sadness, waiting to descend upon her and fasten her even closer to Phillip, to share his distress. She knew it would come to that. Also, as she left she wondered whether the bookbinder knew the story – had he sat down and read it all? *What difference does it make?* He said nothing and she didn't ask, hoping he would at least not show it to anyone else, or copy any of it but also wondering again what difference would it make if he had. She would collect it, hopefully as good as before, in a few days; the mystery was solved, and the process of solving it was complete apart from the one thing she could never resolve – had Phillip really opened up the cover himself and put the note there?

: : :

In early September 1825 Phillip was very much in love with Janet, and since the beginning of that love, in the April of that year, he'd thought about keeping a journal. There was much to record. He wanted to write it all down – his feelings and hopes, and the little diary he carried with him was too small for what he was experiencing. So in that September he took the short walk from the harbourside at Mardyke, across to St Augustine's Back and on into the city where he found a bookseller who directed him to a bookbinder, halfway along Maudlin Lane. He wanted a journal, a quarto-sized book of plain pages bound in black leather, and he wanted something special: he asked for a note he'd received from

Béatrice in 1816 – and kept so carefully since – to be placed under the leather of the back cover. An unusual request, but easily done, he was told, on the understanding that it could never be recovered from its hiding place unharmed.

So on that day, in a dingy workshop in a Bristol backstreet, he said goodbye to the only physical connection he had to Béatrice Fleury, apart from the returned necklace she had briefly worn. His reasoning was that if his journal were to be discovered, the story of Béatrice would be revealed but the only words she had written to him – his sole connection with her – were safely hidden for ever, being far too precious to share. It would take a hundred and seventy-two years, a trick of the light, and the skill of a bookbinder for her words to be read again.

She had sent the note two weeks after seeing Phillip for the last time in April, having addressed it to 'Captain Phillip Rossetti, Master of the ship Florence, Bristol, England', and given it to a trusted friend sailing for England shortly from the port of Antibes, near to where she was kept by her parents, in dejection.

It arrived four weeks later at the Mardyke office and was left with John Parrish, who kept the envelope until his master returned from sea at the beginning of June. John was already curious about Phillip's time at Morlaix, which had seemingly filled him with joy then cast him into despair, and as the envelope came with a very French gentleman a connection seemed likely. It was given to Phillip, whose immediate reaction was one of intense interest as he took himself away from the office to read it. He had sailed to Antibes looking for Béatrice while her note was sailing to England, and was in despair at finding nothing there but an unsettling, low-key hostility from some of the people he'd asked. She was known there, but definitely *not* there and he was effectively warned off any further attempts to find her. He had left the Mediterranean Sea for the last time.

The note was devastating, and he went away from the harbour for the rest of the afternoon, sitting up on Brandon Hill until almost dark. France was too big, too unexpectedly hostile, and even if he found her, there would be, as she'd written, 'a life full of worry and pain for us both'. He was not able to forgive her parents, and would be unable to for many years to come.

Finally, at the end of that awful afternoon, and with the heaviest heart, Phillip agreed to let her go.

: : :

January had begun with days of frost, of winter stillness as the valley sat through the shortened days. There had been no snow to speak of, no hindrance to Jon's daily journeys to Filton where he worked towards his uncertain future, unable to share his feelings and hopes with Alice; he could continue in the factory as a qualified engineer, earn good money, and settle down for life. Or he could follow his heart and be more of an individual, happier outside the tight clique that the engineering department appeared to him to be. He felt his time with Rolls Royce was running out, and soon a decision would be made, either by him, or for him.

Alice is alone in the shared room. The double bed sits comfortably under a pattern of light from the window as she kneels at its side, as if in prayer, over the opened book. The sunlight refreshes the pale pages. She is half-dressed, pulled away even from that basic task, and is fully awake, sensitive to what-is and to what-may-be, to the words before her and to the slightest sound from the passage beyond the room – she would not want to be caught. She feels her Captain leaning over her as she reads again from her chosen text, from the third of April, 1828:

'The Hopes I woke with that morning were dashed but I resolved to return & follow this Lady who had taken my Heart from me in such a way that I could not ever forget Her, but it was a full month & more before I could again undertake a voyage to find Her. In my dreams Béatrice was my Lover.'

She's struck by the last line, as she always is. *In his dreams she was his lover.* In the isolation of her room Alice closes the book on its bookmark, rises to her feet and puts it away – *Rest now, my Captain, in my bottom drawer. Of all the places I could put you! Be safe.*

She goes to her dressing table and sits at the mirror, preoccupied. Moments pass, moments of searching the accustomed face, pausing, looking for the beauty she hopes is still there. She stops at the eyes and leans closer. The staring stared-at eyes, focused, mesmerising, becoming beautiful... *You have beautiful eyes,* her lover had said, and she is aware of the seamless metamorphosis of Phillip into another: the dream has become real.

She's fragile and suddenly afraid, but the mirror holds her. Without looking her hand goes to the open box, and takes out the necklace: the silver chain and the frail magical ship of Phillip Rossetti lie in her open palm. She wants to put it on again, to see this symbol of love beautiful against her skin.

Not hearing the door open, the voice startles her.

"We should go."

Her hand closes. She sees her estranged husband in the mirror as he turns away, leaves the door half open, and disappears. She believes he doesn't notice it, this rediscovered beauty; even her naked back with its promise, all is lost to him.

She doesn't wonder any more how this can be, as she replaces the necklace and closes the box; nothing around her neck today, but soon, *soon*.

She says quietly to herself, "Yes, I'm coming".

They walk to the car without speaking, and begin the six-mile drive to her lover's house (her lover's house? A special sentence, a reminder, about Alice: she longs to be loved. She's longed for the real love she married for, three years and more ago, but it's gone, lost somewhere in the space between her and her lost-love Jon, floating there – waiting to be caught again, she used to think.

Too poetic. Too hopeful.

It's long gone, unreachable – and now, just now, after all her dreaming and wanting, Alice has a lover).

PART TWO

...a pause in my everyday thoughts,
a short space,
is all I need to think of you again.

TOM AND CONNIE

Tom Fisher, at twenty-one, thought he was in love, but Connie James, at the same age, really was in love. In June 1974, and a month before they graduated, they met on the same campus at Sheffield – he an engineer, she a clothes designer. She was smart: in her head, her body, and the way she dressed, and she liked his trousers – no, she *loved* his trousers. She saw him in the lunchtime cafeteria queue and she stared at them, longed to touch them, and only after falling for them did she consider the person inside. It was a shock for her, after a few seconds' distraction, to see their owner, an interesting boy, also looking at her. He was standing in line with his tray, and she was sitting a few tables into the crowded room with her camomile tea and muesli. He looked at her as if a pivotal moment had arrived.

He'd seen her here and there on the campus and once in town, fancying her from afar, silently approving of her as one of the special girls he'd singled out. She'd noticed him before but without much excitement. Like a car enthusiast, Connie generally examined the outside before the person inside and now, after the enticement of his trousers, she smiled at him.

That was a smile. For me. Suddenly removed from the banalities of the queue, his eyes and ears stopped working. The array of food, the people in front and behind, the background of voices and tinkling cutlery all left him as his senses centred on the girl at the table. He looked back, and she was still looking at him, still smiling. He smiled at her.

A close disconnected voice brought him back.

"What are you having?"

His tray was empty. In the seconds of seeing her he'd moved blindly with the queue, past his usual bacon sandwich, but there was no going back and he had to ask for it. The familiar girl behind the counter took a few steps, reached for the sandwich and dropped it on a plate onto his tray. He studied her distractedly, out of habit. She poured tea into an almost-clean mug then moved, expressionless, to the next in line.

What do I do now? The smile was still there. As he passed her table he glanced at her and said hello as casually as he could, then looked away.

"There's room here."

He stopped. Her tone was not *would you like to.* It was *sit here, please,* her open hand extended to the empty chair across from her. So he did as he was told, and that's how Tom and Connie got started – in the chatter and bustle of the cafeteria with the early afternoon sun streaming through the windows onto them, their differences apparent even then: *bacon sandwich, muesli.*

They would both agree later that 1974 was a time not to be revisited, and for many reasons, some much worse than the strikes, power cuts, and platform shoes of the Heath/Wilson changeover year. There had been IRA bombs, set against the hangings-on of flower power as the war in Vietnam entered its final year. Much going on in the world, but it left them alone if they chose to ignore it – and most did, working and mingling as life went on, petty grievances often more concerning than the momentous events on their TV screens.

There were so many students, spread across the campuses and the city – twenty-odd thousand in all, and Tom and Connie were a tiny part of the several thousand of those who would graduate from Sheffield Hallam that year, but having just met, they were more absorbed with each other, as one would expect. Biology was having its way, while Tom tried to think. He'd heard that Connie created things, 'concepts' as she called them, then justified them with an intensity that made people unsure: talented or imposter? He hadn't known her but he settled for talent. *Surely, talent.* She looked fresh and new and always dressed well, showing her curves rather than hiding them as a lot of the other girls did beneath their billowing Laura Ashley outfits. He'd never heard anything about her, good or bad, apart from her confidence in her abilities, which was fine if those abilities were real – nothing sexual, no tales of anyone exploring those curves; she was a girl going through university, keeping to herself.

She was a little shorter than average, but noticeably shorter than slightly-taller-than-average Tom, and attractive: a face too round perhaps to be called beautiful, but which was always smiling – and the rest of her was fair-proportioned, almost petite, and caressable; there was no heaviness in her, and the bobbed honey-blonde hair darkening into pale brown was a unique colour, he was sure.

As they sat there that lunchtime she told him how much she liked his trousers and he didn't know what to say. He just watched and listened until she allowed him to talk, allowed her confidence to stand aside and let him tell her about himself. But as he talked he was aware that there were too many delights in her, and before long he asked her again about herself, unwilling to overdo his own story.

He watched as she spoke, defying the urge to reach into her hair as it fell over her cheek, to feel the softness of her skin on the palm of his hand. But above all it was her eyes that sealed it for him, not anything else. Perfect, clear, wide open eyes, and not sky-blue but the colour of the ocean, or rather the sea, like the Mediterranean he'd seen on a postcard. It was the first time he'd really noticed someone's eyes. The year before he'd had a girlfriend for a few months but had forgotten hers, and his mother's eyes, surely gazed into so many times, didn't count. Connie's eyes stunned him, and briefly eclipsed his interest in the rest of her.

He must have her. Why not? Somebody would, very soon, if they hadn't already, and he had the trousers for it... he gazed at her across that cafeteria table, their eyes almost level. He was dark, slim, anxious; short unfashionable set-in-its-ways curly hair, earth-brown eyes to complement those Mediterranean-blues, and a thin, sensitive poet's face.

He asked, knowing the answer, "So what are you studying?" He hoped he sounded sincere.

"Fashion – history and design."

"You design clothes?"

"Yes. I plan to start my own business." Her eyes lit up as she said it, and he was impressed with her excitement, her resolve. The warmth went back and forth between them. He was captivated, staring across at her and knowing this would go further, but it was late in the evening before they met again. They'd both had meetings to go to, and as he walked with her through the tree-lined streets to her lodgings afterwards and met the girls she shared with, it was all a bit strange – a hurried, surprising kiss on the doorstep, and an invitation for supper tomorrow... not quite what he'd expected, but then he wasn't sure what he'd expected. More intimacy and a bit less talking, perhaps.

They'd walked – she clinging to his arm – and he'd seen for the first time an underlying desperation, a need for him that he wasn't sure about and as he'd walked the half-mile to his own place – across an invisible frontier and onto a less favourable, treeless street – he'd hoped the clinging would stop.

The next evening ended when she let him grope his way to her bed, by way of a supper shared with her housemates – three girls, friendly but intimidating. There had been an unsettling buzz around the table, the presence of three other females, and he'd thought about each one in turn, sizing them up, undressing them, even while being smitten with Connie. *It's what men do. Distracting, but okay.* Connie appeared unaware of it, simply happy to have the only boy in the house. Later they went to her room, locked the door and tried to be quiet, imagining the other girls listening in, and she asked him to stay. Her narrow bed was barely sufficient.

And yet, the next morning – their first waking-up together, when the sky should have been blue and all well with the world –

he crossed his fingers, hoping already to uncommit himself now that the act was over. The lust that had quickly filled him and overcome his caution, was, for the time being, displaced by alarm. It was new, and extraordinary. Those first days with her, and those hours in her bed, had not produced the soulmate he hoped he'd found in the cafeteria two days before. So many things wrong with this new romance, he told himself. Most of all – *she talks too much, this girl.* He especially didn't like the chattering that followed their lovemaking, when he wanted to lie still and quiet. *Is she glad it's over? Is she liberated, relieved? Will she always do this?* Whatever it was, the girl he'd had the year before had been the same and it had worn him out in the end. *Just let me be.*

But Connie was in love, and could not let him be. She fell so quickly, so hopelessly and in such a spirit of welcoming that all else went out of the window. In a short time everything depended on this boy, her present existence and the long life stretching in front of her: all revolved around Tom Fisher. She loved the way he looked, the way he spoke, the way he moved. And while she was distantly aware of her chattering, it was already so natural to be lying beside him, talking in the darkness.

"Are you happy Tom?"

"Of course. Aren't you?"

And she would fall again, inwards, away from the spoiling world beyond her door. She gazed at him moon-eyed (with different eyes, now) but all he wanted to say was, *It was great, Con. You're a lovely person, but please... let's just be friends.*

That morning after, Tom became aware of his problem: he couldn't bring himself to speak his mind with her, against her; unexpectedly, he felt responsible for everything about this girl, especially her happiness, and there was an inconvenient duty to protect her now that he'd *used* her – because that's what he feared he'd done. Used her, took her to bed, even though it was more her that had taken *him.* He reasoned it wasn't a big deal, they'd had sex a couple of times, and slept the rest of the night together, and that's what people do. It needn't be permanent.

And yet it was very particular with him, this feeling of being kind to her, and not to drop her the morning after. It had been so different with the other girl, the year before – she was easy to leave when the time came, but in the space of a day he'd seen that Connie was softer, and fragile... oddly troublesome traits that needed looking after: a hesitation had appeared when talking about herself, as if she were not quite good enough for him, and could never be his equal. It was unexpected after her bold beginning, but true – she was in awe of him, and simply too vulnerable to abandon.

Before he left her, standing at the door of her room, she wrapped her arms around him and said *I love you* for the eleventh time – bizarrely, he'd counted – and all he could do was smile at her. How could she say those *I love yous* and not press him to say the same back to her? He'd said it twice, that's all, and it worried him that it didn't seem to matter to her – that she had no doubts that they were in love, and hopelessly.

In the following weeks he slept with her, at her place and his, but there were nights when he needed to be alone, away from the flood of affection and concern for him. If he had been in need of keeping her down, or of such adoration, it might have worked, but he wasn't. Her manner had become oppressive, yet she allowed those nights off without a fuss, and with a simple *That's fine Tom* she took away the showdown he might have allowed himself. And as the days passed it turned, this adoration, into something else. He could not criticise her, and so he allowed her to criticise him with almost complete impunity: carefree, confident comments lacking in tact – about his music, his reading, anything – that he countered with an amiable smile and therefore gave her the small confirmations she needed, while knowing he should ask her to be kinder. But Tom hated seeing anyone hurt, especially by getting something wrong, so the asking was not done. He tried, and failed: a rare wounded look from those eyes and he would melt. So Connie lived her new life alongside him believing they were both winners, carelessly exaggerating herself in her new freedom. They were early days, and always he would be patient, trying her out, while mostly, sadly, he was disappointed, and troubled. Connie, duped by this dishonesty, was elated.

: : :

Constance Evelyn James was a Hereford girl, *Connie* from birth, and Constance only to her grandmother, who equated this shortening of her name with sacrilege *(Why call her Constance, if you're never going to call her that?)* – this grandmother simply liked the name though, and overlooked her tolerance of her own name being shortened more dramatically than Connie's – she was Janet, forever called *J* by her husband, and *Granny J* by everyone else.

Granny J lived down the street from Connie's family, a close and dependable link for the girl as she grew up, without brothers or sisters, in that quiet street in the middle of town, the cul-de-sac that ended – fearfully for a while – at the cathedral gates. Fearfully because Granny J's husband died just beyond them when Connie was four years old, a tragedy for everyone and a great loss for the child, who would never forget him, her father's father, an occasional but profound presence in her life who fell without warning from high on the cathedral one sunny morning while she played in her garden. His perfection in stonecutting, which had brought him to Hereford in the first place, contrasted with the imperfection of the scaffold he worked on; an ankle, turned on the biding edge of a board, surprised him and as his hands were full he had no opportunity to save himself. He fell, with his perfectly-cut coping stone, onto the grass at the edge of the path far below. Poor Connie, truly his greatest admirer, cried for a whole day then said nothing for a week.

The Cathedral School took her as she approached the age of five, and taught her across the road from where she lived, and away from the shadow of the huge building that had taken her grandfather from her less than a year before. Her other grandparents – her mother's parents – were long dead, having moved to northern France, to Brittany, in the fifties and died there of simple old age just three months apart. Every summer her father loaded the car and drove his small family south on a long twelve hours' trip, via Saint-Malo and the hushed graves of his wife's parents overlooking the sea, and into the warm and welcoming arms of Limousin, and the rambling house to the west of Limoges. It was Granny J's house, and was unused by her after her husband's death, her holiday spirit having died with him.

Those trips were the highlight of the year for Connie, by then (at the end of her first decade) a quiet and almost withdrawn child who was far more comfortable with people she knew than with strangers, who would close her down, and make her hide behind her parents. Changing to the Senior School at eleven – in the Cathedral Close she once feared – woke her up; her schoolfriends went with her and within half a year she came to embrace them and their outgoing ways, rather than tag along in shyness. A sea-change for Connie, welcomed by her parents, and as the years passed she turned into the normal child they had hoped for rather than a problematic, introverted one. She blossomed, but a slow blossoming, a measured and guarded process towards being open and friendly – flirtatious, even – and her shy awkwardness was overcome by the time the Sixth Form arrived. She belonged at last, and after a couple of short-term boyfriends en route she left Hereford in the late summer of 1970 for a different world. Her parents drove her the tedious hundred-and-fifty miles to Sheffield with her suitcases and boxes, and settled her into her room in the leafy backstreet semi a short walk from the University, all in a swirl of fuss and excitement and promise.

They hugged and kissed her then drove reluctantly away,

leaving her standing at the roadside in unknown territory feeling unconnected and suddenly alone. Within the space of five hours her life had changed; her long held and solitary hobbies of fashion and drawing had taken her from childhood, through school and to the earnestness of university. The eighteen-year-old would rush through those years, and at the end of them would graduate on the same stage on the same day as her lover and soon-to-be husband.

He was to be her first real love, the first one to properly reach her heart, and those two days together ending in her small white bed at the end of the second, were an idyllic omen for her future: *he loves me, loves whatever I do, never tells me otherwise, so all's well. And so what, if I don't like his music? It's only some of it anyway, and he doesn't mind. We'll be okay.*

After a month together Tom still didn't think he could accept her as she was. His soulmate was not Connie, not yet, and he was troubled by how long it would take to be as content with her as he thought she was with him. Maybe never. He struggled with himself as their relationship settled onto the unsafe ground that his new lover appeared utterly unaware of: *poor Connie, Everything Is Beautiful; poor Tom, Not Waving But Drowning.*

∷

Tom's growing-up was done on his father's farm, *Pentwyn*, a few miles north west of Monmouth, at St. Maughans. *Wealth made by hard work, is the best wealth of all,* he remembers. It should have been carved on the bedhead. Tom's father was a strong man, a farmer risen from the ranks of farm labourers through farm managers to farm owner. The only luck he ever had (he was fond of saying) was the thousand pounds his own father left him in 1939, barely enough to make a start (his biggest luck was really his choice of wife, which he realised, in time).

So young Thomas Francis Fisher – the *Francis* from his father –

grew up in the rural stewpot of wet cold sweaty hardships as he followed his brother Geoff along the mapped-out trail that leads to inheritance, taking over, and carrying on for the next generation. Frank Fisher was no slouch – we must admire him for that – he worked with his wife without rest or holiday for twenty-three years.

In the early sixties he slowed down, paying others to do the hard work, but dreamed of his sons carrying on after him. It was painful to contemplate Tom's drift away from the farm-dream, but not catastrophic: Geoff (two years older) was already safely gathered in. Still, two boys are better than one. It was in innocence that ten-year-old Tom had announced over Sunday lunch, on a spring day in 1962, that he'd probably (*probably*, mind you, as if he'd had any doubts) like to be an engineer of some sort when he grew up.

His father, already uncertain of him, listened to his talk of aeroplanes and engines and cars and machines, then calmly said, "Well, you know Tom... plenty of machines here, too."

They talked back and forth, amicably, father and son (Frank was no fool, nor bully), under the amused gaze of Geoff and the anxious gaze of his mother. But he was lost to them even then, this boy who preferred to be indoors or in the workshop out of the cold and wet, and who'd never happily learned the outdoor ways, even to climb trees, or to swim easily. Where he'd come from was a mystery to them all, and as time went on, as the eleven-plus loomed, Frank knew in his heart that Grammar School could take him from them for ever, and in due course it did.

: : :

Oh mother Mary, oh father Frank, I'm sorry. Sorry for my different needs, my treachery. Geoff will carry on your name at Pentwyn. This saves me, or part of me at least, from dying; I suffer too much for you both.

His parents died together on a fine day at the end of July in 1974, in their new car on the hill down to Rockfield, a week after Tom's graduation in Sheffield and the day before his twenty-second birthday. His father was sixty-six, his mother fifty-nine. No seat-belts, and the steering lock was on, because the key was out... Frank had pulled the key from the ignition while they coasted down the hill because the glove box key was with it, and Mary must have needed to open the glove box, because that's where the keys were found.

"Power-assisted brakes, sir," the policeman said with exper-ience, "they won't work very well with the engine off. And the steering lock. The key was out, you see..."

Yes, he did see.

He had to go to Bishop's to look at the car, mad with himself for not warning them of something so simple, so basic – and why hadn't he insisted about the seatbelts? A stupid end, caused by a friendly human gesture, and he couldn't stop thinking about it: *Here, it's on here, it's the small one...* Crushed by the tragedy, he would be further upset by the thought of his father laughing about it, if they had come out of it all right.

So Tom's fortunes changed, for worse and for better, at the age of twenty-two. His father had allowed for him, a surprise muted by his soaring guilt over his desertion; he feared he was out – he was reconciled to it, even though his mother had assured him: "Your father will look after you, I promise you that." She'd looked hard into his eyes, almost had to shake him.

They'd met Connie at the graduation in Sheffield only the week before, and this brought him a little closer to her, the fact that she'd met his parents so soon before he'd lost them, and also that they approved of her. One of the last things his mother had said to him as they parted outside the University was, "She's a lovely girl Tom. Be kind to her," and that went a long way towards set-tling it for him.

Twenty-three thousand pounds, and Pentwyn was entirely for Geoff.
Neither complained. Twenty-three thousand pounds was a fortune, enough to buy a couple of properties, a nice car, and have a
lot left over. When he knew how much had been left him he sat
down in disbelief. His life had changed. It would soon change
again: six weeks after their first meeting and two weeks after
losing his parents, he met Connie's parents for the first time
when she knew for sure she was pregnant (she'd looked at him
with tears in her eyes and he'd felt no anger, in spite of his shock.
Yet there was no immediate reason for him beyond extraordinary
forgetfulness; later that day however he wondered how someone
could actually forget to take that pill... and not once, but two days
in a row, apparently. None of it made sense to him).

They were staying at Pentwyn with Tom's brother in the otherwise quiet and sombre house, and one morning Connie had got
up before Tom then came back to him ten minutes later.

"Tom, I have to tell you something," was all she'd said, hoping
he would understand everything and make it easier for her, and
after some convoluted talk she'd come to the point. Then the
tears, the remorse, the apologies, and the numbing realisation
for him. He'd held her in his arms, sitting on the edge of his bed,
and she'd wept.

She moped around all morning, helping in the house, feeling
desperate and alone as they went around each other with their
thoughts. Tom had choices. He could refuse to marry her and pay
all his life for a back-and-forth child, or he could enter the
darkness of illegal abortions – no more than a fleeting thought
for him, and quite impossible. For her, there were no choices.
Her own rules, and those of the day, meant they would marry for
the child, for better or worse. A bad start, but she would make it
all up to him somehow.

She called her father at midday. "We look forward to meeting
Tom properly," he'd said, with the level tone of disappointment...
and things would work out. So that afternoon Tom went in a daze

with her to Hereford, and found her parents to be the same slightly odd, old-fashioned couple he remembered from the graduation and his own parents' funeral just weeks before, who now instead of being upset with him – or Connie – talked at great length of the wedding, as if it were normal for her to be pregnant, or had expected it to happen any day now... it was bizarre, and Tom struggled inside his new mapped-out world. He drove away from Hereford that day leaving behind a subdued Connie, who was aware that Tom was utterly shocked by her parents easiness over her pregnancy – *Why are they so HAPPY?*

She'd apologised for them, for their enthusiasm: "I hope you can forgive them, Tom." But he would, of course. It was easy when he thought it through. There was no other way for those particular parents to go. He knew he should be grateful to them, but it was too hard that day, especially coming so soon after his own parents' deaths; being genuinely happy would take time for them all.

Added to the loss of his father and mother was the loss of his freedom, his privacy, his promising future, and all because he'd had sex with Connie, because she became pregnant. His lust had been expensive. He longed to step back into the dream he used to have of happy years of study and work, of settling down at the right time and starting a family. Three or four years ahead, maybe – years of knowing someone, of feeling she's right for you, of feeling free, of making a decision, but those opportunities were gone and now he was resentful of Connie, the girl he'd once chosen for her loveliness, and he was hurting.

And he'd stepped back from *her* feelings, naturally and without guilt, because of what had happened. In his mind he was harder with her and argued with his doubts over her motives, if motives beyond loving him were involved.

So she cries... well, I would expect that.

He didn't know her and it was too difficult to work out, so he ended up in a private place where Connie's feelings were less important than his own. But she would tell him that pregnancy had not been a part of her plans either, and she felt a failure while also mourning the loss of those precious in-between years. In time she would cope differently with it, and much later, with disturbing hindsight, Tom would see how he'd let her down, how he could have changed their life together by accepting her and the adjustments that came with her. He would think, for most of his life, *why doesn't this get any better?* – while knowing in his heart the reason.

After leaving Connie with her parents, Tom stayed at Pentwyn, in his old room in the now too-empty house. On the first evening he shared his troubles over a simple supper with his brother in the cluttered kitchen, still heavy with memories, still with the anticipation of his mother or father walking in.

The talk was mostly one-way. Geoff listened as Tom unloaded all his doubts and regrets, layering them on top of the still-raw grief they both felt over their parents, and made worse by his doubts over Connie.

"Two days in a row, she said. She actually told me that. Who would forget two days in a row?"

In spite of that revelation, Geoff said, "Well, she did. Anyone can forget." Tom said nothing. "And why would she admit to *two* days? She's honest, and I'll bet she loves you Tom. That's the main thing. Don't imagine things that aren't there."

So he told it all to his brother, who listened, with his father's patience, to this boy who seemed to be at the beginning of a lasting unhappiness. Geoff sat through it all; he was marrying his own girlfriend, his fiancée, in September, and it looked like his brother would marry long before then. Tom talked especially of his mother being so happy he'd found a girl like Connie – so caring, so obviously in love with her precious son. But his doubts over her forgetfulness would not go away and ran alongside his suspicions of her wanting his money, the promise of a comfortable life. *Don't imagine things that aren't there.* Easier said than done.

Talking had been helpful, and Tom wanted to move on. Three days later he moved with his doubts into a small bare flat that smelled of dust and the faint tang of old cigarette smoke, above a newsagents on Monmouth's main street, and brought Connie down from Hereford the same afternoon. His stoicism was his master, and guided his actions without him realising, so in the heat of August they made the four rooms the way they wanted them, with mostly secondhand furniture, rugs over the gappy floorboards, and clean paint on some of the walls as the hollow emptiness of the place slowly receded.

As he and Connie bustled around, Tom would sometimes stop and stare out of the window over the busy street, the people and the traffic, the constant movement by day and the little groups of wanderers and pub-leavers in the late evening, and wonder about other people's lives and about how his had changed so starkly in a few short weeks. And they made love when they felt like it, on their new big-enough bed, afterwards talking quietly about this and that, relaxed for a while before the reality returned; Tom was warm then, and Connie had calmed, leaving her strained chattering behind her – but secretly she was unsure and in awe of him, in varying amounts of wonder and dread, hardly knowing him – the father of her child – and wishing above all for him to love her.

Through all that August the tiny flat was hot, and they lived with the sounds of the town through the open windows as they unpacked their different and precious belongings and laid them out around the rooms, bits and pieces sitting together, silently sociable as their owners got used to each other.

At Abergavenny Registry Office, on Friday the twenty-eighth of August 1974 at two o'clock, with a few people around them, they were married. And they were both relieved to be married, for it to be over – security for her and stoic acceptance for him – the end of the possibility of escape; Tom had walked around Woolworths to kill time before the event, a buttonholed BSc Eng with barely thirty minutes of his old life left. Later, at the reception, they seemed to him an odd assembly, his friends and hers, brought together too soon in celebration of an unplanned future, and for Tom relief was mixed with regret. *What if I change my mind? What if I start to grieve for my freedom all over again?*

But he was already grieving: in the depths of his soul time was what he still wanted – more time, and a big part of him clung to the vain hope of some miraculous liberation from his new life.

Connie had appeared with her parents and friends, smiling, welcoming, and together doing their best to avert the despondency that threatened them all, the feeling that it could, or should, have been better. Before the day Tom had imagined embarrassed handshakes, understanding smiles all round, but there was no real disappointment that he could see – it was all in his mind; the outward reality was one of happiness, and he was grateful to them for keeping it in, as he was sure they had.

Connie – in an unusual, floor-length and almost-white ensemble of her own design which would have looked far better in a church – clung smiling to him, a little dazed by it all. She was happy on that day, regardless of its relegation from church to Registry Office, and regardless of the facts of their lives and the forgetfulness that had brought them there.

Because it *was* forgetfulness, on those blissful nights when they'd made love and her head was full of him and not of the pills she'd taken for a couple of weeks then overlooked. They were there, almost in front of her, and after missing the first it was easier to miss the second – her eyes never saw them again until the end of the third day when she'd picked them up, disbelieving.

She'd counted the times they'd made love in those few days – five times, five chances to become pregnant, possibly, *probably*.

Married life began with the convoluted process of getting on with each other. Tom missed his privacy, Connie mostly wanted to talk, and the little flat in the middle of Monmouth became a strained proving-ground for their needs, and both of them would suffer – the confidence she had with him would often be knocked by a careless word, and she would look at him in silence with the wide open stare of a child, wondering what he meant, or which way this would go, and then he would feel guilty for saying it.

It was soon clear that music was a problem. They were on far-apart parallel tracks, converging slightly with some of the Beatles songs, but he was always deeper. Connie's *Paperback Writer* to Tom's *Long and Winding Road*. Compromise was usually bearable for both, but with his classical stuff, impossible; she disliked most of it and in her easy way she called it miserable, boring, dead, *sends-me-to-sleep*. When he was lost in Debussy, she would be similarly lost in The Jackson 5, or T Rex. She sang in the tiny kitchen without thinking (inexplicably, to him) that he could hear her voice and her radio, her own spoiling music, above his own; but in truth she *was* aware, and on the day they returned from honeymoon, in their first September, she'd surprised him with headphones (happily, the very ones he would have chosen) but he hardly wore them, disliking the isolation and wishing the flat could be filled with his undisturbed music as it was often filled with hers. Despite her perfect gift, inwardly there was no pleasing him.

He moved around their small flat as autumn began, sometimes happy with her presence and sometimes not, never arguing with her over anything, but allowing his disappointment with her to steadily evolve; a poison tree was growing which after a dozen years would have its shadow fixed over soft, warm Connie, and all because of his private intolerance of her ways, and her own hopeful complacency.

: : :

After a week of distraction in North Wales, half-a-dozen refreshing days of remote, astonishing silence in the foothills of the lesser mountains below Snowdon, they returned and stayed in Monmouth until the end of September, when Tom took the irreversible step of finding a house for them both. He was ill at ease, but composed enough to focus on the necessary move – he could not imagine living in the tiny flat for much longer, not with Connie and certainly not with their child.

The nearly-new house he found was in the Wye Valley on the riverbank below Redbrook, and on an unforgettable day he took Connie to see it, and the memory of that day would stay with them both for ever, long after the other excitements had gone – the start of their move from country town to countryside, and the start of proper married life.

The house was startling: a stark square single-storey brick and aluminium structure on the sloping meadow close to the river – the front part on ground built up against an unlikely flood – and contrasting sharply with everything around it. Expanses of rough peppery bricks, interrupted here and there by tall narrow slits of glass – except for the wide picture windows overlooking the river and unseen from the road that ran at a higher level behind the house. The grounds spread level in front to their boundaries; neat beech hedges on each side, the river in front. Dotted across the lawn, delicate maples shivered in the cool October breeze.

The forest covered the rising ground beyond the road and across the river, and their new home with its silver-grey roof sat in the valley hollow, set fast in the greenness, carelessly clashing with all around. Tom was impressed, and Connie was delighted. It was different, modern, open and clean, and in that autumn they began filling it with the things they largely agreed upon together – their tastes in furnishings were similar and it was a time of reprieve for Tom, an escape from the life he'd feared. They were getting on together. He spent his money without any resentment, going here and there with Connie, discussing and agreeing easily, and in a month it was done. The new house was ready to give them the comfort of being settled after their restlessness, to welcome the accidental child, and to be lived in for ever.

They called their home *Rivendell*, after the deep valley realm of Tolkien's Middle-earth, a magical name for Connie, and while it overstated the deepness of their particular valley she was very set on it. Tom thought about it, and after saying he didn't like it, the next day said he *did* like it. He felt he should sometimes go against her, but it was a little power game that when it went his way never felt like a victory, and in time he stopped doing it. For Tom it was always easier to give in, in spite of his irritation, and in those days he was too busy in his mind with getting the house straight to dwell too much on it. But in unguarded moments, in his heart he wished above all he could bring those irritations to a halt, and accept his wife as she was.

Connie did not look for work. Her dream of starting a business fell by the wayside, her life being full enough with new husband and new house, but Tom had expected that and didn't mind at all. They didn't need the extra income and he found it appealing, having a future presence in the house to come home to, and knowing that all day she would be there unless she'd gone into Monmouth or wherever to shop or visit the friends she'd made in the summer. It was comforting for him, stabilising. Her parents had given her a car after the wedding so they were both free to come and go, which is what they did, until in November Tom made the move he'd been hoping for since the summer... he tried for the job he'd coveted for months before. The company was Sims Flight Instrumentation – *SFI* – a small family-run business in the niche market of instruments and test gear for the aviation industry.

He'd said, "I have an interview in Chepstow," and she was shocked at the thought of losing him, of being at home in her small world without him.

There was no vacancy, but he was taken on – mostly because of his sheer enthusiasm – but especially with his First in engineering; he'd visited the factory near Chepstow several times, just looking, just hoping to be allowed to work there while indulging himself at Rivendell. He became part of a team, but on his very first day he'd known that what he'd really wanted was to be number one, the top man at SFI. Once he'd started work Connie's concern was replaced with excitement for his ambition, while Tom genuinely felt closer to her and as the weeks passed, in the newness of everything their tracks converged a little more, and a little more often. She busied herself as her pregnancy progressed, waiting for his return each evening to give him news of what she'd been up to, the big and small details of her day. Then, barely eight months after their marriage baby Rachel Mary arrived, and Tom fell properly in love for the first time in his life.

The phone call came soon after lunch, and he was with her in twenty minutes; another fifteen and Connie was in the little hospital in Monmouth, and within the hour the child was born and handed, wrinkled and bawling, to her mother, and laid on her breast. She settled against her, and Connie was too full to say more than *Isn't she lovely...* soon after, the nurse lifted the child and she cried again in protest, as at barely three minutes old she was handed to her father and he took her carefully, a strange, stiff, struggling creature, howling a lament much bigger than herself. But when he took her she stopped as their eyes met, her wide un focused gaze close to his, and she was quiet again. He kissed her bruised forehead and still she was quiet, fists clenched to her face as she looked up in wonder at him.

She was his daughter and she had captured him without trying, and he was overwhelmed.

WE'RE IN LOVE, AREN'T WE

Three miles north of The Wondrous Gift is Bigsweir Bridge, and three-and-a-half miles further, the village of Redbrook.

Rivendell is before the village, low on the river bank meadow, seen for a moment beyond the lay-by at the top of the gravel drive when travelling north, and only glimpsed with difficulty through the hedges along the road. The house is remote from the village, on its own apart from a few houses lost in the trees across the river, the short quarter-mile before the sudden arrival of Redbrook being enough to give it its apparent isolation.

In early 1997, when life at The Wondrous Gift was settled in its cheerless ways, Tom and Connie had been upriver from it for twenty-two years, and both families, while aware of each other's homes, knew nothing of each other's lives. Alice had looked down through the hedges at Rivendell a thousand times from her father's car as he'd taken her to school every morning, and Tom had forever driven past The Wondrous Gift twice a day en route to and from Chepstow. Familiar but unknown, the two buildings stood alone – fixed parts of the valley – and were given a glance each time, perhaps, but more often they were at the periphery of vision, only vaguely registered as they went by.

Those twenty-two years were Rachel Mary Fisher's lifetime. From her birth in early April of 1975 to her twenty-second birthday, Rivendell had been her home, apart from the recent back-and-forth years at Edinburgh University – too far away for everybody when she'd announced her place there, but latterly perfect for her, and she looked forward to a future in the beautiful city. Her parents had come to terms with her desertion but kept her room as it was, the way most parents do, in readiness for the next visit or a permanent but unlikely change of mind.

The years of her upbringing were often confusing in her memory, at least the earlier years, before she understood the tensions or could read her father's mood or her mother's responses and find reasons for them. She was a seven-year-old, blaming herself when her parents were cross, being short with each other, or silent. She felt excluded at such times, her parents missing and replaced with physical replicas she didn't understand and could not relate to. The reason, she concluded, was that they didn't really love each other, and it was most likely her fault – why else would it be? But by the age of eleven Rachel knew their behaviour, had stopped blaming herself, and overall it wasn't so bad. They bickered, they made up. Or silences, followed by healing – and none of it was aggressive. And sometimes they were great together, warm and friendly; by then she hoped they loved each other, but was never sure. She was sure they loved her though, each in their own way – her father unquestioningly, even when silent and withdrawn, and her mother with reservations: mother and daughter, too close in biology, sometimes far apart in expectations. But overall, the good times were plentiful and looking back over her life brought more comfort than sadness.

Six years after starting at SFI, Tom Fisher had taken over the manager's office from Alfred Sims – the company owner, *Alfie* to everyone – and three weeks after that had the manager's job itself when Alfie finally decided he'd had enough of work, went home one Friday evening and never came back. It was a feeling that came over him as he passed his seventieth birthday, that he'd rather be doing something else now. So he left it all to Tom, who'd been effectively running it for the past year anyway, and stayed at home with his wife and his garden. Connie was overjoyed when she knew for sure that Tom was running the entire business, overseeing six people, and answering only to Alfie Sims, the owner. It was a dream come true for her, and a big step forward for Tom, who had real hopes of buying the business – after years of work-talk with Alfie, and sensing his wish to eventually wind it all down, he'd made a few cautious comments about taking it over. Alfie was interested, but not yet, perhaps. Tom had said nothing to Connie about his dream, a real possibility now, especially as Alfie and his wife were without children, and he was the new manager. The next step was only a matter of time, and he would surprise her when the time was right.

: : :

Oh Connie, I wish you wouldn't come here.

She said, "Thought I'd bring these up for you."

She put his morning mail on his desk, hugged him, kissed him. He smiled, suffering. They were both aware that his secretary could see them through the glass partition.

"I'm on my way to see Marge," she said. "She'll probably ask us to lunch on Sunday. We ought to go Tom, it's been ages." She waited. Tom turned away from her, put his hands in his pockets and walked to the window. He hoped his secretary wasn't still watching. Too bad if she was. He stood looking out over the workshop, and said quietly, almost pleadingly, to the glass, "Con... let's have Sunday in, shall we?" *No scene here, please.*

He turned back, and the look on her face was enough. "Oh, Tom..." Her tired response; her unattractive, don't-spoil-it-for-me routine. She sat down in his chair; he would have to give in.

Later he stood back from the window, looking down over the machines and the men as she went unseen down the stairs at the side and he saw the heads turn, thinking *You've made your point, they'll remember you. Please stay away from here Connie, you embarrass me.* And that led, as it usually did, to a short period when he went over all the reasons Connie was wrong for him, a time of annoyance with her and wishing things were different. It was a regular and damaging self-indulgence. Today he stood at his window and for some reason remembered her saying to him, shortly after their marriage, *"We're in love, aren't we."* He did not recall his answer, but it would have been positive, regardless of how he'd felt at the time. It was one of the many deeply-held memories he'd turned into grievances, that he could bring out when she had upset him in some way. As she left the building he went back to his desk and his mind turned to other things, but the usual vague feeling of guilt would take a while to go.

That was 1982, when Rachel was a wondering seven-year-old and both Tom and Connie were sadly remiss in reassuring her. Their differences were so commonplace by then, so normal, and they muddled through their not-so-private lives in front of her, only rarely pulling themselves up for her sake. Guilt would come and go. Connie, at home with the child far more than Tom was, felt a responsibility she wasn't quite sure of delivering, and usually felt a fraud telling her not to worry about Mum and Dad.

Once, around that time, she'd had a drink too many without realising it, sitting alone with a book on her lap. She'd looked up at her wine glass – empty for the third, possibly fourth, time – then spent some time staring at the label on the bottle, as if at some place of great moment, some turning-point in her life. She got up and put the bottle away: *that is not going to happen. Not to me.* So on that day Connie avoided alcoholism, which scared her far more than having a child hooked on believing that parents really were like this.

A year later, Tom Fisher became the owner of Sims Flight Instrumentation. He'd waited that year for Alfie Sims to commit to selling, a time of uncertainty which ended on a late autumn afternoon when Alfie overdid his gardening, fell over, and died.

His wife removed the uncertainty by following her husband's directions, put together months ago but kept from Tom because he was not ready to let it go. She sold it all to him, the building, the machines, the stock and the orders, and it was only days before that happened that Tom told Connie. He also asked her for money.

The death of Alfie Sims and the seamless continuation of the business all happened over a period of two months, and by Christmas the Fisher's lives had been transformed. Now, at last, Connie considered her physical life at Rivendell fulfilled, and Tom was elevated in her eyes to the summit of importance. Her input for the venture was eighteen thousand pounds, given freely by her parents who'd sat on a mountain of money since the death of Granny J and the sale of her houses in Hereford and France. It was a worthy cause, but that Christmas of 1983 was memorable to Rachel for just one reason: her parents got through the season without apparent conflict.

::::

In early 1997 Tom Fisher was settled, his business thriving, his daughter grown up, and his wife bearable. Replace 'wife' with 'husband' and the same could be said of Connie. Their situation was stable, and that thriving business, she felt, was half hers even though her contribution fourteen years ago was rather less than half. But the business was not half hers. Tom was the sole owner, and he overlooked any sensible reasons for sharing it with his wife. He was content with Connie being his sole beneficiary should he die, and the contingencies he'd set up for her put him at ease with what she may or may not do if that happened; he looked upon his possessions as being finite, as his life was, and what happened afterwards was irrelevant so long as Connie was spared any legal nightmares she couldn't cope with. She was, above all, a generous person. He was certain she would take care of Rachel, and his reasoning, knowing his daughter was more savvy than his wife, was that they could decide together to keep the business or let it go. They were grown-ups. His job was to keep it profitable and during those fourteen years of ownership, Tom had travelled every weekday down the valley to Chepstow and the small factory just outside the shadow of the Severn Bridge, and done exactly that. Connie had stayed at home. Rachel had grown, been sent to school in Monmouth, ended her time there and relocated to Edinburgh, first at the University, then at Leith Academy outside the Old Town, where she taught, albeit in a supply role. All was well.

The Fishers were a success. But before all that, before the business was his, Tom had struggled with a double life – his precious ambition rubbed along with his intolerance of Connie, through years of learning to get on with each other which had resolved itself into the often cheerless stability they now had. Within five years of their marriage, they had separate beds – the mark of royalty, or perhaps the aged, unwilling or unable to share the closeness of bodies in a double bed. It was the saddest thing for Connie. They stayed in the same room, and the gap between their new beds was kept clear and sometimes love would return in one of those beds, quietly or in a blaze, and last for a little while, before the weariness came back, like the love had, the cycles spinning slower until only the more familiar of the two, the weariness with each other, was left. They became set in their ways, apart, but the gap between their beds was kept clear, an ever-present and wistful hope for Connie. The hopeful symbolism was lost on Tom, who thought about taking to one of the other rooms, but stopped because of the effect such a final separation could have on his daughter.

His depressions had started around that time. Often he would not talk with Connie, preferring to lie on the couch in his study or even take to his bed at a silly time in the evening. He would very occasionally forego his supper, and then the next morning wake out of his stupor as if nothing had happened. So life went on, and Connie accepted her husband as he was. And the ups were always more plentiful than the downs.

His evenings were spent usually in his study, his head lost in the gloomy poetry Connie feared he read, or cut off from the house by the headphones she'd bought him years ago in an effort to give him privacy. His music was his own, not to be shared. In those days it was still Debussy, or Joni Mitchell. Debussy was lost on Connie, which he saw as her disregard of beauty rather than a simple preference, so it was impossible to play through speakers, ever. Joni Mitchell was shared, up to a point. He'd bought *Big Yellow Taxi* in 1970, when he was eighteen, but he'd bought it for the B-side, for the depth of *Woodstock*, and was quietly horrified when much later she'd said she preferred the A-side. It was impossible. He simply could not see how anyone could compare the two, let alone prefer the one she did, and that was how he got the message that his own music was perhaps not perfect for everyone – but that was hard to cope with, and soon led to his reluctant and singular musical life between the earpieces of his headphones.

Connie had taken to interior decorating, and at least one room was always in progress, unable to be used, empty and bare sometimes for days as her mind flitted from one theme to another, and at times she found it hard to continue. Even the annual holiday had degenerated to a single fortnight in the sun, usually France or Spain, and at best around fifty percent successful.

Tom's brother Geoff had kept all their postcards – the oldest of them now faded and curled – on the side of his fridge in the kitchen at Pentwyn, in homage to his unhappy brother; the thoughtful early enthusiasm had steadily slid into curt, token greetings as the years passed. Tom's affection for Geoff could not overcome his glumness while on holiday with Connie, and now Geoff could look through all those cards and trace the decline of their twenty years of married life behind bright and garish images of Saint-Tropez, Biarritz and Valencia. Sun and silence, and doing one's own thing, mostly; it didn't matter any more to appear close in front of strangers in foreign lands. Tom loved his solitude, looking forward to the times Connie would leave him alone in the big house to wander the rooms and garden with his thoughts, or to just sit with his music. It became a need, an irritating loss when it didn't happen, and yet at the same time this apparent need sometimes faltered when Connie was away for any length of time. She routinely stayed with her cousin in Stratford for a long weekend once a month, and Tom Fisher was often surprised by loneliness while she was away.

The new year of 1997 brought resolutions – unshared, private resolutions – and as usual Connie's involved a new start with something she'd left off the year before. This time it was to finish the decorating, then start with the outside, on the insignificant amount of timber visible amongst the brick and aluminium and glass. It was modest, and feasible.

Tom's resolution was the same as last year's: to lose himself in his work at the factory. So at home and away they were settled in their expectations for another year, but one day soon in that settled future, in a move that would change their lives for ever, SFI would lose two men to Rolls-Royce and gain one from it. A disgruntled Jon Greerson would jump ship as he'd thought he might one day, and Tom Fisher would take him on.

Her calls were desperate. Aku had gone, in an instant, through the doorway and up over the car park, curving away from her towards the bank of trees at the back of the hotel. Alice was distraught. She ran around from the front but couldn't see him. She'd taken him out of his cage as she often did, but this time she'd unwisely opened the front door a little as part of her plan for today, certain it was too narrow to let him through. She was wrong, and instead of his usual tight circuits of the corridor then coming back to her arm, he'd bypassed her and with a skilful and flashing fold of his wings was through the impossible gap and away. She stood beside the hotel with the trees towering before her, shouting his name. Aku had flown.

One hundred and fifty years before, the same thing had happened to Phillip Rossetti. That first Aku had escaped, through the same doorway and into the ancestors of the same trees, and it was next morning before he'd decided to come home. Deciding to come back was what was needed – because the decision was the bird's, not Phillip's. Alice knew all this. She had read of his despair at losing his companion. With Phillip it was late afternoon, and after a few minutes the bird had settled in full view up in the branches of the highest tree on the bank. He would not come down, not for anything.

As twilight approached Phillip tried, by offering food or showing him his cage, but after a while Aku stopped his occasional screeching and settled down for the night. He became quiet as darkness fell and Phillip went inside, despairing at his loss, fearing that their love was one-way, that Aku did not love him as much as he himself was loved. But a troubled night was followed by joy at first light as Aku was still there, looking down at his master, and after a few times of calling his name he'd left the branch and swooped down towards him. A few wide carefree circuits at the front of the Inn, and he'd flapped down onto his shoulder, sitting quietly, preening himself, wondering what all the fuss had been about. And Phillip had the broom – worn-out, almost without bristles, that he'd taught his Aku to come to every time it was held up for him in the corridor, a high welcoming perch, in anticipation of being taken outside. The broom had not worked for him though on that long-ago afternoon.

Knowing all this, Alice peered into those trees, and called. It was mid afternoon, and dusk was two hours away. She chastised herself again for her stupidity. Her plan had been to take him briefly outside, show him the world around him then take him back in. Just like that. Her naïve expectation was that he would behave better than that first Aku, and she'd wanted to replicate Phillip's later success with him. At worst he would fly around a bit, then settle in a tree and be happy after a while to come back to her, but now she wasn't so sure.

He'd been outside twice before today. Each of those times – the last being three years ago – was a lucky break for him: a door opening at the wrong time, a dive past the shocked person who had opened it, and a mad chase through the hotel until a conveniently-open window was found. But now, this time, what had she expected to happen? He was not a young parrot any more (he apparently had the mental development of a four-year-old child, and they can be wilful) so was it a surprise that he'd looked for adventure? He'd waited patiently for years for that slip, that slightly open door. Still, it was a long time to nightfall.

For all of her life, Alice had known Aku. Her mother had found him the year before her daughter's birth, the result of her long-held wish to return a new Wondrous Gift to the hotel and to have another Aku in his cage at the bottom of the stairs, as he had been with Phillip at first, before being elevated to his room. So Alice grew up with the young parrot, and achieved the sort of bond her mother had wished for herself, but had always been too busy to make happen. Aku needed contact with people. And Alice discovered that attention given to him was well-rewarded; by the time she was six or seven, *her* Aku (for that's what he had become) was a competent speaker, copying what she said, rewarding her patience with far more than *hello* or *bye-bye.* She kept a list of his words, which by then was fifty-two, and which would grow to more than four hundred as Alice reached twenty-five. Many phrases and four hundred words, not always used correctly – but that was her fault, for not being thorough with him – and colours, no problem with colours. And through those twenty-five years she'd known that he needed her as much as she loved him.

She knew that African Greys will fret if left alone for too long. They seek human companionship. Since biblical times they had been kept as pets, as companions, and the stars amongst them were always the ones given the most attention. So for a while after those escapes Alice had let Aku out of his cage every day, always when windows and doors were closed, to fly through the corridor and around a few selected rooms, but in the last two years her routine had slipped. Nowadays other things distracted her and it was once a week, if that, but after a recent bout of feather-plucking she had at last resolved to widen his world. Feather-plucking was distressing, for birds and owners, a self-harming that meant more attention was needed. She would take him outside. He'd said his usual hopeful *"Going out now?"* as his cage was opened, and soon after she'd raced outside in panic.

Then she'd seen him in the branches of a tree on the bank – the same tree he'd gone to on his previous escapes – and talked to him, hoping he could hear her. He could hear. She went back in for his broom (as equally tatty as Phillip's had been) and he screeched as she disappeared, then sat quietly observing when she returned. She felt silly, hoping no one was watching and fearing a repeat of Phillip's trauma, of the bird not caring for the broom just now, thank you – of having to wait until morning; she was standing at the foot of the bank when her grandfather drove into the car park, wondering why she was there with the old and tattered broom at her side, but then he knew. Before he got out of his car she pointed up to the tree, and he nodded, amused at her, resigning himself to a long wait.

He walked over to her and she said, "Aku's up there."

He said, "Thought so."

They discussed the situation at length. Everything she'd read about training these parrots seemed irrelevant now. The bird was free and most likely would stay out until morning. He sat on his branch, looking down, and the two humans gazed up at him; the situation was stable, at least. But then, as suddenly as it had started, it was over.

As they stood together Peter said, "You know, that bird's not very bright. He's not going to get his freedom ever again if he doesn't come back." And he looked up again and shouted, "Come down Aku! We'll trust you then!"

On cue, Aku left the branch and glided down.

He circled three times to assert his mastery over them, then landed easily on the broom as Alice held it up at her side, and the day was saved.

"Well, that was easy," said Peter.

They went different ways – he to his car, and Alice to Aku's cage as a darkly meaningful eye settled on her, and she realised she would have to keep the bargain her grandfather had made with him. Aku hadn't come back for *her* – the infidelity hurt – but she was also annoyed with herself for abandoning his welfare, his simple parrot needs, and with a slightly worrying sidestep she imagined him waiting at the same time tomorrow, and every day after that.

She was still in front of the cage when Peter reappeared, smiling, carrying something in bubble-wrap. He held it out for her. She took it, and saw through the plastic the cover of a book, with writing she couldn't make out.

"Is this... *your book?"*

His smile widened.

Aku muttered behind them, very quietly, *"Your book Alice."*

She said, "How did you get it printed so quickly?"

"I have friends in Bristol. I had them in readiness – a couple of weeks, and it was done." And Alice's mind touched on Phillip's bookbinder, also somewhere in Bristol...

They went into the kitchen and stood at the table where Peter took off the wrapping and there, in front of her, were the fruits of their labour, their collaboration. On the cover were the words:

A Personal History of Our Family, From Rossetti to Bennett,
1757 to 1996

Silver script on blue leather, like Phillip's first diary. They sat down together with the book before her, and she turned the pages reverently, aware of the newness, the perfectness of the white paper and the printing.

"Forty-five thousand words," Peter said, "can you believe that?"

Yes, she could. It was a huge lump of history and recollection, long stories and short, mostly of people Alice barely knew existed, and his sense of achievement was unmissable. She knew he'd barely slept towards the end, wanting to get it done.

They sat turning pages for almost half an hour, neither even thinking of putting a kettle on until Peter got up and did it, and two minutes later the door opened and Jon came in. They both looked at him in shock. He was home two hours early. He crossed the room, with no kiss for Alice but a flat "Hello" followed by a slightly brighter "Hello Peter".

It was rare for Peter to see this – the way they were together – and it was instantly sad, as Jon sat down opposite them at the precise moment that Elena came in, carrying an empty tray. She stopped in her tracks, surprised by the full kitchen. She greeted them – but Jon was home early.

"Is everything ok, my love?"

He looked at her with his usual doleful expression, and the optimism of the room, the warmth of his mother-in-law, the comforting background noises of the hotel and the perfect timing of the kettle clicking off did nothing to separate him from his melancholy. Even there, he felt awkward and seemed to be looking for a means of escape, bound too tightly to his situation with Alice.

He said, "Yes. I have some news."

They all stared at him; he hadn't gone straight upstairs as he usually did... *he has some news.* Elena put her tray down.

"I'm leaving Rolls Royce," he said, almost mournfully.

It was big news, but the way he'd said it had them all staring at him as if it were bad news. Alice was thrown. This was out of the blue... why hadn't he talked with her about it? *Has he been fired?*

In the seconds of silence she felt lost with him, annoyed almost that he had not shared it with her. But her feelings went very quickly from irritation with him to doubts about herself. It was a few seconds, that's all, but she felt bad at the end of them and returned his look of mournfulness until he said, "I've got a job in Chepstow, starting in two weeks." Relief all round. Alice managed a rare smile for him.

He told them he'd taken the afternoon off and gone to see Tom Fisher, the owner of *Sims Flight Instrumentation,* with the hope of working there... two men had started at Rolls-Royce the week before, and they had come from Sims, or *SFI* as they called it. He'd phoned a few days later and spoken to Tom, who sounded enthusiastic.

"Come and see us," he'd said. He had, and he'd got the job. As the conversation paused Alice said, "It's all a bit sudden," then felt feeble for saying it.

The tea was made and they sat together, a quartet of hopeful people, as Jon lightened his mood and smiled at last. A glance around him told him he was indeed among friends, and his injured relationship with Alice stepped back as he enthused over his new job. It was what he'd wanted for the past year, probably longer (and he'd told himself many times, *there's more to life than this – but beware of the wishes of others – the ambitions they have for you*). So he told them it was closer to home, the money was better, and he would save on the bridge tolls… but above all it was what he wanted. Nobody questioned it, nobody seemed to mind him leaving the prestige of Rolls-Royce, but Alice thought, *I knew nothing of that; he's been unhappy at work, and I didn't know.* She felt unexpected sympathy for him as he sat opposite her, this man of hers, lately deserted. He was having a new start. Her grandfather's wonderful new book was still in front of her, and in a moment of friendliness she turned the book around and pushed it across the table to Jon.

"Look at this," she said.

He read the cover, and ran his fingers over the leather.

"So this is it – the long-awaited book."

"It was a lot of work for us both Jon," said Peter.

Jon looked through it, opening here and there. "It's beautifully done. So is this the only copy?"

"No. This is Alice's. I had two made." Then, looking at her, Peter said, "I'm sure she'll let you read it though."

She was touched that he'd made one for her.

"Yes, of course I will."

It had been a comforting hour for Jon, and afterwards, alone in their bedroom, he thought of the day and of the changes. He'd brought the book up with him as Alice had asked, and he put it on her bedside cabinet, with a sense of oddness to be in the room a good hour before he normally was. It was an hour of freedom, and precious, to be used and not wasted. His surroundings were warmer and more welcoming, and all because of the way she had spoken to him, and smiled at him. His new job was the topping on that, but not as important. She was everything, and he longed for her to know it. *Keep telling her you love her.*

He stood in the room and looked around. *Like a room in a museum, where nothing changes,* he used to think, and gathering sadness rather than dust, day after day. The late afternoon was clear and bright, light still flooding the room though the sun had long gone from this side, and soon dusk would come, then the night, and she would be here with him again.

He sat on the edge of the bed, on Alice's side. Yes, the room was warmer, more friendly – it was Alice, and the way she had reached out briefly to him at the kitchen table, talked easily with him about his work and the book. It had ended when she'd pulled herself up, suddenly realising that this was not how she should be. She'd gone back, away from him to wherever she was these days, but for now he was sitting on her side of the bed, not angry with her, and remembering her smiling at him.

: : :

The third of February was the day Jon would start at SFI. His last day at Rolls-Royce – a Friday, having been let off without pay for the Saturday morning – was a muted affair, lacking the usual jollities and camaraderie given to leavers. He was reckoned to be unsociable, and not much fun, so no point in going to the pub after work, no point in anything special for the day. He said his goodbyes in his own way, without the back-slapping and drinking – and he doubted he would be missed, without realising the gap he was leaving behind him... a small gap in a company that size, but a gap nonetheless.

Three weeks earlier he'd left after lunch, northwards over the bridge towards home, and turned off the roundabout into the industrial estate after the sign he'd seen and wondered about a thousand times before on his way home from Filton – a patriotic square of red, white and blue with the words *Excellence in*

Instrumentation across the bottom. The words alone inspired him – not that Rolls-Royce was any different, but he was so ready to be a part of that smaller, particular excellence.

He would remember the first time walking into the workshop – a fraction of the size of the one he'd left behind – and the shock of seeing only five men working there, moving around, and the quietness of the whole affair with soft, almost humming machinery and a heavenly, unblaring radio somewhere.

Tom Fisher was always ready for over-confidence, for the cocky know-it-all approach supposed to impress but which turned him off. Jon Greerson was not cocky, and he got the job. *Chief Engineer,* if you please, an unexpected second-in-command because of his qualifications, his quiet approach, and his obvious knowledge of what he saw as Tom showed him around. He was unfazed.

On his first Monday he drove into the industrial estate and parked in the space kept for him – in front of a very tidy and discreet sign announcing: *J D Greerson, Chief Engineer.* That's what he was now. From being one of many, he was now on his own and couldn't help thinking that Tom was indulging him with the title; he was twenty-five years old, and *Chief Engineer* filled him with pride and fear in equal amounts. He would be responsible for so much more than he had been at Filton, and would be above five others, three of whom were older than him, hence the fear... but he'd left the crowds behind him.

: : :

At ten o'clock precisely on the eleventh of February, 1997, Jon first saw Connie Fisher: a Tuesday, a never-to-be-forgotten sun-showery Tuesday, and the shock of seeing her was absolute. On the stroke of ten (her appearance being announced by the beeps on the radio), her brief smile changed him from a deserted, fed-up husband to a refocused, something-to-live-for husband, to the detriment of his wife and his marriage.

Jon had been in his new job for a week and a day when Connie appeared – petite and striking with her bob cut hair, tight jeans, low-top sneakers and a loose, untucked denim shirt. She was carrying her coat to show off her figure, but that did not occur to him then; he was just wondering if there was a bra underneath that shirt or not. She tapped up the steel steps to the mezzanine – watched by them all – then looked down at him, smiled an automatic smile and like most unhappy men he thought it meant *I like the look of you... I would like to sleep with you sometime.* From then on Connie Fisher – his employer's wife – and Jon were hopelessly bound together by his longing, and her non-appreciation of it.

He turned back to his work, and had three goes at calibrating a simple transponder, something he'd done a hundred times before. When he'd done it, he let his gaze and his thoughts wander – at that stage of his struckness, even before being closer to her than thirty feet, he would have given anything to be in Tom's place, to have this new wonder-woman in his bed. His lust was immediate, and in those moments of astonishment she had eclipsed Alice. His wife had gone from him.

He tried to busy himself, needing to calm down, until after ten minutes Tom appeared at the top of the steps and beckoned him up. He followed him into his office and was introduced to Connie, and shook hands with her – and once again in his life he was exhilarated by the first touch of a woman. This was not Alice.

He'd guessed she was in her early forties, and now he thought she was easily as beautiful as Alice was at half that age... as lovely as any of the girls he had dreamed up in his solitude, all of them younger, and all of them ousted by her. The successful executive's wife – the perfectly casual clothes, the perfect honey-blonde hair, the looked-after figure. A step up from what Jon would call *smart*. Her face, so different from Alice's, more full and round and sensual... voluptuous, even. He was besotted.

Tom stood back from them with his arms folded as the handshake took place, then in the small talk Jon felt himself leaving the unchanging life he had with Alice for a higher plane, to where this woman was. It was all he could do not to give himself away by being too enthusiastic. She had been unmoved, but pleased to meet him nonetheless and she would never know how significant she really was – a distraction arriving at the right time, sweeping out Alice and her problems.

The rest of his day went smoothly after she had come down the stairs and walked through the workshop, with half-a-dozen furtive pairs of eyes following until the door closed behind her. He was keyed up, but was he just one of many who had gone through the same thing? A hopeless lusting after the boss's wife? The looks he had from a few of them when she'd gone gave the answer – *Well? What do you think, Jon?* – and all he could do was smile back. Alice, for the first time in months, had left the front of his mind. And he was still wondering about that bra.

On the day that Jon met Connie, Julia phoned the hotel with some news from France. Her life in Fréjus had progressed gently through the years since Alice's time in 1989, and the two had only met since on the four occasions when Julia had come over, and to the wedding. She'd been told about the *baby problem,* as Peter called it – and of Alice's coming back to life in December but, like everyone else, did not know the reason for it. The news was that Olivier Canac wanted to see Alice again.

"Elena... this bothers me. I wish he'd stay away, with Alice as she is. Should I speak to him again? What do you think?" He was coming to Bristol, a mere thirty miles from her.

"Well you can't stop him coming over."

Neither mother nor great-aunt were happy to imagine Alice's wrath, if she ever found out.

"It's a secret I don't want, Julia. He's not going to forget her."

Elena found her daughter and gave her the phone. She tried to listen in from a distance slightly too far away, so heard nothing. Julia would tell her later.

How are you, good to hear from you again, then, "Alice, I'm sure you remember Olivier." There was a slight pause, duly noted.

"Yes... of course I do." *Olivier.* The name pulled her out of wherever she was that morning.

Julia's tone was almost apologetic. "Well, he's teaching at the new High School here – the *Lycée Albert Camus,* if you please – and he's going to England next week with a group of students. In *February,* of all months. Haven't spoken to him for half a year then he calls me saying he'd like to look you up. Sorry if that's a problem, but I could hardly stop him."

"No, that's not a problem. Be nice to see him again."

A teacher? Olivier?

"What does he teach?"

"History."

"Ah... no more gardens."

"No, apparently not."

Julia couldn't help herself. "He knows you're married, by the way."

Alice was amused. "Oh... thank you Julia!"

"Well, I have memories of you two, you know. A close-run thing, that was. You know he married his cousin soon after you left – well he tells me he's happy with her but I'm not sure. Something about him now." As she said it she cursed herself for being honest.

"So he hasn't worked for you for a while?"

"No, not for years. I bump into him sometimes at the market. He still lives in the same place."

"So what makes you think he's not happy with her?"

This girl. Julia mentally cursed herself again. "Don't know." She wanted to say *I think he'd rather be on his own.*

"I never see them together... not that that means much, I suppose."

"So why exactly did he ring you? What did he want?"

"Just some news of you, I suppose, before seeing you. Preparation, my dear."

Alice smiled into the phone. *Same old Julia.* "Well I'll expect a visit. Did he ask for my number?"

"No, and I didn't offer. But he'll find it. Not that many hotels in Brockweir. It shouldn't worry me really, because if he had designs on you he'd hardly have let me in on it, would he?"

Designs on me? Really? "No, I suppose not."

Then Julia said, "All the same, I hope it doesn't become a problem Alice. There's a big part of me that's a bit unhappy with this."

Alice was calm. "It was a long time ago Julia, and I'm not seventeen any more. He's just an old friend. Don't worry about me."

"I'll try not to," she said, knowing she would. "He says he'll call first, won't just turn up. Anyway my dear, that's the news from France. What's happening your end?"

After the call Alice sat down in the kitchen as her pulse slowed from racing to merely fast, and mused on the possibilities of a visit from Olivier, now twenty-seven, married – maybe not happily – and maybe with *designs* on her. She was severely distracted, her obsession with Phillip not swept aside, but here was a real flesh-and-blood man. In a couple of days he could walk into the hotel and ask for her – how would that feel? Or a phone call, handed over by her mother perhaps – the familiar voice from long ago, asking how she was, and could they get together somewhere. And then she thought about making love with him. She would have in 1989, if he'd gone along with her.

Then Jon popped annoyingly into her head but she ignored him, stepped over him in an instant. This was more important, yet through it all she felt traces of the irrational, fuzzy head-filling confusion she'd had before finding the Journal. After the reawakening of December, suddenly her new, reordered life was threatened by a visit from an old friend.

That's how it was on the few days after Julia's call, as Alice waited for Olivier in her busy world of hotel work and overexcited imaginings. Her mother said, "Julia tells me your friend Olivier is coming over to see you darling... are you looking forward to that?"

She was surprised, but said, with detachment, "Oh yes, it'll be nice."

Elena wanted to say, *You must bring him here to meet us,* but with things as they were... life was awkward enough as it was. So they would meet somewhere else – and knowing where that could lead she asked anyway, "Will he come here?"

"Well he hasn't called me yet. We'll probably have a coffee

somewhere. And I won't keep it from Jon, don't worry."

She sounded thoughtful for her husband as she held plans and hopes against him, but Elena was desperate to be heartened – and the threat had lifted a little. She dared to think it wouldn't be a problem after all.

A long two days later Olivier called the hotel, and it was Alice who answered. The voice was the same, for them both.

"Alice, it's so good to hear you again. How are you?"

So she told him how she was, while she was far away and already in his arms, already being loved. She tried not to sound too excited.

He said, "Would it be possible to meet you? For coffee, or a little drink perhaps?"

"Yes, I'd like that." She had already worked it all out, where to go – and where to go after that, if things went that way.

She asked him where he was staying. "In Bristol first – Filton? We're there for two nights, then Gloucester for another two. Then north to see the Vikings in York, then on to Scotland. Three weeks and a few days. It's all cultural. What do you think, will you be able to see me?"

Filton. Jon used to be at Filton. "I think so. I can be flexible, but an afternoon is best for me."

"Well how about next Wednesday? We'll be settling in at Bristol, and I could get away for an hour or so. What do you think?"

"Okay, yes… if you come across the bridge we could meet in Chepstow. I know a place, it'll be nice to see you."

It was a hurried call but they arranged their meeting, swapped phone numbers and said *au revoir*. Again, Alice's heartbeat was almost audible. It was done. This was not an imagined lover, this was a real man – and although she had Jon all she thought was, *my Captain won't mind*. The reality was that she had no real, grounded thoughts at all, only the wonderful expectation of love coming her way, and sweeping aside the life she had.

For Alice, the success of her meeting with Olivier depended on certain things, and on one in particular. During the eight years she'd had him in her memory he'd become an enduring symbol of love, sitting at the back of her mind as she'd lived her life. She'd met and married Jon with Olivier there, constant and true... but she had always wondered, *did he love me?* and the danger now was that he would not be the person she remembered, but some travesty of him, some stranger. In her world it was quite possible to be without fault, and that alone promised him the harshest of tests as she counted down to the Wednesday afternoon.

On the weekend she told her mother, who asked, "Is Jon okay about it?"

"He'll be fine."

"You haven't told him yet?"

"It's not a problem Mum – I'll tell him tonight." But that night drifted by and the next evening she told him.

"You need to know something," she said when they'd gone upstairs after their supper together – and while she busied herself so as not to face him directly – "and it doesn't mean anything. I'm having a coffee on Wednesday afternoon with an old friend I met in France a long time ago. He was the gardener where I stayed in Fréjus. We'll be in Chepstow, at *The Lookout*. Just so you know."

She had his attention. "Why would I think it means something?"

"I don't know. You may."

A pause. "Should I be worried?"

She glanced at him, then looked away again. "No. He's just an old friend. Nothing more."

Jon thought this through. *Why aren't you looking at me?* The feeling was one of alarm, yet he found himself saying, "You're free Alice. I don't hold you down." Then his politeness stepped in with a cheerless, "But thanks for letting me know."

Alice simply said, "Okay," before going back downstairs, but as she left him his words filled her head: she's *free*. The word felt new and liberating, as if she'd been tied down in some way. It cheered her. Permission from her husband, freedom given – that's how it felt, and suddenly Wednesday was different, the promise of it.

Jon actually thought of taking an afternoon off – to follow her, to spy – but decided against it. Yet under such a threat it was alarm that troubled him, not jealousy, and within a few hours he was imagining the scenario of properly losing her and being left empty, with just his infatuation for Tom's wife to comfort him. There were no more words between them that evening, but later he lay next to Alice as she had her dreams, there was no room in his head for Connie.

At five past two on Wednesday afternoon Alice drove away from the hotel. Twenty minutes later she parked outside the café she'd chosen almost a week before, the car park looking out over the rooftops to the Severn estuary sitting heavy and grey in the distance, and at the graceful arching bridge that would bring him to her. She was early, so she sat at a table in the corner and waited. The few minutes were slow, like hours, dragging by: she was facing a clock on the wall and she found herself drawn to it every few seconds, hurrying it along. She was ready. She thought again about having sex with him. Would she, if he loved her? How would she know he loved her? *Well, she would know.* She would see where this leads, and not think of him having to lie to his wife, which would surely happen, as she would have to lie to her husband. She thought of the Filton coincidence, and of how she was at that moment less than a mile from Jon, and how Olivier also would be, soon. Odd coincidences connecting these men somehow, but ultimately meaningless - then he was there, coming through the door.

He came towards her as she stood up. "Hello Alice."

The voice she'd remembered had returned to her. They

hugged. There was a kissing of cheeks, and they sat down opposite each other. They were both cheered by what they saw. He looked the same, and she looked softer to him: her hair, her skin, her eyes – but on top of all that she looked grown-up, which surprised him. The eager seventeen-year-old had moved on. But after eight years Olivier was exactly as she recalled him, apart from his clothes. Growing up had not changed him: he was the Olivier she knew, and she was delighted. They drank coffee, and talked.

He'd arrived from Nice that morning. Three *minders* – his word – and twenty-two students.

"Three weeks, and much travelling. But it's good."

He'd gone into teaching the year after Alice left Fréjus – it had been his choice in school and college, and gardening was a sideline – and now he was travelling with teenagers.

Alice listened, letting him talk, realising she knew nothing of him beyond his gardening, and guessed that Julia hadn't told her more because she didn't know either. She felt a slight disappointment, losing her gentle gardener. History was fine though – just the remote threat of being dry and dusty... but surely not with him, not with Olivier.

"History is life," he said, "the record of it. Real people, real places. It fascinates me to imagine how things were. Something I learned recently – did you know there were seventeen pubs in Brockweir, once upon a time? And a hundred and nineteen in Monmouth?"

She was smiling. *He's been reading up.* "No, I didn't. You sound happy with your job."

"I am. I enjoy it very much."

Small talk, back and forth, avoiding the depths of their feelings as they both skirted around the no-go areas, the spoiling facts of their lives as coffee was replenished, and a few modest cakes came and went. Then the moment arrived as Olivier suddenly leaned forward in his chair and said, "You know Alice, as I walked away from you I was so sorry. I could not stop thinking of you, even years later. I wished I had said yes to you."

Her eyes never left his as she reached for his hands, as he'd once taken hers across that table in the sun. "Oh, Olivier. I'm sorry."

"We're both sorry, I think."

She said, "I've always wondered how you felt."

"You mean, did I love you?"

"Yes."

"Yes, I did. And after you went that could have gone two ways. It could have become unbearable – which would have brought me to you much sooner than this." He smiled. "Or it could have faded, and become hopeless. Which is what happened. I could not have you. I was in a bad place, Alice. I was... *betrothed?* – to my cousin but she was happier than I was." His voice became detached, further away. "But I had promised to marry her you see, and that made the difference. I had to think beyond you, and after a while, well..."

She said, "I caused you all that pain, and I'm sorry."

"Yes, it was painful. But also for you, I know." He brightened. "And now I have my life, and you have yours. I assume you're happy? Can I ask that?"

"Yes... happy enough," was the best she could do, "and you are not?"

A long sigh. "Well, I could talk philosophy to you, talk about stoicism, about happiness coming and going, but we would both be bored, I think." Then he paused. He looked down to the table, then back to her eyes.

"I haven't come to seduce you Alice."

It should have shocked her perhaps, but it didn't. They sat, hands clasped together and with all the complication of their lives piled up in their heads, gazing into each other's eyes like the young lovers they never were. She couldn't help smiling as she said, "So why *have* you come?"

A broad smile from him. "Well, to see how you are, of course."

"And what do you see?"

"Oh, Alice. I see a girl, in a garden..."

His broad smile softened. "But I also see you grown up, and married, and happy enough."

Happy enough. He was either a lover or a confidant. He could not be both. She'd always imagined that to have a lover and discuss your husband would be the worst thing. The sort of thing other people did.

Then he said, "So I married a florist, and you married..."

"I married an engineer."

He nodded slowly, as if it confirmed something for him... his wonderful Alice with this *engineer* – their conversations, their common ground; he didn't know who would be right for her, but this was still a small shock.

"He's kind," she said, "and he does his best with most things."

So she tolerates him, as I tolerate Delphine. But the bitterness of the thought pricked him and was immediately followed by, *be good now, Olivier Canac, be good.*

He said, "You have children?"

She tried not to sound disappointed. "No. Not yet. What about you?"

"No, and no plans."

"No plans?"

"We have agreed to wait, but I don't know why. So we wait."

After a moment she said, "It's okay to have something to wait for."

There was a time of silence, before he went back to the garden in Fréjus: "You know, I did actually say yes to you – at the window – what I said was that I wished I could go with you. You didn't understand. You couldn't understand."

A very heavy pause. "Is that really what you said?"

"Yes."

The revelation changed him in her eyes, and took her back to the days after leaving him in Fréjus, and the height she'd elevated him to. "And you were unhappy with your cousin."

"Yes, I was."

So she was right. *Duty and loyalty.* What else could it have been? It never occurred to her that the nineteen-year-old might have been afraid to take that step, afraid of consequences. There was only chivalry.

"So why did you marry her?" *Your eyes are beautiful...*

"Because of my promise." But that sounded too virtuous, and he said, "But also – it sounds crazy... I married her to forget you."

"To forget me? I can't believe that."

"It's true, it's what I did."

"But, you didn't forget me."

"No, I didn't."

She was in a different place with him now. Empathy had modified whatever hopes she'd come with. Hopes, thoughts, dreams – *so would I really like to go somewhere with this man, hold him and kiss him, lie down with him, give myself to him? Yes, I would.*

In the long silence that followed she felt sorry for him, and for herself. He was trapped in his marriage as she was trapped in hers, and here was an opportunity for release – a hurried, secret fling to settle their old passion for each other. Just that, nothing more needed, perhaps. She looked at his hands, resting in hers: the gardener's hands, now softened by teaching, and she imagined him in front of a class giving his knowledge away softly, and thoughtfully. But then, as she studied those hands, quite suddenly she saw the pale, narrow band around his finger where his wedding ring had been – very pale, almost invisible. There was a shock as she realised he'd taken it off; she stared, then a familiar despair rushed in. It gave her the same alarm as her *baby thing* with Jon had, an impossible to ignore shift in her perception of the man in front of her. Why would he take it off? Was he hiding her from Delphine? Her sense of chivalry was offended as she dwelt on that feint band around the finger of his left hand that held the *vena amoris,* the vein of love, that ran to the heart. He'd taken off the ring that encircled and protected it, left it vacant in the hope that Alice would connect with it. That was what she concluded, in those few seconds of silence. The sounds around her, – the low talking, the clinking of cutlery – all faded as a familiar disappointment returned. She'd gone from anticipation to failure. Things had collapsed, just as they had with Jon in that long-ago moment, but none of that came back to her then. She was firmly in *this* moment, and the small detail of his missing ring had become huge.

He didn't see the slight change in her. Still the smile, as she looked back to his face, and him unaware of what was going on behind that smile. She glanced at the clock – they'd been talking for twenty minutes. He would have to leave in another fifteen.

She looked into his eyes. "Did you mean what you said just now?"

He wasn't sure what she meant. "I've been honest with you, Alice."

She doubted him. Why wasn't he honest with her? She would never take off her wedding ring to deceive someone, not ever. She sat with him, on the verge of walking out, driven by her own mixed-up sense of loyalty.

She said, still holding his hands, "So when do you go back home?"

He smiled, missing the disappointment in her voice.

"In three weeks. But I have a free afternoon this week, on Friday. We'll be staying in Gloucester then."

She waited, and he said, in a quieter voice, "Perhaps we could meet up on Friday, Alice? Have lunch somewhere?"

Suddenly it was sleazy, an *arrangement*. So – lunch, then sex, uneasy and without joy, in some hotel room maybe, or in his car, his borrowed car. Suddenly his own words came back to her from the garden in Fréjus. They were perfect then, and perfect now.

"I'm sorry but I worry my husband will be unhappy if I go out with you again."

He gave her a faintly puzzled look. "But you're out with me now."

"And he knows I am... and where we are. Doing it again might be too much."

"How so? Would he really mind if you had lunch with an old friend?"

"It wouldn't feel right. I'm sorry."

Olivier knew he had not managed to be honest with her. He had given in to a brief and meaningful lowering of his eyes, and the statement *I haven't come to seduce you*; the words were a noble aspiration but not true. He'd come from France through necessity, to a coincidence that put him within reach of her, but when he met her he would tell of his unhappiness with Delphine... it would be hard not to, even while knowing that the sympathy that would surely follow is a cheap way to a woman's heart, and a pitiable way to her body. He should not use his unhappiness like that, but in his heart he wanted the girl he'd lost in Fréjus, the girl who would have given herself to him. He looked long and hard at her face, taking in everything he remembered of Alice Lindberg, familiar and almost unchanged over the years. But changed she had. Seventeen was a world away from twenty-five, and there was nothing he could do about it. He had no idea what had gone wrong. He gave a long sigh – in her eyes, giving himself away to her again – and said, "Well, Alice, can I get you more coffee?"

A short time later, standing next to his car, they felt quite different from half an hour before. Now, their smiles were slight.

He said, "Should we keep in touch, or should we not?"

The joy had gone out of her voice. "We're friends Olivier, so why not?"

He nodded in agreement, "Yes, we're friends."

They joined hands again, facing each other. He looked down

and said, "That's a lovely ring, Alice. I've lost mine. Or mislaid it somewhere. I take it off to wash, and sometimes I forget..." Her heart skipped a beat as he turned his hand over to show her. "It will be in the bathroom in the hostel, I think. *I hope!*" He looked back to her face and smiled. "It would not be good to lose it."

She stared at him, speechless as her mind reset itself.

Olivier felt the change in her, a sudden coming alive, but could not explain it. Suddenly she wanted to say *Yes... yes! Let's meet again on Friday!* but she feared he would realise what she'd assumed, and think badly of her. So they said their unwilling goodbyes, then hugged and kissed cheeks like friends do in France and he drove away into the grey afternoon, leaving her standing in the car park looking after him, her heart racing.

As she drove home, Alice was preoccupied, but less with the excitement of having seen him again than with her automatic leap to the wrong conclusion. She'd messed up. *So is this me, when things don't go my way?* Suddenly she was aware of doing this before, with Jon. She feared she was abnormal, or at best a spoiler of relationships, someone who expects too much then puts the blame on others when she's disappointed. He wasn't trying to deceive her. *I was prepared to have sex with this man, then it was off because he removed his wedding ring. What's the matter with me?* But no answer came, because that was her, that was Alice. She moved on. She would put it right. She drove alongside the dull river – trees, houses, life going about its business, all unseen as she passed through and as she turned into the car park she knew: yes, she would put it right. Her assumptions had been wrong, and now the idea of sex was not at all sleazy. *I'll call him, I must call him.* She went into the hotel, and seeing her mother in the dining room splayed her fingers at her and silently mouthed "five minutes," then went straight up and sat on her bed. She waited as long as she could, wanting him to have arrived at Filton. *A few minutes more perhaps, then he'll be there.* He answered immediately.

"Olivier, it's me."

"Alice! Are you okay?"

"Yes..."

"Wait please, I have to move."

She heard the babble of voices around him, the spoken French that always took her away to warmth, and sunshine.

"Okay... sorry."

"Olivier, can I change my mind, about Friday?"

His reply was instant.

"Alice! Of course!"

She asked where he would be staying in Gloucester, and said she would find somewhere close to meet.

"So... is it okay with your husband?"

"It will be," she said, but as Olivier rejoined his students he felt the first pangs of doubt about Alice Lindberg, now Greerson, now not quite the same; uneasy with his own deceptions, he was suddenly uneasy imagining hers.

Alice would spend the rest of the day circling her impending adultery, fully aware of what she was doing but not finding the will, or even the need, to turn away from it.

: : :

"This is Charlie. He's two next month – the Terrible Twos!"

She was about the same age as Alice, and her beaming husband leaned closer to her as they shared the photograph. They were seated at the far end of the Dining Room and during some small talk they had been keen to show her their children. Some people, she knew, always wanted to do that. The urge to show the wonder they had made – *look how lovely he is... such a clever boy...* And then another photograph, an equal of the first, this one a girl of four and everything Alice could want in a child. Her heart melted, in ignorance of any faults these creatures could inexplicably have.

She had dipped into the motherhood she had been denied, and feeling hard done by she left the couple to their meal.

As she walked behind Reception and into the office her phone rang, and it was Olivier. She saw her mother at her desk and answered him, "Oh… hello," then turned and walked back out and into the car park.

He was putting off their meeting.

"Alice, I can't help it. We have to leave Gloucester tomorrow morning now, so I won't be able to see you." And Alice, her head suddenly emptied of beautiful children, faced a new disappointment.

"We're coming back down to Filton again next month. What about the fourteenth – can we meet then instead?" He felt her distress. "What do you think Alice, can I see you then?"

It was three weeks away, a lifetime.

"Yes… we'll meet then."

And that was that.

: : :

"Jon – Sunday – would you and Alice like to come to us for tea?"

Nothing special, Tom said, just something informal away from work. Jon had said yes, and later a preoccupied Alice had also said yes and the Sunday morning, when it came, found them in bed thinking very different things.

It was towards the end of February, and they had both woken early; there was the merest shimmer of frost on the window and the first sun of the day was bright against the glass, but only one of them was lifted by such a morning, only one of them felt promise in the day ahead. It wasn't Alice. She lay on her side, looking across the room, trying to level her thoughts and to work out what was the matter, but the matter was Olivier.

VISIONS OF LOVELINESS

For some weeks now there had been a dulling, a barely-noticeable shift away from the exhilaration Alice had felt every time she'd thought of Phillip, and she opened his journal less often these days, having read it through a dozen times or more since the heady days of December. She became concerned that her affair with Phillip Rossetti would eventually run its course, that it would end instead of lasting for ever; but this movement away was small until Olivier had called and then, in the space of ten days, the French boy returned from her past and one obsession gave way to another. What she'd thought was set in stone was not so and she considered putting the Journal away, back to the attic, to clear the way for him, but that was a step too far for her.

On that Sunday morning she did not look forward to the invitation for tea – meeting strangers and playing the loving wife, to pretending: the *pretending* was the killer, and she wished she didn't have to do it. But she would get through the day, work her Sunday routine then make herself presentable and leave with her husband for the barren journey along the river to Redbrook. She lay there thinking of her French boy as Jon was thinking of his boss's wife – Connie was simply a rush, an arrow of lust to his starved male soul, but the dangers in lusting after the boss's wife were obvious, and non-negotiable.

Jon's dealings with Alice had changed in that time. Above all, he'd stopped telling her he loved her, and he justified it by blaming her, which hurt him all the same. He'd let go of his resolution to tell her every day – the regular, unanswered event – and it saddened him. But it struck him that not speaking of his love was surely the first sign of that love dying of neglect, and in spite of everything he didn't want that. So he'd thought again of Alice, but in a businesslike way, intending to tell her again at some point in the day that he loved her – but it would still be somewhat mechanical. He knew he should try to open his heart again, and all this while Connie reached into his thoughts whether there was a vacancy there or not – she was exciting but unreachable, a treat for the senses and the imagination. He looked forward to his Sunday afternoon.

At ten to four, Jon drove with his wife out of the car park of The Wondrous Gift, and eight minutes later pulled off the road into the drive at Rivendell. It was four o'clock exactly when Tom opened the door to them, and thought, *So this is Alice. Well, I had no idea what to expect.*

There were three of them: Tom, Connie and their daughter Rachel – down for the weekend from her supply teaching in Edinburgh. After the introductions they were led through to the big room at the front, overlooking the lawns, the river meadows and the river itself, and they all sat, one couple opposite the other, on sofas that looked expensive; a low glass table was between them and Rachel lounged in uninhibited fashion in a chair to the side. Best behaviour was apparent from the others, and observed by Rachel – her parents at such times would be trying to find tolerance for each other, but how long they could keep it up? She had long played this game of observing, being able to disconnect herself from them enough to not hate it, to watch in detached awe at the erosion of their togetherness in front of others as the minutes passed.

The day had warmed up after the cold beginning – a gorgeous early spring day, and the view to the river and across was remarkable and unlike anything from the hotel. The windows stretched the full width of the room, and from floor to ceiling – a glass wall broken by the slender uprights of the frames and a sliding door at the one end opening out to the garden – and after a few minutes Connie had invited them to stand and look out over the lawn with its borders, hoping for admiration. The curtains were not entirely open so she walked to the side and opened them fully with the press of a button, a demonstration for her new and gratifyingly impressed friends as Tom watched in embarrassed silence. There would be more marvels to show them as the afternoon moved on, and which would much later prompt Alice to say to Jon, *It's just a house, with fancy bits. We could have them too.*

Tea arrived, and cakes on delicate dishes, and the talk went around everything as they got to know each other. Tom looked at Alice, first with a man's eyes, and a maudlin phrase came to him – *a vision of loveliness.* Indeed. The thin dress – too summery perhaps, and more fitted to garden parties on hot days than very early spring afternoons, and the clear, pale complexion, the green eyes, the blonde hair. So lovely, like a girl from somewhere foreign he'd seen and remembered, leaning from a balcony in a white and blue polka-dot summer dress, unknown, unreachable, unforgettable. He looked, then wondered about her mind, hoping for some depth to complement the vision, to provide the greatest stimulant for him, of beauty and gravitas.

Alice thought him attractive, possibly too sensitive, though for her too much sensitivity was not a bad thing; the world was full of men without it, pretending to be without it, or afraid to show that they had it. The way he moved was thoughtful – as if needing to get it right – and he was tall and slim like Jon but his hair was not straight, though their eyes were the same; and he was older, of course. She guessed at forty-two and was short by three years.

She left the comparisons and felt herself relaxing, letting go of the concerns she'd woken with that morning. She was allowing herself to enjoy the afternoon. Connie did the talking for everyone it seemed, and was less attractive to Alice, with her obvious need to impress, and she soon became boring. Alice thought about the downside of living with someone like her, even thinking *poor Tom.*

Nothing in the room was out of place, and she imagined Connie spending so much time arranging things, from the perfectly-fanned magazines on the table to the orderly books on the shelves above the sideboard – art books, travel books, lavish and large and expensive. It was all expensive. A scene popped into her head of Connie going around with a tape measure, ensuring equilibrium and symmetry. *Poor Connie,* more like.

"So you're home for a few days, Rachel? Your Dad tells me you teach children." This was Jon, making conversation.

"Yes, but far away from here. In Edinburgh." Jon knew, but Alice didn't. Edinburgh was the other side of the world from the Wye Valley.

He asked, "Do you like it there?"

So Rachel described her life and the friendly small-talk went around as the tea and pastries diminished, but all the while she waited for the fall, and at last it came as Connie was showing Alice and Jon one of her treasures, a sublime and beautiful silver hand mirror, carelessly lying on the sideboard.

"It's Lalique," said Connie, "René Lalique. Nineteen-ten, which makes it *Art Nouveau.*"

"Only just," said Tom in the background as the Greersons were listening and looking, neither daring to touch it. He came up to Connie and said quietly, "I'm sure they've seen a mirror before, Connie." Then, to them both, "Don't be too impressed, it's not that rare a thing."

"Oh Tom... I'm not trying to impress them!" Her voice was at the tipping point of petulance, and Alice quickly said, "Well, I *am* impressed. Lalique is a very famous name," as Connie gave her husband a look of barely-hidden frustration. Jon was also impressed, with the mirror, but more so with its albeit flustered owner.

Before he left them and went back to his sofa, Tom said, "Don't worry you two, we do get on, in our own quiet way," and Connie gave a small embarrassed laugh. Rachel, still curled into her chair, looked on and wondered how something as beautiful as a Lalique mirror could have caused such discord.

Connie was lovely. Through the first cup of tea, then the guided tour of the room and its half-dozen treasures, Jon had looked hard at her, sized her up, imagined her. That perfect hair must be ruffled now and then, surely... *what does she wear in bed? Anything at all?* He was aware of his uncommon enthusiasm over everything, feeling out of place, a stand-in actor unable to leave his character, but had anyone noticed? *Alice, for sure. The others don't know me.*

He hoped all eyes would be on Alice, his beautiful wife, and not on him. He watched Connie with relish as she moved about, observing her from all angles with approval and without finding fault, thinking again how lucky Tom was to have her, while ignoring the increasingly unsubtle chafing between them.

Alice picked up on everything, every tiny sign of their irritability with each other. Connie was attractive, but again the truth came to her that beauty was no guarantee of happiness: they were not happy together, and it was a shock, a disappointment. And yes, she saw Jon's interest in Connie, the way his eyes followed her around the room, and his slightly embarrassing and faint praise for everything she showed them. *He's a man,* she thought, *and he'll have male feelings. He obviously needs to impress her*. But that was a new thing, to have her husband interested in another woman, and it was a touch uncomfortable. So she experimented with Tom with the same eyes, testing him, but she did not see a potential lover – she was not aroused in that way by him but weighed him up all the same: *are you a good lover, Tom?* But then she let the half-hearted thought go, bored by it and almost ashamed. Yet he was good-looking. It was his eyes, the depth of his eyes. So was she any better than her husband, feasting on Connie? A little, maybe. Jon was more focused.

The comparisons had returned, the differences between *them and us,* the Fishers and the Greersons, with only Rachel being immune – but did the Greersons also have their problems? There was something about the two of them, and Rachel sensed the maladjustment, their slight awkwardness with each other.

So they drank tea and talked of the house, the garden, the hotel, the weather and the world... but the world especially, and Connie said, "There's so much sadness in the world these days, don't you think?"

"Humans are very basic sometimes," said Tom, coming into the room with a milk jug, and he stood there as they recalled the greed, the disasters and deaths of what was an average year so far, and the apparent urge of so many to defraud others, and the also apparent urge for people to harm those who disagreed with them. Connie was aghast at how the conversation was going. She'd made a small observation, and now they were discussing criminality and death.

"Can we change the subject, please?"

"It's how it is, Connie," said Tom. She switched off, picked up a magazine and settled back with it, ignoring everyone; Tom said, *"Connie..."* then left it.

Alice asked, "So how can we overcome all of that?"

Tom put the jug on the table and sat down heavily next to his wife. He sighed. "I don't know. But love conquers all, doesn't it."

Alice felt a jolt go through her. *Love conquers all.* They were amongst the first words she'd read in Phillip's journal. She stared at him, disbelieving what she'd heard, as Connie flipped through her magazine, watched by Jon as he sipped his tea – what had caught Alice had not touched either. Suddenly very engaged, she said, "Do you think it does?"

"Well yes. Can you imagine the world if everybody loved everybody else?"

Connie, touched by it after all, and without looking up from her magazine, said idly, "You're being the big idealist again Tom," but he reached for his tea, sat back into the sofa and said, "Love Conquers All was a song by Deep Purple, Connie. It's not that profound you know, nor idealistic... it's a fact. Love overcomes everything bad." And all Alice could think of were the words: *Love conquers all.* The exact phrase. *Deep Purple?* She hadn't known that.

Connie was talking again, putting her magazine down, but Alice heard nothing. She was taken back to the early days with Phillip, to the helpless love she'd felt with him. She still looked at Tom, not knowing at all what was happening to her. She was awakened by those three words, but after a few seconds she snapped out of it, and was looking again at the Tom Fisher she only slightly knew, feeling shaken out of herself, almost foolish. *Just a man, Alice. A man who knows a song by Deep Purple.* She relaxed back into the sofa, as the thunderbolt that had hit her slowly dissolved.

She sat in silence as the others talked, recovering from her brief journey; *I shouldn't be like this,* she thought, as her few second's absence troubled her. But there was no explanation, just the aftershock of finding and losing, the whirlwind of her up and down emotions.

From beside her Jon said, "Love is important – of course it is," and Alice came back. She looked at Jon, wondering to whom he'd said it, then Connie replied, "But it's a strange thing, don't you think? It depends on so many things being right."

Tom said, "Well yes. But it depends on one thing, I think. It depends on being loved yourself. Then you can love someone else."

"Very simplistic, that," said Connie.

"But it's true. Love conquers all. If you feel it you can give it."

For Alice it was all too strange, this talk of love. *Why so complicated?* These two were in knots over something so simple to understand.

As she listened to them, Jon thought about what Tom had said – *so if Alice loves me, then I should feel it from her. Is that right? Yes... of course. But I don't.*

"Love conquers all," Alice said calmly, "I agree with that," and Tom said, "Thank you Alice."

"Shall I get more tea?" Rachel had spoken, as if to pull them all back.

"I'll get it," said Connie, a little too curtly, but stayed where she was.

There was a silence, and Alice looked up to the shelves above the sideboard. "I love your books. We don't have enough... not enough shelves. Books need shelves."

Connie nodded sideways towards Tom and said, with an edge of irritation, "You should see his study – more books than he could ever read."

"I'll do my best to prove you wrong there, Connie."

Their conversation was degenerating in front of their guests and Alice wondered if this was their quiet 'getting on with each other'.

Connie went on, "Well you'll read yourself into oblivion dear, with the stuff you've got there." Her *dear* was less than sincere. Another silence. Jon kept quiet. Alice ignored the discord and asked, "So what stuff do you read, Tom?"

"Mostly poetry."

Connie pulled a face. "*Poetry.* I don't understand any of it."

"Yes you do Connie," Tom said, then, with a smile and without inhibition, "I like Elizabethan poetry – Herbert, Marlowe, Jonson, Donne; especially Donne."

Connie sighed, got up and went into the kitchen, with Jon watching her and wondering about Elizabethan poetry, of which he knew nothing beyond knowing that Alice liked it. But Alice was staring at Tom, again.

Donne. John Donne.

Tom turned to the kitchen and said, loudly, "They're mostly love poems Connie," but there was no reply. He looked back to his guests with a resigned half-smile that said, *that's how it is here, folks. Hey-ho.* Rachel had gone back to observing, after asking about the tea.

Again, Alice was moved. The likelihood of another coincidence, another shared interest, seemed impossible... but here it was, and it was special.

She stayed calm. *"No Man Is An Island* is a good starting point for *love conquers all,* don't you think?"

"Oh... you know it?

"Yes, I do. It's wonderful."

And he looked at her with slightly different eyes, she thought. Jon sat on the sofa, feeling out of it, as Rachel said, "I think you've found a soulmate at last, Dad," and Tom said, with a smile for Alice, "Someone who actually likes poetry – whatever next."

As Connie came out from the kitchen with both the tray and her mood replenished, Jon said, "I like poetry, but some of it's very deep. I find a lot of it too heavy, if I'm honest," and as she put the tray down between them Connie said, with her own smile to him, "You can be *my* soulmate then. We'll stick to stuff we can understand."

So there were smiles all round, for differing reasons.

The five of them sat in the warmth of the big room with their small talk, their tea, and their glances out of the wide windows over the lawn to the darkening forest and the already black river, as twilight crept closer. It was lazy, and agreeable, but Alice's mind was far from idle; no thunderbolt this time, but a slow re-kindling of the embers she always carried with her; a confirm-ation of her belief that someone somewhere would have interests like hers. In quiet moments and whenever she could get away with it she looked at Tom, and when he sensed her looking and looked back she kept her eyes on his, saying nothing until he looked away; Jon had a flicker of awareness, a short glance away from his focus on Connie to Tom staring at Alice, then Alice staring in silence at Tom... a surprised moment, but a flicker, not quite enough to cause concern.

"Anyway," Alice said out of the blue, and with a smile, "please don't read yourself into oblivion, Tom," and there were other smiles as Connie's statement lost its bite while Rachel, watching, noticed it all – the interest in her mother and the interest in her father. She excused herself moments later and went to her room for a break, and soon after was called back as the Greersons left.

Such a revealing two hours, thought Tom.

And then he wondered, Will she be coming back? Those times when he'd been so fed up with Connie, when he'd been wistful about a different life with someone else, were now less than trivial. Alice was real. He tried to imagine how she would be in everything she did, while leaving Connie on the sidelines – dependable, predictable Connie, safe on the sidelines.

Jon drove his wife home to the hotel. Connie had loosely invited them again, but Jon wasn't sure that next time would be so looked forward to; seeing her alone would be something else though, even if the thought slightly scared him.

Alice tried to work it out. She felt the need to plan, to think ahead, and she became oddly more concerned with the route she would take than with the man possibly waiting at the end of it. She went through a process in her head that was quite unfamiliar and removed from her usual waterfall of emotions. This is another woman's husband. This is not Phillip, this is a real person. And her analysis included Olivier. He badly wanted to see her, and she knew none of Tom's needs. So, what to do? She didn't know how she would deal with any of it... Olivier was three weeks away, and who knows what might happen in that time?

And that is my problem, that is why I've lost my husband. Will it be the same with Tom Fisher, this man I hardly know beyond him liking John Donne? And is that all it takes for me – that we share a liking for a particular poet? It would have been so much simpler if Olivier had seen me again. I could have had my unsleazy sex and maybe that would have been enough. A start, and an end. So much simpler, and perhaps Tom would then have just become a friend instead of the lover he could be. A lover? Really? Oh, how I suffer...

She went about the hotel, struggling with the events of that Sunday, with *love conquers all* and with a dead poet he happened to like. She wasn't sure she could love him. There were many things she'd noticed about him, and not all of them were appealing... especially the way he played with Connie, the calm put-downs that clearly hurt her. Why should Alice love a man like that? For his poetry? For the deepness of his eyes? But by the middle of the week she badly wanted to stop struggling.

: : :

"You must come again," Connie had said to them as they'd left Rivendell that Sunday, but before that happened the Fishers were invited for coffee at the hotel the following Saturday morning. Jon was keen not to make it too special. He did not want to outshine them, especially Connie, and Alice and Elena went along with that, up to a point... perhaps the best crockery could be left in the cupboard and the home-made pastries could be mixed with more ordinary fare; they were amused by Jon's concerns, but would indulge his wishes regarding his new employer.

Rachel came with them. They all met at the reception desk, with handshakes and the slight kisses of new acquaintances, then moved on together along the corridor to the Conference Room, – their equivalent of a sitting room – passing framed photographs of the hotel from years ago, a few aerial pictures, and two of Elena and David on their wedding day in 1971, then the latest, of Alice and Jon on their own wedding day. It was an excellent photograph. Head and shoulders, perfectly framed by the arched doorway of the church, and Elena couldn't help herself; she reached and took it down, desperate to show their visitors the way those two had been, the happiness they once had. They all looked at it, at the two happy people smiling at the camera, the mixed emotions of the onlookers briefly overcome by the loveliness of the image.

Tom said, "That necklace looks special, Alice."

"Oh," she replied, "that's very old. From my great-great-great-great-grandfather... *four greats!* It goes to each bride. Mum had it before me." Alice had brightened up, while Jon stood back from them all, separated from that lovely bride.

The picture went back onto the wall and they walked on, and before going for their coffee Alice took them into the narrow passageway that led to their staircase, and she introduced them to Aku. He was motionless apart from his eyes, which swivelled around them all as his mistress went from one to the other, saying their names. Connie, Tom, Rachel. In that order. She knew he would remember, for a long while anyway, all their names. After some polite one-way small talk, there was no reply from him until they said their goodbyes and turned away, when he said a very friendly and sing-song *Bye-bye everyone* as they went back along the corridor.

The Conference Room was a world away from Tom's idea of how such places usually were. There were no plastic chairs or formica tables. It was plush, and cosy; there was a big table of dark mahogany but they sat away from it, on sofas and armchairs, in a relaxed huddle as coffee was brought in.

Jon sat next to Connie on a sofa, inches away from her unwary flesh, as her eyes went from furniture to wall panelling to oak-beamed ceiling, from oriental carpet to gilt-framed pictures. It would not have helped Connie to know that where wealth was concerned the Fishers were some way behind the Lindbergs and, by extension, the Greersons, so it was all down to looking around and wondering. It wasn't quite opulent, but it was quality, and she realised that she did not have the monopoly on nice houses. This one was splendid. Very different, but splendid.

Such a lovely place, don't you think, Rachel?

You see Mother? We're not so special.

Alice, you look even better to me today.

I think I could love you Tom.

Alice, I wish you wouldn't look at him like that. When I look at

Connie I'm not planning anything. You look as if you are.

: : :

Late on Wednesday afternoon of that week, Tom walked into their kitchen and Connie said, without looking round at him, "I saw Alice this morning, at the Leisure Centre. Playing squash, would you believe." She was standing at the window, facing away as she prepared a salad, and her absence irritated him, as it always did. He thought she was speaking without thinking, not even looking round at him – disconnected impersonal babbling. He never considered the safe and relaxed connection it was for her. She glanced at him as he put his empty mug into the sink. He turned away and she said, "She certainly looks fit. Do you think I should have a go at squash, Tom? It's a bit energetic. Am I too old for it, do you think?" She looked through the window as she turned the salad spinner, and Tom's mind turned to Alice. He stopped at the table and flicked blindly through a magazine.

After a moment he said, downbeat, "It would kill you, I think. Stick to swimming." It was without humour, but it happened often, this response, and as always she would skip over it. She said, "She's a nice girl. I quite like her."

Again, downbeat, "Yes... she's nice."

"Tell you what though, if you'd seen her shorts your eyes would have popped out dear. Hardly worth putting them on. Why do people dress like that?"

It was so matter-of-fact, so detached and so unknowing of the effect it would have on him. He was transfixed. Staring at her back, an electrifying image filled his mind, of Alice in her shorts, – *were they tight... or just tiny? Or both?* Why would she give him such a cue, such an image of another woman? *Is she taunting me?* But it didn't matter, – idle gossip, innocent or not – it instantly focused him. He wanted to see her like that, to stand close to her, to look her over, *to touch.* He felt a rush of excitement as he left the magazine and the kitchen, and knew that some line had been crossed – his heart was pounding and he was thinking of Alice, as good as naked in those shorts, as Connie continued her salad-making at the window, occasionally looking languidly out over the lawn to the river.

: : :

"So you want them here every Sunday."

"I think it's a really nice idea," she'd said and Tom, always preferring Sundays untouched by visitors, had agreed, but if Connie had gone deeper into his acquiescence rather than just being happy about it, she might have wondered *why*.

INFATUATION, AGAIN

The month of March, and the morning outside their window was clear and kind. An extra half-hour in bed for Jon, but Alice had got up at the same time as on other days... the specialness of Sunday mornings therefore being lost, beyond the feeling of freedom it always had for him: a free day, but now without his wife to share it, except in the moments of her day when she could break off and they would be around each other. He went down to the kitchen for breakfast, and he would usually catch Elena and David there and spend time with his in-laws while his wife was working elsewhere. He had surprised himself with his urge to share the kitchen with them, but it was a brighter start to his Sunday, an easy and pleasant half-hour before sauntering into the usually unplanned morning.

Alice's parents, Jon had long ago discovered, were reasonable people with a moral compass he could relate to, and lately they were open to his predicament. He had been forgiven in the light of their daughter's extreme response; their embarrassment was palpable, and they looked upon Jon as suffering because of the wife they had produced for him. They felt they should apologise for her and that, when he detected it, was gratifying. They were on his side.

Their shared breakfast mornings were far from being routine, and usually rushed except for Sundays, when warm fresh bread or croissants were produced to celebrate the day. But the half-hour was never enough, and it was always Elena who had to get on with work and the others would be left to themselves to finish the bread and preserves and coffee; very relaxed, but on this Sunday Alice was not there. So Jon talked easily with his father-in-law about everything from school to work to gardens to cars. They would however never get near the space he had in his life for Connie, his very own secret; they would talk while she sat at the back of his mind – delicious, indulgent compensation for his distant wife.

The relaxed breakfast was eked out until nine, when the big table was cleared and both men went their separate ways. The afternoon promised uninterrupted Formula One for David, sitting alone in front of the sitting room TV, and a quite different pleasure for Jon.

It's six-and-a-half miles, they both know, and it takes just under eight minutes; parallel with the river and crossing it once; onto the gravel welcoming drive, and the newly-familiar private rush as the car stops and they go together but separately to their secrets.

Connie is there with Tom as the door opens, as smiles are exchanged, and passions are roused; their daughter is back in Edinburgh, in the middle of two weeks away, which they say is long enough. Alice gives the flowers Jon had bought the day before to Connie, and they are allowed to lead the way through to the big room at the front and sit down together. The Fishers and the Greersons are not at the beginnings of a love triangle, but rather a square, with one diagonal alive and the other only half alive, with wives and husbands being excited, complacent, hopeful or confused, which is the common run of things when attracted couples encounter each other, and sure enough three out of the four people here are struggling silently with their emotions. There is much going on, and only Connie misses it all; she feels the tension but lives too far from her husband to catch anything in particular or work anything out, and isn't tuned in to the others anyway.

But still she feels something, so she asks, "Is everyone all right?" in a thin, superficial tone. Tom looks at her, and wonders.

Jon says, "Yes... we're fine, aren't we, Alice? It's so nice to be amongst the civilised again."

Alice cringes inside for her husband and smiles apologetically at Connie; Connie smiles back then glances at Tom, who is smiling at Alice. Jon is smiling at them all. So, everyone's all right... but what is the matter *with everyone today?*

Music came from somewhere. Alice knew the voice, but not the song; it was Joni Mitchell, and she was coming from Tom's study – the unmistakable, effortless voice. The volume was low, and she found herself straining to hear.

"It's Joni Mitchell," said Tom, seeing Alice looking towards his study. "Hope you don't mind."

"No, I approve. What's the song?"

Jon was also trying to hear.

"It's *The Dawntreader,*" said Tom.

Before Alice could say anything Connie said, "It's music to die by, I'm afraid."

"Or to die *for*, maybe?" said Tom.

Connie ignored him and said to the others, "Just so you know, I wanted something a bit more jolly."

The strain was already there this time, without the preamble of pretending to get on with each other. Jon wasn't sure what to say, whether to agree with her or with his boss so he just smiled at her as Alice said, "It's fine... it's jolly enough for me," and Tom was pleased with that.

Connie brought tea and cakes, and the afternoon passed much as the first one had with varied talk, a little deeper this time, a little wider. They discussed Rachel in her absence – her move to Edinburgh and how it had freed them up, though privately neither were convinced it had. Small talk for a while, and poetry was avoided. That morning Connie had requested no work-talk, *please*, between Tom and Jon... so boring, so out-of-place, and Tom had requested an avoidance of showing off what they had. There wasn't much left to impress them with anyway. He'd upset her when he'd reminded her of what the Greersons and the Lindbergs had, and she'd snapped at him, "How do you know what they've got, if we didn't see any of it?"

He'd given up on that, but as he'd walked away he'd said, "And please don't read in front of our guests."

So an agreement had been irritably reached to behave better for them, and halfway through Tom thought it was going reasonably well. A few barely-noticed minor bitchings, back and forth, but on the whole pretty good. Also, Jon was talking more this time, and not about work. They were all getting used to each other.

"Eric Clapton, Bryan Ferry, Queen," Jon said, when Connie asked him. "Lots of other stuff too." She was pleased he was out of Tom's deep and dour realm of music.

"I like songs with a bit of life in them," she said, "I want to be cheered up, not depressed." Then – while fearing her visitor's tastes were more in line with Tom's – "What about you, Alice?"

"Oh… so much, really. I suppose I prefer songs with a message of some sort. Paul Simon's quieter songs, lots of classical things. I like lyrics that make sense to me. And melody… I like melody."

Jon looked sideways at her and said, "I think that's right. You like quieter things really. Quieter than mine, anyway." He was relaxed enough to talk to his wife like that – closely, intimately, like the old friends they really were. It felt good. He saw her then, eyes closed, lost in that melody and those lyrics. He imagined it well, but she didn't answer him. Tom was also imagining her.

They talked disjointedly of music but after a while Connie suggested they go out while there was still light and see the garden, in the hope of impressing them after all, so they went out through the sliding door and down the bank onto a lawn which was as perfect as it could be after the winter, and before its first cut of the year.

"It must be cut at the right moment," said Connie.

Tom hoped he would be ready for that *moment*. He said, "I'll be ready with my mower," but she ignored him, instead waving her hands towards the parts she wanted them to see.

The borders were tidy, mostly green, mostly dormant, and half a dozen young spindly trees were dotted here and there to break the expanse of grass; Connie's hopes were almost realised when both Alice and Jon commented on the openness, compared to the closed-in garden they had on the bank behind the hotel; it was refreshing, they said, that openness, but poor Connie had hoped for more than compliments on empty space.

They walked to the end of the garden, to the low fence that separated it from the footpath that ran alongside the river a few yards beyond and below, then turned back. Connie went along the border towards the house, stopping here and there, talking with Jon, hardly noticing Tom leaving them and heading with Alice towards the other border. Connie talked gardens to Jon, but Tom, thirty yards across the lawn, spoke with Alice of other things. He wanted to know her. They walked, parallel with the other two, slowly towards the house, as those other two were differently engrossed... Connie with her garden and Jon with Connie; he examined her as closely as he dared as she moved and talked, savouring the closeness of a different woman, imagining different flesh, catching the faint scent of her perfume and wanting so much just to touch her, just once, even accidentally... but it wasn't long before he was pulled back and gave a wondering glance across the lawn; Alice was with Tom, alone, and it bothered him. Connie talked of plants, as Jon struggled to share his focus with her and his wife.

Tom had thought of little else but Alice for the past week, endlessly running a script through his head for the unplanned moment when he would be alone with her. It had been like a holiday, a time away from the familiar, a few days of excitement in being somewhere new in his mind – but what he wanted was vague and unformed beyond wanting to touch her, which was not possible, not the way he wanted to. He wanted everything from her, her entire life, given to him in an instant, for him to pore over.

He said, "Are you into gardens?"

"No, not much."

"What *are* you into?"

They had stopped walking; the borders were neat, no stray

leaves, no stray anything. She didn't know, but Tom would not be interested in making a show garden. He liked tidiness but he was a grass cutter, a labourer. Alice moved on slowly and he followed.

"I'm into hotels, it seems." She was smiling. "But as for hobbies... I suppose I have my books and my music."

Of course, he knew she would say that. He just knew.

They walked side by side, stopping then going on, and they talked of her interests, many of which were shared with his. It was uncanny, he thought, the similarities. Paul Simon – yes, okay. Sandy Denny, Fleetwood, her classical stuff, her medieval obsessions, her poets – she reeled it off to him and he could relate to it all. And now as the minutes passed she could see him properly, could see how he wanted her – it was unmistakable: his attentiveness – and his eyes, how they searched her face. Connie's immaculate borders went by unnoticed.

He said, "So what's your *favourite* music?"

"I don't have a single piece, not really..."

"So what's the last thing you listened to?" He pushed sweetly for what he wanted. She thought of last night, when she was alone, very late in the evening.

"I have a collection of poems, and songs. Joan Baez... you know her?"

"Oh yes."

She felt she should warn him though: very imaginative, she said, but not always the best rendition, her voice being better suited to the songs than to reading poetry.

"But I'll lend it to you, if you'd like."

"Yes, I'd like that. And you can take my Joni Mitchell... see what you think."

But she was thinking of him wanting her, and how that might turn out.

They all arrived together at the vast expanse of glass that was the living room window, and Jon was relieved. *Those two were not looking at flowers.* The surroundings – the perfect garden, the river, the woods beyond and the early spring beauty were all lost, as he silently welcomed her back into the safety of the group of four while being uneasy – or was he jealous over her, for the first time ever?

When they were back inside Tom went straight to his study and got the CD for her. She took it without too much obvious pleasure.

"It's Joni Mitchell," she said to Jon, "Tom's lending it to me."

Joni Mitchell, he thought. *Big Yellow Taxi. Really didn't think she liked that stuff.*

"And Alice is lending me one of hers," said Tom, making light of it. Connie caught Jon's eye and raised her perfect eyebrows, and smiled. He smiled back. It was all okay.

Fifteen minutes later the Greersons were thinking of leaving. Connie went through to their bedroom to look for a book she thought Alice would like, while Jon sat with a thick book on his lap, distractedly reading of walking in the Pyrenees. Alice took the last of the cups and plates into the kitchen, and she was putting them into the dishwasher when Tom came in.

"There's no need to do that, Alice," he said.

"Oh, I may as well put them down in the right place."

She stood up and he moved towards her. The kitchen was quiet. She would remember that there was no sound, nothing from inside or outside. She didn't move away from him. They were close, and face to face. He thought he would kiss her then, but his courage failed him and instead he looked down from her face, lifted her hand, kissed it softly and released it. In the brightness of his kitchen, and careless with privacy, he kissed her hand as she stared blankly at his face, too stunned to throw her arms around him as she'd imagined she would. Her hand stayed where he'd left it, in shock, frozen, as another thunderbolt went through her – a real one this time, a heart-stopping thump which cleared her mind completely. She made no response, and he gave her an uncertain look then turned and left her without a word. It was over in seconds, and Alice stood there as he went back into the lounge where his wife was coming in, annoyed at not being able to find the book. Jon sat with his own book in his lap, looking up at Connie, both of them unaware of the painful birth of intimacy in her kitchen.

Alice came back into the room but did not sit down.

"I really should get back, Jon," she said.

Tom stood in front of the wide window, hands in pockets, looking at nothing, giving hopeless glances at Alice. He was certain he'd started something but spoiled everything, and wished he could take back those few astonishing seconds.

Neither said anything, standing apart and quiet amongst the chit-chat from Connie and Jon, then they were all at the door – handshakes and kisses, thank-yous and goodbyes; Tom's hands lightly on her shoulders; a veiled, brushing kiss on her cheek, and Alice was gone. The last thing he saw was a soft look from her which said, he hoped, *Please don't despair.*

: : :

She'd listened to the CD late into the night, alone in the study and curled up in her dressing gown on the sofa, headphones keeping the music for herself in the low light, as Jon slept next door. The songs were from before Alice was born and Joni Mitchell snared her, was right for her in her solitude and yet still she tried – thinking she should – to separate the music from the man who'd given it to her, concerned that it was just something else to turn her head, a distraction, along with the words and the poetry.

Tom was being imagined, dissected, looked at in detail, and she feared – from her frail position of scrutiny – that it would be both wrong and easy to fall for him because of those things. But more than music and poetry had happened, and as she went to bed that night she knew it wouldn't be wrong. It was all part of the man.

: : :

There had been no *frisson* with Tom, as there had been with Olivier. There was a wanting, a need to be lifted away from the drabness of her life and that need was now mingled with the kiss, possessing her as she went over and over what had happened. And above all she felt sorry for Tom's attempt at seducing her. She feared he would never be open with her again, and she was trying to think of the best way out for him, to restore the balance, now heavily in her favour. She'd tried to soften his pain with her glance as they'd left Rivendell, but she could not begin to guess how he was feeling now. And as for *love* for him... how did it feel? Well there was no missing it. It became better in her memory, the simple beauty of that kiss, and the way it was done: hopefully, carefully, then doubtfully, but all without threat: *Please love me, Alice.*

Yes, she could easily love him.

Throughout Monday, as she worked, there were many moments of searching for insight, of bringing herself to a halt in whatever she was doing and staring into space – usually in some quiet place, the top of the stairs, or the corridor, or at a window somewhere. The verge she was on was unique – always she'd jumped, or fallen quickly into love but this was different - the biggest considered leap she would ever make, inescapable once she'd committed to it. Olivier was being overridden and there would be no going back.

Her work needed doing and it was all she could do to concentrate, to function with her mother and everyone else, and when Jon came home at six her mind was set. He smiled at her and said hello, and she said hello back to him. Strangers now, almost. She looked after him as he went through to the stairs carrying his winter coat and his briefcase full of mysteries, remembering him as the man she'd chosen and married and feeling a helpless sadness as he disappeared up the stairs to their rooms. But she could not at all think ahead to any resolution, so busy was her mind with Tom and what had happened. Jon had gone, and she was soon back with the man he worked for and had said goodbye to, half an hour before; a bright web was being woven, not yet so tangled, but the deception made its mark. In spite of it she deliberated.

Connie would be away at her cousin's that weekend, and Rachel was in Edinburgh, *so Saturday – it would be Saturday.* She would take Joan Baez to him. He would be alone then, in the early evening. And she would see him again the next day with Jon. She was driven by sheer excitement, hardly able to dismiss him from her mind when she had to. Saturday would make everything clear. She wove her web.

∴

On that Monday night Tom came to her in a dream. He touched her face and then they were alongside the river where she'd first lain with Jon, and the day was warm, as it had been then. They were talking after making love, and then he was gone; she was on her back looking at the sky, at the wheeling gulls that sometimes came upriver from the estuary, and when the gulls left she was alone, surrounded by nothing but her intense desire for him. She cried in her dream, cried out of frustration and longing, and when she woke from it she had stepped over the verge. This was not Phillip, not a character on a page, and not Olivier, and in the morning as she left her empty bedroom for her work her doubts had gone. There would be no living without him. Alice's obsession with Tom had begun.

∴

Above her excitement, now and then she thought of Friday, and Olivier, and the simple plan she'd had for him in the weeks before. She would keep her promise, but the hopes they'd both had would fail and they would share lunch and reminiscences, but nothing more. He would be the slightest distraction in her inevitable journey to Tom the following day, when her plan was to go into Monmouth for the small items that were always needed, – extra wine, cleaning stuff – anything the hotel was short of that week, and to call in with the CD for Tom on her way back. The trip was a weekly thing and not the Manager's duty but she would say she fancied going, and when Saturday afternoon came her mother would say to Jon, "She's getting the extras from Monmouth for us. Let her have a break." And Jon would think nothing of it.

"So you didn't tell him."

Olivier, sure in his assumption, smiled as he said it, and she didn't know if it was a smile of conspiracy or conquest, or both. He knew it was neither.

He'd texted her the day before with the name of a restaurant on the Gloucester Road, and his three question marks begged her approval. She knew the place however, and replied along with three carefree exclamation marks; they would meet at two, and have two hours from then before he'd have to leave her. Driving to Bristol she wished she'd cancelled. At the very least she wondered about the wisdom of those three exclamation marks, and what would he make of them. She didn't want him to be hurt.

The Mirabelle was a restaurant she'd been to a few times, a warm place with flowers on the tables and a good choice of music in the air; as she'd walked in it was a low-key Charles Trenet and *La Mer,* as if to punish her for her coming rejection of Olivier, and France. He was there, at a table against the wall, and he'd stood up at the sight of her and they'd hugged and kissed cheeks before squeezing into their chairs. There were more tables than she remembered.

After what was one of his first comments she smiled and said, "I did tell him. And he's fine about it."

Already he was doubtful, and not just about her telling her husband. As they talked she was happy, but too distracted, not truly focused on him. And she had dressed down today – not dowdy, never that, but not to impress him either: plain clothes, a roll neck jumper up to her chin, a heavy coat, unspecial jeans, no jewellery, no make-up to speak of – but still she could not make herself other than beautiful to him.

They talked as their food came and went, and again, because of their limited life together, it was of Fréjus and business – his job, his students, her job, and the hotel. But Olivier was curious about her wider life. "Tell me about your husband – what exactly does he do?" So more work-talk, and the Filton connection was made more interesting than it was.

"I don't pretend to know anything about his work. It's all gobbledegook to me." There was no enjoyment as she spoke of him, no pride, no embroidery of her husband, just a telling of facts – and it struck Olivier that he would also find it hard to enthuse about Delphine. That particular spark had left them both.

He wondered what was happening in her life. *Something* was happening, for sure. She was a little too cheerful, and he didn't feel it was for him, and it was not because of Jon. There had been no hand-holding this time, and after a few seconds of quiet reflection he said, "So. Marriages are interesting things, don't you think?"

"They are, yes." It would do no harm now so she said, "Mine is not good. But I suppose you realised that."

He lost his smile. "I knew there was something. Can it be made good again?"

"Perhaps. I don't know."

Last time they'd met she'd told him about the Rossetti history, about Phillip and the necklace, and after a little thought he picked up on it, feeling hopelessly virtuous.

"I think your necklace tradition is great. I wonder, could you give it back to Jon? I mean, for him to give back to you again? Something symbolic... a new start, maybe?"

She was uncomfortable now.

"I don't know. That would be very hard for us."

"Too hard?"

"Too difficult." It was a dead end for her. How could he imagine that would ever work?

He wanted to ask the reason, feeling a vague but real urge to do better for her in some fantasy where they were together, but instead he said, "Give it to the one you love, Alice," realising straight away that her husband may not be that person at all. He wished he hadn't said it. Her response was a tolerant smile, and a wait for inspiration which turned out to be the subject he didn't want.

"Tell me more about your wife."

He found his own version of a tolerant smile.

"My wife. Well, Delphine is... *Delphine.*" A slight shrug of his shoulders. "Everything is the same."

There was nothing she could say to that, but earlier, one of the first things she'd said was, "You found your ring," and he'd said, "Yes. It was where I thought it would be."

In her usual way she'd been heartened by that, by the loyalty he felt to his wife... or was it duty? Something he wasn't so bothered about? She wasn't sure. *I am also wearing mine. How unreal this all is.*

Now, after a few seconds of studying his face, she said, "You know we can't have each other, Olivier."

A disappointment, but not a surprise. It was the way it was going. After a moment he said, "I didn't come to seduce you, remember?"

Without a pause she said, her eyes fixed on his, "But I think you would you know." She smiled then as he took it in. Being French, he would in the end tell the truth about such things.

His own smile became disarming, and after a little thought he admitted, "Yes, you are right. I would."

There had been the slightest embarrassment but no shame with his admission, because it was the truth. Seduction had not been a big reason for coming, but it had become so as soon as he'd seen her. So feelings were confirmed for them both, up to a point; he did not give up hope but shortly he would leave, and he was losing her.

Their meal was finished, coffee was over, and Tracy Chapman was singing *Baby can I hold you.*

Olivier said, "I have to go soon."

Again they were at the point of parting, without any final

resolution, and she was sad for him. "I'm sorry you're unhappy with Delphine."

He said nothing, but she knew he would feel the same about her and Jon. They went out to the car park at the rear, a crammed-in space alongside the narrow lane that ran parallel with the Gloucester Road, behind the shops and offices, a crowded, harsh space. A radio was blaring from a backyard opposite. It was a world away from their intimate table against the wall and it was a rerun of last time, a parting in a car park. They kissed cheeks again, then as they stood alone next to his car, his hands still on her shoulders, he asked her.

"Alice..." A pause, then, "Would you let me kiss you?"

And in her mind she said yes, but no. And then yes. So she smiled, and he took her head in his hands and kissed her on the lips, a slow, deep kiss, a complete surprise. She put her arms helplessly around him, and as the kiss ended they stood hugging each other.

Again, her plans had gone awry. *How beautiful, how strange.*

She was as close to him as she could ever be, holding him tightly, her head on his shoulder, and he had kissed her, properly, the way she'd dreamt of since meeting him for the very first time, eight years ago – *but how does this go on? What happens now? Please help me Olivier.* But all that happened was that he kissed her again, as lingeringly as before, and with the same careful, muted passion. For him, the next step had never been in doubt, but could he still ask her for that? Would she get into his car with him – drive somewhere quiet with him? Could that happen now? He had no idea of how his kisses had shocked her, and how even in the midst of it she was not for turning, would not allow it to happen. *The plan has changed Olivier.* She would have to let him go, even now. So in hope he waited for her, without knowing that this had been her fling, the best she could do, and it was over.

They were still in each other's arms, and she smiled, softly to herself, almost a smile of love, but all he could think was *Alice, time is short. Why not?*

She said, almost in a whisper, "Olivier, it's so difficult now. I can't change the way things are."

She pulled herself gently away from him, and they faced each other. Her smile had gone to melancholy and she said, "Could you face seeing me again, ever?"

"Alice, I could be with you always."

His words just made her more sorry for him now, and she tried to be upbeat.

"Then we should see each other again some time, when things are different. I've always believed in happy endings."

He saw how she was then, in that moment, how Alice the dreamer longed for happiness with someone, but also how hopeless it was. He saw how his physical need was no match for her romantic need, and he doubted the two could ever be content together.

He said, "Yes, we should perhaps."

But this felt like the end for him. He knew that she was with someone else, but had he known the way Tom Fisher was burning in her mind he would not even have tried with her.

Eventually she said, *"C'est la vie,"* and what could he say to that?

:::

Olivier coped with his disappointment, his looked-forward-to meeting with the only woman he'd ever wanted so badly, but his coping was a harsh process – *is she really so shallow? Did we want such different things? She was so keen to meet me.*

It was painful to think he'd misread her. He asked himself why he'd wanted so much to see her again, knowing she was married, knowing she was eight years older and possibly very different from the Alice he remembered in Fréjus, but it was simple – he just wanted her.

And yes, the memory brought me to her. From the moment I knew about coming here, it was settled. And now that first memory is perhaps better than it really was, but I have it; she was different then – seventeen, and so incomparably beautiful, and she could have been mine, she could have been mine.

Tomorrow he would fly back to Nice then take the long road down to Fréjus, but tonight he would have a strange dream of the day – of how she had gone with him in his car after all, sitting next to him as they left the city. Then they were stopped, with nothing outside the windows, and just Alice inside. She was naked, and the car was big enough for her to lie in front of him, passive, eyes drowsy, looking up at him as he looked at her. She was as he'd always imagined her, perfect, entirely perfect, but he could not touch her; it would break the spell of the discovery, and all his imaginings would spoil with even a light caress so in that strange consuming dream he just kept her, pure and untouched, until it was over and he'd awakened from it into the darkness of his narrow bunk in the dormitory at Filton, surrounded by others quietly lost in their own dreams.

∶ ∶ ∶

"He's just a friend Mum. I don't love him in that way. Please don't worry."

She'd told her mother the day before, and thought she'd done a good job of making it sound matter-of-fact – just a meeting for lunch with an old friend, again. After her first meeting with Olivier she'd been asked how it had gone, and Alice had been blasé, after a brief and unkind thought of saying *well Mother, he didn't try to rape me.*

"It was nice. Lots to talk about."

But after this time he would go back to France, which was a comfort. And Jon? When she'd told him, also the day before, he'd shrugged his shoulders and said, "Fine. Have a nice time."

As she drove home from the Gloucester Road she dwelt on everything, her head spinning with events, all surrounded and suffused with her longing for Tom. She'd known there would be no horizons to cross with Olivier, as she was once so certain there would be – no adventures, no discoveries waiting, just the man himself. She would meet him, and leave him; but she would continue as before, keeping in a place in her mind the unfaded memory of him amongst the roses in Julia's garden, standing in dismay outside her window before he left her – the last and flawless image of him from that time.

As they'd met today she'd thought that what she was doing was somehow noble, to turn him down for the sake of someone else, and she was unable to see her own faults for lack of a mirror, or eyes, or both – and at the end, after overcoming his kisses, she felt righteous for refusing him. Yet out of the three rivals to Jon's love – which still included Phillip – Olivier was the most poignant, the one who at the moment she believed would miss her the most, and the one she felt sorry for. She thought again about his new start with her precious necklace, the symbol above all of new beginnings, but she could not see her husband as part of the equation she had to balance; as she crossed the bridge back into Wales over the wide, deserted estuary, it really was only Tom she saw, and only Tom she desired.

It was after four-thirty when Alice left Monmouth and took the valley road towards Redbrook. *Please let him be there.* The afternoon was mild for the middle of March and the sun should have been shining instead of the grey overcast, and yet as she drove alongside the river the tops of the hills each side were softened and lost in the mist, and she felt the whole world was enveloping her, and keeping her safe. She went through the dreams of her childhood as she left one life for another, to meet her prince in her grown-up world, and to possess him.

The road twisted and turned ahead of her. *Everything must work out. It must.* A few minutes later she was at the top of Tom's drive, and her thoughts became grounded as her prince suddenly became real. *I'm here. And Tom is here.*

The gate was closed so she parked in the lay-by and went through the side gate, down the drive to the house. It was a dull day but there were no lights showing from inside. A short time after knocking the door the kitchen lights came on, and the door opened.

"Hello Tom."

There was a moment almost of disbelief.

"Alice!"

"I brought this for you."

She held the CD out for him and he took it, and she watched him standing in his doorway, looking down at it in his hands. There was a silence, a slight awkwardness but it saved him, removed him from the difficulty of the first words he'd imagined they would have. He read the cover, then turned it over to the playlist on the back, while feeling that he should do something, or say something to her. He studied the list as if it would keep him from harm.

"These are lovely poems," he said, still not looking at her, "the ones I know, anyway."

"I hope you enjoy it."

He suddenly pulled himself back. "I'm sorry! Come in, please." He stood aside for her, and she went in front of him towards the lounge.

"Go on through."

He walked behind her as she crossed the kitchen, and as he watched her move he remembered Connie's careless words, but the body he'd imagined was not evident through the loose clothes she was wearing. There was no skimpiness there. His mood was shifting from anxiety to anticipation. He was reprieved, surely.

As they went into the lounge he said, to her back, "Alice... I should apologise, for the other day. It was wrong. I'm sorry."

The desire came to her to spin around and take him in her arms, to kiss him and be done with it, to cut short her plans but instead she turned, half expecting to see him reaching for her but he'd stopped too far behind. She smiled at him.

"It's okay Tom. It was a lovely compliment."

They faced each other, in front of the wide window to the river. He said, "Please, sit down," but she stayed as she was.

"Well Tom, I was wondering, would you like to go for a drive? Do you have time?"

He answered with the slightest hesitation, "Yes... I have time."

In the seconds before he'd imagined a different outcome, now that he was over the fear of her response. It was all right now. She had forgiven him, so he'd switched from transgressor back to hopeful seducer and he wanted to take her hand and lead her sweetly to his bedroom, to take off those loose clothes, to see her lying on his bed. But he was surprised, and disappointed to be asked away from the comfort of his house, away from the warmth, the solitude, the safety – all this in a moment's thought.

He said, "Where shall we go?" and his own words were instantly startling to him, charged with certainty: *where shall we go to be alone?*

Her eyes never left his. "There's a place I love. You've been there, I'm sure."

As they left the house and got into her car, everything he knew went from his mind. Everything. His entire life, all that had gone before – his wife, his daughter, all that he had... it all left him. He had no thoughts for the world outside that car, in the same way that Alice had none; they were enclosed, separated from all other humanity and from all burdens, focussing solely on each other. They drove through the village, towards Monmouth.

: : :

Later that evening, Alice sat upright on the couch in Phillip Rossetti's study. She was alone, Jon having gone out that afternoon to Chepstow, to meet up with a few friends from Filton. He would be late back. There was silence, no music for her; the only light was from the turned-down lamp on the desk, and there was darkness outside the window.

What had happened tumbled through her mind, disordered and wild, not a dream but better, and fuller, and vivid. It had really happened. She tried to put it all into some order, to make sense of it – the most intense event of her life, a deep, dreamy mix-up in her mind and the culmination of her desires. She was in the grip of her obsession: the passionate, angry ecstasy and despair of wanting Tom, the desperation for him to accept her. She sat in the empty room, feeling nothing but the anguish of being away from him.

Let's go for a ride Tom. Will you come?

The car on the road, my car, towards Monmouth. The almost-empty road, quiet for a Saturday, and talking talking talking... but a touch of wrongness from you, just a touch, in your voice. Happy but not quite right. Is that how you are Tom? Happy but not-quite-right? What's wrong? Five minutes and we're there, climbing the hill, steep to the top. Walking, together and apart, through the trees. I want your hand, in mine, please. Now we're there, sitting side by side, looking down the slope through the tangle of trees and moss-covered stones, with twilight coming soon and surely a waiting moon somewhere above us. The town lies in front, below the layer of mist, and the greyness is beautiful: it's smoke and half-light, and the air is soft, and quiet. A touch of mist up here too, in the trees. No one else Tom, just us. Side by side, hands together, arms touching, no talking now. Look around you Tom – isn't it lovely here? Isn't it perfect? And suddenly the warmth. I lean towards you and kiss your cheek but you don't respond... you're slow, you take a little while to turn your head to me. Then we kiss and move on together, your gentle hands touching me, undressing me. You tell me I'm beautiful, and I'm delighted.

Oh, Tom.

The coolness of the air made no difference to us. Your warmth, your urgency. No roughness, no taking, no asking, no words at all, just loving me. Beauty, of course – a wonderful thing. I've been lucky, I'm willing to bet I've been lucky. And that place Tom, that's where it first happened you see, so many years ago, and that was perfect too, I'm sure of it; I haven't told you about my Captain yet, or his Lady. I love you Tom. What happens now? The clouds will be dark above the mist, and the softest rain begins as we walk back. Hold my hand, please. Be happy.

We go home, and you brighten up as we drive down the valley. Could you love me? Could you? Too soon, we stop at your gate, and I wonder if you will tell me. I wait. We kiss in the silence, your hand in my hair. I remember you saying, "You have beautiful eyes." And I remember your eyes Tom, in the grey light. You tell me not to text you, to keep our phones clear of each other, and I know it's for the best. Then the misty rain falls as I watch you walk down to the unlit house, the man I love, and I know how it's going to be now... a pause in my everyday thoughts, a short space, is all I need to think of you again.

This cannot go wrong. It cannot.

: : :

She'd got back just before six, unloaded the car and gone straight upstairs after a few words with her mother. Much later she was asleep when Jon came home, and much later again she woke in the dead of night with a dream filling her head – a delectable dream, and she went over it and through it until she was wide awake and dizzy, consumed by her two lovers, one real and one dead. She'd dreamt of Phillip Rossetti, and in the strange way of dreams he was merged with Tom – faces, voices, situations entwined and made one. They blended in the brightness into a great and single presence, the surreal love of her life; in her sultry bed Tom gave flesh to Phillip and she gave the best points of one to the other, refining to distraction until it all exhausted her and she came back to Olivier, who had come into her dream with his quiet concern, his exquisite eyes and the hair she'd once longed to run her fingers through, and smiled at her, a knowing smile that told her all would be well.

It was after four when she dropped off again, while Jon slept in another world beside her, dreaming of trying to find the hotel as darkness and snow were falling together, and finding no roads leading home.

: : :

The next morning Jon was helping to clear the high ground behind the hotel, raking piles of dead scrub and throwing it all down the bank to his father-in-law, who dragged it across to where a bonfire would later be started. Alice watched them from the high window at the end of the upstairs corridor. She watched them as if they were strangers. *How odd this is now. How wonderful.*

She was filled with energy and with longing for four o'clock when she would see Tom again, yet there was always a part of her mind that would open at odd times to reveal her husband, loitering with intent, and suddenly there was a perverse urge to be nice to him. Soon after, she went out to her car for no reason but an excuse to have a chat with them as they drank coffee before going back to their tasks. She'd reasoned it would be more natural to include her father.

She left her car and walked over, feeling out of place in her smart suit as they stood in their old clothes. The Mistress instructs her gardeners, almost. She stood across from her husband.

"You two are doing well! Much more to do?"

"Oh yes," said her father. "More than one Sunday's worth."

"Sorry to take Jon away this afternoon, but we have an invitation."

"Ah... tea with the boss, eh Jon?"

Jon smiled, but his wife was embarrassing him. He lost his smile, looked pointedly at her and said, "You sound happy, Alice."

She lost the brightness in her voice. "Just thought I'd say hello."

"Well that's fine, but don't be friendly just because your Dad's here."

"Jon! I'm not doing that!"

David looked from one to the other, but Jon was walking away with his mug of coffee and leaving Alice with her father, who gave her a very sorry look.

"Well... what was that?" he said. "I think you need to try a bit harder with him, Alice."

She was shocked.

"I didn't mean it like that at all."

"Well that's how it came across." He put his coffee down, came up to her and put his arm around her shoulders. "Forgive him, Alice, why don't you?"

But she just wanted to get away, even from her father. Her small mission had failed. She pulled herself together, said she had to get back, and left him. So he finished his coffee, standing alone in the car park.

In the middle of the afternoon, Alice sat at her mirror, Phillip's necklace in her hand. The exhilaration of the night before was still there, and as she looked from her reflection to the necklace her thoughts went from Phillip Rossetti to Tom Fisher and back again, two lovers tangled in her mind. *You have beautiful eyes,* one of them had said, and the other, *In my dreams Béatrice was my lover.* But Alice no longer dreamed about finding a lover.

"We should go."

Jon had silently opened the door behind her, and startled her. She finished dressing, put the necklace back into its box and said quietly to herself, "Yes, I'm coming", then sat on her bed and with sudden anxiety sent the only text she would ever send to Tom: *Jon doesn't know about my visit, nor the CD.*

They walked to the car without speaking, and began the six-mile drive to Rivendell, where Tom Fisher stood at his kitchen window looking out along the river, waiting and wondering, until at a few minutes after four the car crunched over the gravel. Tom turned from the window and opened the door to them. They crossed the kitchen, Tom leading this time, and he put them next to each other beside the big lounge window then went back to make the tea.

In the time since being with Alice – the night and the morning – he'd come back to earth and he wished he could treat them like strangers, and start again with them both. He had a situation, a complex, ongoing situation that scared him. He stood in front of the kettle as it boiled, leaning forward on the worktop, head lowered in thought. *It's here. This is reality. I have to deal with it.* It would be two unending hours of anxiety, just because Connie had said, "Have them without me," and he'd obeyed. He'd thought about calling Alice that morning at the hotel, sounding her out, maybe putting her off, but he'd let things be. He'd regretted that, especially after her text came in, which he'd deleted in horror as if Connie had been looking over his shoulder. *But I want to see her again. Somebody help me here.*

Husband and wife sat, a few inches apart, and thought their thoughts. A big unframed print was invisibly fixed to the wall opposite, of Merlin looking up with dark bewitched eyes at the loveliness of the Lady of the Lake. They had noticed it last time, but now it dominated their vision as they both faced it. The wall was clear apart from the print – an expanse of wine red that stretched from kitchen door to window and gave the look of a gallery, missing only the description card next to the picture. A perfect, clinical wall with a centrepiece which made them both feel small in front of it. It was surely Connie's idea. The painting was new to Jon, but not Alice. She'd had a bookmark of it in school, and knew the story well. Jon didn't know it at all, but thought it interesting enough as he tried to make sense of the Lady's proportions – her head was surely too small for the rest of her.

Tom came in with a tray as Jon was staring at it. He tried to sound cheerful. "It's *The Beguiling of Merlin*. She's casting her spell on him. We've always loved it."

Jon kept quiet about proportions.

Alice cared not for the picture; her focus was Tom, and only Tom. Her heart had not slowed since they had come down the drive, and now she was disappointed because Tom sat in full view the other side of Jon in the chair that Rachel had curled up in, and she would have to look across her husband at her lover. But maybe that was best, as she could see when Jon was noticing her looking – and she wanted to look all the time. Her awareness of Tom was acute, from the smallest movement of his eyes to the way his mouth moved when he smiled. There was no fault, no weakness, but she desperately needed him to notice her above all else. They talked and drank tea.

"So when does Connie get back?" Jon was remembering Connie as she moved around in her fussy way, as he wallowed in the comfort of the sofa and the temporary separation from Alice's troubles.

Tom's voice was soft, a little resigned. "On Tuesday. Teatime, usually."

There was tension, a touch of coolness as Tom spoke to Alice and more than a touch of animation as she spoke back to him. A curious conflict, and again Jon wondered. He sat between them as their unbalanced exchanges took place. So Tom talked with him, trying not to engage with Alice while under the intensity of her gaze.

His lust had wound down and turned into a tangle of regret, guilt and fear, along with confused moments of excitement as he thought again of being with her on the hill, but things had changed and he was thinking more and more of his wife and daughter. They were far away, but as the clock ticked he knew they would return – they were just there, and inevitable, a few hours and days away. And then, after managing to dominate the conversation, keeping it away from things only he and Alice should know, she said, "So, are you managing on your own, Tom?"

In his mind the smallest slip between them would be enough, the tiniest deviation from the story she'd told her husband – and he didn't know what she'd told him.

"Yes. I wander up to The Boat, if I get lonely."

And she imagined him walking alongside the river, up to the pub across from the village, over the old iron bridge. She thought she could walk with him, keep him company. Then suddenly it was too much. He put his cup down with finality, stood up and said, "I cut the grass for the first time today." They followed him through the glass doors and down onto the lawn and Jon said, weakly, in the background, "It's early, to cut grass..." Alice was oblivious to him; *Tom, I want to know what you think about me.*

Tom's reluctance to talk with her made no difference to how she felt, but their conversation was easier to steer for him as they ambled, a trio of misfits, up to the river and back, looking without interest at the daffodils in the borders. Tom's discomfort was obvious, and Jon was hopelessly out of it.

"You okay about Plessey tomorrow, Jon?" Plessey was meaningless to Alice, as she tagged along.

"I'll be fine Tom. I'll talk them through it."

"You can have Bill with you."

And so on. Work-talk was back. Connie would not be impressed, but Alice's comments were warded off even if her focus was not, and after ten minutes they came back inside and the three of them stood in front of the beguiled Merlin again, with Tom dismayed at how his own Lady of the Lake had captured him – and now wearied him – so well. Jon felt the exclusion of his wife, as she felt anything but excluded, in the company of her lover. *Work talk is fine, Tom. Just look at me, notice me.*

Tom was relieved at the afternoon being over and as it was almost six o'clock they said their goodbyes and went back through the kitchen to the front door, but Jon was allowed to go first and in the few seconds it took, in her feverishness Alice reached for Tom's hand and pressed the small box into it, then closed her fingers briefly over his. It was a moment of vital importance for her, and it was done.

Behind the closed door, Tom opened the box and saw the necklace.

THIS CHANGES EVERYTHING

The drive down from Edinburgh is long, and on that Sunday evening Rachel was on the last stretch after almost seven hours on the road. She would be home by nine, she'd thought, but she'd stopped somewhere unplanned and now it would be more like ten. She called her father, and after some happy banter she drove on.

While his daughter was coming home, in the quietness of his house, Tom Fisher looked around him at his life now. Everything was there – his books, his music, the pictures on the walls and the furniture once thought about between him and Connie, the colours agreed upon, the bright kitchen full of the small things that take time to be found and bought over the years. *Everything.* Wherever he looked, there he was, in some way, and there Connie was too. Regardless of his unhappiness with her it was a marriage, a joining of sensibilities and of needs and likes, however different. But the necklace Alice had given him was a mystery, a strange and unsettling thing, and he'd put it on the kitchen table and left it there as he'd moved around, tidying up. He remembered it from the photograph at the hotel, and now she'd left it for him with no explanation. He picked it up and held it, gently, imagining it lying on her skin, thinking briefly of her again to the exclusion of everything else, but he could not imagine what she wanted, or which way his life would go now; her gift, if that's what it was, confused him. It was a puzzling lack of thought from her, and what had been easy to understand was now complex. The necklace was not for him, and could never be. It was the Rossetti necklace. What was she thinking? What did she want? It made him wonder again how on earth he ever thought it could work – a short, secret affair, without complications? He was ashamed of himself.

In the space of a few minutes his life had become unbearably complicated. He realised with anguish that their brief time together had passed and he was being left to his previous life. Her obvious passion for him could only be destructive. He would never be free. Never again could he talk easily with his wife, never again would his head be free of Alice and what had happened with her.

In the silence he went over his options.

With crushing certainty he knew that the cost of the little hour he'd spent with her, of his adultery, would be the unending hours he would now have to spend with Connie, and also with Rachel – a time of lies, of deceit. So after the temptation, the longing, the dreamlike differences of her, he must return as a weakling to those he'd deceived, and keep secrets from them for ever. That was the true cost of his infidelity. He could not see how he could do it, how he could forever carry that weight in his mind. His precious daughter would be home soon, and his unsuspecting wife would return in a couple of days. He looked again at the necklace, in the palm of his hand.

Rachel arrived just after ten, found the house unlocked, and a note from her father on the kitchen table: *"Darling girl, sorry to miss you. There's something nice in the oven. Just popped up to The Boat, don't wait up. Dad."*

The *something nice* was lasagne, her favourite, but as she sat down to eat, it was odd he wasn't there. She'd been away for two weeks, and they were always so happy to see each other again after a break like that. She sat and waited for him. If he left the pub at eleven, he'd be back by quarter-past, but quarter-past came and went. She wandered out into the garden and onto the riverbank, looking upstream past the village, but the darkness hid everything. His car was outside the house, of course – only ever in bad weather would he drive up to the car park, and tonight was damp, but still, and mild. She went back inside, waited until half-past, then phoned him. She keyed his number and a moment later his phone rang in the lounge, making her jump. That was unusual, not to take his phone – uneasy now, she sat in the kitchen and waited. At a quarter to midnight she couldn't think straight – *should I call the police? How long should I wait... how stupid it would be if he's talking with someone in the village. He thinks I've gone to bed. But how long do I wait?* So she took a deep breath and called The Boat, apologised for the lateness, and asked after Tom Fisher – what time had he left? After a long half-minute someone came back and said he hadn't been in at all. They knew Tom well, and he hadn't been there – and now it was different; in great alarm she went out again, across the garden to the river, scanning with the torch up and down the path – she saw him then, a touch of something light-coloured in the tangle of reeds near the bank below the house. She ran, scrambled down the bank, dropped the torch and pulled him from the water. She slipped backwards on the muddy bank and he fell across her, his head on her arm. The world slowly spun as she tried to make sense of things; she looked down at his face, feeling calm now, not quite believing as she stroked the hair from his eyes and wondered at his lifelessness, his change, from warmth to coldness, from everything he was to this. Then in the darkness she saw the dull necklace in his hand, and uncoiled it from his fingers; she reached for the torch and in the midst of her horror saw in her hand something beautiful. It was the necklace in the photograph at the hotel, the one her father had asked about. She couldn't work out, within the numbing confusion in her head, what had happened here; she wanted to scream, to deny what she could see and to wake herself from this nightmare.

Soon a heavier rain began to fall as Rachel lay with her father on the muddy bank with her feet in the water, weeping for the loss of him.

: : :

The next morning Elena found Alice in the car park, fetching something from her car; she put her hands on Alice's shoulders and said, "Darling, I have some very bad news," and suddenly Alice knew what that news would be, before her mother could tell her. Great sadness often follows great happiness. *It was Tom. Yes of course, it was Tom.*

Elena took a very deep breath. "Jon just phoned. Tom Fisher's dead. Rachel found him in the river last night, poor girl. Jon's on his way home now."

Alice looked at her mother, whose voice was already distant: "I'm so sorry Alice. You were with him yesterday."

Then her mother's arms were suddenly around her, but Alice could only lift her own arms weakly from her side before letting them drop again, looking beyond her mother and the hotel at the drifting white clouds far beyond the horizon. Her mind had already turned, away from the brilliance that was Tom. It couldn't last, and now she'd lost him. She was aware of her mother's voice, somewhere far behind her, outside her head. The words were indistinct – *"Jon... here soon, Connie's... shock, dreadful."* All the words she'd expect at such times, but mixed up, tumbling together. The morning was mild and sweet, and she felt a slight breeze on her cheek as her mother still held her. A beautiful morning.

They went inside, and she left her mother and went up to the study. She stood in front of the window and looked at the river as the sun caught the water – untroubled, but guilty of two deaths now, guilty by being there, of being used. The same water that took Janet has taken Tom, and look at it – no one would know. It looks the same. The crowding in her head overpowered her, and she lay down on the couch and closed her eyes.

Oh Tom... oh Tom.

She closed her eyes, and went back into the dream that was Tom, but it was short-lived. She jumped at Jon's voice - quiet, almost breaking. "I'm going up to Redbrook. Are you coming?"

She stared at him in shock.

"Alice, are you coming? You don't have to."

"No... no."

It was too much for her, this change from Tom to Jon, but as he turned and left the room she jumped up and called him back.

She hugged him tightly, almost painfully, and cried into him as everything overwhelmed her, both the dreams and the reality. They stayed like that for a whole minute, supporting each other, he on the verge of tears and she weeping against him. And again, the unforeseen and strange inevitability rose in her, as it had earlier in the car park with her mother. *It was bound to happen, this loss.* She held her husband and cried softly for her lover, before long finding herself somewhere else, a comforting place, where things would surely be sorted out for her now in the certainty of it being over, but it was fleeting, and soon the loss returned. She cried as her husband held her, without feeling what she should have felt, in his arms at last – she cried for Tom and for her own helplessness. She would afterwards tell herself that this is how love is.

She went with him, silent, up to the house on the riverbank, thinking she could cope with it all but she couldn't leave the car, so he parked in the lay-by up on the road and she sat there as he walked down the gravel drive. Her husband went down to the bright and opened house as Tom had gone down to the closed and darkened house two evenings before. She saw him embrace Rachel, then go inside.

There were other cars there, and a police car arrived minutes later. Her love – her *lover* now, was gone, lost in the river and probably far away and cold in the back of an ambulance, or covered with a sheet on a slab in some dead, brightly lit room. Hard and colourless. It was a strange morning of no thoughts and many, of being unable to put things properly together in her head as she sat there in the car, watching comings and goings and waiting for her husband. *Is this my fault? Did I have anything to do with it? How could I?* She thought of him now in the car with her: his eyes, soft, wondering, looking across to her in the semi-darkness and the pure and guiltless thoughts came to her: *Yes, he will be perfect, and with me, for ever.*

Some time later Jon came back up the drive and got in next to her.

"Well," he said, in a voice she hadn't heard from him before, "how terrible is that, to find him in the river."

They sat quietly together, staring over the house towards the village and the forest beyond.

He said, still looking ahead, "Connie's not back yet," then he lied for her – "Rachel asked after you, I said you'd see her soon."

"Thank you."

He tried to make sense of what could happen now. She said nothing. But then he turned to look at her as she stared ahead, a sideways look that she felt but could not return, and she was suddenly afraid.

He said, while looking across at her, and almost under his breath, "You know, this changes everything."

She stayed looking ahead, but he kept his eyes on her for too long, and after a few seconds she closed hers, fearing his thoughts. Reality was closing in for Alice. People would think differently, would ask questions, would wonder, and they would be real people, real questions, real wonderings. For the first time she knew for certain it was not a dream, and she was in the middle of it. She would not wake up to something different. And her unimagined guilt was closing in.

Jon roused himself, and started the car.

"You sure about not going down?"

She nodded, not even finding the word *yes*.

An hour after supper Alice went into the narrow corridor leading to their staircase, and in the dim light, and to the background sounds of the dining room, she stood in front of Aku's cage. He was thoughtful. There was no tinkling of the bars from Alice, no cheery hello from either. Her sorrow had preceded her and Aku had picked it up, without knowing its cause.

She looked at him and said, softly, "He's gone, Aku," and he just looked back at her. It was something bigger than he could imagine, and for those moments all he could do was give her his complete attention, and all his affection. She left him, after covering his cage for the night.

:::

As that awful morning began, Rachel had to deal with the world alone. She left her father at the water's edge and went back to the house and made the phone call. She sat in the kitchen, wet through, shoes and jeans heavy with mud, until the police arrived after some fifteen minutes. She let them in, oblivious of the state she was in, carrying mud and water through the house. An officer stayed with her as two others went across the lawn to the river. She was concerned about the mess on the floor from the front door to the kitchen and began to clean up the worst of it, when a more senior officer arrived, and said, "I'm sorry. You'll need to leave that until later."

They sat together at the kitchen table, the other policeman standing across the room from them. It would not take long, he said, then she could sleep; just a few questions, and after the usual enquiries about when and where and how, he asked, "What did he have with him... anything? In his pockets?"

"I don't know. I didn't look."

"And did he leave anything here? Anything he should have taken with him?"

She didn't mention the phone, or the torch. "Not that I'm aware of, no."

"He has a mobile phone?"

"Yes, but that's here." Then, untruthfully, "He didn't always have it with him." Already, she felt the need to protect him.

"And what about a torch?" He glanced across to the worktop, where the torch was. She said, "No, he didn't take it."

"If he went along the bank he'd need one, wouldn't he?"

"I suppose so. But he knew the path very well."

"Did he take a different torch, perhaps? Did he have one?"

"He might have, I don't know, sorry."

"Okay." He sat upright in his chair. "And I have to ask – was there a letter, or a note?"

She wasn't shocked at the inference. "Just this."

She showed him the note she'd found on the table. He read it, and gave it back to her.

"Nothing to make you concerned about him, in any way?"

"No."

He thanked her, told her again how sorry he was, and offered to make the difficult phone calls for her. She declined, and smiled weakly at him as he got up and left her. An ambulance came soon after, and she stayed at the kitchen table as things went on outside that she heard and imagined but didn't want to see, and her father was eventually taken away. She overheard that there were no obvious injuries, nothing to suggest violence.

She was aware of a search being made along the path up to The Boat as more people arrived, and there were lights along the bank. She was alone in the kitchen apart from the other policeman who stood at the window, hands clasped behind him, looking out at the goings-on by the river. How many times had he been through this, how many tragedies has he seen? It was not a job she would like.

At half-past two things quietened, and the policeman suggested she go to bed, and they would see her again in the morning. She knew she wouldn't sleep, couldn't sleep with the night as it was, but she pulled off her shoes and socks and went anyway, threw her clothes on the bathroom floor and stood in the shower for ten minutes. Under the hot water she slowly came back from the empty despair she'd had for the past few hours, and began to think about what to do next. She would call her mother in the morning. *Let her sleep.* And her grandparents.

The loss stepped back as she went over what would have to be done now. So many people needing to know, so many things needing to be done, to be tied up – the loose ends of his life. She got out of the shower, dried herself and fell into bed, her head full, her grief held at bay. People came into her thoughts and went, but always she came back to the same place: *the necklace in his hand.* And because only she knew about it, she thought it probable that the eventual verdict would be misadventure, a slip from the muddy bank in the dark. He was, after all, not a good swimmer. She thought she'd never sleep. The necklace lay beside her on the little table.

At seven-thirty she was wide awake, so she got up and went to the window. A police car was parked alongside the house. She guessed they'd been there all night. She put the necklace into a drawer and dressed, then tidied the bathroom, stuffing her dirty clothes into a bag and cleaning the mud from the floor. She thought again of the mess she'd left from the front door, suddenly afraid of her mother seeing it, but her mother didn't know yet. She put off calling her and went through, hearing voices from the kitchen, and remembered saying it was okay for someone to wait in the house until morning, and wondering if she'd had a choice over it.

Two new officers were there, standing by the window as she went in. The senior of the two reached for the kettle and suggested she eat something, but she suddenly found courage and said, "I need to call a few people," and went back full of anxiety to the phone in her parents' room, sat on her mother's bed and called her, and to her relief it was her mother's cousin's voice. She asked her to stay close. Connie was impossible. She went entirely to pieces as she was told, and left the phone to her cousin for Rachel to properly explain what had happened.

She would be driven back home that morning in her cousin's car, and they would worry about her own car later. Rachel then called her grandparents in Hereford, who met the news with expected quietness and stoicism. They would be with her soon.

She walked outside. The rain of the night had cleared, and it was a beautiful morning. There was a police van parked at the side of the house which she hadn't seen, but it was empty, and she could see people standing together on the riverbank where she'd found her father. *Such a mess now.*

Suddenly she realised that she should call the factory – it was eight-fifteen and they would be wondering why Tom was late. Jon answered, and was lost for words beyond saying how sorry he was. He would do what was needed there, he said, and be with her as soon as he could. She felt better for making the calls. She cleaned the floor, and felt better for that too.

It was thirty minutes later that she accepted a cup of tea and a piece of toast – the limit of her giving-in.

During the next hour her grandparents arrived, and soon after she saw Jon coming down the drive. She went to meet him. After a few words he followed her back inside, into the living room where her grandparents were. It was difficult talking.

At the very top of Rachel's mind was the necklace – *his wife's necklace,* but she couldn't say anything to him. When Jon arrived he'd said that Alice was in the car up on the road, and was too upset to come down, and she'd said nothing – there was no response from her. There would be another time for Alice.

Connie was on her way home, a day earlier than planned, and her parents, shocked and quiet, would wait for her. They all sat away from the big window, but looking out, as if the beauty of the morning could take them away from where they were. The bank opposite was bright at the top with the morning sun, the trees beginning their new growth with the spring, with nothing to spoil it. *Round and round the seasons go.*

Jon sat with them for an eternity it seemed – the longest forty-five minutes, certainly the saddest he'd ever known. He would need to talk with Connie, but until then he would go back down to Chepstow, and carry on as best he could.

At the factory Jon was met with questions and despondency and the general feeling that he would be the one to keep things moving, which appalled him. Afia Kouassi, Tom's secretary, a capable woman who'd been with him for five years, was deeply in shock. Twice she asked him, "What shall we do?" and twice Jon replied, "I don't know. We'll manage."

They went together onto the factory floor and Jon told the sad group that came to him all the news from Redbrook, the dreadful details of the death of their employer. He didn't know what would happen now, but someone suggested they simply carry on with things, and he agreed. Afia went up the stairs to her office with him, and they sat for a while, thinking and talking in the quiet before the machines started up again downstairs.

Afia was African, a warm friendly woman from Ghana and before today he'd asked what her first name meant and she'd smiled and said, "Born on Friday," and the simplicity of her answer had delighted him. *Born on Friday Kouassi*. "It's what we do," she'd said. Her ancestral town of Elmina was famous for the wrong reason, being a slave town as far back as the 1500s when the horrors of the Atlantic Trade gathered momentum. Her father had brought her away from it as a baby to escape the dire economy, finding work in the Harbour Offices at Bristol, and she'd never been back to Ghana. Nowadays the only bow to her ethnicity, apart from her colour, was a yellow and purple headscarf she would wear along with her English clothes when she felt like it and which always cheered everyone up - a bright splash amongst the overalls and white coats. Today, there was no headscarf.

Tom's office was next door, behind a glass wall, empty and threatening. Jon told her he thought it was probably useless to wait for guidance from Connie, and Rachel was so young, and without ambition for this. They agreed they could keep things going until a manager was brought in, or until the company closed down. He left Afia and wandered around the factory with altered eyes, seeing everything in a different light and feeling the weight of expectation from everyone, his mind flitting from fear to acceptance to desperation as his surroundings became twice as significant as before. He talked with the others, trying to reassure them while being full of doubt himself, and then Afia had given him a certain look from the mezzanine and he'd climbed the stairs, gone into Tom's office and sat down at her bidding, cautiously, in Tom's chair.

She'd found her strength. "You must sit here. We have to make a start."

So he sat there, lost. The desk was full, not cluttered but almost covered with neat piles of papers. Tom had simply left it all, all the work in progress, the letters needing answers, the orders needing to be placed. He looked around him at the unfamiliar room where a couple of days ago Tom Fisher was in control of the thousand things that Jon knew nothing of, and it seemed impossible to even begin to pick up the threads. As he sat wondering, Afia scooped up half the papers from the desk, took them away then came back minutes later with a neat folder containing three orders for him to sign, which shocked him. *Orders?* Surely a secretary could sign on her employer's behalf? But there was no employer, and he was the Chief Engineer so he'd calmly accepted and it was that – the signing – that brought it all home to him.

He was under her wing, but she'd wanted him in charge, in that chair. It could not stay empty. They would work together in the office, and with the five men down the stairs, themselves working and wondering. He didn't want it, and wished he could recall Dave Fletcher from Rolls Royce, one of the men Tom had lost but who would know how all this worked, and who would surely be happy to sign, to take over. Through the day he sat with Afia, and when he left for home the desk was almost clear, but he knew it was deceptive – she'd cut corners for him, found the strength and carried him along.

That evening he went with Alice back up to Rivendell, to a full house and people they didn't know, friends of Connie who were there to support and commiserate, needed or otherwise. Alice walked into the lounge with Jon and they were all sitting around the edges looking in. Someone had moved the chairs to the walls, even under the wide window as if expecting more, like a doctor's waiting room. The air felt stale and heavy. Facing them as they went in was the unintended focal point: two shockingly large women dressed in pink – mother and daughter, surely, and next to them an older and thinner woman with her equally thin husband were perched on the edge of a sofa. Another woman, vaguely familiar to Alice, smiled sadly at her, and half a dozen others sat glumly staring into space. There were occasional dull murmerings, restrained and respectful, with no one wanting to break the pattern of reverence, but conversation was a little awkward anyway, with chairs too far apart and no one actually face to face with anyone else. The atmosphere was depressing, even under the bright ceiling lights. They did the rounds of low-key introductions, not helped by Rachel, nor Connie, who was sitting in a corner between her parents.

Before sitting down Alice went over to Rachel, touched her shoulder and gave her a soft smile. Rachel looked up as if she hadn't seen her, and said, "Hello... thanks for coming," unable to hide the flatness in her voice. Their eyes met briefly, but Rachel did not get up nor offer her hand to her. Alice kept her smile and backed away, then Jon was there. He offered his hand and Rachel took it as he asked how she was – he was outside of something here, some unfriendly knowledge shared between these two, and he glanced at Alice as she went to talk with Connie, as Rachel ignored her and asked him, "How are things in Chepstow?"

Alice dismissed her by thinking back to Tom in this room, just days ago. She left the sad circle and went into the kitchen, and stood at the window looking down at the river, still feeling his presence in the room where it had begun only a week before. She imagined him, felt him, standing there as people came and went behind her.

Rachel came in and looked with disdain at her back and said pointedly as she walked back out, "There's coffee out here, if you want it."

Alice turned her head to her and said a simple thank-you, but she'd gone. She followed her, back into the living room and the dour small talk.

Jon needed to ask Connie about the future at Chepstow, but guessed it would be impossible. She was safe between her mother and father and he'd gone down on his haunches in front of her and said, changing his mind, "I'm so sorry, Connie." His hand had rested on her knee as he'd looked up to her face. It felt innocent, but all the same he was mildly shocked when he realised he'd done it even though the intimacy was for her grief, nothing more. Her spell was broken; this was the woman he'd wanted – maybe would still want, on a better day – but for now she was Connie the grieving widow, and sexual interest was put aside. All she said back to him was, "Thank you, Jon."

He got up, leaned over and gave her a hug and left her to her parents, then talked briefly with Rachel who said, "We're in at the deep end Jon. Mum won't be interested, but we'll work it out. We'll try."

He sat with Alice and the others, until at around nine it was time to go. Connie's parents left for home – at the last moment Connie had stopped them, grabbed a few things and gone with them, intensely upset and not able to face the night in her empty bedroom alone, but Rachel ignored their pleas to leave, and stood her ground. She would stay.

"You could sleep at the hotel, if you'd like," said Jon on impulse, with an enquiring glance at Alice, who said, "Yes, of course."

Rachel simply said, "No."

They were the last to go, and left her at the door as the worst day of her life came to an end. As they started walking up the drive Rachel went inside and closed the door on them, and on the world.

"Why was she so cold with you?"

Jon asked her in the car, and she replied, "Was she? She seemed okay."

He shook his head. "She was not okay."

"Well, who knows."

Indeed, he thought, *who knows.*

And Alice, in the midst of everything, felt a quite different and urgent need. Her dream-world had collapsed, and she worried about the future. On top of all the grief and loss there was a real-world concern: what if she's pregnant? But a safety net was easy to arrange. The bedroom was warm, and their lovemaking was as urgent as the first time on that sunny riverbank, but this time there was a different edge, the vague feeling of helping each other, like old friends in a time of mutual need. And she actually wanted to be frank with him, but could not. This could be the start of the child she'd wanted but in the end it was sex between strangers, almost, and slightly awkward. Afterwards they talked quietly into the night, strangely ill at ease in each other's arms, and they went over the events of the day – one wanting to keep her secrets, the other desperate to know them.

Jon said, "Rachel's having a hard time."

"Yes."

He asked his question again. "Why would she be cold to you?"

"I don't know that she was, Jon."

And he couldn't miss the tiniest irritation. He lay quiet while he wondered about going further with her, and risk spoiling the peace they had. But he left Rachel alone, and they said nothing more.

Alice could not sleep easily with her thoughts. Was she a monster of some sort, an outsider with no thoughts of the damage she had caused? *No, I am in love, and love does not cause damage. Love heals, and grows.* Her delusions came and went, and her feelings for Tom were as intense as when she'd left him that Sunday with her necklace. But she thought onwards from there and wondered where it was now, of where Tom had left it – and what if it's found? Would it be remembered by Rachel, or Connie, after that brief glance at the photograph? She found a desperate optimism. *It may be found, but not wondered at. It will be a piece of jewellery perhaps from his mother, or someone else long forgotten.* But still she wondered if he'd left it in the kitchen, or on a shelf somewhere. She told herself not to regret giving it to him, nor losing it; she was separated enough from reality to expect to be understood if she ever had to explain – and anyway, what had Olivier said? *Give it to the one you love.*

Jon went over his life now. After the miracle of being back together, he switched off from the bigger doubts about his wife and thought of his work. Would he be alone with the managing of the others, which he'd never wanted to do? He could not imagine Rachel being useful. In spite of Afia's efforts he thought about simply shutting it all down, stepping back and waiting for some miracle of reorganisation, but that bothered him. There was work in progress, things to be finished, contracts to be honoured – and that was the problem. So he would let them all work on, like an orchestra without a conductor, going through familiar actions which they knew better than he did; he was the best qualified but the least experienced there, and this would maybe level them all, and help him. He would lean heavily on Afia, and he would talk to solicitors, accountants, bank managers – whatever was needed, and take advice. He didn't look forward to it, but he would do it because it was all worth saving, and because he had been fond of Tom.

: : :

The next morning Alice walked to her car. She got in, closed the door and leaned sideways to put the key into the ignition when the passenger door opened and Rachel got in beside her, pulled the door closed and straight away offered her open hand to Alice. In it was the necklace. After a few moments she said, calmly, "This is yours."

As Alice stared in horror at her necklace, her grandfather Peter was readying himself for the short journey down the valley to the hotel. Elena had called him the day before, giving the news he would have missed in his isolation at Celyn. He was unhappy now, and suddenly for more reasons than the tragedy: he held a secret to himself, not telling Elena, but keeping it.

On the Saturday evening, the day before Tom's death, he'd driven past his house and by chance seen Alice's car parked at the top of his drive, and he'd seen two people sitting in the car – he was sure of it. One of those people would have been Alice, and the other would have been Tom. He knew from Elena that Tom had been alone, so who else could it have been? His heart was heavier after hearing the news, and he didn't like his imaginings... (Oh Alice, please don't let that be true. Let it be innocent). He went out to his car, unaware of his grand-daughter's peril at that moment, of her imminent descent into the realities of her life.

Alice, frozen in disbelief, stared at the necklace.

Rachel said, "You gave it to Dad, didn't you. It was in his hand when I found him." She moved her hand closer. "Take it."

But Alice was unable to move, desperately thinking through what this meant, of where it may lead... *in his hand?*

"Take it back."

She was caught, wanting to open the door and run back into the hotel, to flee to the safety of her room. As her tears came she made the smallest movement of her hand towards Rachel, who tossed the necklace into her lap.

Then, quietly, "Do you realise what you've done? *Do* you?"

Alice stared across at her, unable to speak.

"All that innocence last night. I just hope you were kind to him. I hope you loved him. Please tell me you loved him." No response. "Tell me!"

In a quiet, frightened voice Alice said, "Yes, yes, I did."

"And do you think he loved you?"

Looking away from Rachel, she closed her eyes. "I know he did."

"And you knew how fragile he was?"

She looked back at her. "What? No, I didn't know anything..." but Rachel spoke over her. *"Listen.* This is simple. Your necklace, in his hand, wrapped around his fingers. Why would that be? Do I have to tell you? My father killed himself. Because of you."

It was all too much for Alice. Tears blinded her, and again she looked away, to the side.

"What were you thinking? Why give him that? Were you going to *marry* him?" Then Rachel calmed herself and after a deep breath, she said, "It's just you and me that know about this – about you and him, yes?"

Another long pause. Jon's look in the car went through Alice's mind, and still she looked away. Her tone was uncertain. "Yes..."

"You sound doubtful. Does Jon know? Or anyone else? Well that's *your* problem. Listen to me. My mother must *never* know. She must never know about you and Dad. And it was an accident, he fell in the river. Don't ever forget that, don't ever slip up."

Then, almost under her breath, *"If she ever finds out, I'll make you pay. I'll destroy you, I really will. Do you understand?"*

The threat astonished Alice behind her closed eyes – horrified her, the cold sincerity of it. There were a few seconds of silence before she found her voice, but still she couldn't look at her.

"I'm so sorry, I really am."

Then Rachel's anger gave way to her own tears. She got out of the car, slammed the door behind her and walked quickly, and in distress, across to her own car and drove away.

Alice sat in her misery. Soon she felt the need to go before being seen, before some unwanted saviour appeared, so she drove the short mile to Tintern through her tears and parked facing the river, in sight of the little church where she'd married Jon in a different world a lifetime ago. The necklace was still in her lap. She looked out across the high water, brown and unwelcoming, and it was as if every injury – all the ills she'd ever suffered – had revisited her at once, in a stifling, crushing mass. She wailed in anguish, alone in her car.

She came back to the hotel after an hour, her original reason for going somewhere gone from her mind. She went straight upstairs, grateful for seeing no one as she went except for Aku, who muttered a subdued *"Alice?"* as she passed him. She washed her face, disturbed by the puffy redness in the mirror, and sat at the table by the window.

There was no one there to help her. She sat alone in that room, her arm resting on the table where Jon worked in the evenings with his unfathomable books. *Would he be ashamed of me?* Yes, of course he would. As would Phillip. Then she thought of Olivier and what she'd been prepared do with him... and Tom, poor Tom. *Happy Endings, indeed. What's the matter with me?*

She sat with her thoughts, with the horrors of the morning and the knowledge that to stay there was not an option. She feared showing herself after so much crying, but after a while she thought better of it – *it's okay to be still upset a couple of days after a friend's death*. Across the river the fields were bright with sunlight as they had been all morning but now she began to see it, and the distant sounds of the hotel returned – things that had gone on without her. She stopped crying, then waited through a slow watering down of her misery until the mirror had returned her almost to normal. She felt fit to be seen again so she went downstairs and found her mother, who had seen her leave the hotel but not realised she was back, and she'd missed her grandfather's visit. There were no questions, but in spite of her strained smiles her despair had passed between them, through their intimate bond and by the stubborn traces of the tears she'd thought were gone. And when Jon returned from work at six she grabbed and kissed him passionately, almost knocking him off balance as she'd done on their wedding day; it was a simple need to have her grief shared.

: : :

Alice and Jon were reconciled, after a fashion, but there was a lot of overcoming to do and Alice struggled to keep her resolve. Jon's struggle was no easier. He would not forget Connie as she was when he'd lusted after her, but her imagined treasures moved to the back of his mind. She had changed from an object of desire to a sad, overturned woman needing to be comforted. He wanted details from Alice so he could live with her again without suspicion, and even if she'd had sex with Tom he felt he would cope with it. *Even if she'd had sex with him?* It was likely, and he'd gone through all the signs: talking in the garden, Tom's final awkwardness with her, Rachel's coldness and Alice's evasiveness, imagined or real. He even confronted the scenario of Tom's death not being an accident, and that he might have killed himself because of her – what an impossible mess that would be. Oh, and if she did have sex with him, were they careful, or not... for all he knew she could be pregnant now. *Too much imagination, Jon.* He feared everything.

: : :

In the middle of that week, on the Thursday morning, Alice needed to get away. Her grief had built up through a sleepless night until it was too much to contain, and after a late breakfast she excused herself to Jenny, by now quite used to her moods, and left in her car with no idea of where she was going. Down to Tintern then up to Lydart, down to Monmouth and back along the valley road, seeing nothing. In her pocket was the necklace, unable to be parted from her since Rachel had given it back.

Then as she reached Redbrook, on impulse she pulled into the car park above the river, an impulse that came from her need for her lover, and the river – his gentle undoing – had become a part of him. She parked the car, walked to the high bank and looked down through the greening trees to the brown swirling water, and the old railway bridge – a cold, grey, hard steel affair sitting on fat columns into the river, the tracks long gone, the bridge now kept for walkers crossing to The Boat. Had he been on this bridge that night? She stood, hands in pockets, the necklace around her fingers, when a romantic notion came to her: *give it back to the river.* In her distress it was appealing, a fitting end. All its memories would go – Phillip, Béatrice, Janet, the other Rossetti brides, even herself, and then Tom. The end of the whole affair, and she had Jon's necklace to continue the tradition in its place. It all added up in her mind. She went down the steps and out onto the bridge with the necklace in her hand. As she stood against the rail her head was full of her lover, her eyes fixed on the slow-moving river below – surely the last thing he had seen before deciding to go from her. She held the necklace out over the water and let the thin chain unravel slowly through her fingers, the slight weight of the pendant pulling it down until she held it over just one finger, above the river. Sunlight glittered on its tracery in a final appeal to her – *Look how beautiful I am!* – as it slowly turned on its chain.

Go back to your river.

Yet even as those thoughts came together, the mess inside her head – the sorrow, the fear, the longing, the wish for easy salvation all fuzzed her decision-making. She stood looking down at the water, and as quickly as it had come the new plan was abandoned. She changed her mind, the necklace went back into her pocket and she turned back to the car in dismay at how easily a resolution came and went, of how ungrounded she was, how defenceless against her whims.

She was alone apart from a few distant dog walkers. Across the road were rows of houses on the bank, houses with life inside, young and old, happiness and woes, all different, all playing their parts but unknown to her. They would have heard of the tragedy. And right here, in front of them on this promising March morning, stood the culprit: a confused figure in the tight, inescapable world she'd made for herself. What would they think of her, if they knew what she'd done?

She sat in her car, watching the high clouds drifting across. A lovely morning, but the world was changing with her moods. How long before she could enjoy such a morning again? The day was bright but her mind was dark, the numberless threads leading in and out of her life each able to give her pain, she feared, and unrest.

She drove home to Brockweir, passing Rivendell, looking down on the squat building on the meadow, at the cars parked outside, and at the deadness of the scene. With Tom filling her head, suddenly she said aloud, "Maybe some day, in a different world, I could have known you very well." But such wistfulness could not lift her mood. *Nobody understands me now.* She could have explained to Rachel about the necklace, but surely mockery would have been added to her anger. *All I wanted was for Tom to give it back to me. That's all I wanted.* How could Rachel, or anyone else, understand that?

∴

The funeral was set for Thursday of the following week, the news coming that there were no signs of violence, no injuries, and no reasons for suicide. On the night Tom died, dogs had been brought in but the heavy rain in the early hours had muddled them. Even so they had stopped and there, under the follower's torches, were the signs of Tom's short fall to the river – a sliding track in the mud down to the edge of the slow, deep water, turned at the very top where his foot had left the path, still visible in the rain. The dogs were certain and the police agreed with them. Near the water they found his small yellow torch, turned on, batteries dead.

Rachel had been interviewed again a couple of days later. No, he was not suicidal. Occasional ups and downs, but then everyone's like that, aren't they? And he was successful, no money worries, certainly no enemies – and of course, we all loved each other. She asked him not to contact her mother in Hereford, and hoped he wouldn't. But Rachel could have been more truthful about those ups and downs; she could have told the simple truth – that she'd often worried about him, seen him so very down and not known what to do, and it was no help to be told by her mother that he was fine. He was always fine for her. Rachel thought she must be used to it, seen him like that so many times, and he always came round. One time he'd disappeared, left the house without telling them and walked for hours – or maybe sat for hours somewhere. But he came back and went straight to bed, early in the evening. Rachel never forgot that episode, but never mentioned it to anyone.

The same officer had called at the hotel and spoken with Alice about the Sunday visit. Again, no indications of anything, just having tea with a friend. Jon was not needed. And as for her Saturday visit, well, no need to tell anyone about that... all the while the fear enveloping her as she sat in front of her questioner, wary of the depths she could be pulled into if the truth came out.

So all that, plus death by drowning from the doctor would bring about the Coroner's acceptance of accidental death. Death by misadventure. No inquest, and Tom was free to be buried.

The tragedy had resolved into a tragic accident. Rachel's silence over the necklace – the risk of witholding evidence – felt safe to her, and didn't trouble her greatly. She was as satisfied as she could be with the verdict, and would live the lie while her mother was alive. She had no idea what she would do if she died.

:: : :

Eleven days after Tom's death, Jon and Alice sat with their parents in the kitchen at The Wondrous Gift, in the midst of the restrained and hushed small-talk of a funeral day. In two hours Tom would be buried at the old church of St Thomas the Martyr, in Monmouth, after a brief service. He would join his parents in the small churchyard above the river, an almost-tranquil spot walled away from the traffic crossing the ancient bridge nearby, and only slightly bothered by the comings and goings and sounds of the market town. It would be over, for Tom at least. For Alice, now, it was far from over. In a couple of hours she would see Rachel again, for the first time since their meeting in her car. She would be expected to embrace her, to be sorry for her loss. How good would their acting be? And Connie would be there, the wife of her lover. She wished she could call in sick.

The week before had been filled with apprehension, for herself and for Jon, who was struggling to hold things together at the factory. Alice found herself concerned for him, and thought of parallels, of how he was in a similar position to John Parrish when Phillip had died, having to carry the business because the rightful owner could not. *So history repeats itself, more or less.* She saw the business going to Connie and being wound up unless Jon – she gave little thought to secretary Afia – could keep it going for her, and she was proud of him for trying; "Let's get the funeral over," he'd said, "then I'll talk properly with Connie."

The talk went round and round, Alice becoming more detached and anxious as the time ticked on. Jon's sister Diane was there, and Peter, and eventually they all drove to Monmouth, in two cars, and joined the crowd that had come for Tom on that bright Thursday. For Alice it was almost unbearable. Some sixty people, family, friends, connected lives, and all there because of her, because she'd wanted him; the entire day, all this sadness and grief, was because of her. She was unnoticed, but there was surely a sign above her which said, *I'm the one. It's all my fault.* She felt vulnerable in an unknowing crowd which could turn on her at any moment if someone should tell them, and she was afraid of being set upon, poked and prodded, asked impossible questions, of being reviled. And she briefly held the nightmarish image of Rachel denouncing her from the pulpit, of people turning in their seats to look at her as she hid at the back of the church. But it was only Rachel that looked at her, and as their eyes briefly met through the crowd she felt a panic, a need to run away; but they moved into the church then and Alice watched as Rachel and her mother went to the front, a safe distance away.

In front of them all, on a shiny chrome trolley, was the coffin, draped in green with two wreaths of white roses laid on top. It was surreal – Alice's lover was there, close to her, impossibly out of reach for ever. She saw the tears, the arms around shoulders. She saw more grief and sadness than she had ever seen, in the confines of that small church. There was Tom's brother Geoff, whom she never knew existed, dressed in the Sunday Best of a farmer, the slight awkwardness in looking smart; he stood at the lectern and gave an overly detailed account of Tom's life, describing him as *a very generous person, a person to be valued,* and informing her of the man she had lost better than anyone ever could, or ever would – showing her that in her blindness she'd hardly known him.

As it came to an end Rachel got up and announced that she would like to read one more thing. It was a poem that Dad was fond of, she said, even though it wasn't in the Order of Service. As she spoke Alice closed her eyes, letting the words wash over her as the lines she knew so well ran their course, lines by John

Donne, the poet she'd shared with Tom. *It's for me, she's done it for me.* She feared what was coming. She kept her eyes closed and bowed her head, and thought she felt Rachel's eyes on her alone at the end, as indeed they were – and Jon saw it: *Is Rachel looking at me? No, she's looking at Alice.*

The last lines came as he glanced at his wife, bowed and cowed beside him: *"Any man's death diminishes me, because I am involved in mankind. And therefore, never send to know for whom the bell tolls; it tolls for Thee."*

Alice sat with her family and friends as the church emptied behind the coffin, unable to look at Rachel as she passed, and as they followed the rest outside Rachel was there, speaking to everyone as they went by. Just seeing her there, with Connie gently weeping next to her, was a vision of hell. In a few seconds she would have to face her, face them both. Elena and David were first, hugging her and Connie and saying how sorry they were. Jon's parents and sister did the same, and so did Jon – especially him, as Connie held his hands and thanked him for helping Tom while he could. Then it was Alice, facing the nemesis that was Rachel, trembling, forcing herself to look in her eyes and not look away. Alice hugged her, and anyone watching closely would have seen Rachel's eyes closed, her set expression, as she'd put her arms around her. "Sorry," was all Alice could whisper before she turned to Connie and hugged her, saying nothing to her then walking away; but Jon had been watching, and felt a confirming measure of unease – their reluctance to touch, their stiffness amongst the warmth of emotion from the others.

The churchyard emptied and the cars left for home. There was food at Rivendell for them all, and thirty or so were there, enough to make Alice anonymous as she tried to avoid talking with anyone. After an hour she left with her husband, and the day was over.

The day after the funeral Peter Bennett stood under the skylight in his studio with a letter in his hands, brought to a halt by the first paragraph:

'Dear Mr Bennett,
I am contacting you with some information which I am sure you will find interesting, and I will get straight to the point. My name is Daniel Barthe-Fleury, and it seems that we share an ancestor, namely Captain Phillip Rossetti, our great-great-grandfather. This is as a result of his brief liaison with my great-great-grandmother, Béatrice Fleury, at Morlaix in the spring of 1816.'

He slowly sank into his chair. The day was forgotten – everything, even the coffee he'd been about to make. His distraction was serious enough to replace entirely the sadness of yesterday's funeral. The writer's address was Saint-Malo in northern France, where he knew no one. He read on:

'Two years ago, after my father's death, I discovered a letter written to him by his grandfather Fabrice which explained factually, if rather obscurely, that our ancestry was not purely French, but mixed. You can imagine my interest in such a statement!'

Just before she died Bèatrice had apparently confessed to her son Fabrice that his father was not the man she'd married. The confused old woman left him with an enigma having uttered *Phillip* and *Florence* but not much more, and later he followed a trail, via her deliberately vague diaries, to Morlaix where Bèatrice briefly was in April 1816 around the time he was conceived. He found nothing helpful there. He wrote to his grandson – Daniel Barthe-Fleury's father – and it was that letter that Daniel found and used to track down Phillip Rossetti – his father and grandfather having been unconcerned with the ramblings of an old woman on her deathbed, and far more interested in the running of their business.

'And how did I find our Florence? Well, first of all I agreed with Fabrice that she was probably a ship, and not a person or the city in Italy, because there were veiled references in her diaries (all lost now, I'm afraid). So I simply chose a country to search for a ship of that name, and the first country I chose was the closest one – England. I came to Bristol, having found a record of three ships of that name at Lloyds, in London. She was the last one I checked, of course! In Bristol I found Florence, her captain Phillip Rossetti, and records of her time in Morlaix when Bèatrice would have been there.'

The letter continued, with the trail he'd followed from those Port records and Phillip's house at Charlotte Street, through the change from Rossetti to Bennett, to Phillip's connection with Brockweir and finally to Peter Matthew Bennett living at Whitebrook... *voilà!*

And he wrote of the sort of person Béatrice was – headstrong, almost wilful – a capable woman trapped by the promise of marriage to someone she strongly disliked. Her options were few. She could have run away, left her family and her fortune and chanced an unknown life somewhere, reviled and ostracised. She chose to stay. But first she found and fell helplessly in love with Phillip Rossetti and made love to him on the low hill above the harbour, a distracted last fling, forlornly hoping that all would be well and that her promised life could miraculously change and accommodate him, but it could not.

Daniel's letter ended:

'She must have known she was pregnant when she began her long life, her sixty-two years of regret. It saddens me, because who truly knows the mind of another? Who knows how another suffers, when that suffering is borne well?'

Peter sat with the letter in his lap, astonished by what he'd read. This was why John Parrish had been curious about Phillip's second visit to Morlaix, and the reason for his comment, 'I have seen Him but once before like this', which had puzzled both Peter and Alice when they had read it in his letter... Béatrice Fleury was his first love, the love that preceded Janet.

He would keep the letter to himself. He would show it to Alice of course, but when would depend on how things turned out. There was an unanswered question about her on the night before Tom died, which needed resolving before he could share something as trivial as some interesting news from France.

THE GENTLE RIVER

Rachel arrived at her lodgings in Edinburgh just after midday. She had split the journey, leaving Redbrook a few hours after the funeral the previous afternoon and chosen the scenic route, as she often did, stopping for the night before Carlisle. From there she went as leisurely as the motorway would allow, and the welcome distraction of Gretna Green was soon followed by the melancholy of Lockerbie, before branching off east to Edinburgh.

In the midst of her turmoil she was looking forward to the evening, of meeting people again, of getting back to work; she hoped it would go well, her getting back, after twelve days of disorder and sadness. She would try to enjoy her return before having to go back to Rivendell to sort things out, as was inevitable. The sunshine helped.

Her mother planned to sell the house, and to stay with her parents in Hereford, apparently for the rest of her life and for the rest of theirs. There was nothing in her now, no spark, certainly no ambition for anything beyond settling back into her childhood home. Rivendell would be emptied, and sold, and Rachel would be the one to do it all, and the sooner the better for Connie. It was assumed that her daughter would not want to live there, and the question was never asked; the feeling of *you'll do it, won't you* was hurtful, but she took it on in spite of offers of help from friends and the well-meant pleadings of Connie's parents. She would again immerse herself in the only real home she'd known, but this time slowly and gently say goodbye to it. One day she would have another home, but not on the banks of that river.

In Edinburgh she was supply teaching, the culmination of her university years and the path to the outcome she'd always planned – *young people, pliable seven-eight-nine-year-olds, quick minds caught before the distractions of adolescence, etc.*

From her idealism as she'd begun her studies, to the challenging reality of her first job, she'd had no doubts about what she should do with her life. Her work was usually close by: temporary work, which she thought – she hoped – would become permanent. It was sufficient for her needs, monetary and otherwise. With great reluctance she'd given up the nine-months' attachment she'd made with Leith Academy in the week after her father's death, but stayed with the agency, foreseeing the flexibility needed to travel back and forth for however long it took. She would also need time for herself; the solitary drive to Scotland, and the remoteness from Redbrook, would surely provide that. She expected a long haul – many weeks, of sorting and disposing, and maybe many days spent with her grieving mother during and after. And there was Chepstow, where Jon and Afia were keeping her father's business alive until decisions could be made. She could not turn her back on any of it.

The interminable hours since her father's death had swung her relentlessly from calm acceptance through helpless grief and anger, and back again. She would not be free, but she would strive to find some time for herself, her friends and her work.

∴ ∴ ∴

Of all the sorting-out she'd done before the funeral, her own room had been the hardest, and she had tackled it first. Filled with the memories of growing up with her parents, of school, her friends elsewhere – it was the sum total of her life up to that point. The room was always ready for her, unchanged since she'd left for Edinburgh, and the emptiness after everything had gone was profound – the hollow echoing space with the wallpaper she'd chosen at thirteen and never wanted to change, now rudely exposed with its vacant hooks and unfaded squares where the pictures and posters had been; the empty shelves, cleared of their treasures; the cold and bare window looking upriver towards Redbrook.

Moving her own belongings to somewhere else – to storage, to charity or to Edinburgh, to pitiful black bags destined for oblivion – was hardly bearable at the start, but liberating at the end when her mind had turned. It had been a process of removing herself from Rivendell, of taking away all possibility of keeping her old life there, before beginning her father's study and the rest of the house. There was to be no moping about. She dragged her mattress from her own room to her father's study (her last linking with him) in the middle of the house, putting her clothes in boxes – all her needs around her for the duration of the closing-down process. She refused help, except with the removal of furniture, which she timed carefully so that no one was left hanging around waiting for her. After almost a week at Rivendell her own room was empty, as was her makeshift bedroom; from then on, she thought, it should be easier, now that her own and her father's things had gone.

She had compared her life to his during the process – her single row of books to his wall of books, her twenty CDs to his hundred and more and his dozens of cassettes, and suffered with the weight of not knowing what to do with it all. She went through his music and his books, putting aside or rejecting as she went, but unable to happily let any of it go. In the end it was impossible and she stood back, tears welling in her eyes, with three CDs and four books and closed the box lids on the rest, vowing not to reopen them and to ask only his brother if he wanted anything. Her mother wanted nothing from her husband's sanctuary.

So the day before the funeral the two rooms were empty, apart from her few boxes and her mattress, and it felt good to close the doors on them. She could leave it all for a while.

: : :

When she arrived in Edinburgh, the big house in Restalrig, on the fringes of the city, was empty. From top to bottom, everyone was out. Her part of the property was on the ground floor, her bedroom and the few rooms she shared, and as she let herself in the relief of returning was overwhelming; all was the same as when she'd left on that long-ago, irretrievable Sunday. She dumped her bags in her room then went into the kitchen, and on the table was a small pile of mail for her. The usual stuff. She wondered why someone would imagine a university graduate needing double glazing. Or a timeshare in Portugal. Then, at the bottom of the pile, the one that had come first, the one that took her breath away for a second. It was from her father. She sat slowly down at the table, with the sun streaming gloriously through the window behind her on that lovely Edinburgh day, in the silent and empty house. She looked at the envelope, at her father's handwriting, and the postmark – Friday the fourteenth of March, a few days before he'd died. It struck her that this would be his last letter to her, maybe his last letter of all, and she dreaded his reason for writing it; she turned it over in her hands, putting off the pain she feared was waiting. She reached for a knife and slit the envelope open neatly, the way she always did – she did not rip letters open – and took out a black-and-white photograph inside a folded slip of paper. As they separated she saw an image that made her heart falter. It was her with her father. She was ten or so, and standing in front of him, his hands on her shoulders. They were both smiling at the camera. Her mother was in the background on a sun lounger, wearing her expensive shades, looking across at them with an amused expression. The picture was new to her, and as she looked at it she was transported into her past, to the happy times; she was wearing a very demure swimsuit that she remembered well, and she took it all in until the tears came. She let her hands drop to the table, and looked away into the cluttered, warm and sunlit room, the soft ticking of the wall clock adding to the calm refuge holding her and her lost father. She picked up the paper, fearing his words:

'Rayt my love, look what I found the other day!'

His pet name for her. She could not manage *Rachel* until she was almost four, and he would still call her Raytel or just Rayt when he was in a good mood, to his wife's annoyance.

'I haven't seen it for years. Albert took it – remember him? Photography geek, everything better in black and white.'

Yes, she remembered Albert, but for one reason only. They'd met him in Alicante, or was it Biarritz... they'd had to keep her away from him after a few days of snapping away. But still the memories tumbled back to her of happier times than now, of warmth and security with people she loved. Her tears were blurring the words.

'Great photo, for your bedside table, perhaps? Hope you settle back in okay. Looking forward so much to seeing you again. Look after yourself. Love, love, love, Dad.'

The afternoon passed slowly, and her appetite for unpacking her few things, or eating – even the coffee she'd looked forward to on the drive up – all left her. She went over and over his words, the few sentences that now meant so much, sometimes weeping and then angry with herself for not seeing it coming – but how could she have seen it coming?

Her flatmate would come home later – Holly would be there, doing her best to comfort her, but until then Rachel tried to understand her father. She thought about the necklace, trying to reason with the facts, to make sense of what happened. Why had he clung to the necklace when it would connect him with Alice if someone else had found him? So did he really love her? There was no answer, unless he did love her and at the end he simply couldn't let it go.

My poor father.

As the minutes and hours slipped by she went over everything again. What should she do about Alice Greerson? Could she ever begin to forgive her? She doubted she could. She was angry with her for taking him away from them, for hogging his thoughts at the end. It wasn't right. His mind was not with his wife and daughter, his loved ones, in his last moments – it was with *her*.

The afternoon came to an end as the big house slowly came to life: people returned – faraway doors opening and closing, feet on stairs, muffled voices. She put his letter and the photograph away and tried to busy herself, to overcome it, but when Holly returned at five-thirty and Rachel began to carry the weight of it all, her tears were for both her father and for herself.

Much later, as she slept, the photograph was beside her bed next to her clock, and among the first things she would see when she woke.

∷

She would never know, but in the end it had been easy for him. All was well. Alice had given him the necklace, and he would keep it after all. His wish was soon granted: the gentle river had taken him, without fuss or apology, and drowned him.

ALICE, IT'S BETWEEN US TWO

As Rachel sat in her kitchen in Edinburgh, Peter Matthew Bennett, painter, father and grandfather, stood at his living room window looking down the blue and green unruffled valley to Bigsweir Bridge, the link that had boosted the traffic to Phillip Rossetti's legacy, The Wondrous Gift. He imagined the scene a hundred-and-seventy years ago, the celebrations as the bridge was opened, the first carriages crossing and the delight of the passengers with the previously unseen view upriver towards him – the placid, mirroring river, the meadows and low green banks, the forest into the distance towards Redbrook and Monmouth, and no buildings to take the scene away from nature apart from Celyn, the old farm then, on the sloping field to the left. It was a common view now, but still beautiful after seeing it from the car a thousand times, still serene enough to calm him, to make him almost stop as he reached the middle of the bridge and risk being honked at by someone. When that happened it was usually the young, he'd noticed – the young people rushing down to or up from Chepstow, the M4, Bristol, London, to or from wherever, with no time to stand and stare.

Had he been the same at their age? He decided yes, he had been. He hoped his own father had known this feeling. And to Peter, young meant anyone under fifty, not just the teenagers from a different world with their gadgets and unfathomable ideas. There was Alice. She was young (*twenty-five* this summer, he thought) and still with her mysteries though her proper youth was long gone. He'd known of her unusual preoccupations from her parents, but overall she'd been a comfortable child to be with and grown into adulthood most successfully, becoming his favourite. She would not have honked at him on the bridge. She was young and he was old, and the gap between them was crucial, the generational distance which bridged over her parents and made it easier for them to connect. He had no memories of how difficult her growing up might have been, only seeing her now as finished, mature, an adult. He'd not had to deal with Alice's teenage traumas, the day after day of problems from school, the petulance and moodiness of growing up. She was always on her best behaviour when he or Clara were around. And he mused on how it wasn't new, this conflict: he remembered his own children and their obtuseness, and further back there was an illustration in one of his books of a stone tablet, incised with the strange barbed Cuneiform writing of the Chaldeans, two thousand years before Christ: *'Our youth is run down and immoral. Young people are not listening to their parents any more. The end of the world is near.'*

But the world had not ended – still it moved on; young people would come with their rebelliousness, grow up, become old and themselves despair of the young as their own parents had. He had a disturbing vision of Alice becoming old, and of her being cross with a beautiful child as yet unknown to him, his great-grandchild.

The teeming summer would return, when the valley would blossom and Peter's struggles with the last few brambles in his hedges would begin again. Then autumn, then winter. He found himself dwelling more and more on the passing of time, on the cycle of years, relentless and rushing, and on his own frailties. It was three weeks before his eighty-third birthday, and there would not be very many more summers, he thought... an odd thought, that he would leave it all behind, all the experiences and complications of his life; everything would turn off and he would end. Peter Bennett would end, long before Alice would end, and he would leave her.

He stepped out of his reverie and back from the window, into the room, uncluttered, open and calm. He was happy here, with his solitude, even without Clara. She was always in his memory but away from him now, and he was coping far better than he'd thought he would when she died. He'd done well, everyone agreed. But now, in some uncertainty, he felt more alone; a few miles from his daughter and granddaughter, yet far apart from them, at least apart from sharing uncommon knowledge with them. The death of Tom Fisher was troubling him. There was no real closure, as they say, for Peter. Tom had fallen into the Wye, and drowned, and the verdict was that he'd slipped on the bank and gone in... but there was more to it than that, for him. Why would they both be in her car in the lay-by up on the road? Saying goodbye, out of the rain, perhaps? But the rain was hardly anything. And saying goodbye, after what? Why was she there? He fretted over it but couldn't bring himself to ask her, and mulled over whether he even needed to, so for eleven days he'd kept it to himself.

The next day, Alice visited her grandfather at Celyn. Rachel was in Edinburgh, safely far away. Connie was with her parents in Hereford, apparently planning to stay there for good, and life with Jon had begun again. The precariousness of her situation played on her less. She phoned her grandfather first, but as he put the phone down he was perplexed, both happy and anxious about seeing her alone.

He went into his studio, for no reason except to think; it was where he concentrated best, where he worked things out. It was cluttered, as ever, with racks of shelving on the white walls stacked high with unframed canvasses, and many more standing on the floor, leaning against whatever was there, all the props and paraphernalia of his trade; the dust of years was layered on the paintings and the shelves, on everything apart from the table and the couple of easels he used, he having long given up trying to keep such disorder free of it. Not much had changed in the room since his wife had died, and that comforted him – never seeing it as clutter, rather as a host of memories – and on the big table where he'd worked with Alice were piles of books, and pages of sketches strewn around amongst pencils, tubes of paint, and brushes standing in Clara's once-precious Wedgwood milk jug, less precious after losing its handle. Colour was everywhere, in the caked palettes and splashed over easels, drips and smudges over the table and floor, the careless evidence of years of industry. He surveyed it all, and sat down in the well-worn leather chair he kept for his ultimate relaxation – no better place in the whole house for him to be comfortable, than to be in that chair and to look out upon the fruits of his life, preferably at the best time of his day, under bright sunlight – warm or otherwise – through the wide square roof light breaking the bare expanse of the studio ceiling.

Sometimes he would play music, for himself and his lost wife and think over the years they had spent there, but today he had other thoughts. Alice was coming – the first time he would see her alone since Tom Fisher had died, and he was still in the quandary of confronting her with what he'd seen, or leaving it. He thought there could be be a simple and harmless answer, but really he needed to know and he feared he could spoil her day – much more than her day, perhaps – so still he could not decide. And there was something new he wanted to show her – that letter from France – but dithering over his question made him want to keep it until he was sure, one way or the other.

Their talks were always easy, always relaxed, but today he guessed they would talk of serious things, of the funeral just past, and of the future and especially, hopefully, of Jon. The old Alice he remembered would return, and she would reassure him; those were his hopes as he sat and waited for her.

After ten minutes she tapped on the front door and came in; he jumped up, went to her and there was a longer hug than usual. They went through to the kitchen and sat at the table, a pot of coffee between them. She looked so much better than when he'd last seen her, two days before at the funeral.

"You're looking well Alice."

She spoke about herself and Jon, candidly and with only a slight edge of embarrassment, and carelessly put their recovery down to Tom's death, the shock, the realisation that there was more to life – the old story of the estranged couple brought together by a mutual trauma.

Then Alice admitted to him, for the first time, her problem, knowing he knew – knowing everyone knew – "I feel stupid now, over this baby thing," she said, "but it was very real. I felt so let down."

"But you're telling me it's past now, your baby thing?"

She didn't mind his levity. "Yes. But it took me over. It was impossible."

"Poor Jon, I suppose, but he should have been more aware of my granddaughter's requirements." She almost laughed at that, but her candour seemed weak to him. Peter watched her as she talked, casual and fresh, in a pale blue shirt and faded jeans, the thin line of a coloured velvet band around her neck. And those green eyes. He recalled his Clara at twenty-five years old, and for some reason wondered if this was the best age for a woman – an in-between age; but then, there would be more in-between ages for Alice as there had been for Clara, and again his thoughts were on the unending cycles of life. Such a shame, if he were to end this now, if he were to say something to spoil it all. He waited, and their talk came inevitably around to Tom.

He saw how animated Alice was when talking of him, how unbothered she seemed. She was almost chattering, something she didn't normally do, and he was bemused but he let her talk.

She spoke again of the Sunday afternoons she and Jon had spent at Rivendell, and what an odd couple they appeared to be, Tom and Connie. Then, while touching on the problems Tom appeared to have with his wife, Alice said, "On that weekend he seemed happier, somehow," referring to his last weekend, when he was alone at home, "so I wonder how happy they were together."

Peter's tone contrasted with hers. "That's sad, Alice. I'm sorry."

"But there was nothing to make us worry about him at all on that Sunday." An innocent reference to Tom being all right, but was it not an accident? Something felt wrong here. So then, he forced the moment. He needed to know. He would ask her, and she would reassure him.

"Yes, well. Did I see you parked at the top of his driveway on the Saturday evening, by the way? Was that him with you in the car?"

She was unable to hide the shock in her eyes. There was panic, a desperate scramble in her mind as she weighed it up. With no time for reflection she could think of nothing apart from, "Yes... he asked me to pop in for a coffee, then he came up to the car with me before I left. We chatted a bit. He was fine." *But why should he not have been fine?* Yet it was said, and now her temperature had risen with the lie, and her face coloured. She was a bad liar, and her grandfather saw it, felt it, like a punch to his chest; he looked long and hard at her, horrified at the possibilities, and as she said nothing more but sat there looking away, he reached for her hand and said, downbeat and saddened, "Alice, be careful my love."

The afternoon, and everything in it, was turned upside down. She couldn't stop the tears coming, so she got up and left him without a word, angry with him and herself for being caught out. He went out and stopped her as she got to her car. They stood in the sunshine, his hand on the open door, as he faced her.

"Alice, it's between us two. It won't go further, you understand? Please tell me."

She said nothing, but stood looking down, distressed. She was pulling the door away from him but he stopped her and gently pulled her away from the car. He put his arms around her, hugging her to him, and they stood together quietly in the warm sun before he had to let her go.

"I love you Alice. Don't hide this from me now."

When she'd gone, leaving him looking after her as she went

down the drive to the lane, he was more miserable than shocked, wishing he'd said more, or less, to her, reassured her more than he had. But most of all he wished for no one else to know what he knew.

She drove back down the valley. It was a beautiful spring afternoon and the roads were busier because of it – a Saturday, people out for the day. She drove automatically, noticing nothing, her head full of what had happened. She knew she couldn't leave it like that. He was the one she felt she could trust entirely, out of all her family – unlike her mother, and able to listen without a mother's ear. It was love without the complications and the sometimes stifling maternal concern. And her father, she'd feared, would want to take things much further than she'd like, to try to sort it all out for her. Surrounded by these different loves, it had to be her grandfather because she felt she could tell him anything, and everything, with impunity, despite the fear and appalling embarrassment she would feel after their friendly talk. And it was him who had seen her with Tom, which was both lucky for her and not… *Don't hide this from me now,* he'd said. She turned the car around, and went back to him.

He came out to meet her, and stood away from the car as she got out. They went inside together without speaking, to the same table in his kitchen and sat opposite each other with the same pot of coffee, now cool, between them. She was calm. He waited as she gathered her thoughts, and finally she settled her tearful gaze on him, breathed out audibly and said, "What I really want now is for you to forgive me."

"Alice, tell me what I'm forgiving you for."

When she didn't reply, he moved the coffee pot to the side, leaned forward and took both her hands in his across the table, a gesture that could have taken her back to a sultry garden, and different coffee, many years ago – a gesture for serious talk.

He said softly, "Of course I can forgive you Alice, of course I can."

The familiar reassurance. She looked into his eyes. "It was an infatuation. That's all it was."

Okay. He nodded slowly. "It happens."

All she said was, "Yes."

She almost broke down then, at that moment, but Peter said, "I can forgive you, no matter what. Remember that." He held her hands firmly in his, and slowly she came back to him.

After a long pause, he said, "Does anyone else know?"

A longer pause. "Jon may think... well, I don't know."

"Does he know you went to see Tom?"

"No."

She hesitated at the edge of telling him everything, and in the end simply said, "There's more, Grandad."

They sat, still holding hands, and she told him about Tom and how she'd fallen for him in her unhappiness, and how she could not help herself from then on. He sat and listened, not quite believing this was Alice, the weakness of her argument appalling him: *Of course you could have helped yourself.*

But she went on, stepped over that edge and told him of her despair regarding Rachel, who had somehow found out about their *friendship*, as Alice called it, and had faced her in her car.

Friendship? Peter listened as, like a forgiven and safe child, she let it all pour out of her.

"She said he killed himself for me. She said it was my fault."

But it wasn't an affair, she said; it was infatuation, an obsession she was helpless to escape, while never hinting at their final intimacy, avoiding the things she was sure would condemn her. She held back those two great secrets – the necklace, and the lovemaking. Things suddenly became impossibly unreal.

"Are you telling me it wasn't an affair? A sexual thing?"

It was a shock – her aged grandfather asking her directly about sex. He'd tested her with the words she'd wanted to avoid, but she had already resolved the question.

"No, really it wasn't."

Peter let her talk, incredulous and deeply shaken by what she was saying. He said nothing more, but as she spoke he saw in his mind a course of events that looked likely to him: *they had sex – what else do 'infatuated' people do at such times? Hold hands? Play cards?* So, guilt and despair – to the likely end for someone like the man she'd described. She'd told him of Tom's love for his daughter and his unhappiness with his wife, and his sensitivity, his despondency. It really was a plausible outcome.

For her it was done, and all she wanted was for her grandfather to live forever, to always be there for her, sharing the weight of those secrets. She hoped she could always talk to him now, whatever came along; it could all be shared – unless, she thought, with a rush of unease, Rachel tells it all. *If she does, my world ends.*

He concealed his alarm, finding the words to tell her not to really fear Rachel, because although he would expect her to hate Alice, nothing would happen while unsuspecting Connie was alive, and he didn't think her hatred would last. He thought she would want to be rid of it and the best way was through forgiveness, he said, not revenge. If what Alice had told him was true, then Tom was comforted by her and if Rachel loved her father, that knowledge would, or should, make a difference. He had faith in that daughter, an optimism for someone he'd never met.

They sat in the sunlit kitchen, she with her head bowed and he looking at the green fields beyond the window, overwhelmingly laden with the tangled mess of her life as it now was, storing her confessions – and the worry of what she hadn't confessed – for unravelling later when he was alone in his favourite chair in his favourite room.

Alice wondered about his real thoughts, behind the mask of kindness - *What do you think of me?* - but to him she was like a child again, trying out people, and failing. Alice slowly stood up. She began to cry again and Peter comforted her, hugging her as they stood quietly in the middle of his kitchen. He knew he would have to forgive her for it all... even the parts he was sure she'd left out. *How did Rachel find out? So you didn't ask her?* It wouldn't really change things now, but in time he would want to know. As they parted he said, "I want you to tell Jon what you've told me. He'll ask you questions, and you must be honest. He won't forgive you if you're not."

She sat in her car as he stood at the open window, and told him she couldn't do it.

"Look, if you think he suspects anything, you must tell him. Think of him not trusting you for ever, or somehow finding out. Tell him, then the three of us will know. We'll be with you, and you won't lose Jon."

"I don't know if I can."

"Yes you can. Do it, Alice."

Peter went back inside when she'd gone, feeling the weight of the world on him. He was crushed – his beloved granddaughter, having a fling with her husband's employer, then him probably killing himself for her; the police led to believe something different, and an angry and unpredictable woman waiting in the wings. *So don't tell anyone, Peter. Keep it all under your hat.*

: : :

The next morning, Alice woke with the resolve to talk with Jon, to do as her grandfather had said. It was early, not quite six-thirty, and as it was Sunday there was no need for her to be up for an hour so they lay side by side, she awake and he asleep. She had slept badly in the first half of the night, being awake until after three, her mind far too active. She'd worn herself out with the possibilities of the coming day; she had promised herself to give Jon the truth and spent hours undoing then remaking that promise. But what should that truth be? It ought to match what she'd told her grandfather – but now she doubted the wisdom of telling the old man anything. If only she'd known he'd seen them together, if only she'd had time to work something out. But if she had, how would it feel to have to keep those secrets for ever? *Maybe it's best like this, half-told, half-hidden.*

In the black stillness she'd lain there, waiting for the old clock downstairs to chime, drifting in and out of a shallow sleep and wondering what a single chime meant – one o'clock, or half-past something? Waiting for the hour, then despairing at the lateness, but in the end calmness had come with exhaustion and she'd given in to it with her resolve in place.

Now she felt the need to wake him, to get it out of the way. She felt strong, determined. Jon was lying away from her as he slept, the way he always did, in good times and bad, so she turned to face him and stroked his hair as he slept, feeling sorry for having to wake him. Slowly he stirred, then turned his face to her. She kissed his forehead.

"I love you," she whispered, as he came to his senses and focused on her. He lay there, looking at her face, and drowsily said back to her, "I love you." Then, without feeling the immensity of what she had to say, she said, "We need to talk, Jon."

He asked what the time was and she told him, and apologised. He sighed heavily and turned onto his back.

Again she said, "We need to talk." He was fully awake now, and simply said, "Okay."

A door slammed somewhere below them, far away, in another universe. Suddenly she was afraid but there was no going back, apart from jumping out of bed and running away.

She pushed the words out. "Jon, it's about Tom."

"Yes, I know."

Shock, and a pause, then, "I don't know where to start with this..."

He said, "Well let me start. Can I ask you one thing?"

She knew what that would be. He turned onto his side towards her. "Did you have sex with him?"

She shook her head slightly and said, without hesitation, "No."

And now he didn't know what to think. For several seconds they lay there, looking at each other, the words they'd both rehearsed over and over not fitting any more. He'd thought he would now be thanking her for being honest, and Alice had lost the thread of her own script, as the reality of her situation returned and crushed her. She turned onto her back and stared at the ceiling. He saw the corners of her mouth go down, and he knew she would cry. She covered her face with her hands and he put his arm across her, to touch her, and comfort her, and her voice almost broke as she said, "Jon, there's a lot more." He stayed as he was, looking sideways at her, and straight away she confessed.

"I fell in love with him."

She lay there weeping and he shook her gently. "Come on, come on." He moved against her, pulling her close. "Alice, talk to me." But she wept under her hands, unable to say more.

Later, when the talking was over, she turned away from him onto her side. He moved closer, legs pulled up and nestled into her, his arm over, his hand resting on her breast. It was how they lay when talking, or thinking, or just feeling close; a restful, sensual closeness, folded into each other. Nothing more was said, then Alice turned to him, quickly kissed him, and got up. She left him there with his thoughts. He watched her as she moved around the room, busy with her morning routine, in and out of the shower, dressing, fussing in the shortness of time she had. But she looked different to him now – the same good looks, but as he watched her there was a detachment. She had stepped slightly but definitely away from being *his* Alice; he watched her every move, but she readied herself as if he wasn't there.

Before leaving she leaned over him and said, nervously, "Will we be all right, Jon?" and he said yes, they would be. It was the right answer. She ran her fingers through his hair, smiled uneasily at him and left the room.

Alice's morning was one of fragile relief. In that hour after waking she'd finally told him what she'd told her grandfather, a re-run of her confession.

"He saw me... in the car with him, on the Saturday," she'd said through her tears as he'd held her, after she'd lied to him over the sex, unsure of whether the lie had worked. As with her grandfather, it had not. It was obvious to Jon but he had to go with it – there was no way now she would change her mind and admit she had.

So her circle had become a confiding group of three, with her parents and everyone else outside, and this was the first day of her new life. She was twenty-five years old. How will things be when she's fifty, or sixty? Her relief remained fragile.

Jon's day was different. A clear blue Sunday, the sort of day that took him outside, to potter, to chop wood or clean their cars. He did the easiest task, the cleaning of cars, needing less focus than wielding an axe. Alice's words as they had lain together went round and round. The day slipped by and they met off and on, both busy, looking at each other with wariness hidden behind half-smiles, and trapped in his head was her pitiable question: *Will we be all right, Jon?* – and the answer he should have given: *I don't know Alice, is the truth. I just don't know.*

In the time since Tom's death Jon had hoped – but without much confidence – that she had gone only one step further than he had with Connie, the step of declaring her interest. Then he'd remembered his own first experience with her, to how in-different she was to unguarded sex. And her eagerness with him, also unguarded, the night after Tom died. The imagined and the real chain of events both made terrible sense to him and he suddenly had the disquieting thought that it was lucky for her that Tom wasn't black, or Asian, or anything other than he was. That would have given her more to worry about.

He'd been horrified and silent when she'd weepingly told him of Rachel's anger in the car, albeit with the necklace edited out; how Rachel had known about them, she wasn't sure, she'd said. He needed time to think, and the more he thought about it the worse it became. He would also be at the mercy of his imagination for nine months if she were pregnant now. And what then? A lovely child, but would it be his? Would he actually want to know? And how would it feel, forever having that fifty percent doubt? And he also thought of her grandfather Peter having the same doubt, and probably Rachel too.

But throughout it all, at the back of his mind loitered the possibility that she'd told him the truth, and any child that came would be his own. He wished he could fall asleep and absurdly wake into a new life, on a sunny day like today where everything was put right and they could start all over again, but the reality was that if any happiness was to come he would have to forgive her, for everything that had happened, and everything that was to come. So although Alice had deceived him he would spend his life doing that, hoping that things really would be all right, but optimism was something else.

Meanwhile, Connie was still big in his mind, and what he would have liked to do with her; she was fixed there, a reminder of his own virtual adultery, a reminder that this situation could have been turned the other way. His feelings for her had changed from desire to compassion, and above all he wished her peace; even thinking of what had excited him about her had lost its thrill. She was his boss's wife and would always remind him of the times his desire for Alice had faded. Connie had stepped into his life, and now stepped out.

: : :

I was spellbound and only saw my dream coming true, that's all I saw. I didn't need to wish for it, it would work. All I wanted was for Tom to give the necklace back to me – I was blind to everything else.

Alice had not shared those things with Jon. The giving of the necklace, that symbol of love, had become impossible – it would never be properly understood. She went through the hotel in her work, the familiar surroundings, every room, the sun-slanted passageways, all the parts of the big house, her mind turning this way and that and as the afternoon ended she had lost the feeling she'd had that morning – her relief had gone. The slate would never be wiped clean with Jon; her position was fixed, and there was no rewind button, as she'd once reminded him.

She worried through the afternoon, but then the end of the day brought a sudden and extraordinary change – another of her deliverances; it all turned around and she wondered why she had even considered telling him more. Her thoughts had exhausted her, and at the lowest point she simply let it all go, all the anxiety, in an instant and revelatory release. She made the crucial decision that those things were far too personal anyway, and would never be understood; so it was simple – she came full circle and would keep the leftover secrets she had. Her grandfather didn't know either, so he and Jon would both have the same understanding. She told herself they were secrets from a different time, from a different person, and could be forgotten... so again, after hours of struggling she had successfully stepped back from it and put her anxiety, along with Rachel and the necklace, into the deep and dark velvet box at the back of her mind.

∶ ∶ ∶

In the time since making love to her lover and her husband, two days apart, Alice had thought she was pregnant. There was something unusual: a slight tiredness, an even slighter nausea, but both too vague to believe and by the morning of her confessions to Jon she thought she'd imagined it, after expecting it, almost. Those feelings had faded, then returned, then faded again in the ten days between death and funeral and now she was free of them. She felt nothing, she felt normal, she felt *safe*.

For Peter, the hardest thing was no longer Alice's brief affair with Tom, but rather that her parents – his daughter and son-in-law – knew nothing of it. There had been times in the last few days when he'd almost convinced himself to tell them, to force it into the open and deal with it. Alice had called and told him about her confession to Jon, so one less secret to worry about even though his next meeting with him promised to be strange, with the knowledge they both had. It was her parents that worried him now. The days of being honest, of sharing, were modified by *them and us*, and the possibility of slipping up terrified him. *Mercifully short, this life of mine.*

∴ ∴ ∴

It was the first day of a new month, and a sublime start to April. Peter followed the river, – glimpsing it through the trees – passed a couple of half-hidden houses, went through Llandogo and a few minutes later turned into the car park in front of The Wondrous Gift. He hadn't chosen a time, but would simply drop in and distract Alice for a few minutes and show her the letter he'd had from France – that was the plan for today.

He found her in the Dining Room, going through a pile of menus. The room was threequarters full and he had the awkward feeling of intruding, of being a trespasser with no intention of eating, and they hugged each other in front of an elderly couple at a table who smiled at them, amused to see the Manager embracing someone, and the slight softening of her authority. She took him away, into the kitchen. He'd promised himself to be upbeat.

"It's good to see you," he said. "Are you surviving?"

She said quietly, "I am, yes."

"Good. How's Jon?"

"He's quiet. I hope he can forgive me."

"I hope so too. I hope all will be well."

Now she wanted to say sorry, to start it all over again, as if it would be better second time around. They stood facing each other, careful with their words as people came and went, both with questions but no safe way to ask them. There was a moment of silence, then Peter said, "I have something to show you. Look." He took the letter from his pocket. "This came the other day." He handed it to her. She began reading, and was as shocked by the first paragraph as he had been. She looked at him in astonishment, and in the warmth of the kitchen they sat down at an out-of-the-way table and she read it through. It was extraordinary. Here was Béatrice, in the flesh, and here was the handwriting of her descendant, describing her life after Phillip. But as she read she realised that Peter had not known of her at all, and a struggle began inside her about the Journal and whether she should tell him about it. She could do without another secret, and if ever that secret were revealed to him she would simply appear even worse in his eyes. He would be even more disappointed in her – his special, *favourite* granddaughter, lying and pretending to him. Béatrice had changed the situation. She finished reading and the words blurred as she kept looking at them, and pondered. Now would be the time to tell him, now or never. The traumas of a few days were overshadowed.

"Well... I don't know what to say."

He was leaning back in his chair, hands clasped in his lap, smiling at her. "That's one surprise I could never have imagined."

Now or never. But still she wavered. "Are there any implications from this? That we have relatives in France?"

"The implications are just that – we have very distant relatives in France. I'll write back to him, invite him over, I think."

She looked across at her smiling grandfather and suddenly it was out of her hands – she would have to let Phillip go, and it didn't hurt as she'd thought it would. She gave the letter back to him; he folded it and started to get up from his chair, wanting to let her get on, but she told him to stay there.

"I've got something very special for *you*."

They stared at each other in silence. Her expression was apologetic. *"I've already met Béatrice."*

Peter's face didn't change.

She said, "Won't be a moment," then left him and went upstairs, passing a pensive Aku, who simply said, *"Alice?"* but her mind was now with the explanation she would need to give her grandfather for not sharing the Journal sooner.

March. She'd found it in early March, she'd say, long after he'd shown her his finished *History* and then events had made her forget about it. Just a few weeks ago. She'd been meaning to show him, but, well... here it is! So another secret would go, helped on its way by another lie – a small, helpful, harmless lie perhaps.

But she had not prepared for this, and in a rush removed all the coloured strips she'd so carefully put in, surprised now at how many there were. Favourite pages went back into the depths of the book. Then, as she went back downstairs with it, Béatrice's letter came to her – invisible and safe now, and she couldn't possibly tell him. It was there, to be discovered again. *Just go to a different bookbinder, please!*

It had taken her longer than she'd thought it would, but at last she put the Journal on the table in front of Peter, as gravely as treasure given away, and in her heart she was certain of its safety from then on. A questioning look, then he opened the cover and saw the first few lines:

The Private Journal of Phillip Rossetti
Owner & Master of the Barque FLORENCE
of Bristol, England
Begun this 12th of September, 1825
Omnia vincit Amor; et nos cedamus Amori

After those magical words he was lost. He said nothing, imagining the treasure in front of him, and as he turned the pages he was as overwhelmed as Alice had been months before, alone in her attic.

She said, "I should have given it to you sooner, sorry. But I've only had it a few weeks." Nothing she could have said would have spoiled his delight, and for that moment, and in the midst of his dark anxieties over Alice, Peter felt that maybe the future would not be as bad as he'd feared. The reverence he'd seen in her as she'd given it told him that this was something beyond special – and she was happy to let him see it, to share it with him. It was possibly another liberation for her.

: : :

Since her father's death, Rachel had called twice at the factory in Chepstow, where Jon and Afia were spending long hours tying the loose ends Tom had left. The business was now Connie's but she was completely out of it, mentally and physically, and far away in Hereford.

"Do whatever's necessary," she'd said – three words to describe a mountain of effort and worry... tiresome discussions with their accountant, visits to their solicitor and bank manager, following the tedious path to Sims Flight Instrumentation continuing in the best way, *the most advantageous way*, her accountant had said – but Rachel had long ago been turned off by the language of business, and longed to get back to her children, impossibly far away in Scotland.

After two weeks the future of SFI was settled, apart from the question of someone to run it all. In quiet desperation Jon had followed his intuition and contacted the men who had left Tom for Rolls Royce, and found interest from one of them who had left with hopes so different from Jon's, and he could come back to the Manager's job at Chepstow if it suited them all. A decision would come but until then Jon was acting manager and would wait for his Chief Engineer slot to return. The business was being saved.

: : :

On that same first of April Rachel sat at her kitchen table in Edinburgh, talking to Jon at Chepstow. Their conversation was more relaxed – there was nothing to be done now apart from welcoming a new manager, and Jon was convinced his man would come from Filton with his precious knowledge and ambition, and make everything easier. The business was proceeding, the future was promising, and their talk was superficial – they came to the end of it and Rachel said, "I'll be down on Friday for a couple of days, then back up on Monday. A bit hectic, but it's how it is."

Jon asked if he could help her at Rivendell, but she said she had all the help she needed, and that led into a long silence, several seconds of something between them. They had not mentioned Alice in the weeks before when they'd met or spoken on the phone; it had all been about the business – intense, and focused. Rachel's anger was still sharp. There had been many tears since, and when alone, which was often, she would travel the routes open to her, going through each punishing scenario of harming Alice or Jon or both... but in the end, after each revengeful bout she came back to the same point, of the necessary peace with Jon, at least until the business was stable again. But what then? Would that be the happy land of salvation? How could it be? Would it be different, simply because the business was safe?

Jon was a big part of her life, like it or not, and if she kept him on board she ought to be at ease with him – at ease with the man whose wife had taken her father from her. *The woman he goes home to each night.* How much does he know? How close are they now? Does he kiss her? Do they have sex? And then a thought she couldn't help – *Did she have sex with my father?*

It was more than two weeks since it had happened, a long sixteen days of relentless effort for Rachel and Jon and Afia, while Alice floated somewhere on the fringes, unmentioned. But now she was becoming impossible to ignore. Jon sat behind the glass wall in Tom Fisher's office, leaning back in the black leather chair, phone in hand, apprehensive and looking for all the world like the executive he didn't want to be.

He took a deep breath. "Rachel, we need to talk."

"I know, Jon."

A pause. "I'm so sorry about Alice."

Good. "What has she told you?"

"That she had, well, she called it an infatuation. With your father."

She closed her eyes. She could have leapt on that word.

"But I don't know how far it went, Rachel."

No confessions from his wife, then.

"And are you coping with that? With not knowing?"

"I guess I'll have to. But you must know more than I do. You were very cold with her."

"I was upset Jon. No one was safe."

"How did you find out?"

And now she had to lie. She'd had no idea before she'd found the necklace, and the necklace was a secret, so far, like the suicide – things she was holding back.

"I found out. There were signs."

"What signs?"

"It was clear to me. And to you, I think."

True. There were signs. "So what happened that Sunday?"

"Jon, I wasn't there."

In those moments it would have been easy to tell him everything, all the things he didn't appear to know - the necklace, her father's suicide. She could spill the beans, make life so much more difficult for Alice – a few more words, that's all it would take, and from the safety of Edinburgh she could put the phone down on their life together and let them sort it out. But there was magnanimity as well as grievance, and after a moment's reflection she said, "I think you know as much as I do."

Not true, he knew, but he let it go. He was more than sorry, and really, this was all she needed to hear from him. Their life was out of her hands now, and it was over – her days and weeks of running and re-running this conversation had come down to a few words.

She said, "I'll get back to my work now. Call me if you need me, for anything at all."

They finished their call, and Jon stared at the wall opposite, at a cluttered pinboard. In the bottom right corner was an old photograph, curled a little at the edges, the colours faded: Tom and Connie with a young Rachel between them, on a beach somewhere, smiling. And once again he wasn't sure that he wanted to know everything.

: : :

That evening Alice lied to Jon again. He had waited two days for her to volunteer more of her story, two days of a different relationship – one of tenderness mixed with anxiety. There was one thing he needed to know, as if it would answer all his questions - how Rachel had found out about her and Tom. His talk with Rachel had given him nothing new.

They were together in their living room, having come up from their supper; the room was slowly darkening, and Alice had put the lights on and gone over to close the curtains when Jon had asked her. She sat down beside him and said the words she'd prepared, outwardly smooth, inwardly despairing.

"She said she'd seen Tom looking at me, when we were looking at the pictures in the corridor." She paused. "And again later, when we were all having tea."

She looked down at his hand and reached for it in the gap

between them, entwining her fingers in his.

Jon said, "So she worked it all out from that? Just a few looks?"

She was unconvincing. "She said it was."

She'd almost cried then, with the hopelessness of what she was saying, but instead stood up, walked away then turned back to face him, and her eyes were shining with tears. Her quiet distress moved him. He stood up and took her in his arms, and she rested her head against him.

He said softly, "Alice, don't suffer like this. We've come a long way now. Can't you tell me?"

He held her to him, standing in the middle of the room, and he said, "Just don't be so afraid of me, of what I'll think of you. I love you."

His hand was in her hair, caressing her, and after a short while he said quietly, "Alice... you did have sex with him, didn't you."

She didn't move. The moment had arrived, as she'd known it would. *He said he loved her.* But she moved away from him and he said, "It's okay Alice, it's okay."

She looked at him through her tears, shook her head slowly and said, "It's not okay. But not now. I'm so sorry," then turned and left the room.

Afterwards he'd gone out into the evening, to the car park, and sat in his car. *So I have my wife back. Alice will return with her secrets, to me with mine, and maybe we'll rid ourselves of them. How to overcome this... I know there's more than sex, more than just a fling, but I can imagine how hard it must be to tell me. So that's love, I guess – to not knock her down. What she did was no worse, really, than my own thing with Connie. If I'd had the opportunity, I would have had Connie. Alice knows nothing about that... should I ever tell her? Would it help her – help us, to balance things out? Connie, Connie... what a secret you are.*

He looked through the windscreen at the hotel – his home now, for better or worse. Elena and David were always kind to him. He saw the young plants in the narrow border leading to the entrance and thought, *springtime. Everything is growing now. A time for growth, for new things to begin.* It was trite, but it helped him see that even if he lived with uncertainties for ever, he and Alice – these two adulterers – could make a new start. Could a fling be forgiven, in the light of his own guilt over Connie? Possibly. Yet the one had happened, the other had not. But there was no anger in either of them now. He wanted her as she used to be, in their first years together – happy, loving, without secrets, and beautiful... always beautiful, in so many ways, before he let her down. On one level he could not imagine what could be worse for her than admitting to an affair with Tom Fisher. But Tom was dead, and there was more – lots more he could imagine.

Maybe in time she could tell her story and there would be no more secrets, but now as the night began and the wind picked up he stayed in the safety of his car. Then, when he went back inside all his doubts had returned: his battle was just beginning, and even after tonight had long passed he would wonder, *am I strong enough for this?*

Later that night, and filled with the doubts of her life, Alice lay with her husband in the warmth of their bed and quietly asked him, "Will you stay with me, Jon?"

They were in each other's arms, and there was no thought of lovemaking. As April gusts rattled the windows they were safe together, but the frailty of her voice almost brought him to tears.

"Of course I will, " he said.

HEREFORD, A FEW DAYS LATER

The road was as Connie had always known it – the cul-de-sac of brick and painted stone houses giving way to school buildings, themselves giving way to the clipped lawns beyond the Cathedral gates. It was still term-time. The weekdays were quiet then busy as the younger children criss-crossed the road, changing buildings and classes, moving the way children do... singly, or in knots, chattering or thoughtful, some rushing but most dragging the time before the next lesson. As a child she had watched them from her window, wondering what school would be like, but now there were no more unknowns; she had grown beyond them, grown up, moved away and married and now she had returned.

The room she left for university in 1970 was hers again, twenty-seven years later; once more, in a replay of her childhood, she watched from that same window as the children came and went, and calmly accepted that this full-circle journey was as far as it would go – that she would grow old with her father and mother, staying on after them and finally being quite alone. She thought that's how it would go.

She had come home with them in the late evening of the day she had lost her husband, three weeks ago now, and since then had thought of little else but how that loss came about. But now her thoughts wandered as she sat at the window, looking along the street on that fresh April day, two weeks after Easter. School term would run another few months then all those children would disperse, spread out over the city and the country for the summer and the street would be quiet again.

She had not returned to Redbrook, to Rivendell, since leaving in disarray that terrible Monday. She'd said she would never go back, and in the three weeks since had not changed her mind. Today though, she was looking out for her daughter. Rachel had arrived from Edinburgh on Friday evening, spent two nights and almost two days at Rivendell, and would break her return journey to be with her mother and grandparents at teatime. There was much to do at the house by the river and Rachel was doing that duty alone, emptying it, readying it to be sold. She wanted no help, and the advice from her mother was simply to sell everything. Connie wanted their photo albums, twenty-three of them – one for each year she'd had Tom – and apart from her camera, a few books, her clothes, and half-a-dozen small and precious reminders of better times, the rest could go... almost the entire gatherings of her life with Tom could go.

She got to her feet as the car pulled up outside. The front door opened and Rachel came in to the atmosphere she'd always treasured – the smiles, the gentleness, the caring warmth of her only grandparents, but now also an almost painful drawn-out hug from her mother. The four of them sat in the front room at the table by the netted window to the street, and had tea.

The little house closed down as the evening ended. As ten o'clock passed Connie's parents tidied everything then went to bed, leaving her and Rachel to themselves in the subdued light of their living room. They sat in the ambience of times-gone-by: the dark pictures on the walls, the heavy curtains, the lack of modernity – an antiquated radio on an antique sideboard – the whole scene only lacking a hanging oil lamp to whisk it back to Edwardian times. It was warm, and comfortable, and it was where Connie had grown up. She was resettled already, and even after twenty-seven years would need few adjustments to slot back in. Placidly free of ambition, the path of her remaining life seemed to be in the surroundings of her remembered childhood, the memories of her grandparents and the unchanging love of her parents, and she was comforted. She had abandoned her previous life and let it all go, even her need to make herself up; her face, clean and clear in the soft light, was suddenly beautiful to Rachel. *She looks calm. Maybe she's found her real home, at last.*

In answer to the expected *Are you managing okay at Rivendell* question, Rachel simply said, "Yes, it's going well," knowing nothing more detailed was needed and that it would all move on without her mother. She looked across at her, and again had the thought that perhaps this was the best ending, the best way for her after a life that was imperfect with a man she loved but often despaired of. Rachel knew about these things, had known them for most of her life; any observer could have seen the gap between her parents, and she was not just any observer; she had witnessed many silences, and barely concealed annoyances with each other – moments of *Okay, okay...*

As these thoughts were going around in Rachel's head, Connie suddenly said, out of nowhere, "You know, I wonder about your father." A long pause. Rachel waited. "I wouldn't be too surprised... if he'd done it on purpose." She spoke the words vaguely, away into space, then looked back to her daughter and said, "It wouldn't surprise me."

She was so calm, so easy about it, this momentous announcement, that Rachel was taken aback. There was no leading up to it, no treading carefully, no mother-to-daughter thoughtfulness – she had simply dropped the unexpected notion of suicide onto her, and it was as uncaring as her father had sometimes been to her. Again, she saw how they had always been too tied up in each other.

There were a few seconds of silence, then Rachel said the best thing, although it would have been unthinkable before his death – "I think it's possible. I'm sorry Mum." She dared not show her relief as one of the biggest of her three-week secrets dissolved into nothing.

Connie nodded her head slowly, and drifted away again. *Death by misadventure.* For three weeks she'd wanted to believe it, that he'd fallen from a path he'd walked hundreds of times before, that it was an accident, but she could not. Since his death she'd looked anyway for the reasons she already knew of, for clues, for any thread that could have led eventually to his suicide. It was not difficult – there were scores of them; twenty-three years' worth of bad omens, a shower of remembrances that peppered their times together. She went over the very first days with Tom – her awe of him, his caring patience with her. Endlessly kind, endlessly forgiving, while in truth his stoical kindness was the veneer covering his intolerance, and in time, she knew it – but what was she to do? She loved him, she wanted him, so she kept him, for twenty-three years. A long time, and through most of it she'd felt a guilt that unknowingly matched her husband's.

They sat in the enveloping warmth, with everything familiar to Connie. The ceaseless, dull, reassuring ticking of the clock had not changed. The soporific dimness of the wall lights brought back the memories of her growing-up, sitting in front of the fire reading in her soft circle of light, away from the darkened corners of the room - the ghost of her childhood, in this very chair.

Not much had changed here. They were comfortable, and through the long silences Rachel felt her mother's calmness. Still distracted and looking away, Connie quietly said, "I know I wasn't his dream girl. So many things we didn't really agree on, but he tried to be kind... I think he'd had enough of life, maybe enough of me, and couldn't really bear hurting me for ever."

It was hard to listen to, and after a while Rachel turned her away from it and went over the memories that made them more cheerful, of holidays, the days when Rachel was a child and laughed with them in the sun. They talked about him with the detachment of a lost friend, reminiscing, and for a time put away the sudden acceptance of his suicide and thought of the other side of their husband and father, the side they could enjoy in the meagreness of their low spirits. They called up the happy times, and smiled as they remembered but the cliff edge was close, especially for Connie, and after a few minutes it brought her to a halt.

She looked into her daughter's eyes and said, "I think your father had girlfriends," as if it just had to come out.

It was close to midnight when they parted, leaving the house in darkness as they went to their rooms. Connie, a little slower, a little older, opened her door and Rachel saw her future in the small friendly house, shuffling around with her thoughts, living out the years.

Connie hadn't wanted to think any deeper about those girl-friends, she'd said, again without concern for her daughter. She'd spoken her mind, saying she didn't know names, or faces, or times... it was just a feeling she'd had for the past ten years or so, but again, it wouldn't have surprised her. But no proof. Rachel listened. "There was a girl in Monmouth – in Wigmore's. I saw the way he looked at her..."

She'd sat through it, taking in one wretched, uncertain revelation after another, while wanting to get up and leave her disconnected mother to her ramblings. Later it came to her that even if she'd told her about Alice Greerson, she would have shrugged it off. She felt a soft relief for her, knowing that this was the endgame and that nobody had won; there would be no last laugh. Her mother had merely survived, and her unhappy father had gone for ever. It was settled.

Rachel lay in her bed listening to far-off traffic, the street lights taking the edge off the darkness, and tried to order her life. It was still messy. She needed to forgive her father for abandoning her and her mother. And there were still secrets to be kept. She wanted more, more things sorted, less to carry forward. Her mother, she thought, was now settled, having shared her husband and closed her mind to other possibilities. They could rest in peace for each other. There was just Alice Greerson. Would it help if she let it go with her? Not complete forgiveness – never that – but a new understanding of them both, she and her father. If she gave him some comfort – it probably didn't matter how – that could also be a comfort to Rachel.

She thought she could overcome the simplicity of what Alice

had done with her father – the affair, however short or long – and perhaps she could begin to forgive her for that. Alice did not foresee his death. Whatever was in her mind with the necklace seemed irrelevant, a silly dreamy thing, but if it tipped him over then that was the sin, and as long as she saw her as the cause of his death, forgiveness would be impossible.

The equation was this: on the one side, the affair – she still felt sure she'd started it – and on the other, the comfort he'd had from it. Could she balance that out in her mind? It just depended on which side she placed his death, which way she tipped the scales, because there was a need for blame. Could she give it to them both, equally? And would that allow her to forgive them both? She was deeply unhappy about forever holding bitterness in her heart. With tears not far away and the rest of her life in front of her, she realised his suicide was probably inevitable, if not with Alice then with someone else as yet unknown.

:::

At the end of that week, and far away to the north, Rachel stood at her bedroom window and looked out at Edinburgh. The sunshine of recent weeks had gone, and heavy grey clouds were scudding across, promising rain. The buildings were drab, the few trees rustling in the breeze as they waited for the rain in the failing light. She was at the end of her week away. She wanted to get her work at Rivendell done and over with, and tomorrow after breakfast she would throw a few things into the car and drive the three hundred and fifty miles back to her mother, and to the house, to four days of her other life. Seven hours driving, two hours eating and resting, then hopefully an early night at her grandparent's house in Hereford. She would leave Restalrig by nine, and be there, in the quiet street leading to the Cathedral gates, by early evening – but the steady finishing of her tasks and the uncertain comfort of her mother had become meagre rewards for the long journey.

The next morning, on the seat next to her in the car was a half-finished letter. She would work on it in the coming days until it said precisely what she wanted it to say, and post it before she left for Scotland again at the end of what would be a week of changes, of winding down. She drove through the wet streets, around the city, away to the west and out towards Carlisle and the south. It was the ending of the hard times – the last few days at the sad house by the river, and the last of the regular stop-offs with her mother. She would leave Connie, as surely as she would leave Rivendell, returning to Hereford in a month's time, she hoped, and then spacing her visits to suit herself rather than heeding her mother's pleas to come back soon; the bigger reason had become the house, and that would come to an end. She would return to Edinburgh, to her work at Leith Academy.

Too early on a Friday morning Alice lay in bed, wide awake. Her mind was on the day ahead, a day she'd decided upon in an almost sleepless night. She would go to Monmouth, to The Kymin Hill, to the place where she'd taken Tom and loved him. She would sit where they had sat, and she would overcome him, exorcise him... she'd spent hours coming to that decision, resolving to bring back a precious hour, to relive it and then let it go, and let him go with it. Alice, quietly dreaming Alice, believed it would happen.

She got out of bed, pulled on her dressing gown and went into the study, closing the door slowly and painfully to avoid waking Jon. She opened the curtains and sat under the window, at Phillip Rossetti's desk. Through the window the world was white, the blanket of mist having crept up from the river during the night and covered everything. There would be pale blue sky waiting above it, and eventually the thin sun's warmth would burn through and bring another beautiful April morning, cool then warm as the day progressed. That's how it would be. She looked forward to her day.

She sat with Phillip Rossetti's Journal in front of her, and it didn't matter anymore if someone caught her with it but it was odd, and sometimes regrettable not to have it to herself, not to have Phillip to herself. Her grandfather had kept it for two weeks then given it back to her, sensing a need greater than his own, and since then everyone had seen it – but it was *Alice's book* to them all, even without knowing of her earlier dependence on it.

The Journal had become the symbol of Alice's return from her dark days, and her grandfather Peter was content to let it be, and not rewrite his own version of their history in the light of it, but rather had tried to recover the life he'd had before Alice's crisis of October. Springtime returned to the winter of his life because she had returned to them all, happy to be seen as recovered in spite of her deep secrets. By now Peter had managed to find a reliable if miserable way of coping – it simply meant he visited the hotel less often than he would like, a sure way of reducing the odds of him making a mistake. He became distant, and found reasons to decline offers of the Sunday lunches he used to look forward to.

He did not envy Jon, moving in the circles he did, forever having to be on his guard. So the three people who knew had somehow reached a way for themselves to cope, different from each other maybe, but a way that worked until the inevitable day when a slip would be made, memories tested, or complete disclosure came from Tom's daughter. That would be a day to remember, and the three souls in the Wye Valley waited and wondered.

Her grandfather had voiced his fears again a few days before, reminding her of the anxiety she was causing, reminding her of his suffering.

"This is very difficult Alice," he'd said, and encouraged her to face the problem before it was forced upon her but she'd replied, "Give me some time... please," and he'd left it at that, incapable of pushing it further.

She sat before the window and the white, shrouded world outside, and opened the Journal to a passage that used to have a yellow marker, one she'd read many times and which she'd decided upon during the night. It was an account of longing and love and warmth, of a castle on the Lake of Geneva, of a moment of realisation for Phillip that all would be well, and it resonated with her. It was profoundly evocative of a very special time, but really it was about forgiveness, the thing she wanted above all for herself.

Looking up from the Journal and across the room, to the closed door between her and her sleeping husband, she realised how lucky she was; she had him, and he was alive and close, not half a world away as Béatrice had been for Phillip. Today, she would try to change her life.

Her mind went back and she was on the train with her parents in the heat from Martigny to Montreux which took her past the Château of Chillon – a place to explore some other time, but she'd never gone back. And now she was reading again about Phillip longing to go there, and she wondered how it would have been in his time, without the railway or the busy roads, only the vineyards and the wooded mountain rising behind the solitary and splendid Château alongside the lake and the dusty carriage road. She began reading from August 1828 – after Phillip's revelations of Béatrice and in the heartbreaking year after losing Janet:

'Some five years ago & in the midst of my unending sorrow for Béatrice, in a short time it seemed that a great part of my suffering was overcome. Until then my thoughts had dwelt overmuch on the conversation We had in that calm place at Morlaix & in particular Her description of Her time at the Castle of Chillon. She told me of swimming there, in the cool Summer water under the Castle walls in complete freedom, & of how such freedom was rare for Her, & I longed to swim in that same water.

'I thought too much on Her being in that place, so well described for me, & my Heart was heavy for not having been there with Her. As I once again indulged my grief while imagining Béatrice there, at last, & quite calmly, a realisation came to me that this was enough & my melancholy could not continue for fear of destroying me. So I was able to let the dream cleanse me, instead of filling me with an even more desperate longing for Béatrice & an equally desperate hatred for those who had taken Her from me. On that serene day of reflection & quite alone in my Study, a large part of my grief came to an end as I unexpectedly did as She asked of me in Her letter, & forgave Her Parents. I left the Castle of Chillon, in more settled spirits than I had met it & though I would on occasion still be troubled by this whole injustice I found that it was always surmountable from that time on. I laid down the yoke I had carried for six years and more & I felt She would surely be cared for now, & forgiven for Her brief attachment to me. I had no doubt that I would always Love Her, & it was a turning point for me because forgiveness, real & so hopefully imagined, had made easier my life without Her.'

And once more, quite alone in that same study, Alice thought about forgiveness. She craved it, but what would make it happen while she lived with lies? Rachel could pull her out of her flimsy box whenever she fancied, and destroy her, and the lovely Alice Greerson would be exposed as a liar and a cheat. She would never recover, and green-eyed beauty would amount to nothing.

: : :

Today, this morning, Alice would change. She thought of what Jon had said, the words that had kept coming back in the silence of the night... *don't be afraid of what I'll think of you. I love you.* And she'd touched him as he slept, but gently, as he'd often touched her without her knowing. She saw that his words could free her for ever, and triumph over all the dreadful consequences of what he'd said seven months ago. And she thought of those *consequences.* She rolled the word around her head, then whispered it out loud. Beautifully balanced, and surely the most heavily-loaded word there is... *there are always consequences.* If only she'd stopped at that moment – held back and tried to think instead of being crushed, all would be well now. If only she'd said to him, *explain yourself;* but she'd wallowed in his words, in the instantaneous wreck of her dreams, and the outcome was *see what you've done to me.*

So she would put Tom, and Phillip, to rest. It would all happen, one thing following another until she was clear and pure again; on this historic morning she would put her men to rest, and then her parents could be faced. To forgive Jon, in the end, had been easy, and she believed now that he'd forgiven her. She recalled the end of Daniel Barthe-Fleury's letter to Peter: '...who truly knows the mind of another? Who knows how another suffers, when that suffering is borne well?' What was true for Béatrice was surely true for Jon. *He has borne me well. He loves me.*

As she looked towards the invisible river, she was filled with love for her husband. She'd had the realisation in the night that Jon was the only one of her chosen men who had ever told her he loved her. The only one, and she would have remembered. From the boy who took her virginity, to Olivier, to Tom: Jon was the constant star, and the one who stayed, after Phillip had faded and the others had gone. There was something in him, something she'd taken for granted, or even not noticed before, a quality beyond mere perseverance. And later, as they parted in the car park she hugged him, an intense and drawn-out hug that said more than words could have done that she was sorry for this.

She asked him, "Can we talk this evening?" in a final giving-in there could be no going back from.

"Yes, we'll talk." He smiled, and raised his hand to her face, to her cheek, then turned and got into his car and drove away to his instruments and complexities, and she stood and watched him go.

: : :

As Alice prepared for her day, Rachel looked out at the same early morning mist with her breakfast plate on her knees, sitting on cushions on the floor in front of the big window at Rivendell. Like Alice, she knew the mist would go in a couple of hours, as it had every other morning that week, and reveal a perfect April day, but she would be gone by then.

The garden – her mother's garden – faded ahead of her to the river, full of colour and at its spring best, but abandoned. Connie had left it, her gentle passion, to whoever came next. Rachel had done nothing to it, and planned nothing; in the weeks ahead the grass would grow longer than it ever had, the roses would bloom and die on their stalks, uncut, and it was okay. It would all be saved by someone, someday. She thought again of her parents, both lost to her now, of their lives together and of how they had all grown up in this house into the discordant couple she'd loved, regardless. After some simple arithmetic she'd guessed early on how that discord had started, with a surely unplanned pregnancy – their marriage ceremony far less than either would have wanted because of baby Rachel, but she was never blamed, openly or secretly. And now she had removed them both from the house they had loved, along with herself.

Her mind wandered as she sat looking out at the morning. She picked up a photograph she'd found in one of her mother's albums, an image she loved, where her parents were both smiling for the camera; it had been in their wedding album next to a similar picture where Connie was smiling for them both, unaware of her new husband's uncertain look. Rachel had taken it out before giving the album to her mother in Hereford, and would deal with its loss – which would be noticed – some other time. It would go onto her bedside table in Edinburgh, alongside the one her father had sent her, and the thought gave her hope. *My life need not go wrong. I will strive to be happy.*

So that morning the house was empty, and soon she would walk through the rooms a last time, the extraordinary bare rooms, stripped of all familiarity. In an hour she would lock the door and drive away and it would be a relief, but it would also be sorrowful: her disconnection would be suddenly fragile, and she expected a shaky farewell, a last-minute, unhelpful rush of melancholy.

She went to the letter she'd left on the kitchen worktop, the letter she'd taken all week to finish. She read it again.

> '...you see I cannot begin with "Dear Alice". You are not dear to me but even so I can't imagine a life full of anger and resentment towards you. My mother will stay in Hereford, and I don't imagine you meeting her again, but she was aware of many things regarding my father that I had no idea of. His death was a huge shock for her but not a big surprise, it seems. My father was not the saint I would have liked him to be, nor as stable in his mind as I thought he was. So you need not fear me unless my mother learns of your involvement and why he died, and I insist that you, and anyone you share them with, keep those secrets. That's still the deal.
>
> 'Forgiveness of a sort is what I give you, knowing only the way he was, and the way I believe you loved him. Love always amounts to something valuable and worth having, so in spite of my loss I wish you well, but you must remember our bargain.'

The letter didn't say much more, and didn't really warrant the hours spent on it. She'd followed many paths and finally settled on half a page of what she'd wanted to say, without any of the anger she still felt showing through. It was honest, and firm. Alice could still be held to account. She read to the end then folded the letter and put it in the envelope; it would arrive tomorrow if she posted it today. *If she posted it.* But the more she thought of what she had written, the more she felt it would be the right thing to do. She put the letter with her keys and prepared to leave Rivendell for Edinburgh, with a thirty-mile detour via her temporary manager at Chepstow.

: : :

Alice would take her couple of hours off. This Friday morning would be no different to any other weekday morning, no less busy, but she would go and be back by lunchtime. Her mother let her go easily. Elena didn't ask where or why she was going. It didn't matter any more, not really, now that Alice was back on board and would return.

"Back before lunch..."

As Alice walked out into the car park the sky above her was clearing, from the early morning pall of mist to the pale blue of April, and her heart was light. She felt different, and new. *A new Alice.* Today would be the first day of the rest of her life – an old truism she reprised whenever she'd needed a new start – and she would keep the words in her mind while looking forward to a future which would be infinitely better. She drove out from the hotel, towards Monmouth.

:::

Rachel Fisher drove along the Wye Valley from Chepstow. She would stop at Hereford, but briefly, and have a light early lunch with her mother and grandparents before setting off again and leaving her old life behind her. Tomorrow she would be far away, and safe again.

The Valley, she thought, was beautiful, as lovely as she'd ever seen it in her long years alongside the river and the countless times she'd driven through it with or without her parents, en route to somewhere, north or south. The morning was as promised by the early mist, the sky pale blue and vast above the confines of the high forested banks each side of road and river.

There was much she would miss. In time she could safely return, when the grief and sadness had truly eased, when the house was taken over and lived in by someone else, by another family, and all she would feel would be the soft ache of nostalgia. Would they keep it as *Rivendell*, or give it another name? Part of her wished for that, for it to become something else and not be so special anymore, not so reminding. She passed The Wondrous Gift without a sideways glance.

Ahead of her, Alice pulled in to the lay-by above Rivendell as though it were the natural thing to do, and faced the gated drive; she sat looking down at Tom's house, keeping the engine running, not meaning to stop for more than a moment – a need for a last look, a wistful goodbye to the man she hoped to exorcise. The house was empty, unlived-in. She sat there as all she knew of him flooded back, but instead of any warmth she felt an overpowering sadness, and regret. There was life here a month ago – life, and a family, and now it had gone and it all looked so grey, and so cold, even on such a beautiful morning. She put the car into reverse and moved back from the gate as a car drove past. Rachel drove by without looking down at the house, without a last look at her past, suddenly overwhelmed by what she'd seen.

It was Alice Greerson's car.

She was horrified. Everything stopped as her mind was filled with the image. She continued the short distance into the village, and pulled over in front of the Post Office as she'd planned. But it was automatic, and the reason for stopping had gone.

It was Alice Greerson.

She sat there, blinded, as seconds later Alice drove past unseen on her way to Monmouth.

On the seat next to Rachel was her letter, sealed and stamped. She got out and walked over to the post box in the wall with it in her hand, and stood in front of it. She was back in the past, in almost as much shock as when she'd found her father, and only because she felt taunted by this woman who had dared to revisit the scene of her crimes. She stood quite still. Then, as her purpose returned she drew back from the letter box, suddenly realising that this was surely where her father had posted his last letter to her, where he had actually stood that day, and in her hand was an offer of forgiveness for the person who had taken him from her. She turned back to the car.

:::

Alice parked at the top, and took the path up across the wide open crest of the hill and on through the wood. She had not been back since being there with Tom. The morning was calm, almost clear, and as she walked she kept her mind on her mission – she would get over Tom Fisher. The manner of his death was not important now. All that mattered was to move on. But her mood was heavier after stopping at Rivendell, and she wished she'd driven past, ignored that impulse and stayed focused. And now she became aware of her footfall, of how the ground she was on held the memories of so many other feet over so many years, and especially of Tom. They had walked this way together; he had been here, in the space she moved through, seen the same trees, breathed the same air; Tom was firmly with her, as she prepared to move him from her life.

In her pockets she had two necklaces, one each side. She took them out and held them in one hand, uniting them, folding them over each other and closing her fingers over them in a joining of all they stood for, a blending of love tokens into what she had thought would be a perfect pairing, a mutual befriending, and not symbolic, but real. They would live together, having been given in the same spirit and standing for the same thing – genuine, unconditional love. Jon's gift was now easily as precious to her as Phillip's had been to Béatrice.

There was no wind, and it was the time between snowdrop and bluebell, when the daffodils held sway further down the hill. Up here the path was bare and dry, and on the bank below, showing through the carpet of last year's beech leaves, the bluebells were biding their time, their thin leaves a darker green than the mossy stones dotted about the hillside. In the familiarity of her surroundings she came to the end of the path and sat on the edge of the bank, on the cold slab where she'd sat that evening with Tom, caught in an unexpected returning flood of fear and guilt. But the growing warmth had melted the very last of the mist from the tops of the trees above her, and she looked up at the blue sky through the thin branches. The beauty of what she saw surprised her, and rallied her: *this is too good,* she thought, *too beautiful to relinquish to fear and guilt. What happened here was perfect.* Love, yes, an abundance of love, never to be denied, never forgotten. *The end is perfect.* She sat under the high branches with their new, bright green leaves, and allowed a last indulgence, a last fling with her memories of Tom and she slipped without effort into the comfortable world she still kept in reserve, overpowering everything that threatened her. Now she was secure, in her familiar world of memories and dreams.

She looked around her at the stones and the trees, unchanged since he'd been there with her – the place where they had sat side by side on a misty and damp evening only a month before, the small clearing where they had made love. Then in the stillness Phillip came to her, and Chillon, and his vision of the woman he loved swimming free in the lake below the Castle, and the words she knew by heart:

'I had no doubt that I would always Love Her, & it was a turning point for me because forgiveness, real & so hopefully imagined, had made easier my life without Her.'

Phillip, pertinent, as ever. Can I ever say goodbye to you?

Her whole life turned in her head, round and round, people and places, love and loss, until her thoughts turned to the necklace and her fatal flaw: *Give it to the one you love... how clever of me, to think it could work with Tom. How could he understand? Where would it lead? My stupidity is astounding.* And she feared that Tom, knowing her as little as he had, would have agreed, and been disappointed in her.

She stood up and walked to the centre of the clearing below the gap in the high branches, and held her arms out from her body – head back, looking up to the sky, as if welcoming the world she now hoped for. She tried to lose herself in that space in the woods. She turned slowly in a circle, a slow dance on that singular ground, and she moved away from the threats, away from the unknowns she could do nothing about. And gradually there was a slipping back to rational thoughts; still she slowly turned in her circle and in the silence, broken only by the slight scraping of her shoes on the earth, she came to her senses. Her arms came down to her sides and she was still.

It will have to end, this life of dreams.

And then, in that strange new mood of realism, she at last doubted herself: *so is this really love, with Tom? Was it ever?*

Time was passing, and, alone on the top of that hill, her head filled again with all of her life. Like a drowning woman she saw her days race past, everything she'd experienced, from the dreams of her youth to the happiness she'd lost and found again, and it all felt real for the first time ever. She would forsake the beguiling, damaging dreams. Regrets were becoming genuine repentance and she craved clemency, complete forgiveness from everyone – and all this as, unknown to her, someone was driving north at that very moment with her parallel flow of thoughts and decisions. Alice would sometime be given a sort of forgiveness, making of it what she would, but in her ignorance of that woman's journey she stared along the path winding away from her through the trees, and she felt the two necklaces in her hand, their chains now impossibly tangled. She looked down at them. She would separate them in her hand but keep them together in her heart, and now she wanted to do that for Jon – sort out those two love tokens, love them both and keep them real, and without mystery. She felt released into somewhere different, a place that really would turn out to be true and honest.

The morning was ending, and soon she would leave for her

home by the river where she would wait for her husband, her lover of three years and more. She would wait the remainder of the day for him. Alice felt at peace. She looked around her on this first day of the rest of her life, eager to leave, hesitant.

Still so many unknowns. But here, suddenly, the questions drop away, and everything is resolved. All will be well. Here and now I am free, and always will be. From now on I can dream of a true future, of things I know for certain; and yes, of the one certainty that will benefit us all, and make everything right: our child will be a dreamed-of girl, she will come in midwinter – a Christmas child – and like me will share Phillip's name, and one day also his necklace. She will be Béatrice.

PART THREE

The more sand has escaped from the hourglass of our life,
the clearer we should see through it.

(Often attributed to Niccolò Macchiavelli)

NEW YEAR'S EVE, 1999

Rachel Fisher

This morning I drove down the Wye Valley, past the house I grew up in, and unavoidably past the place where Alice Greerson lives. Two years ago she had her child – a beautiful girl – and they are settled now. It was just after her child came that I met her grandfather, who needed to sound me out over my threat. It wasn't even a year after my father killed himself for her. It was still raw and what I didn't need was an olive branch from him or his granddaughter – but that's not what he brought. He knew nothing of my letter to her, and the 'forgiveness of a sort' I offered her then. So over coffee we talked it through until we were almost equal in our knowledge. Almost equal because I decided to keep quiet about the necklace, although I told him I believed my father killed himself because of her. Then he said he already knew that from Alice, who'd confessed most of it to him soon after I'd confronted her in her car. But she'd not told him about the necklace – he would have mentioned it if she had.

I'm sure I'm helping her by keeping that secret, so that counts for something. I told him how easy it was to imagine my father killing himself over something like this, and I asked him to promise to keep it in his immediate family. It was an accident, and that's still my line for anyone who asks. And the child need never know any of it. Even so I told him I hoped never to meet her mother again, fearing just a glimpse of her would undo the resolution I'd made, and I still feel that. My mother's welfare was important to me – still is, after two years - so I'm afraid I allow his granddaughter to languish in her fear of me. Still, I wonder if my mother knew everything that happened, would she even care? I must assume she would. But now, in truth I feel softer, the anger has left me, and I trust the great secret will be kept.

Jon Greerson owns my father's business – a gift from that grand-father, who told me he'd bought it for him. A gift indeed, and my mother was relieved to let it go, and so was I. I'm happy for him, particularly. I called in at the factory a month ago – still SFI, still a small enterprise – and talked with him. I don't know which secrets he's left with, so we skirt around them and keep our friendship. Afia, lovely Afia, had told me of his child two years ago and of his happiness since – and now I write this in my own state of happiness, from above the sea in Dartmouth, far from Redbrook and a whole country away from Edinburgh. I think again of the child. Grow up strong, little girl! Maybe I'll meet you one fine day or maybe never – my possible, unknowing half-sister. Would I know who you are? No matter. Be kind, and happy!

My mother – oh, my mother. She grows old before her time in Hereford, still in ignorance of her husband's final days. Quite difficult to see her as she is but I believe she's content in her own way. Her parents are still there. Her talk is all of the past, as she thinks nothing of her future, and she refuses to go around the pain. She is rare hard work for me now, but I always have the sad luxury of leaving her when I need to.

Today's diversion was for nostalgia, to see it all again. I was driving from Hereford to Devon, to a new life with a man who reminds me so much of my father that again I felt a double shock of recognition when I saw him. I love him, and I'm doing my best. I look forward to a very different life by the sea, where I'll teach new children and be happy because in early summer I shall marry him – I'll be a sailor's wife! He gives me love that I can feel, and I'll embark on our life together with resolve. I could tell you much about him but now I'll go, because it's New Year's Eve and from the other end of the house he calls me to supper. The new century promises much for us all.

: : :

Alice Greerson

Today is my daughter's second birthday. Béatrice Rossetti Greerson is two years old and we are all ready to welcome a new year, a new century, a new millennium... but oh, where to begin!

The secrets of two years ago have gone, almost. In those days we had a pyramid of secrets – from my parents who knew none of them, down to Jon and my grandfather Peter who knew some of them, and then to me who knew them all, and that situation went on until Béatrice was born, when my grandfather went to see Rachel in Hereford. He'd had enough of secrets, but I really couldn't see a way of explaining it all to anyone. Cowardice, that's all it was. So he upped and went. Jon told him she would be there – Peter texted her and they met up for a coffee. She'd largely, but not completely, forgiven me – just as she'd hinted at in her letter. She was working on it, she'd said, which is more than I was doing with my own life. She will be a good friend to many, I think.

So my mother learned from my grandfather, instead of me. He told her of my brief affair – that's still a word I dislike – and how Rachel blames me for his death, which suggests suicide. He told me straight after telling my mother. Job done, no way out. I wept in anxiety and relief, as he apparently feared to be exiled to his empty house upriver by my wrath. But I was calm, and we went downstairs with Béatrice in my arms, to see her. It was intense, the relief at shaking off those secrets, mixed with my shame and embarrassment. And I was able to look in my mother's eyes as I faced her, which was more than the tacit admission I'd given to Jon and my grandfather. That was three days after Béatrice was born, and I guess he'd waited to see her before making his move. As it was he saw some likeness to Jon, as we all do even more as she grows.

My father and Jon came home to the news, ten minutes apart – a shock for one and a confirmation for the other. I'd waited in the kitchen, waited in shame for the horror of telling my father most of all, because I knew Jon would not be so shocked. But it had to be, and it was my mother who simply said, "You need to know something." She stood in front of my father, and didn't mince words. Then in the silence I stood up, and he took me in his arms. He had difficulty believing it. I was in pieces, unable to stop weeping. And Jon held me for a long time, close to tears. Somehow we all got through the day and from then on I could live easier again. Two years later those days seem unreal and gone for ever, unmentioned now by anyone, and there are no questions. I love these people for that, for the way they held on to me when they could have let me go or at least told me what they thought of me. That never happened, though I deserved it. They keep their own secrets – my shocking fall from grace and all that went with it, and they understand the need to keep it from Connie. Rachel is far from here, and we are hoping her forgiveness will last. It seems that Rachel did not mention the necklace, as my grandfather said nothing about it. So a liberating kindness from her, and a secret I will always carry.

What else? Well, Olivier called me in late summer, a rare call. We text now and then, but always I feel sad for him. He said I was 'the other side of his life' and I wish he could get over that, get over *us*. Can't believe it was ten years ago. I told him if I'd known about Delphine I would not have hooked onto him like I did. I was feeling virtuous when I said that, but I think it's true. I hope it's true. He didn't believe me when I said I wouldn't fight for him in that situation, wouldn't want to spoil a relationship – and he sounded disappointed. Better to be fought for, I guess, but I'm not really on board with that. I sometimes wonder if he really loved me. There are times I feel I could meet him again, but I know it's best to leave him in my past. But I am sorry for him.

Daniel, the Frenchman who wrote to my grandfather Peter with Béatrice Fleury's story, visited us in the summer before our own Béatrice was born. He is one year younger than Peter, and as the generations have kept up with each other in both countries, it feels as if I have another grandfather! It was wonderful to see them together with so much in common to talk about, and we all feel sadness that Phillip was unaware of the child he'd longed for. We went over to Saint-Malo last summer, and met Daniel and his family.

Jon has moved forward with his work and now owns SFI outright, my beloved grandfather providing the funds, and the enthusiasm Jon perhaps lacked in taking it on. No regrets though. He's very happy, sometimes hands-on and sometimes at his desk, and it all works well. We are thoroughly reconciled. If he has any inkling that I'm keeping something back from him he hides it well, and leaves it with me. I'm very aware of his love. So the four people I live amongst all know the facts, except for the necklace. I know it's bad for me to keep that secret, but it stays with me because I fear knowing about it would make those I love unhappy for ever, and I know I would not get off so lightly. I'm humbled and grateful at the same time, but in the background still fearful over Rachel, and will be for as long as we both live. So those consequences stay with me.

The most valuable thing I have now is my happiness with Jon and our daughter. I feel such love for Jon sometimes, I fear it must throw me over. It appears stronger than the everyday love we share, and I have no doubts for our future. I can say *Love Conquers All* and truly mean it.

$$\Omega$$

THANK YOU

First of all to my wife Evi, for her patience,
her support, and her very close reading

To Edward and Marian Drzymalski,
for introducing me to Aku, and his ways

To Dorothy Tennov for her book *Love and Limerence,*
(Stein & Day, 1979)

To James Thomas (francisboutle.co.uk) who expertly
provided the Occitan translation on page 66

To Serif Ltd, of Nottingham, England,
for their *Affinity Publisher* software

: : :

Also by Gordon Williams

UPRIVER
Peter Matthew Bennett's History
A companion volume to
The Gentle River
providing an in-depth background
to the historical characters and events of the Novel

SEVEN SHORT STORIES
Seven short stories to intrigue, and entertain

www.gordonwilliams.uk

Printed in Great Britain
by Amazon

45123542R00202